ON

ACCOUNT

of

CONSPICUOUS

WOMEN

Dawn Shamp

ON ACCOUNT of CONSPICUOUS WOMEN

Thomas Dunne Books
ST. MARTIN'S PRESS ≋ NEW YORK

This is a work of fiction. All of the characters, organizations, and events portrayed in this novel are either products of the author's imagination or are used fictitiously.

THOMAS DUNNE BOOKS.
An imprint of St. Martin's Press.

www.thomasdunnebooks.com

www.stmartins.com

Book design by Elina D. Nudelman

Library of Congress Cataloging-in-Publication Data

Shamp, Dawn.
    On account of conspicuous women / Dawn Shamp.—1st ed.
        p. cm.
    ISBN-13: 978-0-312-37997-1
    ISBN-10: 0-312-37997-8
    1. Young women—Fiction.   2. Female friendship—Fiction.   3. Suffragists—Fiction.   4. Virginia—Fiction.   I. Title.

    PS3619.H3543 O6 2008
    813'.6—dc22

                                                        2008005775

First Edition: May 2008

10 9 8 7 6 5 4 3 2 1

to Jim

Note to the Reader

*N*orth Carolina's Person County got its name from Brigadier General Thomas Person—a liberal Whiggamore—after the Revolutionary War. It's a flawless four hundred square miles made up of nine townships, bordered on the north by Virginia. On a map the county resembles a perfect grid for a game of noughts and crosses; or, a challenging plot for hopscotch. And at the very center lies the diggings of Roxboro, a little crossroads hamlet—the sweetest cherry in the center of the cordial—where, in 1920, the concept of city mail delivery was less than a decade old, and where impermeable bricks on the local stores were not yet old enough to render an image of natural beauty. Tobacco was the backbone. Bootleg liquor was the rest of the skeleton. And the skin of the growing body was cotton, miles of it woven at the local mill. If you lived on Main Street, you had a hard-surface, short walk to town. The street was paved between the Methodist church at one end of town and the Baptist church at the other. But beyond those two markers the riding was rough, the packed dirt full of irritating shirrs and puckers. It was like driving over politics.

Well-behaved women
seldom make history.

—Laurel Thatcher Ulrich

1919

Bertie Stumps
for Suffrage

Men with clout are all alike, but some of them are worse, Bertie thought, as she sat at the kitchen table tying freshly roasted peanuts inside squares of burlap sacking.

Her younger sister, Alta Ruth, sat across from her and helped, between them an aluminum pan of unshelled goobers accompanied by a slotted spoon. It was a thirsty summer evening, the middle of July, and the heat indicator on the Victory stove registered over 300. Behind the glass that covered the thermometer's white face, the spring-loaded needle pointed between the *H* and the *O* in the word *Hot*, though to Bertie it felt more like it should be stuck on the *Very Hot T*. The little ivory Westinghouse whirring from the countertop didn't provide much in the way of remedy. A second batch of peanuts had been out of the oven and cooling for more than ten minutes, but still the kitchen felt stifling.

"It's hot enough to scald a hog," Bertie said.

"What makes you think I can get them to come outside and hear what you've got to say?" Alta Ruth asked, bumping the toe of her Rough-and-Tumble play shoe against the table's leg.

"Because, little sister," said Bertie. "There isn't a man alive who can resist a heavily wadded sack." She jostled one of the palm-sized bags in her hand. "There's as much potency in gripping a fistful of roasted nuts as there is in, say, toting a gun or clutching a newspaper. You'll find out soon enough the foolish things that men find power in." She gave the bag another shake before placing it on the table where a bouquet of the brown sacks was already assembled. *A little ingenuity is all it takes to get a man to listen*, she thought, scooping peanuts from the shallow pan to the center of another burlap square. *Sometimes it can be as little as the promise of free nuts*.

Aside from her regular job as hello-girl for Wheeler's Telephone Company,

Bertie had ventured into a side business of her own, selling five-cent bags of "home-cooked" peanuts, and once a week she set up an elaborate production in her mama's kitchen, aided by Alta Ruth and a standing order from Sargeant and Clayton's Grocery of a 100-pound bag of fancy green peanuts—straight from Bertie County, she was proud to tell her customers.

She was the eldest daughter of Brud Daye (God rest him) and Lalura Wise Daye (heaven help her)—nineteen years old to Alta Ruth's twelve. After their papa's bizarre hunting death in 1908, Miss Lul, who was not outwardly fazed by the tragedy and who, thanks to Bertie, still retained the affectionate nickname that Brud had bestowed upon her, opened the house to boarders. But two months had passed since the last boarder moved out and no one else had come to knock. People weren't as stationary as they once had been; they were becoming more mobile (Ford himself had seen to that). And as money in the Daye household was not a thing to squander, and as they were the kind of family that made every effort to help themselves, Bertie felt it her duty to put her meager salary as a telephone operator toward keeping creditors from bothering Miss Lul. But that didn't mean Bertie had abandoned her fondness for frippery. Every silver coin she earned from peddling peanuts was like a holy stone, because nothing tells you more about a person than her clothes. She who gives close attention to herself has a fixed regard for other things, too. You have to be fashionable to be unfashionable. If you're gonna be a bound-breaking individualist, you've got to bring it out from behind a great deal of self-respect and dignity. And as a person bent on making a sweeping change in the world, Bertie believed herself in possession of a healthy supply of both.

She was already the only woman in Person County with her own Model T. It had taken a fair amount of hornswoggling, starting with twelve jars of Miss Lul's prized damson preserves that she snuck from the pantry and miraculously made an even dicker for twelve jugs of white lightning. So dumbfounded by the bargain that she could've peed crosswise, she then turned right around and swapped the jars of lightning to backdoor tavern owner Rufus Small for cash and guns (two muzzle loaders and a carbine), which she parlayed into four acres of land from a man named Gatewood who had more than four hundred, which she then sold to Augustus P. Shaw for cash that she took directly to Clyde Bumpass who she beat down till he gave her a great deal on the used Model T.

"Have you told Mama what you're doing?" said Alta Ruth, winding a snip of twine around the burlap square in her lap.

"No, and don't you either," Bertie said.

Alta Ruth grinned. Bertie knew she enjoyed being an accomplice. Anything questionable or that involved sneaking behind Miss Lul's back was grand entertainment. And if there was one thing Bertie liked when it came to her way of thinking, it was unanimity.

She was staunch as a hound in her support for female suffrage. Always one for asserting independence, even at the risk of embarrassing Miss Lul, Bertie had an opinion on everything, including church, Negro rights, matrimony, and men, and considered every one of those opinions worth listening to. And ever since April, when Muriel Yates Simmons (a high-horse-riding Baptist and proud Daughter of the Confederacy) organized a local branch of the Southern Rejection League, Bertie's prosuffrage sentiments had grown louder. The heart of the League's argument was that a woman's natural role was to be a wife and a mother; they were intellectually inferior and too emotional to be trusted with men's business. And the League had proof that God was backing them up, all the way to the Senate chambers, where they had held a rally in May and flown a banner that proclaimed, "Politics are bad for women and women are bad for politics!" Bertie's opinion? Nuts!

But now that Congress had endorsed the Nineteenth Amendment by one vote and sent it to the states for ratification, the heat was getting to Muriel Yates Simmons and her ilk. And they had every right to be scared, since thirty-six votes were all that was needed.

Bertie had a plan. But she wasn't ready to share it with Miss Lul, who, just then, appeared in the doorway to announce that she was off to church for her evening meeting. "Would you look at the peanuts! That little side business of yours must be doing all right, Beatrice. Did Mr. Sargeant give you a fair price?"

"Bartered a couple jars of damson preserves for this bag."

"Not *my* damsons?"

"Yes, your damsons."

"Do you have any idea how much work went into that last batch?" Miss Lul huffed. "You should've asked me before you went and did that."

"Can't undo what's done now," said Bertie, and blew at a lock of damp hair that was stuck to her forehead.

"You sound more and more like Brud every day. *Every day.*" An observation that didn't seem to please Miss Lul. And because her tone came across as being less than pleased, and perhaps even caused her a bit of religionist guilt, she tried to make up for it by stammering, "No matter, I— I probably would've suggested the damsons myself. In fact, I most certainly would have. But still, Beatrice, you should've asked me first." And now that she had righted herself, she once again found it necessary to be firm in the presence of her daughters. "This little hobby of yours better not interfere with your duties at the telephone company. You need that job."

Bertie waited till Miss Lul had left, then raised her eyes at Alta Ruth and winked.

She was at a juncture in her life when she had the coign of vantage. And she knew it. Mr. Wheeler worshiped her (albeit sometimes too closely). She had been a godsend to that office, and not one person could deny it, coming in to take the place of ninety-two-year-old Miss Jacobs, who'd been as fixed as a mantis in that office—and as slow as one—in various positions, for some twenty-odd years, and who had sadly succumbed to the influenza last winter along with more than a hundred other unfortunate townsfolk. Mr. Wheeler, upon hiring Bertie, was like a dog that'd been parted from his pecker and had suddenly got it back. He knew he had secured a special gal from her very first day, her very first hour on that clock. Her strong but not too gravelly voice, her command of the language, her memory for numbers made her a natural. Her first week on the job a caller went silent in surprise on the other end of the line, expecting to hear Miss Jacobs's voice. Bertie's response: "Speak ass, 'cause the mouth won't!" It established a marked improvement in Roxboro telecommunications efficiency.

When they had tied all the peanuts into individual bags and gathered them into a couple of woven-splint corn baskets, the sisters loaded up Bertie's Model T and headed toward what had been Small's Pool Hall and Saloon before 1908, when North Carolina became the first southern state to outlaw the evils of whiskey. Now it bore the lean-witted name Small's Cathedral of Ladder Day Masons. A unique secret society that had more to do with brotherly drinking from Mason jars hidden on high shelves behind silly hats than it did with charitable stone cutting.

The air whizzed by the open-body Ford as Bertie and Alta Ruth passed through town, their curls blowing up a storm smelling of coconut oil shampoo. Alta Ruth's feet barely touched the floorboard. When they approached the Palace Theater, Bertie tooted the horn causing crooked-backed Mr. Matherly, who was clamped on to the ticket box counter, to jump as if a thunderbolt had crept up on him. The sisters laughed.

Most of the plank sidewalks in town, but for a small section at one corner, had been replaced with concrete, and as Bertie turned the sputtering Ford from the main road, a square of walkway was cordoned off with rope and two-by-fours where men had mixed and poured and smoothed wet concrete during the day. Evidence that they'd be returning the morrow to finish the job was propped against the building: bags of Portland cement, sand and gravel, a screed board for leveling, a bull float for smoothing, and a push broom to make straight strokes for traction.

"No reason not to start with the most difficult of audiences," Bertie said. "What? Don't screench your winkers up at me! I'm talking about the immoral element, Alta Ruth. Whiskey-drinking gamblers. Every last one of them is opposed to women getting the vote. And I'm planning on changing that."

Bertie pulled the black Ford just beyond the swinging doors of Small's and instructed Alta Ruth. "Now you run in and tell them whoever will come out and listen to your sister speak on suffrage gets a *free* five-cent sack of peanuts."

"That's the plan you're sticking with, huh?" Alta Ruth said. "Them men'll laugh me right outta there."

"I know what I'm doing, now slide your pie!" Bertie pushed her sister out, then slipped her own two feet over the running board and onto the plank walkway.

Alta Ruth brushed the wrinkles from her gingham frock and faced the entrance to the tavern. She was a bright little biscuit-headed girl who had inherited her mother's attributes: legs as skinny as a two-year-old tree and a neck so spindly it could've made a turkey chuckle. She was often pleased with herself, and oblivious to any upset she might be the cause of. Making others angry rarely hindered her enjoyment. "Mama'll have a fit when she finds out I stepped foot in this place," she said. A devilish look came over her and she dashed toward the doors.

"Oh, and Alta Ruth?" Bertie called after her. "Gird up your loins. This is court week, so they're liable to be rowdy."

With a flick of her hand, Alta Ruth waved to Bertie and disappeared through the swinging doors.

Bertie hiked the hem of her dress and climbed into the rear seat of the Ford, a yellow Equal Rights for Women banner splayed across the back, and waited to give her open-air speech in support of the cause. She had her papa's stature, Brud Daye's large hands and thick wrists, his bull of a waist, and his firm horse buttocks—though on Bertie, the expanse of her hips was considered fetching. Her nose was as wide as a squash blossom, and because her nostrils had that permanent flare, one sensed she possessed Brud Daye's air of somebody to be reckoned with. The reediest thing about her was her mouth, though it was no fault of her own: those shrill lips had been handed down to every last Daye. She liked to paint them red in defiance (but also because it looked good).

She thought of her papa now. How he had loved to argue for the sake of arguing! He would've made a great philosopher, she thought, on the likes of Bacon. Funny—he loved bacon. That one memory of him at the breakfast table, while he and Miss Lul discussed some point or another, Alta Ruth in her highchair, pulled up alongside Bertie. She could still hear his voice, how loud it grew, and that image of his fist hitting the table. "Anybody that takes things as they come lacks push!" he shouted to Miss Lul. Alta Ruth began to cry and Bertie, who was eating a slice of banana-and-walnut bread, got a piece of nutmeat stuck in her throat.

Thanks to her papa, she would never be one to simply "take things as they come."

The door to Small's swung open and Alta Ruth came out, a tangle of men trailing behind her.

"Go ahead, Bertie," she said. "They're all cocked."

And so Bertie began, with no thought of how long she would speak. "Gentlemen! It's only a matter of time before our state rules in favor of suffrage for women! Your own President Wilson supports it, and you should support it, too!"

"You can talk that nonsense all you want, but these men ain't changing their minds!" The brusque voice belonged to none other than Augustus P. Shaw, Roxboro's chief political bunkoman and known enemy of suffragists.

If Bertie could've gotten her hands on a good-sized grapefruit, she would've tossed it at his head. Instead, she gritted her teeth, leaned over, and whispered to Alta Ruth, "What are you waiting on? Start doling out them peanuts." She then stood up straight and went back to addressing the audience. "This is an injustice that affects you all, too! Ever stopped to wonder why your wages are paltry? The fact that women are underpaid holds down your own wages. Giving us the vote will change those conditions for the better."

"Aw, that's the craziest thing I ever heard!" said Old Man Rubley.

"Ain't you got enough at home to do?" said a scowling Robert Linwood, and waved his foul-smelling pipe in a farewell.

The crowd laughed.

"Give us a kiss!" called out young Calvin Worley.

"Hush!" said Hoyt Yancey. "What's it hurt to listen."

"Thank you, Hoyt. You gotta see things in perspective," Bertie continued. "Sure, it sounds crazy. But it can be put to good uses—"

"I don't see nothing good about my wife neglecting her duties," said a red-cheeked John Jeffers, standing off to one side.

"Amen!"

"Or Coloreds getting the vote neither! Do you, fellas?"

There was more laughter and rumblings among the men. Bertie grew hot. What a shame it was that sweet little boys had to grow into such unlikable excuses for humans, she mused.

"Our own local government ought to be allowed to decide what's right for this here community," Augustus Shaw said. "Uncle Sam should just stay out of it."

"Aw, to devil with state's rights!" said Bertie.

Several men in the crowd whistled and clapped, proof that a vulgar tongue can get attention.

"That argument has been going on for years," she persisted, "and the ones arguing for it are the ones right-thinking folks wouldn't give you two cents for. Every single one of them is wrongheaded. Take that dingleberry congressman we got in Washington who's afraid of the colored vote." Then she paused for dramatic effect. "Now I know you all here have more sense than that half-bake to be scared of a colored woman voting. Y'all *are* more intelligent than that, aren't you? I can rest assured that you've done your homework, can't I, and you know that giving women the vote is the only way to ensure that whites remain dominant."

"What's she talking about, Augie? That true?"

The expression on Augustus Shaw's face resembled one of intestinal distress.

"I imagine Mr. Shaw here doesn't want to sound all uppity around you men," said Bertie in a loud whisper. "You don't want your buddies thinking you're some kind of thinking machine, do you, Augie P'Shaw? No sir, what with all the numbers I have no doubt you collected from the Census Bureau. That's why I'm here, so we can tell them together"—her voice raising with her fist—"that there'll be over fifty thousand white women who'll vote over and above all the colored men and women put together."

The crowd began to murmur.

Bertie, seeing Alta Ruth had not handed out the first bag of peanuts, leaned over and muttered, faint but firm, "Shake a leg, child, and start tossing out them bags. I think we're about to prosecute this to a winning conclusion."

"But they don't want peanuts."

"It'd be different if all the women were like you, Bertie!" Hoyt Yancey said.

She put her hand to her ear. "How's that?"

"Smart, rational—" but before the astute Mr. Yancey could finish he was interrupted.

"Yeah, now how 'bout that kiss!"

"That just ain't the case," said Augustus Shaw. "If we was to go giving women the ballot box, this country'd end up in one big mess. Why, they'd have us menfolk tending to our own young'uns."

"Hear, hear!"

"I say women got more than they can handle at home!"

"That's right! They ain't got no business in politics."

Bertie felt the isolation of standing on an ice-capped mountaintop.

"Just think of the corruption we'd be in for," said Rufus Small, who had been propped against the tavern door, chewing on a toothpick the duration.

Give her something to fling, throw, or hurl, because now she was getting combative. "That's kind of a shock coming from you, Mr. Small," she said. "Everybody knows that law enforcement leans to the lenient around here. Now myself, I enjoy taking a snort from time to time, but word is, the only changes you made since things went dry was to switch the name on your sign right there. And I bet if I was to step inside I'd see that you're making a profit out of violation, 'cause I know you fellas ain't pressing flowers beyond those swinging doors."

The crowd howled. Mr. Small's face colored.

"All I'm asking is for y'all to have faith in the government," Bertie said.

"Why? So they can round us all up like Palmer did and label us as Communists?" a voice cried out.

"Don't be crazy, John," the man next to him said. "I told you: nobody thinks you're a Communist. Fitts doesn't even sound Russian."

"Alta Ruth! If you don't start handing out those bags right this minute!"

"I've heard enough," said Calvin Worley, pushing to the front of the crowd. "I don't know about y'all, but I'm ready for that kiss Little Sister promised us. Go on, sweetheart, plant me one right here," he said, and came at Bertie with buttercup eyes and pursy lips.

"A kiss? You can kiss my foot!"

He made a playful swipe for her ankle and the rest of the crowd took their cue from him. Bertie shrieked. She jumped a hurdle from the back seat to the front, and hollered for Alta Ruth to get in. An upheaval of arm swinging and shoving ensued, but the electric starter came to life and the sisters managed to pull away.

"What just happened back there?" Bertie shouted as dust whirled skyward behind the chugging carriage.

"I told you they didn't want peanuts."

"So you thought you'd turn my flivver into a kissing booth? Don't you pull a cockamamie stunt like that again, you hear? We'd been in a heap of trouble if this machine didn't have an automatic starter!"

The warm night air whipped and whistled as they headed toward home. Alta Ruth raised her voice over the flourish and put a question to Bertie.

"Did you really mean what you said back there, about Coloreds voting? You know, about more white folks and all?"

Bertie put a little pressure to the left foot pedal and slowed the Ford down. "The numbers I cited to that gang of social hiccups are factual. But sometimes, little sister," she sighed, "you gotta squint a little to get people to see things your way."

She couldn't say why or how, or just when exactly, she had become so headstrong in her fight for woman's suffrage. Her mind had always been a moving, shifting landscape, her attention passing from one side to another, searching for someplace to settle. And now it finally had.

1920

Chapter 2

After Ina Fitzhugh's Beloved Drops Dead

$\mathcal{S}$he was lying on a Louis XV sofa, comforted by pillows square and pillows round, all made from European fabrics. Barely two weeks had passed since her husband, Harlan's, sudden death, and ever since, Ina Skipwith *nee* Fitzhugh had been lying perdu.

The dark oak door creaked open, and her mother and father came into Ina's deep mauve- and yellow-schemed room. She could hear them (she had hardly slept), but the heavy velvet drapery was pulled in such a way as to shut out all fraction of light, and Ina's eyes were closed just as tightly behind a lavender satin sleep mask. Only Miss Flick, the long-haired gray cat curled at her feet, could see their motive: they were Lord and Lady Fitzhugh crossing the Aubusson rug to their eldest daughter.

"Sakes alive, Mother!" said Dr. Fitzhugh, hooking the toe of his right shoe on a slight ripple in the carpet. "Find us some light, won't you, dear? Ina, are you awake?"

"Yes, Father. I'm only resting."

"Your mother and I have just had a chat with Dr. Weldon. You remember Dr. Weldon, of course, a classmate of mine at Johns Hopkins. He's of the notion, and we agree, that you need a significant period of rest."

Ina pushed the satin mask from her eyes and compressed it to her forehead. "Isn't that what I've been doing?" Indeed she had, ever since returning home three days early from her New York honeymoon, which was two days after her wedding, and precisely one day after her beloved Harlan dropped dead at her feet from a ruptured appendix. She had returned home inconsolable. (And completely unaware that she was about to be thrust into her very first libidinal rut.)

"Yes, dear," her mother said, "only, not here."

Ina uprighted herself on the sofa, and in the course of doing so, upset the cat. "I'm not sure I understand."

"Let me handle this, Mother," her father said. "It's not that we don't want you here, Ina. Dr. Weldon, you know, is, well, he's a big believer in changes and chances. And sometimes one has to adapt to—or checker their—or give a turn to—well, what I'm trying to say is, Dr. Weldon thinks the best place for you to recuperate after such a loss is Sunset Mountain. And your mother and I agree." Her father had always been a man of so many words.

"But I feel right at home and rested here."

"Yes, dear," her mother said, "but Sunset Mountain is the perfect place for rejuvenating the body and spirit. It's a wonderful hotel, dear. It's not at all like one of those horrid—horrid—"

"The word is *institution*, Mother," said Dr. Fitzhugh.

Mrs. Fitzhugh conceded. "And we understand that Calvin Coolidge was once a guest there, so you should feel right at home." Ina's mother had a dainty waist, and like most women of her generation who had dainty waists, impression was everything. "Consider it a late Christmas gift, dear."

Her parents spoke as if a daily regimen of calisthenics and clabbered milk at a rustic mountain lodge were all that were needed to cure the devastation she felt over the death of her husband, a man she'd only had the pleasure of referring to as such once. They had been seated at dinner in the Algonquin's Oak Room, seduced by the low sconce lighting, and dizzy over shrimp puffs in choux paste. Harlan was left-handed and Ina right, enabling them to give one's hand to the other across the linen-topped table and indulge in puffs without interruption. That is, if one didn't consider the maître d'hotel. Each time he approached their table Ina felt an inclination to withdraw her hand from Harlan's. It took some getting used to, this displaying of affection in public, and more than once she had to remind herself that she was—that they were—now wedded.

Harlan Skipwith had the kind of look that some women would refer to as "fit for a boudoir." On first impression he seemed to be the brooding type. He had a naturally down-turned mouth when he wasn't smiling—though he could be made to do so easily—and his hair was thick and cowlicked, making it difficult for him to manage. His ears complemented the shape of his head; they were the perfect cup of harmony and didn't dominate the rest of his features. His eyes had a particularly starry cast to them, but that was on account of the day-blindness in his right, and a touch of night-blindness in his left. And when it came to his own striking good looks, he was as sightless as a mole. That alone was attractive to the women who knew him.

When the headwaiter had returned to their table to inquire about dessert, Harlan said his wife would have the Chocolate Opera Cake.

"And for you, sir?"

"My husband," Ina said, taking advantage of the pause, "will have the Pecan Tart with Bourbon Cream."

"Excellent choices."

The two smiled at each other. Harlan gave Ina's hand a squeeze.

But all she had now were memories. And for her parents to think of sending her away to what amounted to no more than a silly mountain vacation angered her. What she felt she needed, more than anything, was to be surrounded by people she cared for most, even if she did prefer to lie in her room, drapes drawn—not even words from a book had been able to soothe her. She wanted the comfort of knowing that when she was ready to come out, they would be there to console her. But she had never used harsh words toward her mother or her father, and was not of a mind to argue with them now. After all, if not for their firm resolve in the matter regarding her education, she could no more *parler le Français* than the man in the moon. And she adored the romantic language. To speak it, hear it, made her tremble. Therefore, if it meant forgoing a visit to Dr. Weldon where she would be tortured by his ridiculous nods and the irritating rapid scratch of his steel quill on paper, she would go. Faced with the choice of those two iniquities, Ina decided on Sunset Mountain.

Armed with a trunkful of new undermuslins and a dozen pecan meringues packed by her mother, she arrived at Sunset Mountain on the twentieth of January.

She stepped into the lavish lobby, tugged at the fingers of her leather gloves until they were off, and began to unbutton her winter coat. Where beautiful lofty people must come, she thought, as she strained to look around at the wall murals and imported marble. A flourish of parlor palms was fanned gracefully throughout for as far as she could see, and above, a chandelier with six shades of gold silk and sequins outstretched its arms toward her.

"I say, dear, there's not a touch of color on you," a voice with an undeniably husky quality called from behind.

Ina turned to face its source. It belonged to an elderly woman of curt height and, presumably, manner. She wore a black velvet poke bonnet, of the type a certain generation wore when motoring, with pink chiffon ties that formed roses at each ear.

"I noticed the moment you walked through the door," the woman continued. "You're much too young to be in mourning. And young women your age don't generally prefer black. These days, they come in here painted from head to toe practically. They want to *be seen* more than they want *to see*. And they wear these awful marmot fur sets that stink to the heavens. Why don't they just beat a woodchuck on the head and be done with it? Sling it over their shoulders, why don't they?"

"Yes, well." Put off by the stranger's manner, Ina advanced to the front desk to announce her arrival.

The woman followed. "No jewelry either, I see. Very smart on your part, that way no one can accuse you of levity in your dress."

Ina ignored her. She retrieved the small suitcase she had set down beside her, a canvas Gladstone that was a wedding gift from her parents, and followed the porter to the boost.

"What floor is she, Jasper?" the woman asked the porter.

"Third floor, Miss McGhee."

"Same as me," and she snatched the key from him. "I'll see that she gets there myself, dear boy. You just see that the rest of her luggage is delivered promptly to her room."

"Yes, ma'am. As you wish."

Stepping onto the lift with the strange, insolent woman, Ina felt her color rise. Who was this bumptious woman? she wondered. Could she be the proprietress? Ina gripped the leather handle on her bag tighter and prepared to lash out, but upon taking a closer look, she saw how the elderly woman's cheeks had depressions like two dropped plums, and better noticed the large velvet rose pinned to her breast. Perhaps she was a lonely old maid. And what else do they have to do but mind other people's business? Or perhaps she was a widow herself. In any case, it was the umbrella the woman was using for a cane, the wooden handle shaped into a handsome dog's head, that ultimately ensured Ina's sympathy.

"You're the owner?" Ina felt a confidence in asking once the door closed.

"Me? This glorified sanitarium? Oh, heavens no!" the woman smirked, and the door to the lift opened with a rending grate, stopping short the conversation as the two stepped into the expansive hallway.

The old woman stopped momentarily to look at the number that was etched onto the brass key. "Three-oh-eight. This way, dear." Upon reaching Ina's room, she put the key in the lock and turned the knob, then placed the key into Ina's palm. "I'm sure you'll want to rest a bit before dinner. And at my age I need the extra time to dress. I'll save you a seat at my table." And with a sure fist around her umbrella's ears, Miss McGhee ambled across the hall, *tat tat tat* on the hardwood floor, leaving the word *sanitarium* to pervade Ina's psyche.

Ina was shaking when she entered the room and immediately took a seat on the bed. She had eaten little on the train; the crusts from a mock-crab sandwich and a cup of lukewarm tea. What would people back home think once they learned of her "vacation"? Would they assume that she had been sent to an institution for the un-right-minded? That she had calenture of the brain? That she was suffering from outright delirium? Her parents would say she was merely away for a rest, but Ina knew people formed their own opinions.

The room was spacious, not so different from her room back home, a confident mix of patterns: a little Persian, a smattering of Chinese, and a wee bit of French toile; and her view looked out onto a garden area that was lightly covered with snow. The remainder of her luggage was brought up by the porter shortly afterward, and behind him a bellhop wheeling a silver tea service along with a tray of *bonne bouches* to help her endure the lull until dinner, compliments of Miss McGhee in 303.

She opened her suitcase and began to unpack. Barely twenty-one years of age and already a widow. How could this have happened? And why to her? Why Harlan? It simply did not make sense. That Harlan's inferior eyesight had kept him from military service was supposed to have kept him safe. He was one of the few lucky ones, and how grateful they both had been. They had survived the influenza pandemic, and the war, of course, was finally over and they were like every other young couple, on the tiptop of the world. All they wanted was to spend their lives together, the way you want something so badly you can already taste it. Cake before it's put on a plate.

She knew she wasn't the first to be overcome with a broken heart. Though she felt she was. As if everything she had ever wanted in her whole life had been taken from her with might and main, with one purpose: to cripple her very soul. It was because she was a delicate child, that was why. She'd always been slight and pale, always lagged so far behind the other children it was a wonder she received any education at all. Once, she overheard her mother refer to her as gingerbready, in response to a comment that Ina's Aunt Priscilla made: "That child is weak as milk." "Why, she's just gingerbready is all."

Yes, she supposed, it should be no surprise that she was dealt this sort of fate.

In the dining room, Miss McGhee was seated at a corner table and waved her over. Too late to turn and flee. The old frail was wearing another distinctive hat, a turban with feathers that added no less than six inches to her stout frame, and looked to Ina as if a poor misguided heron had settled directly onto her head. Her dress was a high-luster sateen foulard with full sleeves and a standing collar that made her look like a queen dowager.

The atmosphere in the dining room was befitting a mountain resort. Glossy hardwood floors, a stone fireplace large enough to stand in, and paddle fans that beguiled the ceiling with languid motions. Stuffed heads of brute creation loomed large in the background. One, a forlorn-looking deer whose eyes seemed dead-focused on the chandelier, which was, curiously enough, made from a tangle of antlers. A curly-horned ram with nearly the same eyestrain hung on another wall.

But the most unsettling of these stuffed mementos was directly in Ina's path of sight when she was seated across from Miss McGhee. A lamp made of deer legs. Each table had an identical one as its centerpiece. Four furry legs topped with a beaded shade at the kneecaps—did deer have kneecaps? The hooves were bound in a perplexed state, pointing North, South, East, and West. Ina imagined a trembling doe giving serious thought to those very directions while staring into the wicked barrel of a gun. And all for an absurd table lamp! If her menu choices were Saddle of Venison or, heaven forbid, Smothered Tongue, she would have to reconsider dinner. She was thinking up an excuse when Miss McGhee commented on the night's specials.

"They have a delightful trout that I always have several times during my stay here. And you can't go wrong with the Orange-Lacquered Duck. Simply scrumptious."

If Ina had any qualms about her lack of knowledge on worldly issues, dinner with Miss McGhee certainly made up for it. This woman was full of all sorts of information, and seemed to take great pleasure in sharing choice bits of tidings with her, especially when said tidings involved the other guests.

Early in their conversation—it was a blessing for the reserved Ina that Miss McGhee enjoyed doing most of the talking—she ascertained that Miss McGhee was not a widow at all. In fact, she had never married. She spoke only briefly of herself, how she had traveled the world solo (she apparently came from money) and had made a career for herself in photography, quite rare for a woman of her time. She was a fixture at Sunset Mountain, having spent every winter there since 1901, and knew the staff and the returning guests. Something about the place fed her soul, she said, revived her itchy feet.

"See that gentleman over there?" Miss McGhee said. "With the soup strainer on his lip? That's Mr. Develin, a confirmed bachelor and fur distributor from Charlottesville. Tinctures his tea with gin, his favorite libation.

And thinks he's fooling everyone by carrying around that silver match safe and pipe."

"I'm afraid I don't understand," said Ina.

"Well, dear, the man doesn't even smoke. That's not a match safe at all. Watch him long enough and you'll see what I mean. And that lady there?" She gestured by tipping her head. "The one with the personality bob? A Miss Perrin. Poor creature if ever there was one. Claims that she suffers from irascible skin during the cold months and that coming here is an amulet for her vanity."

"And you don't believe her?" asked Ina.

"Dear heart, take a look at the book she's reading. Can't see it? Well, I can tell you this much: it has either been penned by Charlotte Brontë or Jane Austen. Miss Perrin is on a perennial manhunt, you see, though she no doubt fancies herself a hopeless romantic. I suppose in that respect it's a shame, because every spring she returns home with her books a little more stained, and herself all the more faded. If only she knew what a ludicrous undertaking marriage can be. Most are no more than partnerships between men and their housekeepers. Of course, we all dream, don't we, of someone who will take over for us, and when that doesn't work out, well, what choice have we?" Miss McGhee gave an exhausted shrug.

Her umbrella was hooked over her chair back, and every now and again, when she shifted in her seat to point out another guest, Ina could see its sculpted head. Something about the hard wooden dog eyes began to affect her during Miss McGhee's speech, as if they went through her with some sort of fatal penetration. For the rest of her life eyes would be on her, she thought, people would pity her, speculate about her state of mind.

Her jaw began to quiver.

"Oh, dear," said Miss McGhee. "I'm afraid you've taken me too seriously." She reached across the table and gave a pat to the back of Ina's hand. "I do like to ramble. Forgive an old fool, won't you?"

"No, no, please," Ina said, waving her off. "It has nothing to do with you or our conversation. I'm the one who should be apologizing. It's just that—my husband—he recently—died." Ina felt a swelling in her throat, and all of a sudden she dissolved into tears.

"Thank fortune!" said Miss McGhee.

Ina sniffled. "Pardon?"

"I knew there was a river in there somewhere, dear." Miss McGhee retrieved an embroidered handkerchief from her purse and pressed it into Ina's hands.

It was the first time Ina had shed tears since Harlan died. She had heard that people dealt with sorrow in different ways. But not crying at all seemed abnormal to her, if not abominably heartless. It was the reason she hid in her room. Her father had said she was simply in shock, and because she was in shock she was numb, and because she was numb she felt indifferent, and therefore suffered from lethargy, and everyone knows that lethargy is a symptom of shock.

"You just can't imagine," said Ina, once she was capable of speaking.

"Oh, do tell, dear," said Miss McGhee, propping her sateen elbows on the table, rapt with attention.

❋

Over the course of her stay, Ina and her new friend became inseparable. When the weather allowed, they wrapped themselves in throws and strolled the garden. Ina confided in Miss McGhee things she had never confided to anyone. She had loved Harlan, but was afraid she was the cause of his death, that somehow she had willed it to happen. Even *that* she couldn't explain.

"Listen, dear," said Miss McGhee. "Any woman can talk herself into loving a man, for a while at least. But it's quite normal to be irritated by his daily behavior. Just because a man sucks his teeth, or has a lock of tameless hair that irritates you, doesn't mean you wished the man dead. I think that's what you're trying to say, and if so, it's absolute nonsense."

They were taking advantage of a sunny, though brisk day, seated on chaise longues in the courtyard. On a postcard they would've looked like passengers on a steamboat.

"It wasn't his behavior that caused me concern," said Ina, thoughtfully tracing her finger along the arm of the chair. "It was my own."

"How's that, dear?"

Ina hesitated. "Naturally, a wife has certain, how should I say—*devoirs?*"

"Duties?" Miss McGhee laughed. "Ah yes! The charm of sex. No need to be delicate on my account, dear heart!"

Ina smiled. "It's just that I—I never allowed myself to look, really. At him, you know? Into his eyes. Like a woman should do when she loves a man, yes?"

Miss McGhee nodded. "It's called critical niceness. It's just another way we lie to one another. It's all about being submissive, letting the male mount the throne, if you will. What did Will Shakespeare say, 'every inch a king'? Women have been taught it for years, and I dare say that's what's wrong with the gender nowadays. Don't misunderstand me, dear, I do mean to include myself, but the older I become, the less tact I seem to have. And I don't believe that it's such a bad thing. Desire, dear, no matter what anyone tells you, is not a bad word.

"And while we're on the subject," she continued, "you're much too young for widow's weeds. Don't be afraid of a little color." Miss McGhee closed her eyes and reclined her head against the chair.

Ina paralleled her actions.

She had dismissed this woman only two weeks earlier in the lobby as if she were no more than a decrepit old maid. But now Ina saw her in a different light. Miss McGhee was a sibyl making a prophecy. Perhaps she was right. Perhaps Ina shouldn't be afraid of adding a flush of color to her life. The problem was, there had always been a weakness to Ina, a part of her that relied on the opinions of others to make even the simplest of life's choices. She had never made one decision that she could truly call her own. Perhaps including her marriage.

For several nights afterward, Ina lay awake thinking about the many conversations between her and Miss McGhee. She was ready to stop feeling sorry for herself. Miss McGhee *was* right. She was still a young woman. Much too young to act a widow. She would need to be economically independent now. She would have to learn to be self-supporting.

Chapter 3

The Preparations

*N*ow Beatrice, you won't forget to pick up Miss Fitzhugh this afternoon, will you?" Miss Lul said.

"No, Mama."

"Because I promised Corena Wheeler you'd be more than happy to collect her from the depot. And that train isn't always reliable. Just because they say it'll be here at four o'clock doesn't amount to a hill of beans in my book. I do not want that girl waiting on you in this heat. She's been through enough torment. Not to mention I'd never hear the end of it from Corena."

"I said I will get her, Miss Lul. Now quit your worrying." Bertie sipped at her coffee while Miss Lul went about cleaning up the breakfast dishes.

"You want egg salad today?"

"Sounds fine," Bertie said.

For days on end all she had been hearing about was this woman, a young widow from Richmond, coming to help that frazzled Venie Duncan rein in the ruffians at East Roxboro School.

According to Alta Ruth, who considered herself one of Miss Duncan's more well-behaved charges, Miss Duncan had always been a teacher easy to addle. And it was fortunate for everyone involved that she wasn't in charge of the overall management of the school. That responsibility fell to Mrs. Wheeler, who was principal and superintendent whenever the need arose— when she wasn't attending to her Woman's Page column for the *Courier*. So how the search for a new schoolteacher came about was quite simple. One day Miss Duncan had to call upon Mrs. Wheeler to settle a difficulty with a self-willed pupil, and Mrs. Wheeler—presumably noticing the rapid erosion of Miss Duncan's mind at the time—had immediately sought an assistant for the beleaguered teacher. And it wasn't long before Mrs. Wheeler had procured one, putting the whole town in a state of overwrought, ridiculous excitement.

Gladys Yearwood had even called up Bertie at the switchboard to say, "I heard her father's a doctor." "Well now, isn't that good," Bertie replied. "Maybe he'll find a cure for blue blood." And she unplugged the line.

Her cousin Guerine was just as bad. "Mrs. Wheeler says she speaks French." Bertie didn't care if the woman spoke dog Latin, and told her cousin as much.

Miss Lul was in a tizzy, too, because the last time a single woman had come from Virginia and boarded at the Daye home was in 1915. The woman, a Miss Jones, was a self-reliant, devout Christian whose spiritual adventures were leading her to a life of missionary work. She'd been inspired, the young woman had said, by the great Southern Baptist missionary Lottie Moon and was collecting on behalf of the Lottie Moon Christmas Offering for Foreign Missions. She was going to China, to Tengchow specifically, to give her offering to Miss Moon directly, place it right in the soft sweet palm of her hand so help her God. Bertie didn't trust a word the girl said (and with good reason since Miss Moon had expired in 1912), but Miss Lul was a self-reliant, devout Christian herself and zealously gave the young woman free room and board and a larder of money on the day she left.

"Heavens, Beatrice, put your knees together!" Miss Lul said, wiping toast crumbs from the table with a damp rag. "I hope you don't sit like that up in that telephone office in front of Mr. Wheeler. I can see the tops of your stockings!" Miss Lul's head faltered. "I know how you can be, Beatrice, stopping to chat with folks and not paying a bit of attention to the time of day." She lifted Bertie's cup and made a final pass with the dishrag. "Do not keep that girl waiting."

Bertie got up from the kitchen table and grabbed the egg salad sandwich that Miss Lul had fixed and wrapped for her lunch.

"And you'll be there at what time?" Miss Lul said.

"Let's see. If the train is due in at four o'clock like you've told me for X-teen times then I should probably get there at least half an hour before because my mama taught me to be punctilio."

"Don't you get smart with me."

Chapter 4

Guerine Gets Her Hair Bobbed

*T*o the eye, the most important thing to Guerine was—Guerine. But for good reason: she had built herself on a firm foundation of parental neglect.

Her father, William Upton Loftis, was a cold, distant businessman who divided his time between his tobacco warehouse at the hem of town and, when he was home, sharpening his pencil behind the door to his study. Her mother, Maude Louise Loftis, spent all of hers in bed. Ever since Maude Louise had bore out a wailing beluga-weight baby girl, early autumn of 1900, she'd been beset with a constant case of tired feeling. The sheer thought of ever giving birth again had led her on a life-long search for sedatives. She was the type of woman who, if she had a fleeting thought about anything at all, felt like she had worked on it all day. Worked. Hard. She was a loyal customer of Dr. Miles' Medical Preparations and had a queer fondness for black hair mattresses. For Guerine, it was like living with two ghosts.

Who then could fault her for having overweening pride? Her parents were practically invisible and she had no siblings to steer her attention toward something or someone other than herself. She was a pretty young woman of twenty with brunette hair and a small coaxing mouth, her eyes were as bright as two sociable honeybees, she had a rather high bosom, and complete run of the house. She was independent, with a great deal of voluntariness (a nicer way of calling her an apple-polishing do-gooder), and was always prepared to outvie any female in the community, so long as the outdoing to be done was strictly related to the feminine—say, having to do with clothes or kitchen. Only it was that other habit she had, of appealing to herself for admiration, that made some—her cousin Bertie, for instance— more than a little testy whenever she was around.

She had a considerable amount of work to do to get ready for Miss

Fitzhugh's arrival, so as soon as her chores were done that morning, after she had fluffed her mama's pillows and served her lost bread in bed, giving her a spoonful of tonic to wash it down, she hurried downstairs and tore a page from her latest issue of *Motion Picture* magazine, shoved it deep into her purse, and marched over to the barber's before things got too busy.

"Looking for your pa, Miss Loftis? You just missed him," said Mr. Gentry. He swiped a bristle brush along the shoulders of a gentleman who sat in the barber's chair reading the newspaper.

"No sir, I'm here of my own volition."

"Volition, Miss Loftis?"

"That's right, Mr. Gentry. I'm here to get my hair bobbed."

Mr. Gentry set the brush on the counter and looked at her, his face as empty as a fish. "You mean, you want me to—"

"I do indeed. And now looks to be as good a time as any."

Mr. Wall—the man in the barber chair, a man Guerine had always thought had more forehead than personality—made no indication of removing himself from the leather chair. When he continued to hold the paper out in front of him, Guerine cleared her throat. "How'do, Mr. Wall. Perhaps you could rush it along, now that you've had your pores restored with that smell-goody stuff." She wagged her hand at him. "I'm in a bit of a scramble today."

He folded his newspaper and reached into his pocket, handed several coins to Mr. Gentry, then quietly made his way to the hat rack, where he grabbed a dusty tan hat that looked suitable for a scout, and stepped out onto the sidewalk, but not before bumping against the doorframe.

"I do believe that bay rum is the spikiest thing about that man," Guerine said.

Mr. Gentry, his hands laced in front of his white jacket, his knuckles in line with the division in his slicked hair, cleared his throat. "Miss Loftis, I don't think I ought to be cutting on your hair unless I got your ma and pa's permission."

"Oh, bunkum!" Guerine plopped into the chair. "When's the last time you saw my mama? No, no, don't even answer. She's been holed up in her bedroom since Woodrow Wilson got president. Doesn't even see the light of day even though she's got a perfectly good window. And well, you know my papa, he wants me to have anything I want." She looked at herself in the mirror and primped her hair.

"I don't know," said Mr. Gentry. "Your pa and I go way back. If he was to take a slight to me—"

"Don't be ridiculous. Now here's what I want." She opened her handbag and pulled out a come-hither picture of actress Elsie Ferguson, pressed it flat against her knee, and handed it to the barber. "Short tresses that curl."

Mr. Gentry was at a loss. And Elsie Ferguson did not do one thing to help, staring back at him like a woman who knows what she wants and gets it.

"Well, go on, Mr. Gentry," said Guerine. "I don't have all day. Proceed, please."

He laid the photo on the counter and reached up for an apron hanging from a peg and half-heartedly fanned out the wrinkles. Guerine lifted her chin as he draped the white smock over her.

"Is that Papa's shaving mug up there?" she asked, after pointing to the row of mugs on a high shelf, each with the name of its owner in black Old English letters. "I declare. I haven't seen that since I was a little girl."

Mr. Gentry appeared to be in deep study.

"Oh, my hairpins." Guerine pulled them out, one by one, until her hair fell down her back in a dark, wavy stream and swept the arms of the chair. "Don't be so nervous, Mr. Gentry. I'll pay you more than the thirty cents you charge for a child's Buster Brown."

Guerine never tired of talking. She talked about the hot weather they'd been having and why did he reckon it was called the dog days, didn't cats and cows get hot, too; and that reminded her, did he hear about that incident with Mr. Bradsher the other day, how as soon as he walked out of his house that awful dog of his attacked his feet, and as it turned out it was all on account of him recently taking to shining his shoes with beef tallow, all because that crazy Mr. Archer had suggested it, can you imagine; and did he know she'd had St. Vitus' when she was a little girl and how her papa had refused to let her use a fork because her St. Vitus made her arms dance and he was afraid she'd put out an eye.

But Mr. Gentry was quiet the duration. He would gently separate sections of her hair with an aluminum comb and pull them toward him, study each section for an unreasonable amount of time as if making a mental note regarding its coarseness and luster, and would finally direct his Heinisch shears in a slant.

The first cut took them both by surprise. Guerine let out an audible gasp, and Mr. Gentry nearly came up off his feet like an unsteady shooter. He took a step back, and Guerine bent toward the glass.

"That's not nearly short enough, Mr. Gentry. Look at Elsie here. Above the chin."

By the time the hair cutting was over, Mr. Gentry was ankle deep in dark hair, and Guerine was busily admiring her image in the mirror.

"I dare Bertie to say I don't have cheekbones now. What do you say, Mr. Gentry? Think this calls for a new cloche hat?" She stood from the chair and gathered change from her clutch. "Forty cents seem fair?" She didn't wait for him to reply, simply clinked the coins on the counter and peered into the mirror one final time. "I would think you'd want to redo your sign out front now."

"Ma'am?"

"Right under Electric Massage. You could add the words 'Ladies' Hair-bob, Forty Cents.' Well, good day, Mr. Gentry."

She strolled down the sidewalk as if she could charm birds from trees. Her next stop was Bottomby's, where she bought a new hat and the latest in sportswear, and then over to Thomas's Drug Store to see if she could find Miss Ferguson's favorite perfume—the haunting scent of Egyptian Oriental. In her exclusive interview with *Motion Picture*, Miss Ferguson admitted as to how "Once you smell it you are pursued by its penetrating odor and the unforgettable illusions it calls to mind." But the closest thing Guerine could find was a one-ounce bottle of Stolen Sweets.

And finally, before returning home, she stopped in at Sargeant and Clayton's Grocery. She had read, she couldn't recall where, that Virginians eat delicacies—even on weekdays. Scrumptious little morsels such as dates wrapped in bacon and Benedictine canapés. And she and her Woman's Club members were already in the thick of helping Mrs. Wheeler organize this upcoming Saturday's affair to honor the new teacher, an outdoor supper with music and games and homemade ice cream. Each member had agreed to bring a dish.

The Wheelers threw these types of socials every summer. It was always an occasion to celebrate something, or absolutely nothing. Last year so happened to be the pouring of the cement out on the Roxboro-Durham Road, and clever Mrs. Wheeler had made a batch of macaroon ice cream (Mr. Wheeler snuck in a little bourbon when she wasn't looking), and the way those macaroons made a bumpy crust and resembled the newly cemented road! Mrs. Wheeler was a wonderment. But that squatty-necked Cora Humphries had took and stole her idea and made the Supreme Chicken Salad when Guerine had explicitly told her that she was doing it, and after going to all that dunghill effort the ol' biddy still left the grapes whole. Some of these women, it's a point-to-point race for them. But she, Guerine, was Bertie and Alta Ruth's cousin, and Lalura Daye was her aunt, and she had every right to impress their boarders before anyone else got the chance. She would make her special dish for Miss Fitzhugh. She'd just make it a day early and see that it got hand-delivered, gain a pull over Cora Humphries.

She entered the grocery and waltzed up to the counter. "Mr. Clayton," she said, "I need all the dates you've got. Every last one."

Chapter 5

Ina Arrives in Roxboro

A train pulled into the depot of a small village in North Carolina around four o'clock in the afternoon. It was August, as hot a day as one could possibly imagine. No hat brim wide enough, no paper fan large enough. The air itself smelled like a fiery flatiron scorching damp cotton.

Ina stepped down from the platform with her train case and waited for the remainder of her luggage. She was wearing a simple ivory blouse of silk georgette crepe, a dark skirt with a sweep just above the ankle, and a becoming hat fashioned from imported forget-me-nots. Everything appeared lit to burnt orange, electrified by the sun. She gave her eyes a moment to adjust, then took in the view of what was to be her new, albeit temporary, home.

Her Aunt Priscilla had given her the idea to come here. Distance and time were what she felt Ina needed, and there was no better place for that than the Courteous City. It had been ten years or more since her aunt had visited Roxboro, and that visit had remained firmly fixed in Priscilla's mind. It was during the completion of the town's power plant when the lights were turned on in the stores for the very first time and all the town had flocked to see. She even saved a copy of *The Roxboro Dispatch* with an article that closed with a line Priscilla had committed to memory: *Be wise and come to Roxboro while dirt is still selling at village prices*. Why, come to think of it, she still had a friend in that charming place, a lovely lady by the name of Corena Wheeler. For Ina's sake, she jotted her a note.

Ina's first impression was something akin to being plucked from big city sprightliness, then set down in an English village where there's barely a stir, sometimes for miles. A far cry from Dock Street on a Saturday afternoon when the heart of Richmond is stirring with locals seeking everything from fresh produce to neighborly chats. She watched as three graying women, who had also been on the train, walked in an agreeable covey uphill. They reminded her of mourning doves searching out seed, sweet, the way they had their heads down and bumped shoulders with one another as they walked.

She had been told by Mrs. Wheeler that she would be met by Beatrice Daye, her hostess's eldest daughter. It was the Daye home where Ina was to board, another detail that Mrs. Wheeler had arranged. Her note replying to Ina's inquiry was written in a delicate slanting hand, her script painting the picture of a rattle-boned woman standing amidst a pecky sea of uncontrollable children. *The school's attendance has grown greatly and Venie Duncan poor dear may not be long on this earth if she doesn't get some assistance. The timing of your letter could not be better. Please say you'll come.* And Ina had agreed, but only for one season.

It seemed the only other rush afoot was a shiny black insect trying to get beyond the stark shadow her train case cast on the dusty ground. The rest of her luggage was now collected and lined neatly beside her, yet still no sign of anyone who looked like they might be looking for her. There was evidence of other life, however, across from where she stood. An old inn skirted in ivy that a whitewashed sign announced, in dull black letters, as the Dowdy. It had a winding staircase on one side, and a lazy oak on the other, and deep within the porch of the inn a woman sat rocking.

Ina took a handkerchief from her purse and dotted it along tiny rivulets that were beginning to trickle down her neck. Surely the woman could see her? And yet she wouldn't so much as wave. Isn't that what people did in this part of the South, wave to friends they haven't yet met? Deciding she would have to be the one to do the greeting—and wanting to share a bit of the woman's shaded porch—Ina left her luggage, stepped from the wooden footpath onto packed earth, and started across the road.

She glanced to her right, where the three women had turned the corner, and noticed a partial store awning, and what appeared to be a merchant's sign—a painted window, if her eyes were being truthful. YOU PAY THE PREMIUM, CLAYTON PAYS THE LOSSES. Insurance agency. People were crossing from one corner to another now, men shaking hands, doffing their hats to ladies in passing. A young Negro boy on a bicycle glided by, his wheels turning like a weaver's loom. In one hand he carried a tray that looked to be filled with icy glasses of lemonade, and here she was, dying of thirst! Not that she had qualms regarding her wait for Miss Daye, but five minutes can seem like fifty when standing under a blaze of heat. She watched the boy maneuver a slight dip in the road without spilling a drop, and then all of a sudden he was out of sight.

"Good afternoon," she said, walking up the Dowdy's steps, into deep shade. "I don't suppose you'd mind if I waited out of the sun?"

The woman nodded, but said nothing. She was nervously strumming both thumbs against her index fingers like one might separate paper. Everything about her was furrowed, the wrinkles in her face, her hands. Even the dress she wore had deep, contorted folds like the tightly clustered blooms on a cockscomb.

Concerned that the woman might consider the intrusion on her space an act of insolence, Ina said, as kindly as possible, "I'm to be met by Miss Beatrice Daye, you see. I was told she'd be right along. We've never been introduced. Perhaps you know Miss Daye?"

Again, the woman nodded. Still, no expression. Ina continued to stand although several rockers lined the porch. The woman made no motion for her to sit. Feeling uncomfortable, but not wanting to turn her back to the woman for fear of being rude, Ina turned slightly toward the steps and peered around the ivy to look up and down the road for a sign of Miss Daye. She felt indescribably anxious. The burden of carrying this one-sided conversation was nerve-rending for someone who had never possessed the gift of idle chatter. Better to be question-marked, Ina thought, if that be the only alternative. But the thought didn't keep her from saying, "Your sun is quite hot here," while waving her handkerchief in front of her face. What an absolutely ridiculous thing to say! Like their sun is any hotter than the one back home. She knew before she even said it, she just could not stop herself.

She heard a crunching sound and was relieved to see a motorcar turn from the crosspoint, the rough road making the driver the sport of dips and ducks. The machine soon sputtered to a stop. Painted on one of the door panels were the words "Eat Bertie's Peanuts—Home Cooked—5 Cents," accompanied by an anthropomorphized peanut pod with curly black eyelashes, flame-red lips, and a pair of red patent shoes. The young lady behind the wheel looked in the direction of Ina's luggage.

"Oh, that must be Miss Daye!" Ina said and ran down the steps. "It was a pleasure meeting you. I'm sure." And before she could say another mulish thing she hurried across the road.

"Miss Daye?"

The young woman stepped from the motorcar and slammed the door. "Bertie, if you please. Hello-Girl by day, Peanut Peddler by night. You're Miss Fitzhugh, I take it." She ignored Ina's extended hand and turned to hoisting the bags over into the boot. "Let's hurry it along if you don't mind, while this girl's still running." She slapped a hand to the car. "Doesn't like to be cranked more than she has to."

Ina didn't intend to stare at her new acquaintance, but she was slightly taken aback by Miss Daye's boisterous qualities. The young woman was dressed to such advantage, in a black and white jersey frock with bone buttons, and wearing ultrasmart black, heeled shoes. Yet, she handled Ina's bags with a man's hands. How unfortunate that they should look like ill-shaped sausage cakes, but to her credit she didn't have them set in eye-catching jewels. In some respects she could have doubled for the starlet May Allison in the movie *Fair and Warmer.* Though a fleshier version, Ina thought, with legs that had the aplomb of a big blonde.

"See you met Eunice," Miss Daye said once the two were settled inside the motorcar.

"Oh, yes! The lady there at the inn. We were having a friendly chat before you arrived."

"Is that right? I'd like to've seen that. 'Specially since she was born without a tongue."

Ina looked at Miss Daye and saw she was grinning. Was this her way of teasing? The motorcar jerked forward, pitching them against the seatback.

"Well, this would be Roxboro," Miss Daye said, turning onto the paved crossroad. "Best not to blink if you wanna catch it all in."

It looked like a picture postcard to Ina, the epitome of an up-and-doing small town. Dark red brick on both sides of the street, cream-colored awnings over the windows of storefronts. People on the go, in one door and out another.

The bugling of the machine's horn startled her. Miss Daye laughed and waved as they passed a group of gentlemen standing outside of Sargeant and Clayton's Grocery.

"The structures look so modern," Ina said. "Not that they shouldn't."

"Yep. We've had quite a flurry the last few years. Lot of the old frame buildings been torn down, replaced with brick. Even paved the road between here and Durham last year."

Ina couldn't tell by Miss Daye's manner whether or not she was disappointed with the town's progress, and before she knew it they were pulling to a stop in front of a two-storied house with a low-pitched roof; a wood frame with decorative cornices and Roman arches above the windows and the door. It resembled an Italian villa.

"Here's home," Miss Daye said.

"My, I had no idea how close it was. I could've saved you the trouble and walked from the depot."

"And lugged bags with those arms? I don't think so. Come on in the house. While you're getting acquainted with Miss Lul, I'll carry your bags upstairs."

Ina reached for her train case and tried to catch up to Miss Daye who was already headed up the walkway. "Miss Lul, you say?"

"Mama," said Miss Daye. "As in Lalura. Lalura Daye, your hostess?"

"Oh, of course. A pet name. I don't mean pet as in animal, I mean—"

Miss Daye turned, suitcases in hand. "Need something cold to drink, do ya?"

Ina took a deep breath. What she needed was to relax.

"Oh, and fair warning about Miss Lul? She's a Christian."

"That's not a problem," Ina said, now more at ease. "We have them in Virginia."

The two shared a good-natured laugh, then Miss Daye—Bertie—turned the knob and opened the door, kicking it the rest of the way.

The Daye home didn't strike Ina as being stately to the point of impressing (but anything was better than that glorified *maison de santé* where she had spent her winter, where human mishaps go to be made new). From the moment she walked through the paired doors into a wide entry, she was welcomed by a dark wooden staircase, soft-colored oriental rugs, soothing wall coverings, and enough coleus and fern to suggest cozy clutter.

Once introductions were made, Mrs. Daye showed her upstairs to her room. It had all the touches of a woman's boudoir. Marble-topped nightstands and a dropfront dresser with handkerchief drawers, a fainting couch at the foot of the bed, a folding screen with silk panels in one corner, an upholstered armchair with crocheted antimacassars on its arms and back. Sturdy straight lines and simple carvings set against pale yellow walls, papered in a French-style pattern. And there was plenty of light. The windows nearly spanned floor to ceiling, the tops arched like eyebrows. But the room was eerily reminiscent of the one she and Harlan had been given at the Algonquin Hotel and it was almost more than she could take.

Before returning downstairs she went across the hall to the bathroom to freshen up. She'd been sitting on that hot, filthy train for what felt like hours, the compartment a sweaty medley of soured silk and boiled-leather Gold Bonds, with a base note of clammy camisole. Not exactly what one would call alluring, she thought, laughing to herself at the very incongruity of the concept.

She stood in front of the porcelain basin, the water streaming a Niagara, and gazed at herself in the glass. How foolish to think a splash of cool water could restore oneself. Where was that fresh perspective she'd had days ago, that she could face the world with the assuredness of a strong woman?

It was all but gone now, perhaps circling the drain. If she could she would stay right here, in this tiled water closet, away from any expectations beyond this luxury of unlimited cleansing. Nobody bothers you when you're in a toilet room. Least of all when water is running.

But her hosts were waiting. Reluctantly, she turned off the faucet, picked up the embroidered hand towel that lay on the wooden cabinet next to the sink, and blotted the water from her face.

❄

While Mrs. Daye busied herself in the kitchen, opening and closing cabinet doors and chipping ice, Ina joined Bertie in the parlor.

"You're probably an MIF girl, huh?" Bertie said.

Ina looked perplexed.

"You know, milk in first," explained Bertie. "Like the English take their tea."

"Oh, no," said Ina. "Iced tea is just fine. Especially on a day like today." She looked around the room. "Such a lovely home."

Before Bertie had a chance to reply, Alta Ruth came running into the house, her dirty-blond hair scruffy, and her pink ribbons lopsided.

"Bertie, Bertie! Come look!" She tugged Bertie from the chair and over to the window.

"What is it?"

"Just look, will you!"

"Where? I don't see anything."

"Ha! Made you look, you dirty crook, stole your mama's pocketbook."

"Very funny. Now quit showing off."

"Alta Ruth, where are your manners?" Mrs. Daye said, setting a tray with a pitcher of iced tea and glasses on the credenza. "And what have you done to make such a mess of those pretty hairbows? We have company, young lady. Go wash your hands. Go on. Maybe you can find a game of some sort to occupy yourself till supper."

The doorbell chimed and Alta Ruth ran to open the door. Cousin Guerine stood on the porch, holding what appeared to be a cake box. Alta Ruth stared up at her for a moment without speaking, as if she were looking at a foreigner.

"Alta Ruth? Aren't you gonna let me in?"

"Guerine's here!" Alta Ruth hollered out, and ran off to entertain herself in another part of the house.

"Not so loud, child!" Mrs. Daye said. "Come on in, Guerine. We're in the parlor."

Guerine stepped down from the vestibule, her shepherd-check suit whisking as she walked. "Greetings, Aunt Lul, Cousin," she said, in a harpy singsong fashion. "I just happened to remember your guest was due today and thought while I was out for a walk I'd stop by and say hello."

"Well, aren't you an apple off a different tree," said Bertie. "New glad rags I see, and somebody has run riot with scissors to your hair."

Mrs. Daye appeared stunned. "Yes. A different apple, indeed."

Guerine nodded to Ina and placed the box on the coffee table. "This is what's referred to as natty, Bertie," she said, her shiny locks peeping out from a satin toque. "If you read something other than that *Woman's Arched Versary*, or whatever it is you're so fond of, you'd see that women are foregoing long hair these days."

"It's called *The Advocate*, Guerine, and if yours is that same magazine you ordered that rubber, chin-strapping flesh reducer from, then no thank you!"

"At least I don't have the same haughty face as Mr. Wheeler's bulldog."

"Girls!" said Mrs. Daye. "Have you forgotten we have company?"

Other than the two cousins being close in age, the only thing they had in common was a softness in the waist. Aside from that they were no more alike than an Indian fig is to a ficus. Guerine turned heads with her looks, Bertie with her emancipated tongue. Their relationship had always been like that of siblings, Bertie assuming the role of oldest (what difference was a few months to her?), thinking it her natural duty to boss an inexperienced Guerine. In truth, their constant arguing was nothing more than a reflection of how important the relationship was to them both. For Bertie, it was a way to demonstrate to Guerine that Guerine was important despite the lack of attention she received at home. And arguing, to Bertie, equaled intimacy, something everyone (except for Guerine) assumed that she was too self-sufficient to need. For Guerine, the kinship was important *because* of the lack of attention she received at home. Bertie had always, in some strange self-deprecating way, made her feel respected.

"Forgive me, Aunt Lul. Bertie makes it hard for even a saint to bite her tongue." Guerine looked at Ina and smiled.

"I'm a little disappointed in you, too, Guerine," Mrs. Daye said.

"Ma'am?"

"I'd expect as much from Beatrice here, cutting her hair when you girls have been taught the Bible says not to, but I certainly wouldn't've expected it of you. I suppose the next thing is you both'll be leaving your corsets in the ladies' room and powdering your knees."

Ina's hand flew to her face, covering her mouth and nose like a fully bloomed zephyr lily.

"I beg to disagree," said Bertie. "You wouldn't ever catch me leaving my hip confiner in a semi-public place."

"How about we not get into this now," Mrs. Daye said, and introduced her niece to the new teacher.

The two women clasped hands.

As Guerine was now able to get a closer look at the teacher, she was reminded of a cameo. It was the young woman's smile and the way her dark hair was twisted into a French roll. But art or no art, sculptures gave Guerine the willies, made her feel like there was somebody inside that marble hollering to get out. A few little corkscrew curls to frame her face, Guerine thought, would fix that right up!

"You can let go of her hand, Guerine," said Bertie. "She's already accepted the position."

"I can't tell you how delighted we are to have you in our township," Guerine said, giving Ina's fingers one last squeeze. "I imagine it will be a change for you, you coming from a big city and all. You're probably accustomed to a lot of social activity. Not a whole lot of comings and goings around here, but I think you'll find we are sociable people. Aren't we, Aunt Lul?"

"Green?" Ina said, repeating the name she thought she'd heard. "Like the color?"

"Oh, forgive me," said Guerine. "I tend to forget it sometimes requires spelling. It's not every day I have an opportunity to meet someone so, *cultured*." And she spelled her name for Ina, not too slow, not too fast. "G-U-E-R-I-N-E. Tell you the truth, I'm not even sure the proper annunciation of my own name."

"Pronunciation," Bertie corrected.

Guerine paused, but decided to ignore Bertie just as she had her earlier comment. "Gwa-reen, Ger-reen, see? Usually folks say it so fast it just comes out Green. I don't fret over it too much myself so you shouldn't either. It was my mama's idea of honoring a couple of her great aunts, Gertrude and Irene. Her way of blending their names together, even though the spelling's off."

"Guerine, honey," Mrs. Daye interrupted. "What's in this box?"

"Oh, I almost forgot. I thought y'all would enjoy a little finger food before supper." Guerine bent over and opened the top.

"What in the hot damn?" Bertie said.

"Beatrice Abigail!" said Mrs. Daye. "We don't fall a cursing in this house."

"Well, look at 'em, Miss Lul. They look scatological."

Ina's eyes lit up.

"Gracious, Bertie," said Guerine, "don't you recognize Bacon Tidbits when you see them? They happen to be delicacies in some parts."

"Parts of what? They're ugly enough to sour milk."

"Not that you would know, but this is food fit for a nightingale's tongue."

"And just when have you ever seen a nightingale?" said Bertie.

"Don't pay her any mind, Guerine," Mrs. Daye said. "This is very kind of you, dear. I'll just go see if I can get them—unstuck. Seems the fat from the bacon has jellied."

"Well, don't just stand there," Bertie said to Guerine, who was standing self-consciously in front of her and Ina. "Rest your saddle."

Guerine sat across from them and cleared her throat. "We all believe," she said, "certainly the members of my Women's Club believe, that having you here, Miss Fitzhugh, will make all the difference in the world to this town of ours."

"Thank you," Ina said, her hands cupping her knees. "But please, call me Ina."

"The educating of our children is foremost," said Guerine. "They're lucky to have someone with the good breeding and grace you have to teach them a thing or two." She looked over at Bertie, who was clearly unimpressed.

"That's very nice of you to say," said Ina. "How old are yours?"

"My what? Children? Oh, no, I don't have any children. I meant our *town's* children. I'm not even married for goodness sakes. Yet. And as far as the little ones go, well, they have a tendency to cling like burrs. That's probably the one thing that Bertie and I agree on. Am I right, Bertie?"

Bertie, sunk into the back of the chair with her legs agape, saw no reason to deny it.

Mrs. Daye returned with Guerine's reheated delicacies, and for the second time that afternoon the doorbell rang. On this occasion it was Corena Wheeler who had a habit of offending the air by atomizing the upper half of her life with Sweet Freesia. She was accompanied by the easily excitable and ever-smelling-of-horehound Venie Duncan, head—and only—teacher of East Roxboro School.

Mrs. Daye showed them into the parlor.

Mrs. Wheeler took Ina's hands in hers. "I feel as if I already know you, my dear. Your voice came to me as clear as a bell when I read your letter. Allow me to introduce Miss Duncan, your—"

Ina was barely able to get to her feet before Miss Duncan, old-boned and short as a tadpole, jumped in front of Mrs. Wheeler with swinging arms and clutched onto Ina's waist like a nipping kit. "Oh, oh oh oh," the little woman screeched. "God bless God bless God bless you!"

The tiny storm rendered Ina immotile. Not until Mrs. Daye invited the two women to sit could Ina reclaim her own seat.

"We were just about to have these nice delicacies Guerine made," said Mrs. Daye.

"How delightful," said Mrs. Wheeler, taking a seat next to Guerine. "What wonderful tantalizers have you concocted here, dear?"

"Just an old family recipe. One that Mama passed on to me."

"And how is Maude these days? I haven't seen her lately."

"Yes, neither have I," said Miss Duncan. "Will she be at the social tomorrow?"

Guerine cleared her throat. She shifted in her seat, rearranging her purse from one hip to the other. "With this heat, you know, it's all according to how she feels."

"This heat is enough to keep anybody inside," said Mrs. Wheeler. "Mister and Missus Whitfield certainly picked a good time to go to the mountains. They're vacationing in Blowing Rock. But surely you all have seen that little item of mine in the *Courier*."

"Miss Duncan," said Mrs. Daye, hoping to deflect the attention away from a topic as frivolous as that gibberish Mrs. Wheeler put in her Woman's Page, "you'll be interested to know that the ladies were talking about the future of our children before you and Mrs. Wheeler arrived."

"Oh yes, the children." Miss Duncan wrung her hands. "We must sit down together very soon, Miss Fitzhugh, and write a lesson plan. Very soon. As soon as humanly possible."

"Of course," said Ina.

"There's a saying about teachers," Mrs. Wheeler said. "One of the Adamses said it, can't remember which now, but I quote, 'The teacher affects eternity. He can never know where his influence stops.'"

"Amen," said Mrs. Daye, doling out cocktail napkins.

One by one the women reached for a tidbit. But, for each, the bacon showed itself to be stubborn. It was reluctant to let go, whereupon a game of tug-o-war ensued until each pork strip had unwound itself from the sticky date and snapped into their faces like wet elastic straps.

Ina's strip hung from her mouth like a sad puppy's tongue.

Mrs. Daye reached for an extra napkin.

Mrs. Wheeler helped her offending strip complete its hurdle over her bottom lip by giving it a nudge. "I do admire your creative effort, dear."

Guerine looked down at her lap and fidgeted.

"Not half bad," said Bertie, reaching for seconds.

"Really, Bertie? You like it?" asked Guerine.

"Sure, why not. It's both salty and sweet. Perfect for the indecisive person."

Guerine grinned, oblivious that Miss Duncan had made a tight fist around her sticky tidbit and was holding it close to her lap.

"Your house is mighty quiet these days, Lalura," Miss Duncan said. "I remember when you had as many as ten boarders at one time."

"More like six," Mrs. Daye said. "But it felt like ten. Preacher Allen even lived here for a short spell."

"Speaking of preachers," said Mrs. Wheeler. "Have you given any thought to where you might be attending church, Miss Fitzhugh? Roxboro Methodist has a number of women who are true beacons of compassion in our community. Guerine herself can attest to that."

"And we can always use one more!" Guerine said.

Ina blinked as a volley of questions and retorts were fired at and, eventually, past her. The women spoke as if she weren't in the room. *Have you given any thought to this, Miss Fitzhugh? Surely Miss Fitzhugh would rather do this.*

"I would think she'd want to attend a church where aid is promoted," said Mrs. Daye. "Aid to the church, aid to the needy."

"There's no finer place than Roxboro Methodist for that," said Mrs. Wheeler. "Why, just last year all the ladies got together and made a memory quilt and raffled it off. Isn't that right, Guerine?"

"No better way to fend off a chill!"

"That was so their preacher could buy a new automobile to drive all of two blocks," Mrs. Daye said, nodding at Ina.

"Now Lalura, you know very well he needs that for visiting shut-ins," Mrs. Wheeler said.

"Oh and don't forget, Mrs. Wheeler," said Guerine, "what was left over he used for sending flowers to the infirm."

"Mount Zion is Methodist, too," Mrs. Daye said, "but their Ladies' Aid Society, which they only began two years ago, already has much to show for it."

"Lalura's right, Corena," said Miss Duncan. "They've had a number of health drives. And just last month, if you recall, they sold brooms to raise money for the Red Cross. Pretty brooms, too."

"True," said Mrs. Daye. "But don't let that alone sway you, Ina. The Baptists are just as conscientious, if not more so. In fact I think we are more conscientious. Why, Roxboro's own Emma Humphries was a devout Baptist. She was a teacher, too, by the way, till she decided to become a missionary."

"Wasn't that just awful?" said Miss Duncan. "To go that far from home to help those little yellow people and then to have 'em try and kill you because you're an American?" She clucked her tongue. "Say, didn't you have a girl stay here one time who claimed to be a missionary?"

Mrs. Daye's face tinged. "And nobody does a better box supper than the Baptists. I saw you buying one yourself if I'm not mistaken, Corena, at the last supper we had."

"Yes, I did," said Mrs. Wheeler, whose own cheeks were beginning to turn as purple as a turnip. "I also donated some items of clothing for you all to give to the poor last winter. But wouldn't you know, not two days after that I saw your Preacher Allen wearing my dead brother Wilborn's motoring gloves."

Mrs. Daye gave a nervous laugh. "My goodness, Corena. A glove is a glove, they all look alike. Why, every man around here practically owns a pair."

"I believe I know Grinnells when I see them."

"Oh!" said Miss Duncan, putting her sticky fist to her mouth and shoving in the remainder of her tidbit.

The ivory fan that was humming in the corner of the room failed to keep the warmth from all those rosy cheeks.

Guerine, uncomfortable with silence of any fashion, spoke up. "Look at us. We haven't even given Miss Fitzhugh—Ina—a chance to speak. Not one of us has bothered to even ask her if she's Methodist or Baptist, or—heaven forbid—Presbyterian?"

All the women drew a bead on Ina and waited for a reply. She mulled their offering of abundant and eternal life, swallowed her greasy date in one gulp, then took a deep breath and straightened her back. "The truth is, ladies—I'm Unitarian."

Their faces were scandalized. No Father, Son, or Holy Ghost? The only divinity the soft, creamy, melt-in-your-mouth kind? She might as well have said Atheist.

Bertie slapped the arms of her chair and cackled. "I guess that's settled. Think I'll take a run out to the Shuford farm and visit with Doodle before supper. Care to go, Ina?"

"I wouldn't mind coming along myself," said Guerine, "if you were to ask."

"Suit yourself," Bertie said.

"Honestly, Beatrice," said Mrs. Daye. "Miss Fitzhugh will think she's been set down in a field of unruly farm boys with all those geese running round her feet. Can't you save that trip for another day?"

"I'm talking about taking a simple drive, Miss Lul. If any one of us is destined to be led astray, I doubt if geese will be to blame."

"I'm only concerned that our guest might prefer resting up after her journey. Wouldn't you, dear?"

"Oh no," said Ina, getting quickly to her feet. "I'd love to go. I'd very much like to get my bearings and see as much of the town as I possibly can."

"And I wouldn't mind the fresh air," said Guerine, following suit.

"Won't Maude be looking for you to come home soon, Guerine?" Mrs. Daye asked. "I know she likes to eat early."

"No ma'am. In fact, she's expected to be unwary. Indefinitely."

The three young women all but ran out the door, Guerine holding on to her hat, trying to catch up to Ina, who was trying to catch up to Bertie. They hopped into Bertie's Ford and urgently ker-chugged through town.

Ina yelled over the sound of air and engine, "So who's Doodle?"

Chapter 6

Doodle Gets an Unannounced Visit

$\mathcal{D}$oodle was walking toward the pen with a bucket of feed for her geese when she saw the black machine coming down her reach of road. It was spanking along, stirring up a squall of red dirt behind it, and as the chugga-wheeze-chugga-puff got closer the driver hung her head out and waved a spirited arm at her. Her friend Bertie, crazy gal. Driving like a politician hell-bent for election. And just like her to put lay to the horn and rouse the geese to a furor. The whole gaggle began to cronk. They rustled their wings around Doodle's feet in an attempt to protect her and their territory from the invasion.

The machine came to a stop in the yard and its front-seat occupants got out first. Doodle recognized Guerine as the person sitting in the rear, but the dark-haired woman who stepped out with Bertie she had never seen before.

Bertie feigned at shooing the geese. They had always been sociable with her, like a cousin come to visit, and soon they quieted to soft, satisfied grunts.

"You gonna motor yourself right into a ditch one of these days if you don't slow down," Doodle said.

"Oh, nuts to you!" Bertie said, tossing a bag of peanuts at her. Doodle caught the bag with her free hand. Her papa loved peanuts, and every time Bertie came out to the farm she brought along a bag special for him.

"Much obliged."

The young woman came around the front of the vehicle. She introduced herself, offering Doodle her hand.

"Ina's the new teacher," Bertie said. "The one I told you would be staying with us."

City skin, Doodle thought. Pale as powder. She was so clean and pleasant smelling that Doodle hesitated to shake her hand, afraid a fleck of dirt or worse would come off on the young woman. And there was the tragedy of her own body odor to consider. She'd been hard at it well before the sun came up. But she didn't want to be rude, so she set the bucket on the ground and wiped her callused hand against her overalls, then awkwardly shook the teacher's hand.

"Back, you feather-flapping scamps! Back!"

"Those geese are not gonna hurt you, Guerine!" Bertie said. "Now get over here and be neighborly!"

"Those birds, I can see it in their beaded eyes, they do not like me!"

"Can you blame them?" said Bertie.

Doodle stared at the teacher during Guerine's flustration with the geese. She wondered if she had stared too long and hard because the young woman looked down at her garments and felt along her waist as if something was loose or missing. She wasn't what Doodle would've expected, though she hadn't given it much thought. Mostly it had been Bertie's talk that put the notion in her mind the new schoolteacher was likely to be spinsterish, an old grass widow. But the woman wasn't that at all. She was young and pretty. So bonny pretty that she could've come out of the *Ladies' Home Journal*, right off a page opposite the Letty Lane paper doll section, a model showing off a new style dress. Not that Doodle spent much time looking at such nonsense, only that Guerine was one for shucking her spent magazines off on Doodle, and some nights when she was still wide awake after reading about the importance of keeping poultry runways clean and hen houses disinfected, she would pick one up. But that was once in a blue moon, and only out of a dull curiosity.

"I understand your friends call you . . . Doodle . . . is that right?" said Ina. "Pardon me, I just have to get accustomed to all these bynames."

"Downright silly, isn't it, Ina," said Guerine, "folks giving their children names like that? I think it's a country thing. You won't see much of that back in town."

That was Guerine, making an impression. And like Bertie, Doodle had her own way of dealing with Guerine's worrisome nature. It was best to play possum, simply act like you don't see the offender. Though, she couldn't help noticing Guerine's latest modification. That girl was always giving a turn to change. Shift, shuffle, turn—whatever she had to do to keep up with the new fashions. It's a wonder she didn't have a chronic case of vertigo.

"Oh, I rather think it's charming," said Ina. "It's very lovesome, actually."

Doodle wasn't one to wait around to see which way the cat jumps, she had plenty chores left to do, and the longer she stood before the three women, the more irritated she became that Bertie had brought this stranger out to her land, to have this woman look at how she lived, and look at how she looked while doing her living. Why would somebody from a place as uppity as Virginia want to come to a place like this anyhow? She bent and picked up her bucket and told the women she needed to feed her geese. They were welcome to follow, though she secretly hoped they'd get into Bertie's machine and leave.

They chose, instead, to file in behind her.

"Bertie tells me you're quite the lady granger," Ina said.

"A what?" Doodle called over her shoulder. She didn't want to have to get ugly.

"That's city talk for farmer, Doodle," Guerine said. "Goodness gracious, don't you know anything? Bertie, what was that nickname Mama and Papa used to call me?"

"Where's that pa of yours?" Bertie asked Doodle. "And that mutt of his?"

He was asleep, Doodle told her. He'd had a dizzy round and a bout with nausea the evening before, leftovers that had sat on the table too long she suspected, and Bugle was keeping him company.

"Good gracious!" said Guerine as she dodged goose poop. "Look at these things, they're big as shotgun shells!"

"Doodle is serious when it comes to her geese," Bertie said to Ina. "She makes homemade dumplings to feed to them."

Guerine's attention was given to the locality of her feet. "You'd *have* to be jug-bit to want to wind your way through this mess every day."

Doodle stepped inside a wooden pen. She and her papa had built the pen together. It was low and square, the ceiling squat so it would be easy to warm in winter. She sat on a box in one corner and set the bucket next to her, latched onto a young gander and held him between her legs.

The three young women stood outside and watched as she peeled the lid from the bucket and pulled out a steamy noodle. She put it in the gander's mouth and worked the noodle down its gullet by rubbing the outside of the gander's throat.

"Are you choking him?" asked Guerine.

"I'm making sure there isn't a noodle left from the last feeding. Otherwise they might go off their feed."

"Sure looks like you're choking him," Guerine said. "Goodness, it stinks in here."

Doodle raised her head, saw that Ina was smiling.

"They certainly are amazing creatures, aren't they?" said Ina. "So quick to sense danger. Did you know that European farmers have used them for watchdogs for generations?"

Doodle was surprised that someone of Ina's ilk shared her interest. She loved birds, had since she was a girl, without ever really considering why. Watching their behavior, the way each species went about acquiring their food, the ability of a songbird to recognize a competitor's song. It was a part of herself she had never shared with anyone.

"But I'm only a novice," Ina said apologetically. "It's just a hobby."

Doodle imagined Ina spouting out Latin words and rattling off a bird's weight in grams. When Ina expressed an interest in the types of feed—why noodles as opposed to seed—Doodle was prompted into a lively discourse on the benefits of noodles while Bertie and Guerine listened.

"Gets them to market quicker," she told Ina. "A little bit of scalded corn-meal, some ground oats and barley, some wheat flour. And a dash of salt, too, like you'd do if you were making bread." Though Ina didn't look like the bread-making sort to her. "I just mix it real good and put the dough through a sausage stuffer, then cut the noodles anywhere from four to six inches long. You have to boil them ten to fifteen minutes, till they float. Then dip them in cold water and roll them in flour—that's so they don't stick. 'Cause they will stick. The tricky part to remember is to pour hot water over the noodles right before feeding your geese 'cause they need to be slippery. The noodles. Makes it a whole lot easier going down."

"That seems like considerable work," said Ina.

"Best recipe I've found. Had a noodled gander one time, almost forty pounds."

There was a pause in the conversation and Doodle felt a wave of embarrassment wash over her. She had rattled on. She had gone into too much detail. Who but herself would care to hear about a recipe for fattening geese? This was exactly why she didn't like people showing up unexpected. There was never time to prepare oneself. With people came questions, and with questions, answers. And it didn't matter your answer, you always risked disclosing too much of yourself.

"Well, enough of this loosey-goosey stuff," said Guerine, scraping her shoe against the pen door in an effort to knock a goose plug free. "We need to be getting back before it gets dark. Ina's first day in town and all."

"That's right," said Bertie, winking at Doodle. "We wouldn't want to corrupt her all in one night. We'll see you at the Wheelers' tomorrow, won't we?"

"Lord willing," said Doodle.

"You might want to think about wearing something besides britches then if you come," Guerine said before turning to go.

"Be sure and give Pa Shuford my best," said Bertie.

"A pleasure meeting you," said Ina. "Nice of you to let us intrude on your work like this, without any notice."

Doodle nodded.

She watched through the opening as the three women walked back to Bertie's machine and took off down the dusty road. "Run on li'l fella," she said. "Plenty more needing to be fed yet." She bent her head and combed her right hand through her hair. She must've been a sight, those greenish-brown stains on her overalls and work shirt, and there was no telling what all was caked on her face. She looked at her hands, at the thickened palms.

It was selfish to want to go to the Wheelers' gathering, as sick as her papa was. She hadn't been completely truthful with Bertie. He'd been ailing for nearly two weeks, and burdened with the extra chores it had been that long since the last time she was able to go into town. But he seemed to be feeling better, not as weak, after drinking the tea she made for him out of butterfly weed. Miss Cara Sue, their neighbor lady up the road, had brought a bundle over and told Doodle how to boil it and strain the leaves, pour in a little whiskey for him. She offered to stay and do it herself while Doodle did the wash, and Doodle had thanked her, but as proud as her papa was, she knew he wouldn't want anyone else looking after him.

It wasn't so much the party she looked forward to—because really, about all those things amounted to were elbow touching and chumming. What she wanted was to not have to fret with chores for a change or have the added responsibility of tending to her papa. She wanted to get herself all lathered up, to finally be able to use that bar of fancy buttermilk soap she had splurged on (more than twice the price of a loaf of bread), and wear something that smelled sweeter than her work shirt. Wouldn't Guerine love to hear her admit that? To think Doodle was finally taking her highflown advice on how to act and dress. Guerine's problem was that she'd rather have you believe she was born wearing finery, not nothing homespun. And scratch, whether it was clothes or food, was something Doodle took pride in. It made her feel good she could do her own stitching, or dig up a potato without damaging roots. So what if she chopped and split wood? Or did anything that most folks thought of as man's work. Bertie certainly never made her feel out of place for it.

She didn't have to be a belle with a new skirt to have wants and feelings. She was still a woman. She was a woman every night when she stood in front of the washstand looking in the glass, sweeping boar bristles through her hair; when she slipped her nightgown over her head and noticed her do-majigs didn't quite swing the deal; when she rubbed Tarleine into her rough hands and pretended it was lavender lotion. Even when she pulled back the sheets on her bed and lay down—wouldn't have hurt her feelings none if somebody was there to warm it.

But as long as she could help it, nobody, ever, was going to see her hanker for anything. Not one thing.

Chapter 7

Bertie's Reverie of the Present, the Past, and Particularly the Future

*B*ertie couldn't sleep. She had sat out on the porch in owl's light with Ina earlier in the evening, after Miss Lul had ushered a malcontent Alta Ruth inside for bed. The two young women had talked about the day's activities, their conversation light and neighborly, like two people trying to find some common interest.

"So, what piece of Americana do *you* bring all the way from Virginia?" Bertie had asked.

And Ina had laughed. "Oh, the traditional lot, I suppose. Loving parents. Was always a voracious reader. Educated at home. And now, just trying to put it all to some noble use. You?"

"Oh, the usual crack of doom," said Bertie. "Raised by your run-of-the-mill missionary-type after the father got his noggin blown off, having been mistook for the wing of a wild turkey. Attended East Roxboro School where I sat on a hard bench and wrote numbers on slate. Excelled in reading and writing and hygiene, though. Wasn't partial to singing particularly, but discovered a gift for wagging the ol' tongue. Trying to put all that to some noble use, I reckon." After which there was an awkward period of silence, with only the sound of crickets feverishly rubbing their spiny wings together. It didn't escape Bertie's notice that Ina had failed to mention her late husband, but she decided to let the matter alone, and chose to blurt instead:

"What's the word with women in Richmond these days? Many wishing for votes?"

"I"—Ina hesitated—"I think some are becoming increasingly interested in the movement."

"Some? Pfft!" Bertie gave the newcomer a curious look, saw that she was fidgeting with a broken strip of rattan on the rocker.

For a few minutes neither of them spoke, and soon Ina was yawning. "Forgive me, won't you, if I retire for the evening," she said, and rose from the rocking chair. "*Bonne nuit.*"

"Yeah, wiener schnitzel to you, too."

Bertie respected a person who took a stand either way. You're either for the cause or against it. But if you're against, you better have a darn good reason. And don't go giving her the "men are meant to be our sturdy oaks" spiel, because that was a bunch of hooey! She hadn't met a man yet who wasn't apt to get emotional over a silly game of horseshoes. What made him more fit to vote than her? She suspected that was the foot rail Ina "Clinging Vine" had taken, though. The ol' angel-in-the-house syndrome. But if she were to ask Bertie, Bertie would tell her she was backing the wrong horse. That's the trouble with this world. Everything is governed by gotnab namby-pambyism!

After Ina went up to bed, Bertie retired to the parlor, where she sat now. She often sat there late into the night when she couldn't sleep. When she found herself lying in bed counting stamps on the ceiling tins and couldn't stomach another scroll or loop or leaf motif, she'd go into the parlor and prop her heels on a fat battered hassock. Sleeping was an absurd extravagance, an event better suited to the wealthy.

She switched on the electric lamp on the end table where she kept her current suffrage journals stashed—*The Woman Citizen, The Woman's Column, The Woman's Advocate,* or an occasional copy of *The Revolution.* Tonight she opted for lighter reading, the feminist humor of Alice Duer Miller, a columnist for *The New York Times.* Mrs. Miller's book was called *Are Women People? A Book of Rhymes for Suffrage Times.* But Bertie didn't get beyond the book's introduction:

FATHER, what is a Legislature?
A representative body elected by the people of the state.
Are women people?
No, my son, criminals, lunatics and women are not people.
Do legislators legislate for nothing?
Oh, no; they are paid a salary.
By whom?
By the people.
Are women people?
Of course, my son, just as much as men are.

She slammed the book shut and tossed it to the table, belching out several choice words in the process, all of which took the form of a sailor's blessing. Mrs. Miller she admired, but whenever Bertie was confronted with the reality that there were many small minds in the world making very big decisions her temper flared like a Fourth of July candlebomb. The least bit of aplomb—if she had any—went napoo.

She knew she had been facetious to Ina earlier, mocking her comment about putting life's lessons to use. But what exactly was she, Beatrice Abigail Daye, trying to accomplish with her own life? Not one person could look at her and think she had a sensitive disposition. But she did. Any matter involving asymmetry bothered her. Take the disparity between men and women, for example. The saga of women was more than a passing interest for her. Just like a nun feels called to the religious life, Bertie's was to see that women gained full equality with men. She had watched Miss Lul go from being barely more than property to actually owning it—and as much as Bertie had loved and admired her papa, still, she had to admit men had privileges that women didn't. It wasn't that long ago, hardly more than fifty years, that the only choice a woman was allowed was her dress. She didn't have freedom of her person, and her husband, well, he was free—free to do with her whatever he damnably well pleased.

She could sit there all night and go on and on. But what she felt she had to do, no matter how frustrating and tedious the process, was to find a way of breaking the chain of custom and tradition. And find something to calm her nerves.

She opened the drawer to the end table and began rummaging for her box of black licorice drops, and discovered that someone—a thirteen-year-old someone—had gotten into them. A loose lozenge was taken from the box, licked, then spit out, and was now cemented to the bottom of the drawer. She shook her head, compelled to clean out the drawer. She pulled out the box of licorice, a squat can of Rosebud salve, and a fingernail file that she used to wedge under the spent drop. Flush to the back of the drawer was the Whitman's tin that she had given to Miss Lul one Mother's Day. Instead of chocolates it now held fugitive clippings from the *Courier* that Miss Lul had saved. Bertie took one from the tin:

SHERIFF TULLY AND BRUD DAYE LEFT HERE TUESDAY EVENING FOR GOLDSBORO WHERE THEY GO TO CARRY ONE DOCK JONES, A COLORED LUNATIC, TO THE ASYLUM.

The date July 5, 1907, was written up top in Miss Lul's familiar hand, her cursive *J* swollen like a teardrop full enough to fall. It was proof enough to her that Miss Lul still held on to Brud's memory. Yet, whenever she asked Miss Lul about him, Miss Lul would get wrathy. "The past isn't for me," she'd say. "Does no good to look back. The only way we survive is to push ahead."

Behind Bertie's chair soon came the familiar quibble of Miss Lul's house shoes.

"I saw the light on," Miss Lul said in a slow tone. "Can't you sleep?"

"Getting closer."

"Like me to fix you a glass of warm milk?"

"Now when have you ever known me to swallow something from an old bossy?" Bertie cut her eyes up at her. "No offense."

"Point taken." Miss Lul cinched the belt of her green robe tighter and sat down across from Bertie. She eyed the sifted contents of the candy tin. "If you're looking for something to help you sleep, I doubt you'll find it there."

"What will I find in there?"

Miss Lul took a deep sigh. "Oh, Beatrice. I'm just saying." She brushed her palms down the lap of her robe and muttered, "I do wish you didn't worship that man so. It's just not healthy to worship a mortal, for you or for anybody. You have your own mind. I'd like to see you use it, is all I'm saying. Now don't sit up too late. If you start establishing bad habits on the week-end, before you know it you'll be a late-night creature of habit. Happens all the time. I see it often in a lot of our shut-ins and it's a hard thing for a person to overcome. Be sure and turn the light out before you head up."

" 'Night, Mama."

It was all a jigsaw to Bertie. Her life, its purpose. She knew the pieces were meant to fit and that some were likely missing. Miss Lul was trying to leave the past flat and here Bertie was trying to fluff it up. And if it took her till the day she died she was going, by God, to get it all figured out. Whether by way of Miss Lul or not.

Chapter 8

Brud Daye's Call

*T*he first time she saw him guised in all that plumage, Lalura was six months pregnant with their first child.

Brud was, in all ways, a ceremonialist.

For hunting strut bird, he wore an outfit he had made himself, coat and britches tightly stitched with turkey feathers, not a square of fabric showing. The feathered get-up was a ritual his pappy started when Brud was a boy, a notion the elder Daye took to show respect for a neighboring medicine man who had cured Pappy Daye of the gout with a spoonful of sarsaparilla syrup. When the little, feather-covered Brud was presented to the aging Cherokee, the Indian shouted in disbelief, "Gee-sah!" (Jesus!) Brud's pappy took it to be an honor of the highest order, mistakenly thinking the medicine man was giving his boy an Indian name. Later, as a grown man, the headpiece became Brud's crowning glory. A dazzling mix of rich-colored body and tail feathers, bronze, copper, and other shades of brown that curried his forehead.

Lalura was bounced awake that morning when he stood to dress, faced the bed, bent over to pull on his britches and unconsciously tickled her arm with turkey feathers. He thought he'd gone and sent her into an early labor—and she thought he had, too! It was that look she gave, with her face all palsied, like one great tom had swooped down and was ready to gobble her up, gobble gobble. Took ten seconds before she could let out a good scream. "Mister Daye!" she had scolded him. "You don't come at me dressed like that, big as your head is! Don't you ever do that again."

Ever afterward he would laugh about it. Used to make her so mad.

The morning of his accident, however, she figured he was too intense for any laughing. The night before, she had sent the children over to her sister's and gone nose-to-nose with him over what she referred to as his "shadowy doings." At the end of their confrontation she gave him strict instruction to never touch her again, then went directly upstairs where she spent the rest of the night in the empty bedroom across the hall. But she didn't sleep, and she suspected he hadn't either. In fact, it was still drop black outside the next morning when she noticed a pheasant-golden light glowing underneath his door.

She heard him rolling his heavy body from the bed like a falling tree, the heart pine floor no doubt putting a chill to his feet. Figured he was staring in the direction of one of the carved pineapples on the bedpost while scratching—in that typical, truly distasteful, manlike way—through his muslin nightshirt.

She could see him just as clearly as if she was in there with him. Easing his feet into the moose-hide moccasins he kept next to the bed before stepping into the hallway and knocking on her door. He knew as well as she did that she was only pretending to be asleep. When she didn't answer him, he called to her through the door, "It's a shame that you don't understand me, woman. All I'm doing is putting folks in their rightful places, making the world a safe place for our children, and here you go and call me a man of moral irresponsibilities. You've always gotta talk that highfalutin talk, don't you? Can't you see you're wrong in your thinking?" His way of making amends. Hmph. He didn't even wait to hear if she had a retort, just tromped downstairs on his way out to the privy.

And was that man ever proud of his privy, for it had louvered doors and accommodated two people—not for handholding, per se; there was a wall between the benches. Naturally a person does have a right to some privacy, except only a fool would worship a shithouse.

She figured—even hoped—he was going hunting for turkey that day. Like him, wild and bearded. Half the time Lalura didn't know what Brud was up to, barely paid him much attention. Unless, of course, on the occasion he would come home after a day of hunting, full of brag, and hold her captive in the kitchen, telling her about a clean shot to whatever it was that he had just brought down. As if she gave a fig about hunting.

All she knew was he had gone to his favorite wooded spot several days before to do some scouting, and came home bedeviled after seeing a rafter of turkeys—more than he'd ever seen together—and didn't have his rifle.

"Any man who's got a lick of sense knows he needs a plan to hunt turkey," he had squalled to her. "Crazy as hell to think you can just wander into woods and have any kind of success. Wild turkey is hard to come by. You've got to get a lay of the land. You've got to look around for feathers and scat, check the area for wing-tip drag marks of fully strutting birds, find a high spot where you can sit and listen for a vocal tom."

Self-control did not come naturally to Brud Daye, so after fending breakfast for himself, day-old light bread and leftover chicken, Lalura assumed that he was headed to his sacred turkey spot.

"You know something, Miss Lul?" He was outside her door again with one more piece, presumably dressed in his feathered get-up. "Marrying you was like buying that grand, chilled plow I used to admire years ago at the Farmer's Exchange: ran steady, had the correct shape, harder than normal steel. But once I got you home was when I realized you weren't adjustable. And ever since you have given me nothing but fits." He waited. "Well, I'll be damned if I'm gonna spend this day worrying over you. I got plenty other pressing business. You'll either come around to my sensibility or you won't."

Only after she was sure he was gone from the house, did she make her way to the kitchen to start a pot of coffee to boiling. At least he had thought to chuck some wood into the stove for her.

She regretted how things had been left, but it was Brud's own fault. He had gone wrong. He had become downright unpardonable, and in the process had pushed her into a corner. Crazy devil. Just had to wear that dumb suit of feathers, too, only to be mistaken for a live turkey. But it was the ill-guided shooter for whom she felt the most remorse, imagining that poor creature, all these years, too afraid to come forward and confess—and to what amounted to no more than an unfortunate accident. That, she believed, was the real pity.

Chapter 9

Ina's Circle of Acquaintances Expands

*S*he took her time dressing this morning and chose her clothes carefully. There was yesterday's heat to consider. She decided on a pale blue dropped-waist dress, and her leghorn hat with the wide moiré sash around the crown, laid both items on the bed, and took a seat at the vanity. She was coiling her hair into a low chignon, admiring the echelon of scent bottles and a celluloid brush and comb set when, for some inexplicable reason, she was suddenly struck with a comforting image of Harlan standing over her shoulder, teasing her by tapping his wristwatch, trying to hurry her along. The image brightened her face.

Once dressed, she grabbed her hat and went downstairs.

The smell of breakfast—*aroma déjeune*—filled the house. Or traces of it, since she wasn't sure whether she had missed sitting down to the first meal of the day with the rest of the household. But Mrs. Daye was surely in the kitchen. Ina could hear her voice.

A swan's breath of steam was coming from the spout of the white porcelain coffee pot. Mrs. Daye was standing at the back door speaking to a colored man who was dressed in a flake-white shirt with long sleeves under a pair of faded denim coveralls, holding a beige cap by his side. The way in which she gave him instruction led Ina to believe that the man was her helper. "Half a dozen cabbages, Johnny Bob, and two jars of Duke's Mayonnaise. Oh, and don't let Mr. Clayton forget to give you the flour this time. I'm nearly out."

After he had pulled the door closed behind him, Mrs. Daye turned then to see Ina.

"Ah, Miss Fitzhugh. I had just about given up on seeing you this morning. Figured that train ride had done you in."

"I hope you'll forgive me," Ina said. "I don't normally sleep to such a late hour." (When in truth that's all she had done for months on end.) She looked at the scene outside the kitchen window. A flick of his horse's reins and Johnny Bob and his wagon rolled out of view.

"You'll be glad for the extra rest," Mrs. Daye said, wiping her hands briskly on a tea towel. "Especially with the affair Corena Wheeler's got going this afternoon. She's all manner of service over there, that one. Loves to entertain. Not your typical cook shack either."

"What's the occasion?"

Mrs. Daye picked up a section of newsprint from the counter and handed it to Ina.

The Woman's Page
Society Editor
Mrs. B. C. Wheeler
Phone 23G

Friday, August 13, 1920

CHICKEN SUPPER SATURDAY TO HONOR VISITOR

Miss Ina Fitzhugh from Richmond, VA, will be honored with a chicken supper Saturday evening. The chicken will be cooked in an outdoor oven in Mr. and Mrs. Bickford Wheeler's yard. Everyone is encouraged to bring a side dish. Miss Fitzhugh is coming to Roxboro to assist our own Miss Venie Duncan at East Roxboro School. We are sure our citizens will welcome Miss Fitzhugh and we hope she will decide to make Person County her permanent home. She is due to arrive today and will be a guest in Mrs. Lalura Daye's boardinghouse.

"I'm sure Beatrice will be dragging you from here to yon afterward," Mrs. Daye continued. "That girl can't sit still to save her life. Always has to be on the go."

Ina laid the newspaper onto the counter. "Where is she this morning?"

"Over at that telephone office. Up and gone before six. She said to tell you to stop in if you decide to go out for a walk later. She's finagled her way out of working late this afternoon so she can go to the supper."

Ina hadn't counted on being surrounded by so many people, especially people who were making such a fuss over her. It was smothering and made her feel anxious. Yes, an airing was what she needed.

"I hope you like country ham and biscuits," Mrs. Daye said. She pulled a tin of biscuits from the oven. "How do you like your eggs? Scrambled? Fried?"

"A biscuit will do just fine."

"That's barely a lick and a smell. No wonder you're so frail-looking. Don't you want some eggs? Maybe a bowl of grits to go with?"

Ina thanked her, but declined the offer. "I'm still quite full from that wonderful meal you made last night." A beef roast with carrots and potatoes, gravy, string beans, biscuits, and a tray of jams and jellies for the choosing. Peach cobbler for dessert, for which she was too full, but ate every morsel that had been put before her. It had been months since she'd eaten like that and she took it as a good sign that she was regaining her appetite for things she thought she would never want again.

"Shame to have all this ham not get eaten," said Mrs. Daye, wrapping the biscuits in a chintz-covered basket. "I'll give some of it to Johnny Bob. He can take some home to Silvia and Zeke. That young man of theirs could stand a little meat on his bones. Sit, sit! We don't stand on ceremony around here."

Mrs. Daye went about the kitchen like a woman who didn't believe in wasting precious hours, opening and closing cupboards, pouring two cups of coffee and bringing them to the table. "You take cream and sugar?"

"Yes, please. Both." Harlan knew her so well that way. He never had to ask, would even stir her cup. "How old is he? Their son, I mean."

"Who, Zeke? Old enough to run errands for the drugstore, and he helps out Mr. Clayton in the grocery. Anything anybody'll let him do really. You can't miss him, the way he rides that bicycle from one end of town to the other."

"He must be the young boy I saw when I got off the train. Riding a bicycle and balancing a tray of refreshments with one hand. I was amazed at his confidence."

"Probably delivering bon-bons," Mrs. Daye said, "that pineapple sherbet they make over at Thomas's Drug Store."

"Does he go to school?" she asked.

"When would he have time?" Mrs. Daye set a small pitcher of cream and a sugar dish on the table. She pulled out a chair and sat down. "This is a good chance for us to get to know one another. Alta Ruth's over at Mrs. Wheeler's with some of the other neighborhood children, watching that big canopy going up. Have you seen that monstrosity? Big as a circus tent." She picked up her cup and blew, then took a sip, after which she spoke without letting up. Do help yourself to food or beverage if I'm not around. Don't open the windows without assistance. Don't keep late hours. And do dress sufficiently high at the top during school terms. This last item she didn't voice, but it was obvious to Ina what she was thinking by the way she glanced at the neckline on Ina's dress.

"Men boarders," Mrs. Daye said. "They're usually less trouble. At least that's been my experience. Not that I'd expect any trouble from you. Though it's only fair you know that I don't allow any goings-on under my roof, no making eyebrows with some cake-eating slyboots, that sort of thing. 'Course that'll be all I'll say on the matter. Like another biscuit, dear?"

❋

It was an ideal day to take a stroll, and by the songs of the birds, perched deep within the trees, Ina wasn't the only one who thought so. The neighboring houses called to her mind loving couples. Perhaps not Romeo and Juliet, she thought, or Aucassin and Nicolette. But romantic homes nevertheless, where artful endearments are spoken, where breakfast is taken in the parlor, dinner in the dining room.

The canopy on the Wheelers' lawn that Mrs. Daye had referred to grew larger as Ina got closer. Outside, men and women were hurrying about, setting up tables, chairs, and benches, unfolding and snapping linen tablecloths. Inside, beyond large panes of glass, people carried dishes and swiped feather dusters. She even heard the roar of an electric vacuum cleaner. The home had the elegance of a wedding cake. Tall, round Rapunzel towers gracefully balanced on each side, and flowerbeds in brilliant colors throughout the grounds.

Beyond the Wheelers' house, and away from the riddle of the vacuum, an odd sound pricked her ears: a clicking overhead that caused her to look up. Telephone wires, of course! Different environments bring forth different curiosities.

The town was a boast of activity. Every awning was at a proud angle. She was smiled at and nodded to as she looked at the wares displayed on the sidewalk.

"Morning, ma'am. See something I can help you with?"

"Not today, thank you."

Under the barber pole in front of Gentry's Barber Shop, three well-dressed gentlemen stood about like male birds. Seeing their communal display, Ina fought the urge to smile, but when they tipped their hats—her impulse by now was to laugh—her hand flew up to her mouth to catch the impending outburst.

Two doors up, she stopped to admire a phonograph.

Master Wingate

PHONOGRAPH FREE

to One of Our Customers

E.D. CHEEKS
The Furniture Man Who Sells for Less

Looking through the window she saw a large shadow moving around inside, and very shortly a whale of a man stepped out. "Two dollars in cash trade and you'll receive one key," he said, sputtering as he spoke.

"I beg your pardon?"

"Rules for the contest, to win this here beautiful Wingate. Got the lock on exhibition inside. When all the keys been handed out, I'll post another notice and folks'll have thirty days to try the lock. Whoever's key fits the lock gets the Wingate, see."

She nodded and continued on her way.

"Keys going fast!" he called to her. "Only two dollars'll get you one!"

Just beyond a sign advertising fresh barbecue at the Wiggly Pig Diner was Sargeant and Clayton's Grocers, the market that housed the Wheeler Telephone Company where Bertie worked.

Johnny Bob's wagon was out front, his horse tied to a post. Seeing that beautiful brown creature there, calm but for a twitching tail, took her back to the days when she and Lucia would groom their horses. Instinctively, she went over and stroked its muzzle. The poor thing looked haggard. Its coat was dull and several burrs were tangled in its mane. She set her purse at her feet and went about slowly, methodically, separating the snarled and twisted hair with her fingers. Perhaps she should tell Johnny Bob about cornstarch, how it works wonders at getting tangles out. All he would have to do is put some in a large shaker and sprinkle it on the mane and tail.

As she worked at freeing the first burr, she suddenly felt a stinging sensation in her left knee and looked down to see that the horse had locked on it as if it were an apple. What indeed! Scream? No. She was in public. She would hold her course and keep her tongue adhered to the roof of her mouth. Give him a wallop? Oh, but she didn't dare. A delicate situation this was. That dickens of a horse had her by the cusp. But the scene was short-lived. Before she could do anything, Johnny Bob came out of Sargeant and Clayton's Grocery with a box of goods, dropped it to the sidewalk, bungling its contents, and swatted the animal with his cap until the horse finally let go.

"I don't know what come over Thomas, ma'am," he said, shaking his head. "I'm sorry as I can be."

She was shaken, but managed to reach for her purse. "My mistake for approaching him like that."

"He's been having some trouble here lately," Johnny Bob said. "Don't see things when he ought to, and sometimes sees things that isn't there." He gave Thomas another swat for good measure.

"No harm at all. As I said, I was wrong to approach him."

A crowd was starting to gather, and a man on the opposite side of the street began to shout. "You oughta take that nag and shoot it, Johnny Bob! All he does is muck up the street with his trots!"

Ina was embarrassed, for herself and for Johnny Bob, and the quicker she could remove herself from the situation the better they both would be. "Please, don't worry yourself over it," she said. "It was my fault, I frightened him. And he taught me a good lesson because of it." She gave an affected laugh, an attempt to cover her bewilderment, and walked purposefully toward the grocery.

An apron-clad man, whose face was pocked like a honeycomb, was sweeping the floor. "Got a special on Swift'ning Shortening," he pointed out to her the moment she entered. "Fifteen cent a can."

She thanked him and noticed a young boy stocking shelves high up on a ladder, carefully turning cans into tin pyramids. Johnny Bob's son, she presumed. Still reeling from the equine encounter, she didn't ask where the door that led to the phone company was, but instead passed down the aisles as if looking to make a purchase. Beauty aids and baking goods, dried beans displayed in glass cases. Bottles of ketchup, mayonnaise, and pork and beans lined in perfect rows. Post-war commerce on parade.

At the entrance came an abrupt tearful cry. "How do you not see a Lane cake," said an ample woman entering the store with a tall, raily woman. "All those nuts and raisins and brandy. A whole cup of brandy, Murlena! Even a blind man could've seen it!"

"Cora's just a little upset, Mr. Clayton, 'cause her cake fell. And right before today's picnic, too."

"It didn't fall, Murlena. You pushed it is what. You pushed it and you know it!"

"That's not true, Cora!"

"Gosh, Mez Humphries," said the grocer, "I like a sad cake, myself."

"No, Mr. Clayton. It didn't fall. It fell. Off the table. My cat Penny's over there right now seeing double on account of that brandied frosting. And it's all because of Murlena's grubby little hands here. You've always been jealous of me, Murlena, and you know it." The baker pouted and her friend clutched her poplin collar and made a face as if to cry.

"Well, let's see if we can't gather you up some ingredients right quick," Mr. Clayton said, "make you an even finer cake. Zeke, you come on off of that ladder now and help Mez Humphries."

Ina picked up a copy of *Progressive Farmer* and pretended to read while the young boy whipped through the store gathering a sack of sugar, a can of coconut, a bottle of vanilla.

"Don't this beat all," said the baker.

"It did make the awfullest splat," her friend said.

"That's another dozen eggs, too, Murlena. You must think my hens lay 'em like they're getting paid spot cash."

"Will you be needing more pee-cans, Mez Humphries?" Zeke asked.

Ina peered over the magazine and watched as the woman broke down in tears. The thought of shelling must've been more than she could take.

"Oh Cora!" Her friend tried comforting. "I got a perfectly good Sally Lunn. How 'bout we put both our names on it? There'll be so many other cakes and pies to impress that new schoolteacher she won't know the difference."

The woman squealed and out the door she and her friend went, leaving the grocer with a blank face and young Zeke to run after the women with a bundle of groceries in his arms.

Ina returned the magazine to the rack. It hadn't occurred to her that the townspeople would make such a fuss over her arrival. It was almost like they'd never seen a stranger before. She needed to find the entrance to the place of Bertie's employment, but she had stood there for so long she felt she couldn't leave without making a purchase. Zu Zu Gingersnaps, Brer Rabbit Molasses, Pepsodent Tooth Paste, Beeman's Pepsin Chewing Gum, Tootsie Rolls. The gum, she decided—good for the digestive processes—but reaching for it she remembered an advertisement she'd recently read, how gum chewing destroys the beauty of the mouth, and continued down the aisle until catching sight of a box of Eagle Thistle Cornstarch. Yes, of course. That was it. The cornstarch would rectify that fiasco with Johnny Bob. She would show him how to use it to remove the burrs from Thomas's mane.

"That be all for you?" said the grocer, plunking at the register's keys.

Ina placed ten cents in his palm, then asked if he could direct her to the telephone company. Outside and around the corner to an alleyway that led to a metal stairwell. At the top would be the Wheeler Telephone Company. "Be careful about climbing them steps, though," he cautioned her. "And come back next Sardee. After the slaughter, we'll have some real fine poke chops."

Chapter 10

Mr. Wheeler's Wanton Ways

*B*ertie was in the midst of a spatial resolution. She had better-than-perfect vision, which allowed her, peripherally, to decipher the five minutes of arc of Mr. Wheeler's fat, fumbling hand.

He made like he was going through customer files in the cabinet next to her—his reason, he said, for sitting so close—but every so often, after having used a salivous thumb to aid in the separating of the folders, he would give his right arm a rest and allow it to wriggle. It was an overcurious arm on an octopus bent on the nearest broad-sterned thigh.

"Touch my leg again, B.C., and I'll knock you into next week."

"Can't be helped, Bertie. The hand wants what it wants."

She imagined the old walrus filling his head with every inch of her private flesh while his slobbering, flea-infested bulldog, Major, panted from the corner. "You better find a way to help it. It's beyond my limit of human endurance and I'm not paid enough."

"You're beyond price!" he said. "Besides. I know you're just being waggish. You're like those raw peanuts you're so fond of. All you need is a little roasting," and he reached for her knee.

She was true to her promise and hauled off and slapped him. "Do I not look serious to you?" she challenged. "I'm downright murderous."

There were two sides to B.C. Wheeler, the puckish one he showed to Bertie, and the staid one he showed to the rest of the world (Mrs. Wheeler included). He was prosperous, which wouldn't have been so bad, except that he was conniving, too, and thought himself to be a Master Man. To Bertie, he was no more than a stinking conformer.

It didn't surprise her that he had frolicking fingers when she came to work there. The world was full of men like him—they were as common as rickety-back cats in a restaurant alley. She'd encountered one or two of them on occasion, who thought, simply because she was gregarious and had a tart tongue, that she was willing to be spiritual with them.

She could handle every last one if she had to. She could easily cause a bruise. Leave behind one heck of a blood bubble to be remembered by. But what she hadn't counted on was B.C.'s dogged persistence. Nothing had stopped him yet. Even when she was ensnared at his switchboard, when she would be plugging from one socket to another. And sometimes when he started up with that funny business she would misdirect calls. Then she'd get an earful from folks the rest of the day. "Sorry, Miss Mamie. Yes, I know you said Hesteen, and Hesteen is forty-four Gee. My mistake. I'll try her again."

B.C. stood and made a motion to close the cabinet drawer, but when she saw him bend over, his face near her face, and his right hand reaching out, she ripped her headset off and flailed it in his direction. Thus began a test of emasculating endurance for B.C. Wheeler, for the headset inadvertently hooked the crotch of his pants.

Bertie—unaware of the territory her headset had ventured into—gave him a stern lecture on respecting the opposite sex. The headset shook in fits and jerks as she cried:

"I am plumb fed up with always having to be on guard with you! Of sitting at this switchboard every day on the defensive! No woman should have to endure this kind of abuse. To be treated with no regard whatsoever! Just what do you think women are for anyway, B.C.? To be thought of as nothing more than playthings to be pawed? That we ought to be measured by how much milk we produce?"

It was then that she realized what predicaments her headset had entangled. "Oh." But, recognizing her advantage in this delicate condition, she lifted the headset in cadence with each point of emphasis in a final statement, taking her time to draw out each syllable: "And I'll tell you something else . . . too. No matter what the . . . law or the . . . Bible says, I will not be . . . secondary or . . . subordinate to any man. Do we . . . understand each other?"

The doorknob to the office turned with a click. Mr. Wheeler was, by then, standing on the balls of his cowhide soles, pooch-eyed, holding his breath.

The sight of the opening door caused them both to turn their heads. Bertie quickly unsnaggled her headset. Mr. Wheeler cleared his throat and settled onto his heels a couple of octaves.

"Come to pay on your account, Miss?" he crackled.

"No, she's not here to pay on an account," Bertie said, getting up from her chair and pulling Miss Eyes and Ears Polite herself inside before she could decide to run out and down the stairs. "Come in, come in."

"Is this a bad time? I mean—"

"Heavens no! This is an office," Bertie said, flashing a blistery eye at Mr. Wheeler. "This is Miss Fitzhugh, Mr. Wheeler."

"Ah yes! Our guest of honor this evening."

He made polite with Ina in a voice he reserved for "furriners," and after a brief spell he told Bertie that he had important business to attend to and would be back later. He retrieved his jacket and hat from the coat rack and called to his dog. "Come along, Major." It seemed to grieve the slack-jawed mutt to get up, but the dog managed, although far from stud fashion, to wobble his way to the door.

"Good boy," said Mr. Wheeler. "Oh and Beatrice, see if you can't work on your inflection while I'm gone. I've noticed lately it's rather crude to our customers."

"That's my telephone voice," she said.

"Well then, perhaps you could fix it. I'm thinking something a little more harmonious?"

Chapter 11

A Palpable Collision

*I*na wasn't sure what she had walked in on. From appearance's sake, it looked as if Bertie and Mr. Wheeler were in some sort of passionate struggle and, upon seeing her, were both put to the blush. She supposed she should've knocked, but the lettering on the door said *Business Hours 8 to 5*, and according to the clock she'd seen on the grocer's wall, it was already approaching ten o'clock.

"Miss Lul got you running errands for her already?" Bertie said.

"Oh this?" said Ina, clutching the cornstarch.

"Don't let her take advantage. Idle hands, you know? Here, pull up a chair."

"Did I come at an inopportune time?" Ina asked, the image of Bertie and her boss still clear.

"Good Lord no!" said Bertie. "That man's morals are as loose as a deacon's vest. Oop! Hold that thought." She hurried to the switchboard, seized a wire, and plugged it into a socket. "Have you finished, Miss Roberson?"

The room was bright and spacious. Hardwood flooring, a high ceiling, and a large glass pane that looked down onto Main Street. Ina got up from the chair and walked over to the window. Johnny Bob and Thomas were gone. Two ladies were pointing at a pair of shoes on display, or perhaps it was the hat next to them they were admiring. She turned her back to the window and waited for Bertie to finish.

Bertie was a fashionable dresser. She certainly knew good shoes—white Colonial pumps with a French heel—but Ina found the style in which she was sitting somewhat scandalous. Her legs were fanned out and her skirt was hiked above her knees. The type of behavior that incited men to say and do awful, awful things.

She gave her own knee a rub, still smarting from the chomp Thomas had given it. She was certain, by now, that it must be pansy purple.

"What's that?" Bertie said. "Of course I can connect you. You think I'm here for my health?" She motioned for Ina to sit back down.

Ina placed the box of cornstarch in her lap and watched while Bertie crocheted her way through a skein of wires, taking a wire from one plug and sticking it into another.

Her work area was possessed of suffrage items, including a *Votes for Women* calendar and a postcard with a sketch of a gruff-looking suffragette smoking a cigar.

It all spoke volumes about the type of woman Bertie was, though it shouldn't have surprised her. She had suspected from the moment they met that Bertie was headstrong, if not something of a dogmatist. Ina simply hadn't considered that suffrage was a real presence in this part of the South, in a town this small. And then, too, she had grown up believing that it's the woman who takes care of everything in the home. Political equality was merely a notion explored in literature. Better left to the authors.

"Miss Warren, are you there? I said, have—you—finished?" Bertie looked at Ina and raised her eyebrows. "Say what? Yes, I'll call you back in fifteen minutes to let you know it's time to take your sausage balls out of the oven." Bertie glanced at the clock sitting atop a walnut cabinet, jotted a note, then unplugged the cord and pulled her headset off. "There. Maybe it'll stay quiet for a minute."

"Your mother says you've managed to get the afternoon off," Ina said.

"Managed?"

"I believe the word she used was *finagled*."

"Finagled schmagled!" said Bertie. "I'm simply getting up from this chair and leaving. Not one soul is gonna be calling anybody the rest of the day. Everybody's gonna be at the Wheelers' picnic." She cleared her throat. "If there's one thing I will never be is heroic for the telephone company. Not like that silly woman in Tennessee. Talk about foggy in the upper story. Wouldn't leave the switchboard till she called up everybody to warn them about a flood. They all got out, and that birdwit drowned. Come a flood here, my fat rear will be the first one in the boat!"

The phone board lit up.

"Number, please!"

"No, I did not know that," Bertie spoke into the mouthpiece. She turned to Ina and whispered, "According to Miss Pulliam, Mr. and Mrs. Darnette just had another squabble."

✵

As Ina came down the steps and turned the corner, she collided head-on with a gentleman who was traveling in the opposite direction on the sidewalk. The two nearly knocked the wind out of each other. His hat took flight and Ina lost her grip on the cornstarch. The box hit the ground and exploded into a white cloud. It chalked their shoes, his hat, her purse, and led them each into a brief fit of coughing.

"Are you all right?" he asked, settling the dust by waving his hand.

"Yes, thank you. I'm afraid I wasn't looking where I was going." Ina instinctively brushed at her dress. "Oh, your hat. Is it ruined?" It was similar to one Harlan had owned—a stylish sennit with a straw brim.

"Not at all." He reached down for the hat, along with Ina's purse, and commenced to clapping the objects together like cymbals in an effort to remove the cornstarch. "I always say a gentleman could use a good powdering now and again." He handed Ina her bag and returned his hat to his head.

Harlan, Ina thought. Words that could've come from his very own mouth.

"Can I reimburse you for the—" He squinted at the damaged box.

"It's quite all right," she said. "It was bought on impulse more than anything."

"Uh-oh, is this your keepsake?" He bent over to retrieve another wayward item from the sidewalk.

"It must've slipped from my purse," Ina said.

"The crystal's broken I'm afraid. What a shame. I can—"

"No, please! Just give it to me." She snatched the pocket watch from him and walked away in a rush with the intention of disappearing.

She was breathless by the time she mounted the steps. Mrs. Daye was in the parlor watering houseplants when she entered the house. Ina excused herself to the upstairs. She needed to write a letter home, she said. Her family would want to know she had arrived safely. "Unless, of course, there's something I can help you with?"

Mrs. Daye scoffed at the idea.

In her room Ina closed the door, took the watch from her purse and carefully placed it on the vanity. Harlan had referred to the watch as a symbol of his love and fidelity when he presented it to her on their wedding day. And now the glass was broken.

Chapter 12

An Out-of-Door Chicken Supper

A simple rule of thumb when attending a potluck party: bring your contribution in a pretty container.

As guest of honor, Ina carried her powder and puff in a brightly colored, drawstring beaded bag that she looped around her right wrist. Then, remembering that she would need her right hand for greeting and eating, switched the bag over to her left wrist.

Bertie carried a burlap sack of peanuts in the crook of her left arm.

Alta Ruth carried a puzzle made of hand-forged iron in the shape of a G clef with a stirrup attached.

Mrs. Daye's hands, on the contrary, were free. She had made a three-pound pail of coleslaw and an angel food cake with golden lemon icing for the occasion but had delivered them to the Wheelers' by way of Johnny Bob earlier that afternoon.

"Why are you bringing that silly toy along?" Mrs. Daye asked Alta Ruth, as the four of them walked the short distance down the street to the Wheelers'.

"In case I get bored," Alta Ruth said. She was working fervently on the solution, trying to remove the large ring that connected the clef and stirrup, tinking metal to metal.

Mrs. Daye's face grew to a fret.

The two had joined issue earlier over Alta Ruth's attire. Mrs. Daye had laid out a perfectly nice dress for the affair, but when Alta Ruth came downstairs she was clad in overalls and a blouse and couldn't be persuaded to change. Ina took the young girl's determination as a good sign. With that type of perseverance, she was sure to be a natural leader in the classroom.

At the edge of the Wheelers' lawn, they were confronted by a barking dog. That the animal was of the fluffy sort gave Ina no relief. Erect ears and stiff legs on a creature the size of a tiger can only mean one thing. She instinctively took a step back.

"That's Babette," Alta Ruth said. "Don't worry, Miss Fitzhugh. She won't bother you."

Apparently having heard the ceaseless barking, Mrs. Wheeler appeared on the porch. "My goodness! Just what is mama's little boobie doing out?" She held the door open and cooed and gootchy-gooed until she had coaxed the dog back inside, then she came down from the porch to greet her guests.

She carried herself with the air of a Magnificent Frigatebird. She had a long hooked nose and her chest was puffed to a brilliant display. "Samoyeds"—*sammy-YEDs* is how she pronounced it—"can't tolerate this heat, but Babette's been so excited what with all the commotion around here today. But don't let's waste another minute. A number of folks have already arrived. Lalura, you and the girls make yourselves at home. I'll see to proper introductions for Miss Fitzhugh, here."

She urged Ina past a privet hedge and beyond the shade of the water oak, where the sunlight flitted off her butterfly brooch and made the wings look alive, to the back of the house where music was beginning to play.

The Japanese lawn grass, so dense and thick, gave Ina the sensation of walking on tautly pulled woolen blankets. One had to take care not to snag a heel. Rounding the corner, it was clear to her that much effort had gone into the planning of the occasion. Mrs. Wheeler had brought her indoor décor out. Fine furniture sat on the grass: chairs with tufted upholstery, an ornate parlor set, occasional tables (so one wouldn't have to resort to balancing a plate on the knees), and a velvet circular divan with eight walnut lion's feet underneath an oak tree. Every piece looked as if it were at home there. She had even brought out her Madame Royale silverware and Chester Rose china, and not simply one silver coffee urn but two.

"Now dear, I know you've only committed to helping at the school through the winter," Mrs. Wheeler said, hooking her arm around Ina's, "but there's a lot of talk right now about the possibility of a new East Roxboro school being built, and it could very well be an excellent opportunity should you decide to stay on."

Ina could no more see that far into the future than she could predict what her mood would be tomorrow. The truth was, she was beginning to wonder if she had made a mistake in coming to this town at all. Yes, the people were friendly and were making her feel welcomed. But there was a strange sensation tearing at her, as it had been much of the day. She toiled about in her room, pacing, sitting, pacing. She felt like a child overcome with a terrible case of homesickness; all she wanted was to be back in the security of familiar surroundings.

What made her think that she could so easily uproot herself in the first place? Maybe she was not as strong as she had thought. Maybe she hadn't given herself enough time to heal from her loss. A settled disposition is far too underrated. She should've stayed put in Richmond is what she should've done. She should've simply stayed put.

"Has Miss Duncan arrived yet?" Ina asked, feeling somewhat timorous.

"No, I'm afraid she's a bit under the weather today. Now, I'm sure you know that Person County has been experiencing much change as of late," Mrs. Wheeler said, speaking in an exhaustingly chatty manner. "You can see evidence of it in town. An ideal place for a young teacher such as yourself. There was a time when we were cut off from the rest of the world, except for a stagecoach that came through once or twice a week to deliver mail and a few passengers. But it won't be long before this little village is on the map. Look, there's Doctor Farrell! If there's one person you absolutely have to meet it is Doctor Farrell. He's a great believer in public education, and if this school does indeed come to fruition, it'll be because of his generosity. Hellooo, Doctor Farrell!" Mrs. Wheeler guided Ina toward a frail-looking man who had one eye askew, making it difficult to determine whether he was looking at whoever stood before him or at the imaginary fly that sat on his nose.

❈

Some might say he had a bit of the clodhopper in him, but Colon Clayton was a man who knew that sustenance and anchorage come from roots. One way to tell was by the shirt he had on, long-sleeved with a spread collar and two chest flap pockets. His daddy wore that same shirt the day he plighted love to Colon's mama. It wasn't as white as it once was, mostly dingied now, and had a hole the size of a pawpaw under the left arm. But that was the sleeve Colon didn't need anyhow, so he kept it folded cross his chest, and real neatlike, tucked inside the placket, right between two brittle buttons.

He pulled up in front of the Wheelers' house straddling an Indian motorcycle—a red Model O with a bit of snort to it that he used for delivering mail. He tucked his shirttail into the old pair of gabardines he was wearing, the crotch sewed shut more than a time or two, then slung a dusty brown Oxford over the seat, combed his only hand through his hair—parted deep on the left and seal-slick with Vaseline—and swiped a finger across his moustache. Standing, he dusted himself off, then reached inside the saddlebag draped over the back of the cycle and took out a pancaked loaf of bread he'd spent twelve cents on at his uncle's grocery.

This wasn't just any ol' high-do the Wheelers were throwing. It had the feel of a real, honest-to-goodness carnival. Music and food and children giggling. There was a great big open-air tent taking up a smart portion of Miss Corena's natty yard, a platoon of picnic tables crowded with all the eats a person could imagine. Colon's nose detected fried chicken. He grinned and squeezed the bread by its scruff, and with the confidence of a sailor on shore leave striddled his long legs toward the crowd.

"So where's this new schoolkeep, Miss Corena?" Colon asked, coming up behind Mrs. Wheeler and giving her a start.

"Colon Clayton!" she said, clutching at her abdomen. "The living daylights! You should know better than to sneak up on an elderly woman."

"Sorry, Miss Corena. But you ain't old. Chicken's still got some life in her yet. Sure got one dandy of a turnout. Where might I set this bread?" He held up the bag and fishtailed it in front of Mrs. Wheeler's perturbed face.

"Go and give it to Eunice. She wanted something to do, so I've got her over there helping my girl Rella." She pointed toward the canopy. "And the schoolkeep's name is Miss Fitzhugh," Mrs. Wheeler reminded him. "You be sure to address her as such. And, Son, you mind your manners, you hear?"

Colon flashed her an impish smile, then took his offering to Eunice, who was shadowing Rella. Rella was arranging platters on the picnic tables and Eunice was following behind with netted bug covers.

He tried handing over the bread to her, but Eunice stood with her arms at her sides and frowned at both him and the flattened loaf, her mouth as determined as a tight-lipped mussel. "It'll fill back in, Eunice," he said. "Besides, it kindly looks like one of them balloon animals, don't you think?"

The two women gave each other knowing glances, then Eunice snatched the bag from him.

Colon turned and looked out toward the wrap-around porch where a wedge of women stood gossiping about a coal-haired beauty. Miss Fitzhugh, he reckoned. He remembered what his daddy told him once about Virginians, that he had never met one that won't in danger of drowning during a rain, the way they strutted around with their noses hovering in the air. Colon figured he would find out for himself soon enough. She was beautiful, won't no denying. The kind of woman that can get a fella all tang-tongueled. She was a right smart photo finish with Guerine Loftis, which made Colon wonder how that was going to sit with Miss Guerine, being's most in the county thought her to be the prettiest bloom you could ever lay your eyes on and always tickled her to hear it.

Garland Bowes and Rainey Holder were commencing with another set of fingerpicking and fiddling over by the Wheelers' recently abandoned ice shed (Mr. Wheeler had bought the Missus an electric refrigerator). And next to them were a couple of ice cream churns, several men taking turns riling the crank.

A pair of tan ladies' shoes swinging to the sound of the foot music caught his eye. They belonged to a slight young woman who was sitting up on the edge of a wagon. He knew her. He delivered mail to her family's farm near the county line, right out by the Person County Bids You God Speed sign. He wasn't good with recollecting names—a scourge for the man of letters—and had to rely on word tricks to help him get by. But he remembered hers, remembered it sounding like sweetener in the ear, knew it rhymed with noodle because Bertie had told him that was what she fed her geese, one noodle at a time; D for dirt, her being a farmer. Had to be Doodle. Doodle what. Her pappy always wore rag-wrapped *shoes* to the mailbox, and said to Colon on several occasions he wished he could afford a *Ford*. Doodle Shuford! That was it! Goodest people you'd ever want to meet.

So was just about every other farmer Colon knew. Ever last one was sterling folk, good as the day is long. He admired that and hoped someday he could buy himself a little farm.

There was something sensible about that gal Doodle, the way she sat there minding her own business, while the rest of the ladies swarmed around Miss Fitzhugh like worker bees vying for the queen's attention. Practical is what she was. Never would pause in the least to look in his direction when she'd be out doing chores, and Colon knew good and well her little scrawny-neck self could hear the snork of his two-cylinder Indian and the extra-loud rattle he purposefully gave to the door of their letter box. But dang if she didn't wash up good, had on a real pretty dress. Maybe he would go over and sit by her, wait till the buzz died down and he had a chance to greet the teacher. But before he could lift a foot, Rella bumped into him, stepped on one of his dusty shoes with the hard sole of one of her bluchers and looked at him like he'd caused it.

Eunice shooed him like she would a fly, to let him know he was in their way. He took leave of the tables and stepped from under the canopy and into the sun. A few of his buddies from town were playing tenpins, but it was the boneshaking bicycle that took his fancy—the front wheel twice as large as the rear, causing the rider to sit high above the ground. Took talent to drive one. A sudden stop and you were liable to find yourself with a mouthful of dirt. That fella looked a little shaky, Colon decided, so he walked over to show the young man just how it was done.

❈

The air felt good to Doodle. Finally, a day when it wasn't downright pea-soupy. Not a flight of clouds in the sky or the least bit of mugginess, just a nice breeze, soft as a cat's paw, stirring the trees and flirting with the hem of her freshly pressed gingham dress. The day couldn't be more perfect. She had drawn back the curtains in her papa's bedroom and opened his window before she left home so he could enjoy the day, too. She thought of him now, propped in his iron bed, looking out on the field to the west as hiccups of air blew across his blanched face. Fresh air was what he needed. Would positively do him good.

She hopped onto the rear of a farm wagon that was parked at the edge of the property so she could be near the banjo and fiddle music. Not long after she had shut her eyes to better enjoy the melody, a ladybird beetle lighted onto the back of her hand. Her mama had told her an old wives' tale once, that whichever direction a ladybird beetle flies when you release it is the direction your future husband will come from. Doodle paused a moment, then gave the ladybug a quick flick.

Waving her legs back and forth to the rhythm of the music, she wanted to be sure to remember every song that was sawed and plucked so she could tell her papa, maybe even warble him a few tunes to lift his spirit, and to tell him how Mr. Bowes had showed her the piece of turtle shell—worn down to no bigger than a quarter—that he used for picking his guitar strings.

She caught sight of the one-armed fellow who delivered letters out their way, what few pieces of mail they got. She rarely had any dealings with him herself, since her papa liked the brief letup from chores, the regularity of walking down to the mailbox and spending a few minutes talking about the weather and whatnot. Colon was his name. Semi-Colon, Bertie called him—but not to his face. In some ways it was a shame that he didn't have so much as a soup bone to speak of, that his left shoulder simply halted to a nub. It's amazing what a person can do when they're short a support.

She watched as he gangled his way over to a young man who had recently arrived on a bicycle. It was one of those velop- veloc- oh heck, she couldn't pronounce it, just knew that it was funny-looking. Colon coaxed the man off it and climbed up onto the seat.

Watching him had a certain familiarity to it, and it occurred to her then that the first time she'd ever seen him with something even more unruly between his legs was last fall, at the County Fair. It was while Bertie was in charge of manning—or in Bertie's case, munitioning—the suffrage booth, and Doodle, weary from the same old suffrage sing-sing, had gone for a stroll down the midway, from concession to concession, and looked at the farm exhibits and livestock. She stopped to listen to a barker announce with flourish that for just a fifteen-cent admission every man and woman before him could lay their eyes on Person County's first and only bobtailed cats. The crowd was aroused. But from the far end of the midway a thundery sound turned Doodle's attention away from the sideshow, and just as the firm red clay beneath her feet began to quake, six boys on motorcycles roared down the middle of the strip making the hem of her skirt nervous. The last motorcycle had a sign advertising Shank's Grill hooked to its tail end, and was being driven by none other than Colon Clayton.

He rode around the yard fast now like somebody past experience, more natural than the man before him, as a team of children ran after him. Doodle grinned, seeing he had a bent for riding rampant things. But it wasn't long before this man of experience hit a dippy chuckhole and he and the bicycle went flying. His face froze crooked and made the thick hair on his upper lip look cowlicked, like he had done one too many belly-whoppers in Hyco Lake. Dern if it didn't beggar all description. That poor fella got himself hung up on that hard handle bar, and Doodle was willing to bet, by the look on his face, that he felt very much like a neutered rooster.

※

Just when Ina thought she'd made acquaintance with every Mr. and Mrs. So-and-So in attendance—and anyone else Mrs. Wheeler held in highest regard—her hostess would whisk her off to meet someone else. At one point, that feeble Dr. Farrell had practically dragged her home state through the mud, telling her how dire Virginia's road conditions were (Compared to what? she thought, for they're certainly no worse than the packed clay I've seen here), and, "Good man, your governor Davis," he said, "but couldn't he be doing more to improve the schools?"

She took a deep breath, longing to be back home. She would be listening to the Victrola, to the Orpheus Quartet singing "Turn Back the Universe and Give Me Yesterday," instead of the farmerish tunes being played by those men with their banjos and guitars.

As luck would have it, Mrs. Wheeler caught sight of her prized Sammy loose again—this time digging a lodge under her roses with Major.

"Bickford!" Mrs. Wheeler shouted to her husband. "Look at what that awful dog of yours is teaching my Babette. Did you let her out? No, no, Babette! Mommy just gave you a bath!"

While Mrs. Wheeler was distracted with *le premier chien*, Ina managed to slip away. She would've hidden if she could've found a place to get away to, but she found a sturdy tree to lean against and hoped that no one else would seize the opportunity to ask her about life in Richmond and whether or not it was true that Virginia is the biggest apple-producing state in their union.

She sighed. On the other side of the lawn, Bertie was standing with her friend Doodle. She had spent little time with either of them and decided to walk over.

"They always cast her as a girl who gives up everything for love," Bertie was saying as Ina approached.

"Who's that?" Ina asked.

"The saintly Helen Eddy," said a pert Bertie, shoving a tin of Bull Durham cigarettes into her pocket. "Her face is on one of these actress cards they stick in with a decent pack of cigarettes. I pass them on to Doodle."

"May I?" said Ina, seeing the card in Doodle's hand. "My, she's lovely, isn't she?"

Doodle's cheeks seemed to color.

"Pfft! Women like that want fame because they want to be admired," Bertie said. "And you know what's pitiful? Every last one of them wants to be mastered by a man who'll drag them by the hair of their heads. Not me. I'll take clothes over a caveman any day."

Ina and Doodle looked at each other as if questioning their own eternal desires. What could be so awful about having a well-bred *homme des cavernes*?

❄

Guerine told Sam—her intended, her Antony—she didn't want to get there too early. What she wanted was to make *an entrance*.

"There is no entrance, Guerine," Sam said. "It's outdoors. And what on earth have you done to your beautiful hair?"

"Don't you like it?"

He took his time replying. "I suppose." He pouted. "But why are you dressed that way?"

"Sam Eastbrook! Because you made this for me. Remember? After I saw that Swagger London model I liked so much? And I shouldn't have to tell you, silly bug, that clothes affect behavior."

"But it's a picnic supper," he said.

"It's an outing, isn't it? And this is outing wear. You don't expect me to show up in garden togs, do you? I thought you'd like seeing me in this." She did a little twirl for him. "Don't you want me to be special? Well?"

"I just think that a two-piece riding habit will be awfully hot."

"This isn't just for riding," she said. "Why, I could climb Hagar Mountain if I wanted to. And anyway, I want to show off your handiwork to folks. It'll help with business. More clientry means more money, and more money means we can afford a bigger wedding. And sooner."

Guerine would have everybody know that Sam Eastbrook was the best tailor in Roxboro. (Not to mention the *only*.) He clothed practically every upper-cruster in the county. And wore his own designs. And she didn't care where he was or what he was doing, he was always well-dressed, so she was stunned when he questioned her attire while standing right before her very eyes in one of his fancy white shirts with a bat wing bow tie looking snappy. He was clever, that Sam, putting detachable cuffs on a shirt. If he got them soiled in the least, all he had to do was take them off in a jiffy and flip them over. Ingenious was what he was.

"Are you ready to go?" he asked her.

"Soon as I find my crop."

As they walked toward the Wheelers', it occurred to Guerine that the scene back at her house—Sam's shock over her new hair bob—was that sweet gentle wooer of hers getting green in the eye. She knew it was only a matter of time, just didn't know what form the old ogre would take in him. Sam was a man who didn't like change, and she should've known that her new look would bowl him over, knock him right off his steadfast knees.

"Don't you want to hold my hand?" she asked him.

"I promised your mother I wouldn't drop her chowchow."

"Oh Sam! You can carry that little bitty Mason jar in one hand. Here. Now don't you worry. I'll stay within arm's reach." To reassure him, of course. Of her complete devotion.

"There're the girls, Sam. Let's go over and say hello. I'm anxious for Miss Fitzhugh to meet my favorite beau."

Sam set the jar of chowchow onto a nearby table.

"Not there, Sam. Put it next to that pot of beans. That way everybody'll see it." Men simply do not know the first thing about laying a table. "Are you coming? Goodness you're slow, Sam. But I suppose one of the things I love about you is your reserve. Not a bit of spaniel in you.

"Hello, everyone!"

"You'll be highly disappointed if you've come for the fox," Bertie said.

Guerine ignored her cousin and turned to Doodle. "Goodness gracious, Doodle. Not often we get to see you in a dress. And what pretty fabric, too. It wouldn't gap right here, though, if you'd straighten your back. That's what working on a farm does to a woman. Before you know it your back'll be as rounded as a plant dibble. Hello, Ina!"

Suddenly faced with having to introduce Sam to Ina, and Ina to Sam, Guerine's confidence left her. She had a troubled feeling. She was also itchy.

Under her collar, around the waist of her riding skirt, and those darn leggings. Her thighs felt like broasted drumsticks! Sam was right. (But you would've had to kill her by inches before she would admit it.)

"Sam? Be a dear and get me some refreshment, won't you. A mint-ade, perhaps?"

"Bertie tells me you two are engaged," said Ina. "Have you set a date?"

"Sam wants to grow his business a little more before we settle down. Is that Prunella cloth you're wearing? Sam says that's a very dependable fabric. You can never go wrong with Prunella, Sam says." She tugged at her collar, scratched at the nape of her neck. "Quite a party, isn't it? The way Mrs. Wheeler descends to particulars!"

"Are you all right?" Ina asked. "Your face is rather rosy."

"Oh fine, just fine."

"That's not wool, is it?" Doodle asked, and began to relate a story about her great uncle Ham who discovered, too late, that he was over-tender to the stuff. "Before you could say 'Jumping Joseph's foot!' his neck swoll up like a bullfrog. Doc Nichols charged his wife a dollar for the house call, all for splitting a cucumber down the middle and rubbing it over Uncle Ham's welts. Any other time, the doctor said, the swelling would've went right down—"

Guerine felt her throat getting tight and her knees start to buckle. She did a sluggard shimmy before everyone's eyes. Her arms soared out to her sides, cropping Bertie on the rump, and right before Guerine hit the ground, Sam sacrificed the mint-ade to the lawn and caught her.

There were only two things that made Samuel Algernon Eastbrook, Jr., nervous. A dissatisfied customer and a beautiful woman. Of course, one could hardly tell, he hid it so well. Whenever a fit of nerves came over him he would pop any morsel of food nearby into his mouth. He found chewing—on any type of viand—comforting, and in his office drawer he kept a great stash of Tootsie Rolls, a waxed sleeve of soda crackers, and a box of California raisins—should he ever need them. By all appearances, he was simply a hearty eater.

He had doleful eyes, the color of cornflowers, an aquiline nose, brows of Spanish moss, and a delightful cleft in his chin. He was a peach, a plum. The cheese, the nuts.

And, he was hungry. So when Mrs. Wheeler scatted him from the house so she could help Guerine out of her clothes and into one of the former's Homestead house dresses, he returned to the party outside.

"How is she?" Ina asked him.

"That gal will do anything for attention," said Bertie.

Sam laughed. "She's already asking me to bring her some Majesty cheese on a cracker, if that tells you anything. Which reminds me, do any of you ladies know what Majesty cheese is?"

"Potted meat and shredded hoop cheese," Bertie pointed. "Over there. Next to the Sunshine Salad. Myself, I'm heading toward the ice cream churns."

⁂

Doodle followed Bertie, leaving Ina nervous and sparing of words in the company of Mr. Eastbrook.

"You must think I'm scant of any courtesy whatsoever, after that scene on the sidewalk earlier today," she finally managed.

"Oh, that? Think nothing of it. Happens all the time. Quite normal behavior, really."

"Is it, now? A crazed woman fleeing the scene of a simple malfeasance?"

Mr. Eastbrook considered for a moment, then gave a quick nod. "Yes, that's about the order of things. We see that type of thing around here a lot. Particularly after a hog slaughter."

Complete tomfoolery showed itself on Mr. Eastbrook's every feature, and Ina chuckled.

He suggested they continue their talk over the buffet tables while he searched for the Majesty cheese, and as they strolled along on opposite sides of each other, Mr. Eastbrook dared to lift every lid and sample each dish.

"It must be tiresome having everyone ask you about Richmond," he said, plucking a melon ball from a bowl of fruit cocktail and popping it into his mouth. "I hope you haven't been made to suffer any embarrassment over the Cabell issue since you've been here."

"The Cabell issue?" said Ina.

"James Cabell and his notorious novel. I understand he hails from your neck of the woods." He bit into a pecan lace cookie. "I say, this is a must!"

Until then, she had made little eye contact, but she stopped and looked up at him. "You've read—" She couldn't say it. She wouldn't say it. To utter the title of a controversial book, written by what some considered an oversexed author? (Or undersexed. She had very little experience, but she supposed there was a very fine line.) And to admit she was guilty of reading it?

"*Jurgen?* Why, yes," he said, and wiped crumbs from his chin and the front of his shirt. "Haven't you? Forgive me, please, that was awfully pre-

sumptuous. I just thought, as a teacher, you must read all types of literature."

Ina looked down and continued the hunt on her side of the table. "Yes,
well. I usually prefer realism over fantasy."

"I must say, though," said Mr. Eastbrook, lifting the next lid, "for dream-
like thinking his prose is quite exquisite. Hmm, baked bean canapés? Eco-
nomical, but not at all bad. Do you see it yet?" he asked. "This Majestic
cheese? I think if we can find the Sunshine Salad we'll be in a decent shape.
Now, what do you suppose Sunshine Salad looks like?" He scooped up a
deviled egg and crammed it partially into his mouth.

"There you are, Sam!" Mrs. Wheeler was calling now. "Guerine is refusing
to rejoin the party. Embarrassed, poor dear. If her daddy wasn't so busy
turning brightleaf into banknotes out at that new tobacco barn of his, he
could be here to help his daughter. Would you mind seeing her home?"

By now, Mr. Eastbrook's mouth was full and his cheeks were distended,
the food was outgrowing his mouth. He assented by nodding, then
snatched up another egg before leaving and held it high as if to tell Ina
good-bye.

Chapter 13

Doodle's Papa Dictates His Last Will and Testament

*D*oodle took a fresh towel from the cabinet drawer and dried the water from her face and arms, then buffed the towel through her wet hair. She had spent another day tending to chores alone, her papa's health continuing to wilt. By late afternoon, after the chicken yard was cleaned and the anti-vermin perches filled with insect powder to stave off bugs, the sky turned somber and the wind started to whip about like an aggravated mare's tail. She was carrying a fresh bucket of water toward the house and had set it on the porch to lead her mule Drucie inside the barn. While putting hay down in the stall, she could hear rain beginning to fall in broken doses on the barn roof, but before she could return to the house the water was searching roots. It pulled all the curl from her hair as she ran across the yard.

She left the towel draped across her shoulders and went to her papa's room to see how he was.

He appeared to be asleep, the blanket pulled snug to his chin. Doodle recalled her mama posturing that same way before she died of consumption, her head sunk into a feather pillow and fingers clutching the cover. That same Bible on the nightstand, too. The entire image made Doodle tremble. She saw that she had left the window open and hurried to close it before more water could splash onto the floor. The sound woke her papa.

"Angels can't gather me to the Father if you close that window," Papa said, his eyes closed.

"You're dreaming, Papa. Go back to sleep."

"No, I'm not. I'm listening to an angel on the roof. Doesn't pluck that harp none too good though."

"I need to get out of these wet overalls and into something dry, then I'll fix us some supper."

"Not for me."

"You have to eat, Papa. It'll help you get your strength back."

Her mama had taught her as much about economy as she had about cooking. There was leftover ham in the icebox, and that, with a couple of thinly sliced potatoes, a tablespoon of butter and two of flour, along with a scant cup of milk, would make a nice casserole. She knew he loved cornbread—thin and crunchy, near burnt along the edges—and even if he didn't have much of an appetite, it was the one thing he wouldn't refuse. She had made it so many times she no longer needed her mama's recipe as a guide. As she went about the tiny kitchen, she hummed a song she'd heard at the Wheelers' picnic, something with the word *tickle* in it. Once the casserole was assembled and in the oven, she placed a skillet on the stove for the cornbread and watched as a dollop of lard melted and sizzled.

Rain baptized the windows in heavy streams and pattered on the tin roof while they ate.

"Looks like we got us a goose-drownder," said Papa. He sat against the iron turnings, propped by two pillows. Cornbread crumbs were poised in the corner of his mouth.

"We sure need it," Doodle said. "Hadn't seen a rain in near 'bout three weeks."

"Your mama used to say the stars were crying when it rained."

Doodle smiled.

She loved her papa, honored him just as she had her mama, but the constant care, the back and forth with a chamber pot, the soiled linens, the baths from the washstand that humiliated him and embarrassed her, all that worrying was wearing her down. How relaxing it had been at the Wheelers' picnic, if only for two brief hours, to enjoy someone else's efforts, to have your greatest care be one ice cream scoop or two, mint-ade or lemonade, pear salad or potato.

A moment passed before she realized that her papa was talking.

"I spent my whole life on a farm," he said, gazing out the window at gray sheets of rain.

She had heard about his life on numerous occasions, but took comfort in hearing the details again—as she did in the sound of the rain and its washday rhythm—of her papa being raised up in the nurture of the Lord by the strict hand of his mother, and of his father dying when he was only five. It was good to be reminded, particularly during a trying time as this, that she came from people of fire and spirit, people who never quit till the job got done.

He was the youngest of ten children who only went to school three months out of twelve, and who each got a pair of shoes once a year. Her papa, John, went barefoot everywhere except for winter, saving his shoes like his mama did pennies. He could read, as could his siblings, and was good at arithmetic. When he was nineteen he married seventeen-year-old Inez Monk and put a piece of money down on a square of Person County land so he could grow tobacco. They had four children, two boys and two girls, one of whom didn't live long enough to see a new moon. Hard work had finally boiled John Shuford down to shadow.

"I ain't much more than a rusted old tool now," he said.

The rain had stopped by the time Doodle said good night. She took the flat-wick oil lamp from his bedside and, carrying it by its finger hold, went out to the porch and sat at the top of the steps where her papa's hound, Bugle, lay asleep. His body was in a lazy contortion, his hind legs splayed skyward like an onion harvester. He was snoring.

This was what she loved, being outside, especially after a rain. She never tired of listening to the tunefulness of nighttime, of frogs croaking and crickets creaking, of a 'possum's grunt, or the sound of a 'coon scrambling up a tree. She loved the dankness, too, the smell of damp grass, and looking up at the sky. It was like looking into a bowl of treasures, and this month was full of them. She had sat in this very spot two nights earlier and watched a meteor shower. Tonight, the moon was riding low, a slender crescent, and the stars—Longfellow had called them "the forget-me-nots of the angels"—were keeping watch over their queen.

The glow from the lamp filled the glass chimney. There was something about lamplight that made the eyes balmy, when the wick was too high, the flame too bright. It reminded her of the woman at the county fair who called herself Madame Palmer and claimed she could look into her crystal Ball jar and see the future. Madame Palmer could, she claimed, for an extra nickel, solve any problem. But Doodle's future didn't surpass any other woman's who had been left alone to labor on a farm and care for a sick papa. And no nickel now was going to change the fact that he was dying. It was true. He *was* dying. All she had to do was look at the hollowness in his eyes. He was going to die and leave her all alone. And what choice did she have, one brother who cared more for drink, and another who ran off with his imagination. How was it that the two of them turned out so different from her? It was as if they had shucked the very things their parents held in esteem, and had done so as simply as snakes shed skin.

Ballard, the oldest, hated being poor. He used to roll his eyes when their mama ran out of coffee and ground scorched chestnuts in the mill instead. He jeered whenever he was served last winter's dried fruit, and laughed at Doodle's rag dolls.

The youngest boy didn't have the same mean streak as his brother. Talmadge was just plain lazy. He complained about everything. It was either too hard or too heavy. Ask him to help saw and split wood and he'd find some way out. Listening to his colorful excuses, it was a wonder he had the strength to pull on a sock. But give Talmadge a bottle and that would stir his stumps: he was like a dog in a fury to tackle a bitch in heat.

Bugle rolled to his side and Doodle petted him. She leaned back and rested on her elbows.

Ballard would've made fun of her if he'd seen her in a dress the day of the picnic. She had never cared what people thought before, but lately, on the rare opportunities when she found herself in others' company, she felt—different. She noticed things, like the fine beads that were sewn onto Ina's stylish bag. There must have been hundreds, thousands of those tiny little seeds, all in bright colors. A purse like that would've looked silly dangling from Doodle's rough hands. But a part of her had wanted to touch it. And she had come close when Ina asked to see the Helen Eddy card that Bertie gave her.

That was another thing, those actress cards that she collected. Bertie had always saved them for her, but this time, when Bertie gave her the card in front of Ina, Doodle felt embarrassed. She didn't want Ina to think she was some pitiful girl who longed to emulate a glamorous actress. It was simply a hobby of hers, like collecting stamps. She was too busy with work to even study them.

The apples! she remembered, a whole peck that she had peeled, cored, and sliced that afternoon, still out back on the picnic table where she had spread them to dry. Eight quarts of work and all that rain.

She turned the adjustment on the lamp, drawing the wick down into the burner till the light shrank to a warm fleck, picked the lamp up and went back inside. Nothing she could do for the apples tonight.

The next morning, after refusing any breakfast, her papa asked her to bring the family's special writing instrument and a sheet of paper to his room. She did as he asked and gathered up the writing box that held stationery and a jar of black ink. She liked having pretty stationery, though most of the writing she did were notes to herself, favorite lines from poetry and daily observations, and the perpetual list that ran the gamut from needed repairs to food items.

She cradled the box in her lap and prepared to write.

"I, John Wilborn Shuford, being of sound mind and memory, but considering the uncertainty of my earthly existence"—an idea he found amusing by the airy sound he made—"do make and declare this my last will and testament."

"Papa," said Doodle, "are you sure you wanna do this?"

"Delores, as executor of my estate, such as it is, I want you to see that all this gets put down. In writing. And then put in the Bible. Your mama kept all our important papers in the Bible."

Doodle obliged by dipping the tip of the black-and-white instrument into the jar of ink as he continued.

"Revoking all others as follows," he said. "I reckon here's where I make a list of items. First, and I know we already discussed this, Delores, I want you to give my remains a proper burial." He was to be buried on the family land, he said, under the sycamore where his dear Inez's remains lay. There would be no funeral expenses, he commanded, other than the twenty-four dollars she was to take from the drawer of his nightstand and give to the cabinetmaker Mr. Chambers for the pine box that he'd already seen to ordering. Mr. Chambers would be delivering it later that day.

"Item number two," he said, "I give and devise unto my daughter Delores Monk Shuford for life, with remainder to her children if she has any"—he cut his eyes in her direction—"my tract of land, containing ten acres, more or less, on which I live, having the land inherited from my mother."

"What about the boys, Papa?" Doodle asked.

"I got no boys."

"Is that all then?"

"No," he said. "Keep writing. If my daughter Delores should die without issue surviving her, then the land herein devised to her shall go to the only son of Broadie Clayton."

Doodle's shoulders dropped. "What?" She couldn't imagine he meant that chucklehead of a mail carrier, the one all the girls in town fawned over. That fella couldn't ride a bicycle without injury to himself. He needed a sidecar on that motorbike of his just to stay upright.

She knew a friendship had developed between the two men, would see them talking at the mailbox on the days Colon came by to deliver letters, and hear them laughing in the distance while she was out feeding the chickens and doing various chores. And later, over supper, her papa would mention some bit of news or interesting fact the boy shared with him, usually laughing and shaking his head in the delight of what it was he was relating. . . . *And you know what he told him, he said, does a cat have climbing gear?* She thought it was no more than an old man chewing the rag with a young one. Not in a hundred years would she have thought her papa would put him in his will.

"I like that boy," her papa said. "He's smart and he ain't afraid of hard work. Says he's been saving up for a farm of his own some day. Used to help Flem Rutledge on his farm till he passed and them boys of his sold the land.

You never know what the almighty dollar will make a man do. Something like that could happen if your brothers were to ever show their faces around here again, they find out I left you in charge."

"Nobody's gonna take away this land, Papa," Doodle said. "I'll see to that."

"That's why we need to get all this down in writing. And I want you to think about letting that boy Colon help out around here," he said. "Me and his pa Broadie go way back. The Claytons is good people, Delores. You can trust 'em. And you're gonna need help, especially when it comes time to carry my raggedy carcass out of here."

Until now that had been the furthest thing from her mind, the task of literally removing his body.

"You'll wanna ask him to come by on Tuesday," he said.

"How come, Papa? Why Tuesday?"

"Because," he said, "I seen a sun dog yesterday. Prettiest halo I ever seen."

The Shufords had always been people of tradition. They planted crops and killed hogs according to the moon. They ate black-eyed peas on New Year's Day for change, and greens for dollars. To stave off bad luck they slipped both feet into their shoes at the same time, and they never, ever swept dirt out the door after dark. So when her papa said he saw a sun dog—a bright-colored spot next to the sun—Doodle knew, within three days, there was to be a death in the family.

Chapter 14

Ina Meets with Miss Duncan

With her application made, her contract signed, the only thing left for Ina to do was meet with Venie Duncan to sort out the smaller details. They agreed to meet at Miss Duncan's home, the home she shared with her sister, to discuss the impending school year and, now that there would be two teachers instead of one crowding into East Roxboro School, how best to prepare lesson plans. Ina wondered about Miss Duncan's approach to teaching. She doubted that the woman was at all rigid. Perhaps she had been at one time, as a poorly paid nineteen-year-old with strong ideals. But with the amount of nervousness the petite woman exuded at their first meeting, flying into Ina's arms the way she did and clutching on to her like a wild-eyed lemur, it was much more likely that the children now ran her ragged. And that concerned Ina. How was she going to work alongside a woman whose mind was as frenetic as a monkey's in the National Zoo?

And what would Miss Duncan's expectations be of her? Ina supposed she would tell Miss Duncan of her firm belief that lessons should be taught by example, not solely by precept, and indeed that was something she herself practiced every day. Of course, anything more than that she was still figuring out for herself, as she had never taught in a classroom setting before. It caused a slight amount of trepidation in her. As did the fact that the children were probably—rural.

She dressed for breakfast, then looked out the window before deciding on a hat. Her mother had instilled in her that a woman should always be peaked properly at the proper time. Naturally, she wanted to present as good an appearance as possible to Miss Duncan, confident but not too expensive. The sun was straining through the sprawled branches of the eastern red oak just outside her window, casting deep shadows of the pointy-lobed leaves onto the lawn. The smaller branches quieted the excited foliage with calming gestures. The pliable saucer-brim beige was suitable for such a warm and breezy day, she decided. Very smart, yet completely unfussy. She grabbed it from the top shelf of the armoire and made her way downstairs.

Bertie had taken the day off from her job at the telephone company—something about organizing a ballot-marking school for women—and offered to drive Ina over.

"If I wouldn't be taking you out of your way," Ina said, dabbing a corner of a napkin to her lips.

Bertie was fidgety as they bumped along the road. In the short time Ina had known her, Bertie's mind never seemed to rest. She rambled on about what women need to know to prepare themselves for November's election.

"Women are gonna have to be brought up to speed," Bertie shouted over the engine and the air whishing past. "A lot of them probably don't even know what poll tax is. Can you imagine?"

Ina was not about to comment.

There was a small burlap bag of peanuts on the seat between them, and every so often, Bertie would shove her manly hand in and pull out a fistful of the crunchy brown legumes, placing the spoils in her lap. She would crack their shells in one fist and pop the little goobers into her mouth. Ina suspected she did it more out of habit since Mrs. Daye had just provided them a more-than-filling breakfast. Corned beef hash made with bacon drippings felt like a lead weight in Ina's sensitive stomach.

She admired the fact Bertie could drive an automobile, that she knew how to operate its levers on the steering gear, and the way she pumped the foot pedals like she was playing an organ. But what she admired most was that Bertie was capable of bringing the motor to life with one good yank on the starting crank. She took into account that Bertie's arms were as sturdy as the cane of a cornplant, and imagined, too, that the opulence of her bosom must somehow contribute. She watched Bertie's hands and feet carefully, never having learned to operate such a machine herself. When Harlan was alive he took them wherever they needed or wanted to go. And before that it was her father's task to see that she found herself to church or the occasional opera. All she had to do was sit with her purse in her lap, one hand placed on top of the other, and look pretty.

Bertie slowed the Model T to a stop in front of a two-story house. "Should I come back for you?"

"I'm not sure how long this will take," Ina said, stepping out and latching the door. She peered in through the passenger side at Bertie. "And now that I know how close it is, and where I'm going, I think I'd rather walk. It's such a beautiful day."

"Suit yourself," said Bertie, and drove off, leaving Ina standing in front of a sad house shaded by black locusts and sweet gums.

It was an odd-looking house, the way it was put together, like two houses that butted into a V—one roof was lower than the other, and the porch was catty-cornered—so that when you stood facing it from the road you saw the front of the house as well as the back. The yard was cluttered with cats and kittens, and as Ina made her way toward the porch, between rangy yellow cushion chrysanthemums and leggy white asters, they all seemed to stop their frisky little games and stare at her.

As she neared the porch, a tortoise-colored creature shot across the path like an ill omen and nearly tripped her. She took a moment to catch her breath, then stepped onto the porch and tapped on the splintery frame of the screen door. One hinge was loose.

She could hear voices coming from deep inside the house, but couldn't see beyond the screen itself. No natural light emanated from within. The voices, as soon became apparent, belonged to Venie Duncan. Seemed she was scolding herself about something she should or shouldn't have done.

She came scuddling up to the door.

"Oh, oh, you are a punctual one, Miss Fitzhugh! Yes, indeed! I was just getting ready to put us on some water for tea and—" She opened the door with a jittery hand and out darted another cat. The look on Miss Duncan's face was one of a certain discomfort. Or was it wide-eyed fear? "Josephine's," she said. "My sister's. Please, come in, but do watch your step. Little sneaks are begetting as fast as rabbits. Funny, you wouldn't think cats even take an interest." She gave a nervous laugh. "You like tea, don't you? You look like you like tea."

"Oh yes," Ina said. "Very much."

It was dark inside. Before her eyes had a chance to fully focus Miss Duncan was scampering off to the kitchen, urging her to follow. Once her eyes were adjusted, the first thing she noticed was the woman's feet, something she had paid little attention to the day of their first meeting. They were elfin, like a toddler's, swaddled inside serviceable shoes, a school shoe that buttoned with low flat heels, cut large at the ankles. Ideal for a baby's thick fat feet. Her dress was even that of a child's. A practical apron with white rickrack braid—the sort that's easy to put on and can comfortably conceal sateen bloomers.

Ina bit her lip.

"We'll be more comfortable in the kitchen," Miss Duncan said, as the two walked down the dark hallway.

They passed a sitting room where several pairs of golden eyes spangled out from an abomination of a settee. The drapes were drawn and there was the smell of longstanding layers of dust, and scales of mossy mildew. *A striped dimity is sorely needed*, Ina thought.

There was a daguerreotype of a man with the same pop-eyed look of Miss Duncan's hung high in the hallway. She wondered if it was Miss Duncan's father, and then a wicked thought occurred—that the poor man was frozen in horror, his homestead turned into a cathouse.

Miss Duncan had the same jitteriness about her as when they had first met at the Dayes'. Then, Ina thought Miss Duncan was simply anxious about meeting her, but now believed her excitability had a great deal to do with her living quarters. She was the proverbial long-tailed cat in a room full of rockers, as if every step she took needed to be taken with care.

"Do you mind if we have Yellow Label?" Miss Duncan asked, taking a small tin from the cupboard.

"I'm sorry?"

"Tea. Yellow Label tea. Josephine's not here, but if she even thinks I've been digging into her Light of Asia she's liable to have a conniption fit. She likes to use that kind for her pussy-cat tea parties on Sundays."

"Oh, by all means then, we should have Yellow Label."

"Personally, if you ask me, I think she's letting them rule the roost too much. But you can't tell Josephine anything. She wasn't never so wild about cats. In fact, she used to be scared to death of them. Till her Albert died."

"Her husband," Ina said, giving an understanding nod, watching as Miss Duncan poised tiptoe on a stool and reached inside the cupboard again.

"No, no, Wilborn was her husband. But he's dead, too." She presented Ina with a box of candied drops. "Horehound?"

"No, thank you."

"Albert was her Australian parakeep. A little sky-blue budgie. She said he told her before he croaked—hanging like he was on that teeny little acrobat bar by his crooked foot—to let bygones be bygones. Isn't that just the craziest thing? Like a bird can talk!" She popped a brown slug of the bitter mint into her mouth.

Did she say parakeep?

Only after Miss Duncan shooed a marmalade cat from the kitchenette did they sit down to business. It was all Ina could do to force herself to place her teacup on the same surface where those filthy orange paws had been. And, as if that wasn't disturbing enough, the awful thought occurred to her that any one of those cats had probably lapped Light of Asia from her very cup! Pussy-cat tea party, indeed! She tried to be inconspicuous. She took the serviette Miss Duncan provided her, and when the tiny teacher wasn't looking, swiped it along the rim of the cup and made a quick mad dash with it over the table.

She expected Miss Duncan to bring a stack of books to the table, *The Golden Book of Favorite Songs*, Webster's *American Spelling Book*, yet there weren't any books in sight. What she did bring to the table was a slip of paper that Ina presumed to be a list of items to be discussed, but Miss Duncan sheepishly laid the paper facedown and picked up the dainty china cup, cradling it with her childish hands, sloshing the tea till it finally found her lips.

"So," Ina said.

"Well now," said Miss Duncan.

This was most uncomfortable, for Miss Duncan sat as unknowing and awkward as Ina, as if she too were a guest in the house, waiting for the conversation to be started by someone other than herself.

Ina cleared her throat. "Maybe you could begin by telling me how many pupils currently attend East Roxboro School, and their ages."

"Yes, yes, good idea!" Miss Duncan took up her teacup again, her arms shaking like sensitive dowsing rods. When at last she set the cup back down she began rattling off the charges' names.

"Let's see now. There's the twins, Dolian and David. Henry, oh, he's a mean one, that boy. Adele, such a sweet sweet child. Victoria you'll need to watch. She comes across all honey, but I caught her out back one day holding Etta under the spigot, and Henry just'a pumping away on the handle. And, of course, you know Alta Ruth. Now she can be stubborn about not getting her way—"

Ina waited for what seemed like an inordinate amount of time for Miss Duncan to finish her thought regarding Alta Ruth. She was certain that the teacher was about to share the secret for handling tempers, but her unfinished sentence skittered over the table like a bat over water.

"So what do you suggest?" Ina asked.

"What's that?"

"On how to deal with any mischief."

"Mischief from whom?"

Ina was growing flustered. "Mischief among the children. You were saying that Alta Ruth can be temperamental, and that Henry, I believe, is the rowdy one."

"Oh dear," Miss Duncan said, now whispering. "There's no dealing with something like that. All those little minds in that little room. It's best if you just let them do as they wish."

"Surely you don't mean that. Children expect a certain order. Don't they?"

Miss Duncan's mind seemed to drift off again, and Ina, seeing that Miss

Duncan needed to be kept on track, suggested they go over their lessons. "And it looks as if you've made some notes for me there."

"Oh, the list, yes!" Miss Duncan said, strumming nervously at a corner of the paper.

"I was thinking we could split the children into two groups," Ina said, "and perhaps that would solve some of the rambunctiousness among them. Of course, I suppose that all depends on how many grades we have, their ages and all. I take half the pupils, you take the other."

She was having difficulty reading Miss Duncan's reaction to her suggestion. She hadn't considered this before, but now she wondered if it was possible that the idea of sharing her pupils and the schoolhouse was, in some ways, disturbing to the woman. After all, she had been the sole teacher of East Roxboro School for a number of years. Was this not *her* bread? And to have a younger teacher, one who never even taught before, step in.

Maybe she was wrong to have used the word *we* so soon. "But certainly, Miss Duncan, I'll defer to what you think best."

"Oh dear!" said Miss Duncan, shaking her head. "I have made an awful mess of things. Oh, just an awful mess! Can you ever forgive me?"

This was it, Ina thought. This was where Miss Duncan would tell her she'd had a change of heart, that she didn't need nor want any assistance after all. It was all a big mistake, Ina was sure Miss Duncan was going to say— that she never should have told Mrs. Wheeler of her inability to handle the load put upon her anymore, and she'd only said it in a moment of exasperation after Henry had tied her tiny body to the bell rope that day and she flew off the floor, a hostage of the belfry. It was enough to put anybody under a strain. But now that Miss Duncan was upright and feeling sensible, she'd had a change of heart. And it didn't matter how many more students came into East Roxboro School. Come one, come all, the well-behaved, the truly unruly, she, Venie Duncan, would gladly nourish their little minds and big spirits!

But believing that Miss Duncan was simply too proud to say it, Ina decided to offer an out.

"Please, Miss Duncan. There's no need for apology. I must confess that I was seriously considering returning home. Virginia is where I belong, and I thank you for helping me make that decision." Ina slid her chair out from the table and prepared to leave.

Miss Duncan latched on to Ina's wrist with a startlingly cold hand. A cold, eeny-weeny, leathery primate hand. "What? Return to Virginia? No! Oh, this town needs you more than ever now. They need a teacher. I'm sorry, Miss Fitzhugh, but it's too late to find another replacement. It's simply too late. Oh, please! I can't go back. They can't make me go back. Those little scallions'll be the death of me!"

Ina walked back to the Daye home appalled, clutching what amounted to a list of farm chores in her hand. Start fire? Draw water? Sweep outhouse? Total responsibility for the overall operation of the school! This was more than she had anticipated. It was more than a botheration. It was . . . it shouldn't happen to a dog!

The very thought of physical labor fatigued her. Dirty-hand drudgery at that. It was atrocious! Here she had agreed to take on one job—a respectable position that promised no unnecessary muss—and now to have it multiply? Granted she did not envision herself sitting behind the desk reading *Godey's Lady's Book* while the children did their lessons, but she had good reason to be agitated. Split wood? Why, she'd have to get up before dawn! She supposed they'd be expecting her to carry a pistol, too. And she couldn't help but wonder if Mrs. Wheeler had known of Miss Duncan's intent to quit teaching all along, if perhaps it was Mrs. Wheeler who was responsible for arranging this whole charade in the first place. Get the girl here then drop the ol' delayed-action bomb on her. She couldn't wait to give her aunt an earful.

It wasn't long before she realized how irritated she was, simply by the erratic nature of her gait. No, actually, it was purposeful, for she was kicking pebbles every step of the way. Every pebble in her path represented everything in life that angered her. Not a gem among them. The little ones, caustic, hard as desiccated peas, were all the minute things that stung her daily: itchy millinery (she immediately snatched her hat from her head), too-tight bust confiners, and any product claiming to maintain youth and beauty. The bigger stones were for all the rest that she had no control over. Every last one a symbol of regret.

She stepped up to one of those scorns of stone and flamingoed her right foot over it. "This has a covered wood French heel," she said aloud, as if to scold. "It has an aluminum heel plate and a flexible MacKay sewed sole. It's guaranteed, you understand, to give me satisfactory wear! I'm supposed to be able to do anything I want in these!" With that she stomped her heel into the gravelstone, grinding and scraping, hoping to reduce pumice to powder, until her left foot too came out from under her and she found herself sitting on her courage in the dusty road. She began to cry. "*Pourquoi? Il m'a promis.* He promised me. Harlan promised me!"

Ina's blinding walk from Miss Duncan's had brought her to the sidewalk in front of the Dowdy Inn, and when she looked up, the old mute woman Eunice was staring at her just as she had that first day when Ina stepped off the train. It was as if the woman had never moved from that spot, for she was rocking and staring at Ina with the same eerie blank-faced look.

Ina stood and brushed herself off, smeared her tears with the backs of her hands. She retrieved the slip of paper from the ground, and next her hat, straightening it atop her head with confidence, then nodded in greeting to Eunice as any self-respecting lady would do, and continued on her way.

And that is how her days as the teacher—the sole teacher of East Roxboro School—began.

Chapter 15

The Last Thing
John Shuford Said

*D*oodle sat by his side all night, while that sad-eyed hound of his, Bugle, kept vigil on the floor next to the bed. Every so often she would dip a cloth into a basin of water and blot her papa's forehead.

He was feverish and slept little. Mostly he talked nonsense. At times he'd be giddy, vividly remembering a scene from the past; other times Doodle wouldn't be able to make hide nor hair of what it was he was trying to relate, his words amounting to no more than mush.

For the past couple of hours she'd been watching him sleep and listening to the soft "sus" sounds he made in rhythm with the ebb and flow of his chest. She stretched her back, then bent over and ran her hands up and down her legs to revive them. She felt a gnawing in her belly and thought about going into the kitchen for a bite to eat. Her papa hadn't eaten for two days. He refused all remedies now, no blood-building teas or poultices of turpentine and lard to rid his congestion. The only thing he wanted was water.

She looked down at Bugle. He lay with an ear to the ground and one eye open. That hound was as bullheaded as her papa. All her life she believed that animals were capable of having a spiritual affinity. And, in her eyes, Bugle was proving it to be true. He, too, was refusing to eat. She had tried coaxing him outside the day before by placing scraps in a pan on the porch, but when the dog finally budged it was only to move from the foot of the bed over to the side, where he could be closer to his master.

As she made to push herself up from the chair, her papa opened his eyes.

"'Member when I used to tell y'all younguns stories?"

Doodle smiled and settled back into her seat. She remembered sitting by the fire on winter nights with her brothers while Papa told them tales of tombstones in cemeteries and stories that involved misdoings.

"My favorite was the one about the robbers," she said.

He couldn't recall.

"You know, the one about your mama on butchering day? She was inside the house by herself?"

He smiled, remembering. "That was Grandmammy who was in the house. Mama was way out back with the rest of us killing a hog. She's the one taught us how to scrape and gut 'em. Said you gotta be careful when you make that first cut not to go through the intestine. She showed us all that, too."

Doodle could see he was getting off the subject. "But your Grandmammy, did she see the men coming or did they knock?"

"I don't recollect." He cleared his throat. "I believe she just seen them acting peculiar, and knew they won't up to no good by the way they were sneaking around. She was a sharp one, though. Grabbed a hog paunch from the drain board and pulled it over her head. Don't you know she looked like a queer potato. Opened the door and scared them boys so bad, they run plumb off the property."

With every word he expelled now, Doodle could sense his body failing him. His lips were drawn, dry and cracked as the spines on an okra pod left on the vine after a harvest. She asked if he wanted some water.

"Just a sip," he said, "then I got one more story."

She told him to save his strength, for what she didn't know, and put the glass up to his mouth.

It was a strain for him to swallow, but once he did he managed, "This is one that needs to get told."

He was what folks called a "note-shaver" back then, somebody you could borrow money from. There was just the one bank in town and they didn't make it easy for a cropper to get a loan. Brud Daye was somebody you could go to, no questions asked. The man would pull a roll of centuries right out of his pocket and ask you how much. And you didn't think about how you were gonna pay it back. All you cared about was how good it felt. Salve on a rough palm.

Not only was he the richest man in the county, but the hatefullest, too. He used to laugh and say he owned every black ass and half the pink ones between here and Danville. Wasn't a body that wasn't afraid of him. Different ones warned me, said they'd rather do business with the devil. Far as I was concerned it was the same thing, but there wasn't no other choice, crops lost and three mouths to feed, youngun too big to tote. I never told Inez, just prayed that when the time come, when the note come due, that me and him could negotiate, work us out some sort of deal.

Ain't right, I told him the day he come to collect. Calling in a note on a man's land for half a payment, wanting to take from me the farm I had worked all my life to have. He could've made two of me, and still I said what I said. "I know what kinds of things you do after dark," I said flat to that stone face of his. "Be a shame if Lalura was to find out that that smoke you bringing home on your clothes ain't from the tavern, but rather the stench of coal oil that's been set afire. To a cottonwood. With a screaming niggra tied to it."

He laughed at me.

And I figured then I would kill him. I would just as soon kill him before I let him take this farm and show me to look weak in front of Inez. Kill him just to put an end to some of this world's evil.

I knew his favorite spot for hunting turkey; a field nearby, just shy of the county line. I laid belly down in a swale at the edge of the clearing and waited. I waited for him just as patient as he waited to set his sight on a war-bling tom. Peaceful, that time of the morning, just before the sun casts a pale glow on things, and listening to the soft yarp of squirrels, looking up into the treetops and seeing songbirds flirt branches.

He couldn't have been more than twenty yards away when I finally spot-ted him, dressed from head to toe he was, in a ceremonious get-up. Any other man would've slipped a rabbit's foot in his pocket. But not him. Takes a self-sure man, I say, to dress like a turkey. That, or a foolish one. Made me smile to see him that way though, a grown man worshiping bird in boys' play clothes. For a second I actually considered there might be a vane of goodness in them feathers.

And to be sure, he was a good woodsman. The man had a keen eye for the least bit of movement. I watched as he eased hisself to the ground and slid his back along the trunk of a tree, propped that curly maple rifle of his against it. He took his call bone out of his shirt pocket, put it to his mouth and kissed. It was a soft and nasally, three-note chirp he made, and before long that crazy cuss had yelped up one helluva turkey.

Sounded like thunder to me, and it was, but of a gobbling turkey out in the open timber. I allowed myself to blink and then I focused on Brud. He was smiling. Sonofabitch. Had a tight chokehold to his rifle. That's the first time me and him was on the same level. I can recall, to this very day, how stingy my chest felt—'bout like it feels now—my heart pushing against my ribs as near and grating as bark on a tree. He aimed for the neck. I aimed for his head. And I wondered then if he felt the same curious sensation I was feeling—like a tarpaulin being stretched overhead and silencing everything. We kept our eyes on the sights and slowly we pressured the triggers. I braced for the kick and the sharp burn that was about to ring my ears.

It was a hot, wet, crackling shock from nowhere and everywhere. Feathers billowed and flittered down like hummingbirds on a battlefield, taking shelter at the base of that black oak. The turkey cried out a shrill alarm, jumped into the air and beat its wings to freedom. Brud, he wasn't so lucky.

I reckon we're about to be on the same level again.

Her field of view through the window this morning was a soothing cope of pink, but the room was yet to fill with more than a gray light. She moved her chair closer to the bed and lit the lamp, deciding to read scripture aloud. Perhaps grace would be revealed in some pregnant verse.

She had read for hours it seemed, until the sun was strong enough to spin dark circles under her arms and sap her strength. Her eyes were growing weary. She had barely shut an eye since her papa told her that story. She didn't know what to make of it, and throughout the night had instinctively reached for the Bible. The words on the page began to jump about like fleas now, and she closed the book and reached for the glass pitcher on the nightstand, pouring water into a jelly jar. The water tasted tinny.

There was a strong, musky odor in the room that followed, and she wondered for a moment if this was the smell of the last gasp, of someone soon to be numbered. Whatever the source, it was heady, rank as spoiled sowbelly. More likely, she thought, the smell was coming from her; her lack of a hot bath these past few days. That, and the gaminess of Bugle, who now began to whimper.

She shushed him, but to no avail. For hours upon hours that dog had lain on the wooden floor like he, too, was dying, and she figured that when her papa went, his dog would soon follow. But she watched as Bugle rolled to his feet and raised his sixty pounds from the floor. He began to nudge her papa's hand with his sharp nose. His whimper grew fretful.

A strange energy entered the room, like a child of the lightning that had struck their barn years before, burning it to the ground, the airy shed her papa had borrowed money to replace. Upward of a thousand and one fireflies electrifying the air. And there was Bugle, measuring length around a worn armchair, his mottled hide rippling over backbone. She wondered if she might be having a fantastic vision from not eating. She leaned over and took hold of her papa's hand and squeezed, and without warning, the cagey hound jumped onto the bed and curled nose to tail next to his master.

Minutes passed and the only sound in the room was her papa's slow rattle. In one final draw of breath, Bugle's best friend finally surrendered. What had been whimpers from the blue tick looped into wailful yowls. And with the same haste that he'd jumped onto the bed, he now sprang to the floor. Through her tears she could see him climb the wall like he was baying a 'coon up a tree. All around the room he went, clattering his claws, splitting paper from the walls, throwing his head back and his mouth wide, letting loose a series of deep howls.

She released her papa's hand and stood on shaky legs.

It took more than simple prodding to get Bugle out of the house. She pushed him and pulled him in hopes of preparing her papa's body for burial in some semblance of peace. Bugle howled from the porch when she first put him outside and shut the door, but after a while he settled down, and all she could hear was the scolding of a wren on the windowsill as she wrung a wet soapy rag and wiped her papa's leaded limbs.

She used his folding straight razor to give him a shave, the corner of a matchbook to scrape underneath his nails. When a search of the bathroom cabinet turned up no amount of hair oil, she ran a palmful of antifungal ointment through his scalp instead.

When the last button was fastened, and the wrinkles smoothed from his Sunday coat sleeves, she stepped back and admired her handiwork. His hair was tame, and his face was smooth as an earthworm. He was a man getting some shuteye before heading out to go honkytonk. He was dressed pretty and laid out like a long pig.

She hadn't given any thought to how she would get him from the bed to the box out back in the shed. And then there was the matter of the hole. Not right to dig before a man is dead. She sunk her knees onto the mattress and looked down at his slumbering face to consider. "Though your body goes the way of all the earth, may God find your soul," she whispered. She would let Bugle back inside, she decided, let him see his friend in all his glory.

⁕

When she opened the door, Colon Clayton was standing on the other side of the screen, ready to knock. Bugle was by his side, and the two looked as if they had arrived together.

"Oh, hey!" Colon said. "Doodle, right?"

She nodded.

"Well, I, uh—I just come to see about John."

Doodle gave him a queer look.

"Hadn't seen him last couple weeks," Colon went on to say. He held out his arm and pointed down the hill. "Usually he's already out by the mailbox, see, by the time I round the corner. Me and him got us a regular bull session going, if you'll pardon. And, well, like I said, I hadn't seen him last couple weeks and thought I ought to just stop up to the house and check on him. Hope you don't mind. I rode my cycle far as the willow. John says them geese can be ornery. I don't reckon I upset 'em too bad by coming up this close to the house. You suppose?"

Doodle remained mum.

"Well," Colon said, rubbing Bugle's head, "I take it he's not home then." He turned and started down the porch steps.

"He's dead," said Doodle. And suddenly the sound of those words washed through her body like a surprise springtime rain, spilling down her cheeks in confused trickles.

❋

Colon stepped inside John's bedroom. "Well now, don't he look tricksy."

Doodle stood in the doorway. "I told him I'd give him a decent burial."

"Looks to me like you done a fine job so far. Fine job, indeed."

"I'm gonna finish it today. Burying him," she said. "Don't see any sense in waiting, hot as it is. I expect you know what I mean."

Colon suggested they let John rest right where he was till they could get the hole dug. Doodle grabbed two shovels, and with Bugle alongside them, she took Colon to the spot out along the edge of the field. The two began digging.

"I could've done this myself," she said, "just so you know. I don't think it's right to start digging before a man is dead."

She watched as Colon put his foot on shovel and pressed his weight into the blade, using his chest for leverage.

"Might've taken me longer," she continued, "but I could've done this myself."

Colon acknowledged her by nodding. He worked with determination.

"You're getting your shirt dirty," Doodle said, slinging a scoopful of red dirt off to one side.

"S'awright," said Colon.

"Well, just so you know, it ain't gonna bother me if you wanna take it off. I'm not at all squeamish. I mean, the fact you're lacking on that side and all." She pointed to his empty sleeve. "That kind of thing doesn't bother me in the least. What does bother me is if you go and get dirty on my account. I got all I can do without worrying over one more piece to wash. And if you get dirty, I got no choice but to wash it for you. That's just the right thing to do."

Colon drove the blade into the ground and let out a heavy sigh. He unbuttoned his shirt, exposing a sleeveless undergarment, slung the shirt to the ground, next to where Bugle was sprawled on his belly and wagging his tail, and went back to scooping soil.

Doodle tried not to stare.

He was burlier than she remembered, his shoulders squarer and his neck thicker. The flesh that covered the nub below his left shoulder was as tight as a ripe tomato. It was as if that absent arm had once been a root and some pesky little worm had come along and eaten it clean off. His skin was tanned, darker on the one arm, just south of the elbow where he rolled up his sleeve—she figured from all the time he spent running up and down the road, out in the open, delivering mail. She could see clearly the lines in his body, the thewiness of his muscles, how they flexed with every fluid movement he made. Looking on him was like mapping a deeply veined cabbage. Come to think of it, his head was kindly pointed like an Early Jersey Wakefield. She let out a chuckle when she realized she was comparing him to a vegetable.

"Something funny?" Colon asked.

"Sorry." After a minute or so had passed, she added, "Just seems peculiar is all."

"What's that?"

"Well," Doodle said, "if you and my papa were such good friends, how come he never invited you up to the house?"

"He did," said Colon, steadily working, sweat dripping from his moustache.

Doodle considered his reply, but after time enough had passed for Colon to explain, she decided not to press further. The rest of the time, they worked in silence.

They took the pine box from the barn and carried it as far as the bottom of the front porch steps, setting it down in a patch of grass.

"Let's raise him off them pillows," Colon said, once they were back inside the house, "then I can hoist him up on my shoulder."

"Wait," said Doodle. She reached across her papa and tugged at the flat corners of the bottom sheet until they loosened from the striped ticking. Slowly, respectfully, she pulled each hem inward, gathering, folding, tucking the cotton, loosely gauzing her papa inside a winding sheet, then knotting both ends, the tails of which resembled pigs' ears. She ladled her hands under the shoulders and slid the body with heart and soul from the iron bed to the rough-hewn floor.

"That's all right," she said as Colon tried to help. "I need to do this. You just get the door."

She strained her papa in his graveclothes over the threshold and out onto the porch. By gentle jerks she pulled the body from the porch, jarring the feet on the steps as she walked backward, tips of toes skimming each riser. In the yard, daughter and father found solace. She took a breath and straightened her back, and waited for Colon to slide the pine box closer. Then they each grabbed the sheet by its playful ears and hefted the body into the box.

"God, I hope we hadn't broke his back," Doodle said, noticing the body had stiffened.

"Don't reckon the man's gonna care one way or another now," said Colon.

When they had finished nailing the top shut, the two made the short trek back to the freshly dug hole, on the green sward next to her mama's grave, this time with Drucie the mule proudly pulling the pine box. A homely procession, Bugle following behind, his nose hooked to a cold path, the box furrowing through the dusty yard, scoring dry earth.

A thick murmur of starlings flew overhead and lighted into the canopies of the surrounding hardwoods while Doodle and Colon filled in the hole.

"May you go to happy hunting grounds, John Shuford," said Colon, patting the last shovelful of soil onto the grave.

If only he knew the irony of what he said.

Chapter 16

Doodle Tends a Lonesome House

$\mathcal{S}$he asked Colon if she could feed him some supper before he took off.

"That's mighty kind of you," he said, "but I reckon my ma's been done put food on the table, and I suspect she'll be worried and send Pa out looking for me if I'm not home soon."

"Sure. I only offered because that's what Papa would've wanted, beings he kept you from delivering the rest of your mail today." She looked over at the satchel of letters in Colon's sidecar.

"I best be going then," he said, and gave a scrub to Bugle's head. "If you need help with anything, just holler."

She stood on the porch and watched as Colon straddled his motorcycle and kicked the engine to life. Bugle took off after him.

"Bugle!" she hollered. "You get back here!" Bugle obeyed, doing a quick turnabout, hightailing it back to the porch where he sat obediently at her side. The two watched as the bike went down the hill and created a cloud of red dust that melted into the night.

Once back inside, she set to cleaning the little farmhouse as if going through every discourse of a Domestic Science class. No use in waiting till morning to rid the distressing pall from the house. Even as tired as her body felt she figured she wouldn't be able to sleep, and this was one time when she didn't want her mind to settle on anything meaningful—which to her meant worrisome. She grabbed the corn broom that hung next to the back door first, and started high and worked her way low, going room to room swiping cobwebs and a grimy layer of stove soot from the stout ceiling, and readied the chimney for winter by reaching as far as the broom would go. Afterward, she tinctured a pail of water with camphor and wiped down all the walls.

The paper that lined the open shelves in the kitchen was torn and soiled and fretted her that she was forever needing to replace it. It ripped too easily, and as soon as something was spilled on it, didn't wipe up good. She had an idea, something she'd thought of doing for a long time. There was a 10-pound bag of quicklime out in the shed, and with that in mind she set out through the backyard, leaving an oil lamp glowing from the porch steps. She threw back the latch on the shed and stepped into darkness, groping about gently until she felt the bag. She hauled it to the back stoop in a wheelbarrow and slaked half of the bag with a gallon of water in a heavy-duty bucket.

While the mixture set up, she went on to another chore, dragging both her mattress and her papa's out onto the porch, where she flopped each over a chair back and took turns whacking them with a wire rug beater. Bugle watched with curiosity as she beat both sides till the excelsior filling no longer uttered dust, and then she hauled them back inside and focused on doing the same to the quilts.

Her intention of keeping her mind blank reached its limit when she returned the bedding to her papa's room. She could almost see him lying there, the pained look on his face, and hear the awful rattle in his chest. Manic in her movements, she took to rearranging what few furnishings were there. She pulled the iron bed in quick tugs and jerks until the headboard was settled flush against the wall on the other side of the room. But the new location didn't suit her, and she pulled on the iron pillars again, this time harder, until the bed rested, at last, catty-cornered. Only after she had slid the oak dresser to another wall, and shifted the washstand, too, did she consider that job done.

Next, she went to the kitchen and began stripping the smirched paper from the shelves and wiped each with a soppy rag dipped in the camphor water. As the shelving dried she removed all the glass chimneys from the lamps, holding each one over the spout of a simmering tea kettle, then rubbing them clear with a soft rag. After the chimneys had been replaced on their burners, she went back outside to check on the lime and water solution. She lifted the heavy bucket and carried it into the kitchen, careful not to slosh the contents, where she whitewashed every bared ledge.

The shelves looked as clean as a new penny when she finished, so clear and tidy that she decided to whitewash every strip of beaded board along the walls, too. Why hadn't she done this before now? 'Course, when was there ever time?

Tiredness was confronting her, but before she would allow herself sleep, she set to mopping the floors. Her head was beginning to feel as if it was caught between the curb and bottom of a cider press. She couldn't recall ever having an ache so bad and blamed the awful throbbing on the information her papa had laid bare. What did he expect her to do with light such as that? Did he want her to tell the Dayes? That he was the one who had killed their husband and father? He didn't tell her what to do with his confession, didn't ask her to relay any message to the family, and she had failed to ask him, too stunned she was by his admission. It was bad enough that *she* knew, but even worse that these were people she genuinely cared about. Bertie was her closest friend. She was a truth-seeker, in every sense of the word, and she wouldn't stop till she knew what had really happened that day. But how do you tell someone you care about that her papa was a monster, that his death was actually justified, when all her life she believed him to be something great? Wasn't she better off not knowing? And anyway, what purpose would it serve? His death hadn't seemed to cause too much hardship on the family. Every one of them seemed to thrive. The boardinghouse had done well over the years, and to hear Bertie tell it her mama enjoyed the busyness that came with keeping the house up and running. Alta Ruth was spirited and smart. And Bertie herself had grown up to be a prominent member of the community. Folks didn't always agree with her ideas, but they admired her courage. She stood for everything that her papa hadn't.

No. She wasn't going to tell Bertie. She couldn't. Even if she had to withstand a lifetime of headaches she absolutely positively would not tell her.

She finally reached an end to her chores.

It was only after she went to her room and stretched out across her bed that she realized what she'd been trying to avoid all along. It wasn't sleep that made her afraid. A person quits being lonely when they fall asleep. It was the time spent waiting on sleep to come, and being reminded of that line in the Keats' poem, *The Eve of St. Agnes*—the house was as "noiseless as fear in a wide wilderness."

Chapter 17

A Glimpse of Doodle's Neighbor

The morning after she buried her papa, after she had put out ground meat meal for the chickens and geese, Doodle walked over to Miss Cara Sue's carrying a basket of fresh eggs. Miss Cara Sue wouldn't have seen the goings-on the day before, their properties screened by a dense patch of woodland—sycamores, serviceberries, hickories—and Doodle was going to break the news of John's death to her.

The old woman didn't have any family to speak of, and her husband was dead now, going on twelve years. He had built Miss Cara Sue a new house the year before he died, with window screens and modern cookstove; a fine frame house with a combination butler's pantry and laundry that housed a gravity washer, situated in the very same yard as the old one, barely twenty paces from the brand-new back door to the dilapidated front door of their log cabin. But when the time came to move from the one into the other, Miss Cara Sue wouldn't budge. Nobody knew why, just accepted it as part of the woman's old-fogyish ways, and for the better part of a year the two kept house under different roofs.

When Doodle was six years old, Miss Cara Sue appeared at the edge of the yard one day with her hands tucked inside her apron pockets and calmly asked her to fetch her ma and pa, that Mr. Brown, it appeared, was dead. A statement as pure and unvarnished as Miss Cara Sue herself. Doodle didn't understand why she had insisted on living all these years in that ramshackle of a place, invaded by critters, snakes and lizards, frogs and flies, and an occasional bird or two, and cooking over an open fireplace when she could be cooking on a stove. Miss Cara Sue had always been a woman of many mysteries.

Doodle and Bugle tangled their way through the woods, Doodle ducking wisteria and Bugle tromping over poison ivy and milkweed, truffling his nose under leaves.

Smoke was coming from Miss Cara Sue's chimney, and by the rich, spicy aroma wafting through the trees, Doodle was certain she was barbecuing rabbit. Miss Cara Sue kept a box set and ready, baited with spoils from her garden. When a rabbit would hop inside and push against the triggering stick to get to the bait, a door would drop, trapping the rabbit. If it had stiff paws and ears, Miss Cara Sue would release it. Only young ones, she said, with soft paws and soft ears, made the tenderest meals.

"That frog'll pee on you," Doodle said when she saw Bugle being nosy over a toad that was resting on the gnarl of an oak root. He looked up at her, decided to heed her warning, and followed her closely the rest of the way through the woods.

Coming out along the clearing, she spotted Miss Cara Sue. The old woman was escorting a long black snake out of the log cabin. She had it gripped in her right hand, just behind its head, and at the edge of the porch she flung the scoundrel as if discarding the dry-rotted hose of an insecticide sprayer. The snake landed in an unruly hedge of witch hazel and slipped down between the branches.

"Still like wandering in them woods, I see," she said, as Doodle and Bugle approached the cabin. She looked like a pioneering woman in her plain blue dress, long enough to sweep the porch. Her hair was gray as a field and parted down the middle, swagged into a bun at the back of her head. She brushed her hands down her apron. "You and Bugle both done picked up a fair share of beggar ticks."

Doodle looked down at the brown prickly seeds that were stuck to the legs of her britches and made a conscious swipe at them, but to no avail. They would have to be peeled off later one at a time.

"I reckon he's gone, is he?" Miss Cara Sue asked.

"Yes, ma'am. Yesterday."

"I figured as much. A man works his whole life, never sick not one day, then gets felled by a piddling chest cold that even illicit whiskey won't cure. Makes you wonder, don't it?"

Doodle nodded.

"Been nice if he could've held on till after blood month." Miss Cara Sue looked out into the distance, and seemed to be taking in the fresh air.

Doodle understood the implication. By mid-November, the Shufords' crop would've been harvested and the rest of the strenuous farming would've come to a standstill. If only he could've outlived one final reaping.

She looked toward Miss Cara Sue's "new" house when Bugle started to howl. His front paws were hooked onto a window ledge, and he was see-sawing his nose against the pane and whisking his tail. Apparently something was inside.

"Birds," said Miss Cara Sue. "They get in, but then the silly things don't know how to get out."

Doodle had been inside that house only once, not long after Mr. Brown died, a day when her brothers, Ballard and Talmadge, had snuck inside strictly for mischief. It was a rarity for a house to be built then, rare that folks had the money to build one. To a little girl in crooked braids, clad in a worn cotton frock and standing barefoot in a dusty road with soil smudges on her face, it was like looking at a life-sized playhouse, and it took her fancy to hear her brothers rustle around inside and rifle through things that didn't belong to them. She had stepped onto the porch, then through the front door until she was standing inside the dark entry. The boys were laughing somewhere, but she couldn't see them, and before she knew what was happening, someone—one of her brothers—had shoved her into a room and slammed the door. "Old man Brown died in that room," she heard Ballard's voice say, then giggles and the sound of feet running from the house. It was Miss Cara Sue who heard her cries and helped her find her way out.

Bugle continued his antics, and Doodle hollered at him.

"Bugle! You get down from there! You gonna bust a window if you keep that up."

"Aw, let him alone." Miss Cara Sue shooed with her hand. "He's just doing what comes natural. Let's me and you have us a bite to eat. Got a whole pan of grit cakes I just took up and was ready to enjoy before that dadblasted snake showed hisself."

She followed Miss Cara Sue inside and set the basket of eggs on the table. "I'm not hungry, much."

"Woman can't expect to do her work on a empty stomach," Miss Cara Sue said. "Even if she is fit and fine."

Doodle could see the skewered rabbit cooking in the fireplace. It was sizzling in a pan, whole and flat and greasy, frying on top of a grate. Red and yellow flames blackened the pan and the walls of the chimney. She watched as they formed sooty letters, but before she could make out any words another flame would lick the lettering away.

It wasn't often that she came over for a lengthy visit to Miss Cara Sue's, and even rarer that she stepped inside. There was always too much work that needed tending to. For years, the two homes had shared victuals of every kind. The Shufords customarily brought eggs over to the Browns—a practice begun before Doodle was born—and in return Miss Cara Sue would send them home with an assortment of vegetables from her garden or freshly baked bread. Neither family had ever gone hungry.

"Ain't got the powder I once had, Delores," Miss Cara Sue said, "but I expect you know I'll do what I can for you, now that John's gone."

"Yes, ma'am, I know. And I appreciate it. But you don't need to worry, I'm gonna make do."

"I know you will." Her hands were arthritic and shook as she ladled the grit cakes onto the plates.

"Here," Doodle said. "I ought to be helping you."

"You sit," said Miss Cara Sue. "Not every day I get to have company." She placed the dishes on the table, along with two glasses of buttermilk she had poured from a crock, while Doodle scraped two chairs along the uneven floor, away from the table.

"Are you churning today?" Doodle asked.

"Indeed, I am. If you'll come back tomorrow I ought to have some butter for you." They quietly ate their grit cakes.

Doodle enjoyed being in Miss Cara Sue's company. Not an insincere bone in the old woman's body; treated everybody the same. She wasn't easily surprised either, and if Doodle had wanted she could've shared her papa's admission without hesitation. Miss Cara Sue was somebody to make sense of that sort of thing, and would've made her feel better straightaway.

"Miss Cara Sue? Mind if I ask you something?"

"What's that?"

"How do you know when to keep something inside yourself when it feels bigger than you?"

The old woman wiped her mouth. "Talk can be selfish," she said. "Depends on why you're doing it—whether it's a burn or a salve. I usually ask myself, is it worth bragging about?"

Doodle laughed outright and Miss Cara Sue got up from the table and went over to the fireplace to tend to the well-cooked rabbit.

"How come you never moved into the house Mr. Brown built for you?" Doodle asked.

Miss Cara Sue turned around and smiled. "Look out that window there and tell me what you see."

"Lilacs?"

"That's right. Lilacs. And if I was to move even ten feet from here, I couldn't smell my lilacs every day they're in bloom. You see, Delores, that house over yonder there, all that is, is things. This here, this is life."

She saw to it that Doodle didn't leave empty-handed. In one hand, Doodle carried the remains of the rabbit, and in the other a jar of pickled peaches. Bugle garnered a used-up ham bone Miss Cara Sue had saved just for this visit. She knew he'd be needing a distraction.

WOMEN MAY NOW VOTE

"The right of citizens of the United States to vote shall not be denied or abridged by the United States or by any State on account of sex." (United States Constitution, Amendment 19.)

This means that women, as well as men, may take part in all elections, national, state, and local, regular and special. Whatever may be said to the contrary, the **women of North Carolina are eligible to vote** on equal terms with men. Provision has been made for the women to vote this year without paying poll tax.

Women are affected, in equal degree with men, by conditions of government, profiting or suffering according as the government is good or bad. Since this is so, it is clearly the duty of women to take a responsibility in their government—they should, at least, contribute their thought and the force of their vote towards making their government what they would like to have it.

In order to vote it is necessary first to register. This may be done any day from Sept. 30 to Oct. 23 inclusive except Sundays.

November 2nd Is Election Day

All women are urged to study the issues of the present campaign, and to inform themselves as to the candidates for the various offices, national, state, county, and city. Investigate their personal and political qualifications and their stand on the issue of the campaign. Every enfranchised citizen has a solemn DUTY to VOTE. Not only that, but to

VOTE INTELLIGENTLY. Let us vote, not blindly with our minds closed by political prejudice, but with our eyes and minds open to a knowledge of conditions and the ideals of good government.

NORTH CAROLINA LEAGUE OF WOMEN VOTERS

200 Chestnut St.   Goldsboro, NC

Chapter 18

Bertie Shares Her High-Spiritedness with Doodle

*B*ertie was about to burst. She didn't know who was more deserving, good ol' Woody Wilson or "Mama's Boy" Burn, but if either one was here right now she'd kiss him square on the lips!

Her initial thoughts went a little something like this:

Do you have any idea what this means? No more picket lines, no more bloodying our feet on the pavement. We have fought the hard fight, ladies, and finally won! The men have always had every advantage. Well, brothers, here's what I say: move over and make way! We are here to stay! Think our brains are smaller, do you? Not equipped for independent thought, are we? Think we're all hysterical and don't know how to behave rationally, huh? Emotional equilibrium, my ample derriere! Just watch and see, you fat-headed dingledoos.

Hell-fired if I'm not gonna see about shortening my days, and a pay raise!

She decided to drive out to the Shuford farm and take a copy of the news to Doodle. It was likely she hadn't received the official word, the way she stayed so close to that farm, day in day out. It wasn't good for a woman to isolate herself, and Bertie had all but told her so the other night, before Doodle took off from the Wheelers' picnic—too early, Bertie thought. She said, "Doodle, what you need is to get away from that farm more regular. You work yourself too hard. Pa Shuford ain't gonna fault you for wanting to come into town and do a little visiting, see your friends." And all Doodle did was smile. Hiked herself up onto that broken-down mule of hers and told Bertie she'd be seeing her. If that girl wasn't careful she was going to end up like her papa, sick in bed, labored to the bone.

At least they could get a telephone, Bertie thought. That way she could check on her every day from the switchboard, provided Doodle was within ear reach. When Bertie got tired of Mamie Yarborough or the rest of those crazies calling up to the office just to have her time their fruit-cakes and muffins, she could simply drop the call, unplug the wire from the board and plug it into Doodle's. *Pardon me, Miss Mamie, did we get disconnected?*

But Doodle was a culture unto herself. Bertie had never known anybody so connected to sod and soil. Her and Pa Shuford both. She had once made the mistake of calling it dirt, and Doodle set her right-now straight, soft but firm about it. "This is earth," Doodle said, almost like a mother telling her younguns why she loved them. "It sustains us. All of us. It's what we're made of, and, God willing, what we go back to. God don't make dirt. Never did. God, whoever she is, made earth."

Bertie thought it peculiar that no one was outside when she got there. Doodle was usually out in the yard, either tending to the geese, or working in the garden while Pa Shuford ran a steady plow. But the yard and the garden were quiet. And it was an odd time of day for either one of them to be scoffing a meal.

She got out of the Ford and looked around. Even that tailwagger of theirs didn't greet her like usual, always finding it necessary to step on the toes of her shoes and leave behind the remnant of a pawprint. The geese, she could see, were down by the water, but not a hide nor hair of Doodle or Pa Shuford.

"Doo-dle! Hey, country gal!" She waited a second, then snatched a bag of peanuts off the seat of the Ford, along with the women voters' article in the *Courier,* and walked toward the house.

They couldn't have gone too far because the front door was open, and as soon as she stepped onto the porch, Bugle came trotting up from the side of the house.

"Woe, watch the togs, Bubba. Or whatever your name is."

She cupped her hands to her eyes and peeked through the screen as if straining through opera glasses. A flitch of light paled from the kitchen and she could've sworn she smelled black salve. "Anybody home?"

Doodle suddenly became visible at the screened door. "Bertie? What are you doing all the way out here? I must not've heard you. I was in the kitchen mopping." She held the door open and invited her inside.

"Some watchdog you got there," Bertie said, hitching a thumb at Bugle. "I know you got work and all, but this couldn't wait." She handed Doodle the newsprint. "Bastards did something right for a change," she continued. "It's official, country gal. We're heading to the polls! All the canvassing I've done, all that distributing of literature at the fairgrounds, every bit of it has finally paid off."

Doodle looked down at the paper and nodded. "You want some tea? I just made a fresh pitcher."

"Nah, don't spread yourself. I can't stay anyway, got too much to do. Oh, I'm about to forget, Pa Shuford's nuts." She handed Doodle the bag. "Where is that ol' harrower anyway? Don't tell me he's still laid up in bed."

Doodle took a calm, deep breath and told her, in a regretful tone, that he had died on Tuesday.

Bertie gave her a sidelong look. It took a moment for the news to register, but when she was finally able to open her mouth the only thing she could manage to say was, "I believe I'll have some of that tea after all."

Chapter 19

Ina's First Day at School

$\mathcal{I}$n the book *The Rural School: Its Methods and Management*, there are listed characteristics that a teacher should possess: Physical Ability, Health (hence, a good constitution), Nerves, Disposition, and Knowledge of Subject Matter. The only reason Ina knew this was because Miss Duncan left a rain-warped copy for her. It was lying less than flat on a blotter pad on top of the desk.

First, the Physical Ability part, since it figured highly into how her day began. The school was a mere half mile from the Dayes', an easy walk, though it soon became evident that decent shoes were going to be a necessity. By the time she swung the door open at seven o'clock that morning, releasing the awful smell of soured books, her heels tingled like they'd been pricked with knitting needles, and her ankles had the beginnings of angry blisters. It would also be fair to say here that it had a profound effect on her Disposition.

It was to be a very long day.

The pupils weren't due to arrive until nine A.M., but she decided it would be best if she headed to the school much earlier, to get the *how of it*, so to speak.

The weather had turned chilly the last couple of days, and the temperature felt even colder inside the little schoolhouse. Her breath atomized the room. She remembered one of the chores Miss Duncan had written on the list, to build a fire at the start of each cold morning in order that the room was warm in time for the children's arrival. What she didn't remember was how to build one. She'd seen Harlan make a fire in the past, but hadn't recorded the specifics in her memory. Wood, obviously, was the main ingredient, and she had seen a small stack of split logs outside. But what was the proper recipe, besides the obligatory match and logs? Paper and kindling?

But how much of each? And which was more pertinent? The paper or the kindling? If she couldn't find enough twigs, would the paper suffice?

The kindling turned out to be no problem, there was a pail of it next to the stovewood. It was the paper she lacked. There wasn't the least bit of newsprint to be seen, but she recalled, during her initial visit here with Miss Duncan, having seen a barely dispensed Sears and Roebuck catalog out in the privy.

She found a box of matches in the top drawer of the desk. But once her fire caught a decent flame, it billowed out a phenomenal draft of smoke into the room that set her to coughing—uncontrollably. She ran and opened the windows, then back to the stove to search for the flue stopper, burning her hand in the process.

Drawing water from the well was another undertaking, but a requisite if she was going to swab the dusty blackboard. She made a mental note to assign, from this day forward, the chore of pumping water to the oldest boy, and to the oldest girl the cleaning of the blackboard.

By the time her students arrived, the floor had been swept, the piano dusted, cloakroom tidied, and pencils and paper placed on each desk. At eight fifty-nine, with her constitution in check and her name written on the board, she stood at the ready to ring the bell. At nine o'clock sharp she gave the rope a confident tug.

There were ten in all. The seven that Miss Duncan had mentioned over tea, plus three she hadn't. Each child carried a used syrup bucket that contained his or her lunch, except for one young girl who was carrying hers in a fashionable drawstring bag. Ina introduced herself first, then moved on to roll calling, looking up from the roster as each child raised his or her hand.

Naturally the twins, ten-year-olds David and Dolian, were the easiest to recognize, though which one was David and which one was Dolian she had not the faintest clue. They were as identical as twins could be. Both wore the same knickerbocker suits and wool golf caps, and they had the same stylishly erect posture when seated at their desks. She decided it would just be a matter of paying close attention to their mannerisms. Aside from roll call, something would have to, over time, give away their individual identities. How else could their own parents tell them apart?

Henry, the oldest boy, stood nearly six feet tall at fifteen years of age. His hair was jet black, racked with grease under a brown, corduroy hunting cap. He was wearing long trousers and a heavyweight denim jacket that buttoned menacingly up to his neck. Even if Miss Duncan hadn't told her he was the most troublesome, she could've discerned that simply by his scowl.

Eight-year-old Adele endeared herself to Ina immediately. Without a peal of explanation she approached Ina's desk the moment she arrived and took from her pail a carefully wrapped square of gingerbread and placed it on one corner. "Why, thank you," Ina said, but the sweet darling, all she did was bite her lips together, blink, nod, and turn to her seat.

The first thing Ina learned about Victoria—with the fashionable lunch bag—was that she often spoke in superlatives, and talked enough to make an eagle scream. "I chose this dress especially for today, Miss Fitzhugh. My mother and I saw it in the window at Bottomby's. It was the most wonderful one they had, and the most expensive, but I told Mother, I said, 'Mother, I have to have that dress.' It's unusually attractive, don't you think? What makes it so unusual is this frill of lace. See here? And it fastens easily in the front, as simple as ABC."

Little Etta, in comparison, didn't talk at all. She was the only second-grade pupil in the class, a tiny titmouse of a girl who sat on her hands with her shoulders pinched to her ears.

The other three children were assigned to fourth and fifth grades; a chubby bungle-footed boy named Lloyd, and two girls, Rachel and Jeanette. And, of course, there was Alta Ruth.

"My," said Ina, "this is a much bigger class than I was anticipating."

"This isn't all of us, Teacher," one of the twins said. "The others won't be here till after they're done with harvesting."

Here was a piece of information that Miss Duncan somehow failed to tell her, thus Nerves came into play. "I see. Do you know how many more we might be expecting?"

"Hard to say," answered the boy.

Victoria chimed in with her own tally, but once she started it was difficult for Ina to get her to stop.

"Well, let's not worry about it now," Ina said. "We should get on with our day."

Fortunately, Miss Duncan had left behind last year's recitation program, and from that she was able to devise a similar schedule, though she made one minor change to the curriculum. She added French. The lesson plan would need to be adhered to rigidly if all the students were to get equal time.

But the first order of the day was to assign daily duties, not only the two previously mentioned. She would need someone to bring the wood inside for the next morning's fire, and someone to be responsible for throwing out the day's trash. When Alta Ruth, as oldest girl, was offered the responsibility of cleaning the blackboard, she declined (only later did Ina discover the reason behind her refusal—Alta Ruth didn't want the others to think she was being favored simply because the teacher happened to live under her roof. Blackboard cleaning was, didn't she know, a coveted position). All arms pointed straight to the ceiling, eager to be chosen for the honorable task, and after trying to follow the trajectory of pleadings and shrieks, Ina awarded the assignment to Adele.

Once the remaining chores were charged, they began with Music. Song singing went far in determining good citizenship she believed, and as this was work that was not beyond her ability or power, and would also afford both her and her pupils an agreeable relaxation (which she felt they already needed), Ina handed out the songbooks and took her place at the upright piano.

Henry raised his hand.

"Yes, Henry?"

"I like that song 'There's a Tavern in the Town.'"

Her Knowledge of Subject Matter waned. "I don't believe that one is in our book, Henry."

"Naw, it ain't in the book. But my pa sings it though. It's about a jilted lover who drowns herself. It's a real sad fine song."

The first French lesson didn't go as well as she expected either. Rather than begin teaching her pupils the whole French alphabet on the first day of class, she settled on two nouns, so as not to overwhelm them—a preview, one might say, of what was to come. Cat and Dog. *Chat* and *Chien*. *Chat*. *Chien*. Just those two simple nouns, yet, when she pronounced the letter combinations, the entire class snickered.

"May I ask what is so funny?"

"That's a ugly word, Miss Fitzhugh."

"Which word would that be?"

"Shat. My ma uses it. She says she dudn't like going in the outhouse after one of us younguns shat. Says it stinks worse 'an a stiff polecat."

Ina granted morning recess early. By then all of her required teacherly characteristics had been put to test and she had a strong desire to lay her head on the desk.

At four o'clock, she dismissed them. She watched from the window as they headed down the dusty gray road, Henry snatching the twins' hats from their heads, hiking the back of Lloyd's trousers with a quick yank to his cross-back suspenders.

There is nothing temporary about nine months. She prayed for fortitude, despite her theological ambivalence.

Chapter 20

Pie and Palaver at the Wiggly Pig

*T*he pie was Bertie's idea, the chatter naturally Guerine's. A fitting finale for four young women's Saturday evening spent at the Palace Theater watching two-reeler comedies. As far as Bertie was concerned, it served three useful purposes: an ideal occasion to boost Doodle's spirits and get her away from that farm; a good way for acquainting Ina to other local habits; and for herself, a necessary vitaminizing pause—a chance for a rare night of relaxation before going it strong into heated political arguments.

"That Harold Lloyd! If he isn't just the funniest thing!" Guerine chuckled as they walked from the theater to the Wiggly Pig. "When he tied that little dog to the carousel and the carousel started to move and he had to run after it. If that wasn't just the funniest thing! And all that trouble he had trying to get inside a phone booth, and that woman, when she handed him her baby—"

"We got the gist, Guerine," Bertie said. "He's a regular gagman."

"A regular gagman? He's Harold Lloyd!"

"He ain't no Chaplin."

"Honestly, Bertie. I wonder if you'll ever have any flair at all. You don't know a thing about discriminating taste, do you? I suppose if a bottle of Romanza Flower Drops fell into your lap, you'd claim it was onion juice."

"Is that that toilet water you got on? You're right, I would."

Guerine tugged at the collar of her effectively trimmed jacket, pulling it snug against the lobes of her ears. "Wish it would snow."

"Don't worry," said Doodle, walking a few steps behind her. "It'll come soon enough."

Inside the café, they seated themselves at a vacant table across from the counter, where a sole elderly patron sat on a stool drinking coffee.

Bertie took up the flimsy one-page menu that doubled for a placemat and looked it over. "Hope you weren't expecting opulent," she addressed Ina.

Ina gave the small café a cursory look. It was painted a light drab, an uninspired egg pattern on the ceiling. She supposed from a sanitary point of view these cold, awful metal tables were easy to clean—but for a splotch of something unrecognizable left behind by the last customer who sat here. Naturally, she would have to be wearing her best velour! She tightened her arms at her sides and focused on the choice of desserts. Jell-O seemed reasonably safe.

"You girls know what you want?" a round-faced waitress with listless eyes asked.

"Apple pie for me, Lois," said Bertie.

"I believe I'll try the Jell-O salad," Ina said. "A small serving, please."

"East, West, Jell-O's best," chimed Guerine. The waitress gave her a grave look. "Why so glum, Lois? Did we catch you close to quitting time?"

"Are you gonna order, or am I supposed to guess?"

"Yes, of course, I'm going to order," Guerine said, removing her gloves. "Wouldn't come here if I wasn't. You know how much I love the cherry pie."

"And you?"

Doodle had removed her knitted cap and was in the middle of trying to reclaim flyaway hair. "Gosh, Delores, I didn't recognize you," the waitress said. "You look like a little youngster under them pom-poms. What can I get for you?"

"Hey there, Lois," Doodle said. "Apple pie, please."

"My mama'll be glad to hear I ran into you. We were sure sorry to hear about your pappy. Coffee?"

"Four," Bertie answered for everyone.

There was a whisper of contentment after the woman turned to go, as if a great load had been taken off their minds and the hard unforgiving chairs they sat in were actually cushioned and cozy. Bertie, already free of her coat, pushed up the bellows sleeves of her blouse. Doodle unbuttoned the sweater coat she wore, revealing a practicable navy blue shirt. Only Ina remained seated in a rigid fashion and gave the appearance of a less than pleased patrician. She seemed unwilling to part with her outer jacket, and kept her hands confined to her lap as if the two fragile butterflies could easily break.

Guerine clacked her purse shut. "Well now, isn't this nice, the four of us spending time together? And getting to know you better, too, Ina. We should make this a regular thing!"

"Don't go making cozy plans for me," said Bertie. "I'm gonna be plenty busy from now on. Thanks, Lois."

Doodle reached for the sugar dish, helped herself to a scant spoonful, and slid the dish to the center of the table.

"If that's the case," said Guerine, "then we better hurry and get on the right side of sisterly friendship tonight for your benefit, Bertie. Which reminds me of this fun little article I recently read on how to be the perfect hostess—"

"Look around you, Guerine. We're at the Wiggly Pig. If we need anything," said Bertie, "Lois'll get it for us."

"Yes, I know that. But the same applies to situations like this one. It's all about being modern these days, and this article had some very good ideas on getting to know people better, like Ina here. For instance, I think we should go around the table and each one of us tell something about ourselves that nobody else knows. It's what they call cultivating."

"Oh brother," groaned Bertie.

"This type of acquaintedness is just as important for you, Doodle," Guerine continued. "I mean, even someone of your upbringing needs to know how to manage more than just planting potatoes. Wouldn't you like to know how to ennoble friends?"

"Well—"

"Ennoble?" asked Bertie.

But in spite of the interjections, Guerine didn't let up. "A woman needs to be fully alive to the joys of friendship. Why, it's as simple as sharing one little thing about yourself with another person. Another woman." Noticing Lois heading their way with a tray of desserts, she broke off.

"Anything else?" the woman asked.

"Looks good to me," said Bertie.

Doodle nodded, and they each proceeded to ting and clank their almost-silver to stoneware.

"Since none of the rest of you are jumping up and down at the chance," Guerine said, "then I guess I'll have to go first. I've never told anyone this—not even you, Bertie—but, as a child, I always wanted to learn how to play the zither."

"What? You did not!" Bertie blurted, prodding her pie crust with her fork.

"I most certainly did. Would've given my eyeteeth for a zither. Mr. Cheeks had one on display at Christmas one year, solid rosewood with pearl inlaid, and I used to go to his store every day and admire it. He wouldn't let me touch it, that big ole fussbudget. All I could do was stand there and stare at it, the whole time imagining the untold glee of being able to play dreamy music and sing at the same time."

Bertie hooted and found herself joined by Doodle and Ina. The old man sitting at the counter turned to stare at the laughter coming from the young women. Sometimes it was better to let Guerine gust, Bertie thought. This evening was turning out to be all right.

"See how easy it is, Doodle?" said Guerine. "Now it's your turn."

"Oh, I don't know," Doodle said, playing with the edge of her napkin. "I think some things are best left untold."

"Quit being so mousy," said Guerine. "Nothing you say could be that shocking. My goodness, does this pie seem done to you all?"

"You might as well play along," Bertie told Doodle. "I can tell you right now she ain't about to let up." It had seemed to Bertie much of the evening that Doodle was acting more self-conscious than usual, and figured Ina's presence—being around someone she barely knew—was likely the cause. Nothing for her to do now, though, but partake in the conversation.

Doodle took a sip of coffee. After the pause, and in a voice that barely constituted a coo, she said, "I've thought to myself on occasion that I might like to write."

"Write what?" Ina asked, the first sign all evening that she was interested in being here. Her dessert sat barely touched, a gelatinous red quiver surrounded by a border of dainty blue flowers.

Doodle shrugged. "I'm not sure exactly. I don't know as I've ever thought of myself as a poet, but I think I'd like to create something meaningful. Something of awe. Like the kind of inspirations Keats writes."

Ina leaned forward and smiled. *"Oh, sweet Fancy! let her loose—"*

"Every thing is spoilt by use—" Doodle spouted.

"Where's the cheek that doth not fade—"

"Too much gazed at? Where's the maid?"

Ina laughed at their apportioning of the stanza, and Doodle blushed and looked away.

"Huh. How about that," said Bertie, staring at Doodle skeptically. It had never occurred to her that her friend yearned for any activity other than what was related to the farm. And that it could come tripping so smooth off her tongue. "I guess you had a good idea after all, Guerine."

"Didn't I say so! And I'm happy to see that my urgings for you to refine yourself, Doodle, are starting to yield results. What about you, Ina? What is it that you've never shared with anybody?"

Ina regarded the table thoughtfully. "Well, let's see. My parents gave me a globe for my birthday one year, mounted on a beautiful wooden stand. Every single detail was impeccable, especially the colors. The oceans were this amazing Copenhagen blue, and I suppose I've wanted to travel the world ever since. North America, South America. Europe, Asia, Africa."

"Tell us something we don't know," Bertie chafed.

"Excuse me?" said Ina.

"Of course you'd wanna go gangleshanking around the world. Who wouldn't?"

Bertie's words visibly perturbed Ina. She stared at Bertie in surly astonishment and said, "I find that highly offensive."

"I don't know why," said Bertie. "I mean, I wouldn't mind taking to the road myself sometime. Would y'all?"

Doodle kept silent, displaying intent only on finishing her pie, while Guerine came to Ina's defense. "Now Bertie, that's uncalled for. What do you mean talking to Ina that way? We hardly even know her. Ina, just ignore her. She's like this with everybody. You've heard of hot air? Well, that's Bertie."

Bertie laughed and shook her head. "Y'all are taking this way too serious. All I was saying—"

"Then maybe you'd care to share yours," prompted Ina.

"My secret?"

"That's right."

Bertie took a swallow of what was now becoming lukewarm coffee. She sat the mug down. "Just so happens, I bought that zither from Mr. Cheeks and the dumb thing never did play right."

Guerine looked confounded. "You what? Bertie A. Daye! How could you?"

"Well, I didn't know you wanted it, Guerine. It's not like I bought it out from under you on purpose. As I recall, I had a few extra dollars burning a hole in my pocket from one of my many business transactions. It's just too bad we didn't play this game fifteen years ago."

"I am your cousin!" cried Guerine.

"How was I supposed to know? Didn't you just say you never told me? If you still want the silly thing, it's at home under the bed."

"If I still want it?"

Good grief, Bertie thought. Take me out of this place. Right away she focused her attention on Doodle, figuring to change the subject. "I've been wanting to mention to you, Doodle—you ought to think about having a telephone installed. It would solve your problem of living on a farm."

"I've never considered living on a farm a problem."

"A blood relation, no less!" Guerine called out.

"All I mean is," said Bertie, trying to ignore Guerine's chatter, "you're liable to grow lonesome now with your papa gone. A telephone will let you keep in touch with your friends and up on the news."

"Maybe we can talk about it another time, huh?"

"No time like now, if you ask me."

"I'll think about it," said Doodle.

"All I liked having was three more dollars and that zither would've been mine," Guerine said to Ina and anyone else who would listen. Ina shook her head and made a slight cluck with her tongue.

"It wouldn't cost that much to install one," Bertie said. "I'll get you some literature on it and drop it by the house later this week."

"Don't go out of your way just for that," said Doodle. "Like I said, I'll have to think about it."

"And I'm sure I would've appreciated it more than you obviously did!" Guerine protested.

The room was getting noisier by the second. And Bertie was growing hotter.

"For crying out loud! Give it a rest, Guerine!" Bertie pushed her dessert plate to the middle of the table. "I tell you all what—some night this turned out to be. Half-baked apple pie and I gotta sit here and listen to a couple of sob sisters. Doodle, are you ready? I'll take you home."

"I think I'll just catch a ride with Lois."

"Suit yourself. Lois, can I have my check, please?" Bertie stood up and shoved her arms inside her coat.

"Mine, too, Lois," Guerine said. "And I want to talk to you about that thrifty pie you served me. Practically indigestible!"

"Thanks for the fun evening, gals," Bertie quipped. "It's been a night that I won't soon enjoy recalling."

"I don't know why you always have to get so riled up about everything, Bertie. Bertie, wait!" Guerine called after her. "You're not gonna make me and Ina walk home by ourselves, are you?"

Her plan exactly. She turned and stomped out of the Wiggly Pig, the bell ringing as she flung the door open, leaving Ina gaping at her colossal nerve, Guerine bickering with Lois about a pie that was nothing to enthuse about, and Doodle hurriedly buttoning her sweater, yanking her cap down over her ears, anxious to make her way toward home.

❧

Chapter 21

Doodle's Problem

*T*hat was all she needed today, to have the clover cutter take a nod. The knives had obviously needed sharpening and now the screw feed was plugged. Used to be she could cut enough clover for twenty fowls in one minute, but lately the long-legged cutter was cutting less clean and not as easy. It was just like her and everything else on this farm these days—seemed one or the other was either on the blitz or out of sorts.

Doodle took a deep breath and considered kicking the old machine. That or spitting at it. Not that either one would've helped matters.

For days on end, she'd been blaming and barking at the least little thing. Even Bugle had gotten the hint and taken to entertaining himself away from her critical eyes during the light of day. She was aggravated and had no intention of hiding it. Ever since being put on the spot at the Wiggly Pig the other night—asked to disclose a secret about herself then and there, just like that! Something she'd never told anyone before. The whole idea set her on edge, particularly knowing what she did about Brud Daye. And then for Guerine to make that uncalled-for comment doubting that anything Doodle said could be remarkable. If she hadn't been sitting on the inside next to the wall, she would've gotten up and walked out. At least she would have if she hadn't had to rely on somebody else to take her home. Lie if you need to, was the first thing she thought when Guerine suggested that silly game. Grasp on to the first insignificant thing that pops into your head and give them that. But that's not what she did. She had exposed a very real part of herself, and before she even knew what she was doing she was spewing Keats over apple pie. That was the last time she was going to put herself in a situation like that, consarn it! There was something to be said for absolute solitude.

She bent over the Gem cutter and began the process of removing the blades, her breath erupting into the air like quick blasphemies as she strained at getting them loose. Easily removable, my eye! What other points of merit were claimed for this machine? Made perfectly for cutting poultry fodder, green or dry, and easy to run. Not today it doesn't! After a brief sweat-beaded battle, she succeeded in freeing the knives, only to slice open her finger the moment she began sharpening them.

"Ouch, dadgummit!"

The loud curse sent her chickens scooting. They flapped and fluttered and fussed at one another, and bumped around like dim-sighted dumdums.

Feeling rebuked, Doodle sat on the ground, her back against a leg of the fitful cutter. She sucked at her finger. Looking at the animated scene, the gossiping hens and chicks, she considered the pause in her life. The day wasn't anywhere near half spent, and already she was behind. Perhaps she was getting exactly what she deserved. She had thought that life would go on as usual after her papa died, and that keeping to herself the knowledge of Brud Daye's demise would have little consequence. But being around Bertie lately made her feel all-overish and anxious, and she couldn't sleep. Her headaches were coming more frequently, and she barely had an appetite. And with this cut on her finger now, it felt like another sting of her conscience.

She took a handkerchief from her overalls, used her teeth to tear a jagged strip from it, and wrapped the strip around her finger to staunch the bleeding. She finished by tying the dressing off with a knot.

The fact was, underlying it all was the reality that not telling Bertie what her own papa had done to Brud was creating a hardship for Doodle. But telling Bertie, she figured, would only do the same. She didn't have the first idea of what to do, and didn't know how—or if—she could get past it. But what was she to Bertie, if not a devoted friend? Truth, it appeared, was a complicated thing.

She heard a motor then, and turned to see Bertie's machine coming up the road.

"That's dandy." Doodle stood and brushed herself off, and turned back to sharpening the blades.

Bertie hopped from the Model T and rushed over.

"Listen to this, country gal! I just found out that Old Man Saunders is running a line out to his place and it won't take much to bring the line on up to your house. Isn't that great? The timing is perfect, and it's completely affordable. The Saunders got more money than God, raising those Morgans like they do, and since they'll be shelling out the bulk of the expense to have a line run, it won't cost you that much. Here's a booklet I got you from the office"—she thrust it at Doodle—"it'll explain all about how a rural telephone works. And in hardly no time at all you'll be able to talk to yours truly here without having to look at her fatso face. Not bad, huh?"

"I guess."

"You guess? I thought you'd be excited."

"Well, I'm busy right now." Doodle folded the thin booklet and shoved it inside her overalls. "I'll look at it later."

"This is perfect for a woman like you, in the country and short on time. Just think of what you can do with a telephone in the house. It'll save you all sorts of time. You can find out almost anything you need to know without leaving home."

Doodle continued sharpening. "Not now, Bertie. Please?"

"You can call up Mr. Sargeant and tell him what groceries you need, and they'll be ready for you when you get there. You can call me, of course—but I already said that. You can check on your neighbors. But more important, if you get sick you can call up Doc Nichols instead of trying to get word to him through somebody else."

Doodle clenched her jaw. "Can't you see I'm wrestling with something here?"

"I don't understand why you're so resistant to the idea. I like privacy myself, but are you just going to shut yourself up?"

"Dammit, Bertie!" Doodle struck one of the knives against the cutter.

It was an image that caught Bertie off guard. "My word! I thought only I was capable of rabid. You know, if I didn't know better, I'd think you were plumb fed up with Bertie Daye." She eyed Doodle as if a curiosity. "You sure don't act like yourself lately. Seems to me whenever we get together, you hardly have a thing to say. Not that I expect you to put on a chinfest like Guerine does, but I was beginning to think that even a snarl would be nice. Now I'm not so sure."

"Bertie, I didn't mean—"

"I can understand that you're still hurting over Pa Shuford. That sort of thing takes time. The man was honorable, the most right-minded person I ever met. A square shooter, you know? And that's hard to come by. What I can't understand, though, is why you'd be taking it out on somebody who only wants the best for you."

Doodle had begun to sob, and Bertie, stunned by this display of raw emotion, patted her friend awkwardly on the shoulder. "I guess my timing's not always so great, country gal. I'll let you alone. You do what you want as far as a telephone."

Doodle wiped her nose with her handkerchief.

"Maybe in a few days we can get us another visit in," Bertie said as she started back to her machine.

"Don't go just yet," Doodle called, pushing hair from her face. "There's a story my papa told me before he died. I think maybe he wanted me to tell it to you, too."

Bertie was at a loss. They had gone inside at Doodle's urging where it was warmer, and sat across from one another at the kitchen table. There, not bothering with the usual courtesy of offering any refreshment, Doodle instead had focused at a single spot on the table, and in a careful if jarring manner, proceeded to tell Bertie about her papa's deathbed confession. It was a short tale, intertwined with a daughter's tears and trembles; of money, and greed, and of a desperate man who could see no other way to protect his neighbors and his family and their homeplace.

"I wasn't going to tell you, Bertie," Doodle said, choking in tears. "But my papa, I'm afraid he wasn't that honorable man you thought he was."

Listening to the story, Bertie had, like Doodle, taken to staring distantly at a sole place on the table, and for a short time had unconsciously polished a finger over it. But she sat motionless now, with no show of emotion, her hands at complete rest and eyes cast toward her lap.

"I'm truly sorry," Doodle said, sniffling. "But I think you deserve to know the truth."

At first, Bertie didn't know what to think. Or to say. Her papa murdered—not an accident—and Pa Shuford the one who'd done it? Since a child she had entertained the idea that there was more to the version she'd always been told. But maybe that was more her simply fascinating about the details of his death to keep his memory alive, because she hadn't envisioned anything like this—that he was evil enough for somebody to actually kill him. Of all the bad habits in the world his had to be greed. Her papa—a money-hungry bastard. It must be true then, because why else would Pa Shuford confess to such a thing? It made her think of her own connection with money, her nostalgic want for it compared to her papa's obvious insatiable desire for the almighty. Money was a means of ultimately being in a position to help people, not a spur to be used for beating them down. And if he had mistreated Doodle's family the way Doodle's papa told her, what must Doodle think of her?

Bertie blinked and took a clear breath. It felt like twenty minutes had passed without either one of them talking, but more likely it was only two. She raised her head and looked at Doodle. How hard this must've been for her, and Bertie suddenly felt an overwhelming gratefulness for Doodle's loving gift of vulnerability.

"What happened to your finger?" Bertie asked.

Doodle's reaction was a downturned mouth. "Just the hazards of country living."

Another brief period of silence, then Bertie said in a soft voice, "Money's like a tapeworm, you know. Some folks can't ever get enough. Guess my old man didn't leave yours any choice."

"I don't know as I agree with that," Doodle said. "It goes against everything he and Mama ever taught us."

Bertie took another audible breath. "Make me a promise," she said. "That you'll never tell anybody else about this. What happened between Brud Daye and John Shuford doesn't have anything to do with you or me. And it would be better if none of this got back to anybody—think of Miss Lul and Alta Ruth."

After a long silence, Doodle said, "I won't, Bertie. I promise."

"It would be too upsetting for Miss Lul."

"Yes, it would."

"And who knows what it would do to Alta Ruth."

"I know, Bertie. I promise you, I'll never tell another soul. It's between us."

Bertie glanced down at the table, then back at Doodle. "We're still us, you know. Friends."

"Of course we are. We always will be."

They got up from the table and hugged, an embrace that was clumsy in both its urgency and its closeness.

As Bertie headed back toward town, Doodle looked out from the porch, hoping she had done the right thing. Their constant friendship had now shifted into a grown-up, tangled version of what they'd had before. And watching the dust left in the wake of Bertie's machine, Doodle hoped that would be for the better.

Chapter 22

The Longest Drive Home

*B*ertie scrutinized the road in front of her as if looking through a tunnel, reflecting on what had just happened back at the Shuford farm.

It explained a lot, what she'd been told. Why Doodle had been acting standoffish, for one thing, but also why no one outside her family had ever mentioned her father to her face. Not a single time could she recall anybody telling her she looked like Brud, never a compliment on the resemblance, or even the slightest amount of praise for having the same go-at-it-ness as her papa—as people do with the sons and daughters of someone they respect. Not one person ever had. Even her mama chose careful words when talking to Bertie about her papa. Not sad words. Short words. Which meant in all likelihood he had grated a number of people, not just John Shuford. Possibly the whole town in fact. People don't like to be separated from their money when they don't get a fair shake. Things like that get around, and she couldn't help but wonder if the sight of her made folks ill at ease. She hoped not. She hoped there wasn't more to Doodle's version of the story.

None of this sat right with her. Call it a barb or a dart, it touched more than a mere soft spot. She felt momentarily deflated. But in no way was it going to keep her from doing the work she had set out to do. No way would she let it. If anything, she'd find a way to make herself even more determined. She'd use it to her advantage.

Coming into the center of town, her concentration was broken by a wildly waving Guerine standing up on the curb, and she pulled the vehicle over.

"Let me in. My feet are killing me. I've been on the go all day."

"Looking at rings again?"

"And that's not all," Guerine puffed, tossing a package from Bottomby's into the back seat before they sped off. "Remember the one at Ingram's I told you about, with the basket setting? Solid gold and it has the fire of a volcano. Lord, Bertie, I wish you could see it! But do you have any idea how much they want for that ring, I discovered? A handsome fortune!"

"I told you so," Bertie said. "Take my advice and look at Hexnite. Put it beside a diamond you can't tell the difference."

"Don't think *I* wouldn't tell the difference! Like I'd even consider cheap! And shame on you for suggesting it. Well, I'm not the least bit worried. Sam Eastbrook would dance on a hot griddle if I asked him."

Bertie grinned and shook her head.

"Just where've you been today?" Guerine asked. "Aren't you supposed to be working?"

"I left early. Had a few things to take care of."

"You and your busy doings! Always on the gad for some cause or another, aren't you? Well, I hope for your sake it'll all be worth it some day. Who knows, maybe you'll change the world and can finally be happy, instead of flying off the handle with everybody like you do. Ooo, stop! There's Sam! I'll walk the rest of the way with him."

"Thought your feet hurt."

"You always take everything I say so literally. Now stop and let me out!"

Bertie dropped her off, then continued another block home. What if she did have a habit of being easily provoked like Guerine said? Maybe people gave her good reason. Maybe they needed to be shook up. And she *would* change the world, too. At least one quick-tempered Daye was going to do something for others' credit. Now, more than ever.

Chapter 23

Bertie's Ballot-Marking School for Female Voters

*T*here are umpteen ways to place a vote. Preferential, proxy, mechanical lever machine, absentee, and the write-in. There's the plural systems and the single systems. Straight tickets, split tickets, party tickets, reform tickets. Joint, blanket, and envelope ballots. You've got your partisans, your independents, your neutrals. Just about anythingarism you could want.

This was the dawn of a new day, and Bertie Daye was bound and determined to make a difference. She was going to educate women. Now that the Nineteenth Amendment had been passed, women would need instruction on how to mark a ballot card. They would need to know what being an interested citizen meant. They would need to be taught the ways and means of political theory.

And Bertie, herself, had been studying and researching policy until she knew everything that was possible to know about the local, state, and federal government (explained the mystery as to why men's minds were uninspired, better suited for a shelf).

For more than a week, she worked at getting word out about her ballot school, a day-long session on teaching women how to vote, telephoning everyone she knew—in spite of Mr. Wheeler's growing irritation that she did it on phone company time and equipment. The only problem was where to have it. Nearly every storeowner in town had allowed her to display notices in their windows—Ballot School for Female Voters—Date and Place to Be Announced—all but for that jackass Cheeks who owned the furniture store. He had stood in the doorway as she approached, wedged between the jambs like a walrus trying to fit into a bluebird box, and wouldn't let her so far as the threshold. "I don't allow no feminist propaganda in my store!" Determined to fix Cheeks, Bertie went on her way, and when she was sure he had squeezed his belly back inside, she returned to the far corner of the storefront window, drew a large X across one of her flyers and wrote "SUFFRAGE SUPPORTERS UNWELCOME HERE," then slid the flyer into view of passersby.

Mr. Long, proprietor of the Palace Theater, suggested the Palace's lobby as the ideal spot for Bertie to conduct her voting class. He was a forward-thinking man (his breed of which was at a premium) and recognized this special opportunity as a profitable collaboration for both. Not only could *he* drum up business, he told Bertie, but *she* would have access to exactly what she needed: a crowd of pliable women. An idea Bertie gloated on. Any place good enough to host the Woman's Club tea was certainly good enough for anybody with post-suffrage flush.

"Now here's what I propose," said Mr. Long, posed in a contemplative fashion against the concession counter, occasionally drumming his fingers. "Weekday matinees are frequented by more of our ladies than on a weekend, when the little ones are home, you see."

Bertie listened and nodded. She had one elbow resting on the counter, the other slantdicular from her hip.

"And I don't know if you're aware of this or not, Miss Daye, but most of those ladies can't resist a certain actor these days by the name of Milton Sills. Me, I'm rather slow about such things, but as a theater owner I try to make it my business. Now if you ask me, he's certainly no Great Lover," he said, referring to Valentino, "*A Delicious Little Devil*"—Mr. Long cleared his throat—"his moving picture, of course. But that's neither here nor there. The ladies, they seem to want Sills."

"Worth penning a quick letter home, I reckon," Bertie said with the same indifference for Milton Sills as had Mr. Long.

"So, if they want Milton Sills, well by golly, I'll give them Milton Sills! They are impressionable, these ladies."

"Swayable," agreed Bertie.

"And as good fortune would have it his latest feature is called *The Inferior Sex*. Now I was thinking we could somehow capitalize on that—"

Bertie found the interplay between the two—the show's title and the significance of her female ballot school—laughable, and with much the same enthusiasm that Mr. Long had found Valentino "delicious."

"Yes, I think you see where I'm going with this," Mr. Long said. "This could be quite an event."

Once they decided on a day, Bertie took out an ad in the *Courier* announcing the class. She had envisioned a half-page plug blazoned across the Coming Attractions section, but what she got for her nickels and dimes was barely the size of a hen's tooth. It was sandwiched between a promotional scene from the film and an announcement of a special Friday showing of a new laugh-sparked, adventurous Charlie Chaplin caper.

But the North Carolina Equal Suffrage Association's involvement with Bertie's Ballot School all but made up for it. When Bertie notified them of her efforts they sent her a box of munitions: banners to enrich the lobby, and souvenirs to award the participants, along with a special invitation for her to join them in October for their annual convention in Asheville. (Her room and train fare were booked before sundown.)

On the day of the big event, she enlisted a couple of young boys shooting marbles in front of the Dowdy Inn to gather up chairs and tables from the telephone office—after she was sure Mr. Wheeler had gone home for lunch. Their labor cost her four hot dogs and two large lemonades. But there was something to be said for getting those two squirrels sugared up. By the time they dredged the bottom of their beverages, they were ready to tackle a six-foot ladder and hang a wide, yellow Triumph of Women's Rights banner high on one of the lobby walls, directly above four glass-cased 14 by 11-inch lobby cards of *The Inferior Sex*.

She was busy displaying the tables with every piece of suffrage literature she had—gold Votes for Women buttons, Ballots for Both pins, and posters with angelic symbols holding torches set against sunbursts—when the lobby door swung open and revealed Mr. Long and his stoop-shouldered son Buster.

"Ready for your voting school, I see," said Mr. Long. "Fetched Buster to come along in anticipation of the crowd. Go on, Son." He coaxed the young man with a gentle slap to the back. "Get that popper fired up!"

"Popper?" said Bertie.

"Didn't I tell you? Got a bargain on a gas-powered popcorn machine. Man sent it all the way from Chicago. Could've sworn I told you."

"Sounds messy."

"Something I've been considering for a while now. You ask me I say movies palaces around the country are missing the boat on this one. I say get 'em to come through the door to buy their popped corn, not from a machine out front. Once they're inside for a bag of the salty treat, they're likely to stay on and take in the show. Looks like more than one of us is going to be making history today, Miss Daye. So how many are you figuring?"

"Don't know."

She was in no mood for talky-talk. And it didn't have a thing to do with nerves. Bertie Daye didn't get nervous. It was simply a matter of putting her mind in a certain temper. One had to have a definite attitude, a moral climate about one's self, when speaking on suffrage-related themes. It required a delicate balance. Not all women were happy to get the vote, and you had to have regard for their opinions (even if their opinions only amounted to hooey) while presenting your own point of view. Posture was just as important as proclivity. And tone should have a respectful quality.

She scrutinized each item on the tables. Mr. Long continued to jaw, following her while she straightened the gold tokens and made sure each one was visible. Strike her dead she had forgotten how gassy he could be! Would talk just to hear his head rattle. She took out extra copies of sample ballot cards, laying them long edge to long edge. She hoped she would have enough cards for everyone, but there was a box of Full Value paper (a donation of Wheeler's Telephone Company, unbeknownst to Mr. Wheeler) so the ladies could take plenty of notes. And for those who liked their rubbers to stay clean there was a hefty supply of pencils with helmet shields covering the erasers, all the leads needle-sharp.

Mr. Long, she knew, had given her a great opportunity, and she didn't want to bark at him as would've been her usual way, but after having his breath behind her ear for ten minutes she finally turned around and said, "Mr. Long, you've got to be the most bablative person I've ever known."

"Why, thank you, Miss Daye. I always say—" but he was distracted by rattling and banging coming from the concession where Buster appeared to be having difficulty with the popper's kettle. And noticing that patrons were already outside, under the marquee at the ticket box, Mr. Long hurried off to put his own mind in a certain temper.

"Crazy clack box," Bertie mumbled.

The sound of a million kernels fizzling and snapping from here to kingdom come added excitement to the atmosphere, as did the hot, nutty aroma. Bertie was ready for the onslaught of her suffrage-minded sisters. At any minute they'd be marching into the lobby and heading directly for her and her tables.

Guerine was one of the first through the door, no surprise to Bertie. She liked to arrive early at the matinees so she could be sure of getting a good seat. In her thinking, the tenth chair in from the left, on the second row, helped to maintain her youthful appearance. By craning her neck like a pig belly up on a turnspit, it diminished her double chin. She was with Maybelle Diggs, one of her Woman's Club members.

"Oh, that's right," Guerine said, walking over to Bertie. "I forgot you're having your little ballot-marking school today. Would you look how fancy!"

"Fancy?" Bertie said. "Guerine, do you not realize the importance of what's happening in the world? You ought to be right here next to me, helping out."

Guerine looked over her shoulder at Maybelle. "I can't be bothered with this now," she whispered to Bertie. "The show will be starting soon and I don't want Maybelle to get my seat. Aren't you coming? No? Well, look, I'll see all your little trinkets when I come out, how about that? Maybe you can save me one."

"You better hope you don't get ablepsy from sitting that close!"

"A what? I don't have time for your foolish word games, Bertie. Meet you inside, Maybelle!" Guerine disappeared through the velvet burgundy curtain that divided the lobby from the theater.

One after another, women entered the lobby. A Mrs. Warren and a Mrs. Pennington. Dorothy Tatum and Margaret Ashe. The two Miss Turners who both showed eager interest despite their aunt admonishing them for dilly-dallying. Most of the ladies were timid about approaching the display, particularly one elderly woman who looked on with uncertainty, like a cat swivel-eyeing a skink. And Bertie had her share of lookee-loos, those who wondered what could be had for free without any commitment.

"Don't be bashful, ladies!" Bertie called out, waving them over. "November second is Election Day, only weeks away, and it's important to have a basic understanding of how to vote! Come on over, let me show you the proper way to mark your ballot cards! It's your duty!"

Louvenia Crumpton, a woman who predated Person County, crept her way to the tables with aid of a cane, leaving her husband to rely on the Palace's handrails. "I'm awfully disappointed in you, Beatrice," she said. "And Lalura, too, that she would let you be involved in something like this. She ought to have you anchored at home. Lot more worthy things a girl your age could be doing."

"Mrs. Crumpton, you of all people should understand," said Bertie. "I've always known you to be a proud woman. You've raised more children than anybody I know. You've killed more hogs, canned more tomatoes, and sewed more, too, than anybody I know. Can you honestly tell me that you haven't, for one minute, thought about what your life would be like if you possessed your own personality?"

Mrs. Crumpton was flummoxed. "Let me just tell you something, young lady! There hasn't been nary a day that I been married to that fool standing yonder when I didn't have to lead him by his nose! My own personality, hmph! What you need is to have a switch put to you. And you can guarantee that Lalura Daye will be hearing from me!" She made haste toward her husband, swinging her cane at anyone who got in her path. "Come along, Franklin. I believe I have lost all appetite for that picture show."

There was still quite a buzz throughout the lobby, plenty of folks who were unable to believe their senses—though it was becoming fast apparent to Bertie that what had most of them wide-eyed and lost in wonder was Mr.

Long's wonderful inclusion of theater popcorn, and not Bertie's Ballot-Marking School.

Once the matinee began and the lobby got quiet, Bertie considered packing everything up and taking leave of the place. But it occurred to her that this was a situation that would have to be handled carefully. This was an argument that was going to take a lot of time and twice as much energy. She decided to plant herself in a seat and wait till the show was over.

As soon as the ladies began filing out of the theater, Bertie sprung from her chair. "Did you enjoy the feature, Mrs. Pennington? Sure you don't have time to let me show you how to mark on the ballot?"

"I think you're opening gates you won't be able to close again, Beatrice," Mrs. Pennington said, and continued on her way out of the theater.

"Seems you didn't get the word, Mrs. Pennington. I opened up those gates a long time ago. And as far as the vote, it's a done deal."

"You always were a mouthy young lady," the woman said and stomped off.

"What is it y'all are afraid of? The conditions are going to better for us now. Is it the masses of Negroes y'all are scared of?" There were a multitude of gasps throughout the lobby at such mention. "I bet not one of you has looked at the numbers, have you? Doesn't matter if they get the vote, they're still the minority."

"I'm surprised she's not out on a street corner," one lady said to another.

"Or a stump," giggled another.

"You only give me ideas, ladies!"

Margaret Ashe walked past with her coat draped across one arm, and reaching the door she turned around. "Unlike some of the others, I'm not in the least surprised. There's always been scandal associated with a Daye." She pushed on the door and walked out.

The lobby was quiet. Between all the migrainous arguing and the smell of just-popped corn, Bertie'd had enough for one day. Her temples throbbed and her jaw ached from strained bouts of gritting her grinders. She began clearing off the table, tossing buttons and handfuls of pencils into the box she had taken them from.

Guerine and Maybelle were the last two out of the theater.

"I don't care what they say about Milton Sills," said Maybelle. "You can give me Harold Lloyd any day. Did you see that crook in his nose?"

"Oh, I don't know," Guerine said. "I think his nose is what gives him his character. Most women are bowled over by that sort of thing. Though I do think twenty cents is a little steep just to have a peek at it—"

"Calling it a day already, Bertie?"

"Yes, Guerine, I'm calling it a day."

"I don't know if you've ever heard Muriel Yates Simmons speak or not, Miss Daye," said Maybelle, "but now there's a woman who has made an excellent point. Her belief is that only educated women should vote. She says it's not the type of thing that should be allowed indiscriminately. There's a certain danger in that, if you know what I mean."

Guerine bent toward Bertie and whispered, "Danger of the colored vote."

"Yes, Guerine. I know very well what she means. And Maybelle, to answer your question, I've heard Mrs. Simmons speak and, wait—" Bertie cupped a hand to her ear. "Do you hear that?"

"No, I don't hear a thing. Do you, Guerine?"

Guerine shook her head.

"That's funny," Bertie said, "'cause I can hear Muriel Yates Simmons crying all the way from Raleigh."

Maybelle was stunned by Bertie's gall.

"Bertie's just tired, Maybelle," Guerine said, cutting her eyes at her cousin. "She gets this way after standing for too long in a pair of dull shoes. We should be going." Guerine took hold of her friend's elbow and led her toward the door.

"That cousin of yours takes herself too seriously," Maybelle said. "I guess that's what happens when women don't find themselves a woman's club like we did."

Mr. Long, whose afternoon had been spent upstairs in the projector room, hadn't been privy to the happenings in the lobby. When he finally came to see how Bertie's Ballot School had fared, Bertie was in the grip of slinging suffrage paraphernalia and spouting a soliloquy.

"Stand here half the live-long day! Like a barker at a turkey draw! I'd have done better playing a game of chuck-a-luck! That's all right. They'll see. It's gonna take more than a few green empty-headed gourds to discourage me! They'll see, all right. I'm just picking up steam!"

Poor Buster didn't seem to have fared any better. He stood behind the concession in a paper cap as deflated as his shoulders, next to a steep mass of puffy white kernels.

Chapter 24

Johnny Bob Looks to Bertie for Help

*W*hen a Daye sets her mind to something, by God if she isn't going to do it. So when Johnny Bob came to her for help after his wife Silvia got turned away from the voter-registration office, Bertie took her lunch break and hot-footed the two blocks over to the courthouse. If what Johnny Bob had told her was accurate—and she didn't have any reason to think otherwise—that Negro women were being denied the right to register, she was damn sure gonna see to it that things were set straight.

It didn't take her a minute to dress down the county clerk, especially with a nickname like Tink. At five-foot two, with arms borrowed from a clothes pole and a face on the edge of appetite, Claude Talley was weedy. A decent slant of wind would've knocked the man over.

"Afternoon, Mr. Talley. Awful quiet in here, isn't it? I would've thought you'd be plenty busy these days, but looks like you hardly know what to do with yourself, other than shuffling those papers on your desk."

He blinked at her over a pair of horn-rimmed spectacles set yaw-ways. "Is there a point, Miss Daye?"

With a sure sense of her usefulness in all matters politic—and not much for hedging—Bertie slammed her hand on the desk and launched into a tirade. "It's downright despicable of you to insist that every Negro woman part with half a week's salary and make them recite the Constitution be-fore you'll even allow them to register, when all any white man has to do is sign his name! Or an X if he's too damned busy to handle cursive. It's de-meaning and it's degrading is what it is!"

Mr. Talley slid about in his seat. He cleared his throat.

"Seems you old boys missed the call for Upright Men," she continued. "You've heard the saying, 'As the teacher, so the school'? Well, as the states-man, so the town, and this town is in need of somebody who can play fair and deal with folks honestly. High time you and your like had an awakening!"

Partway through her rant, a redheaded Augustus Shaw stuck his head in the door. "Well, well. I thought I heard the Mouth of the South. I bet Brud Daye is rolling over in his grave. Don't you reckon so, Tink? His own daughter taking up for niggers!"

At the sight of his crony, Mr. Talley smiled and relaxed against his chair.

"What's that supposed to mean?" she demanded, looking to both of them for an answer. "My papa had fine moral principles"—she had said it now, too late to backtrail—"and I dare you to say otherwise, Augie P'Shaw!"

"Ain't nobody here saying he didn't. He was one Daye who had the discretion of knowing when and how to act. Wouldn't you say so, Tink?"

Mr. Talley nodded.

"Proud of yourself, are you, Augie? Well, you can say what you want about me. All I know is my papa could've taught you two jerk-waters a thing or two."

"True," said Augustus, nodding. "Fact, he very well did. An eight-coil knot, near as I can recall."

Mr. Talley giggled like a barmaid just goosed on the buttocks.

"What did you say?"

"Well, what can I tell you, Bertie," said Augustus. "You said yourself your papa had fine principles, and you don't see me and Tink here disagreeing with you on that point. Man knew how to take a buck by the horns. You're a smart gal, I'm sure you get the *hang* of what I'm saying." The two men looked at each other and began to laugh.

"You don't know what you're talking about. And I don't like what you're insinuating, Augie. Not one bit."

The purpose of her visit had been reduced to the likes of a train wreck. This had gotten her nowhere. But rather than pick up Mr. Talley's Eureka staple driver—that required absolutely no skill at all—and bash it over those two snickering spoon heads, she pushed past Augie and left. Their laughter still echoed through the hall as she departed the building.

She stamped back to work, grinding her teeth the entire way, her face fiery and her mind going in a hundred directions. She was burnt plumb up by that scene back there! She heard everything Augustus Shaw said, and what he didn't say was crystal, too. Not only did those two wiseacres make her bristle, but she was mad at herself, for not accomplishing what she had gone there to do, and at Miss Lul, too, for allowing her to believe all these years that her papa had been a pillar of the community, defender of principles. That money-hungry business had been merely a hitch-in-the-get-along and she'd had no intention of telling Miss Lul. But this! This was out and out connivance. All these years her distorted conception of what kind of man her papa was, and every last bit of it had been a lie.

Damn John Shuford for not killing him twice!

Passing by the Palace, she bumped into Eunice who was just coming out from a matinee viewing of *The Tale of a Goat*, stealthily holding on to a half-eaten bag of popcorn. Eunice looked up, her mouth in a pinch like the butt end of a raw wienie.

"Pardon me, Eunice. I'm full of fight right now." Bertie continued walking, but then turned abruptly to face her. "Eunice," repeating the mum woman's name as if it were an afterthought.

Eunice stopped and looked at her plainly.

"You," said Bertie. "I bet you know every weewowy thing there is to know about every single body in this town. Don't that ever jolt you?"

Eunice placed a handful of popcorn in her mouth and set to grazing.

"Must be useful sometimes to be mute as a mackerel," said Bertie. "All the poisonous knowledge you must have, right up here"—tapping the side of her own temple—"and the rest of us won't ever be privy to it."

Eunice chewed. Bertie gave an ironic snort, then took off down the sidewalk, changing her direction and making a beeline toward home.

Brushing through the front door, she found Miss Lul rubbing a series of bold circles along the banister with a dust rag. The house smelled high of pine deodorizer.

"I know good and well you didn't forget your lunch this morning," Miss Lul said when she saw Bertie, "'cause I clearly recall sending you out the door with a deviled ham sandwich. So what, pray tell, are you doing home at this hour?"

"Why do you think it is that me and you live like cats and dogs oftentimes, Miss Lul?"

"Wouldn't have to if you weren't so contrary. Now what is it you forgot? I don't have all day. Uh-oh, curse of Eve?" Miss Lul stopped dusting. "I've told you time and again, Beatrice, to keep a supply of Curads in your purse for when you need them."

"That ain't why I'm home, Miss Lul."

"I'm sure there's a box upstairs in the water closet."

"No, Mama. Only reason I'm here right now is to get something off my chest."

"I don't have the first idea of what you're talking about," Miss Lul said, "but what I do know is that I don't like your tone."

"You've watched me do everything I can, neck or nothing, to shape woman's destiny and see that we get the vote. And the whole time that I've been fighting for what's right, I've been thinking that I'm just like my papa, down to the marrow. And I've been proud of it, too, knowing that I was the daughter of a strong man with strong beliefs. And you've known all along, Mama, that I wanted to be like him, determined, not just somebody who stands by and consents to things. Instead, I have to find out from two born fools who ain't fit to breathe, people we ain't even kin to, that the man was a bigot."

Miss Lul couldn't find her voice.

"All I've ever wanted to do is reach for the truth, Miss Lul. You know that. And you insist that me and Alta Ruth show you respect. I just think it would've been nice if you could've done the same for me." She felt a sting welling inside her nose—an indication that tears were forthcoming—and pinched the bridge as if to stave off a nosebleed. She swallowed hard. "Well, that's all I wanted to say. I need to get back to the switchboard, so I'll plan on seeing you at supper."

Bertie's thinking was, if she waited till later in the day to pay a visit to Johnny Bob and Silvia, and give them the news that she had failed at the registration office to make things right, she would've had time enough to simmer down and sort through her feelings. In some ways she wished she could've just been kept in the dark. It was always going to be there, a truth that would hang on—damn that word—and follow her everywhere. Not the kind of thing you could shut your mind or close your eyes to. At least giving Miss Lul something to think over had partway set her mind at ease.

During supper, by way of apology, Miss Lul related a suffrage-minded anecdote to her that she had read in the newspaper, tossing an apparent bone toward shaping a new course for their relationship.

But later that evening, sitting with Johnny Bob at their kitchen table while Silvia stood between them and poured three cups of just-perked cof-fee, Bertie was still reeling from Augustus Shaw's comment. *I bet Brud Daye is rolling over in his grave. His own daughter . . .* That's what her big mouth had gotten her, laughed at and insulted.

Out of respect for Silvia, she tried to keep her emotions—and her tongue—reined in. The whole situation was delicate ground, and Bertie had never been one for walking among eggs.

"I reckon you got your answer," Silvia said to Johnny Bob after hearing that Bertie's efforts failed. "Best leave it alone now."

Johnny Bob wrapped his palms around the blue enamel mug and stared down at his dark reflection. Himself, he was used to the rigmarole, the game of fast-talking men doing anything they could to catch him up and keep him from voting—or any hook on civilized life. He had hoped some change was coming, that this new law allowing women to vote would at least open a door for Silvia. Only now was her turn to face the same type of ridicule and discouragement that he'd experienced. Unwelcome, she'd been intimidated by those very men and sent on her way. "My daddy used to tell me about a time when a Negro could vote," he finally said. "I don't know how we let it go."

Bertie diverted her eyes to the corner sewing stand where Silvia had recently been busy piecing a quilt. Swatches of fabric were draped over the stand, and Bertie reckoned it all to be from used clothing—a torn pair of Johnny Bob's dungarees, a shirt once worn by a growing Zeke, an old skirt of Silvia's. A warm account of the family's life.

After several minutes of respecting Johnny Bob's silent reflection, Bertie looked up and addressed Silvia. "I've set this thing forward," she said, "and I'll go there every day and be a thorn till they change the process. I'll come to blows with every last one of 'em if I have to."

"That's what I'm afraid of," said Silvia. "Folks round here are talking hard. They're scared. That's why I didn't want Johnny Bob involving you in the first place. We have Zeke to think about. In any case, we thank you. Just let's be done with it for now." And that woman with the flood of pride—who was afraid of any repercussions that were likely to occur because of Bertie's interference on behalf of the colored community—quietly, stoically, set about slicing a buttered apple pie.

Any other time, Bertie would've gladly inhaled a wedge. But she left, graveling over the situation all the way home. No matter the hardships that lay before them, she pondered, the Johnny Bob and Silvia Johnsons of the world exemplify, throughout their lives, strength and the finest of fine moral fiber. And no woman cut in ivory was ever going to change that.

Chapter 25

All Hallow's Eve

*A*venerable Joan of Arc in her olive-green, hooded tunic with chain-mail sleeves was Bertie. With a gold cross emblazoned on her chest, and the Civil War sword she carried, thanks to the generosity of Mrs. Wheeler. But those wrinkled gray tights! They made her legs resemble two bull elephants trunk wrestling—and she would've defied anyone to point it out to her.

Ina's Lady Pilgrim paled in comparison, she was perfectly aware. She had pieced her costume only that afternoon, uncertain of whether she could attend Guerine's party. Her teaching contract strictly stated that she could not be out past eight o'clock on a Sunday, but Guerine had seen to it that she was allowed an exception this night—without disclosing the details to Ina, only confiding it was a good thing for her that Mrs. Wheeler thought of Guerine like a daughter.

After donning their costumes, Bertie and Ina drove out to the Shuford farm to collect Doodle, who was waiting by the mailbox, just as she had told Bertie she would be, pink-cheeked, her curls bundled into a kerchief, wearing a dress of yellow percale and clutching a wire basket with six brown eggs.

"Hop in, Sunnybrook," Bertie chirped, and the three were off.

"Ah, the fair frauleins!" Sam greeted them at the door.

"Step aside, King Richard," said Bertie, pushing past. "Some of us are dry."

"The Pope, actually," he said, slightly put out of countenance. He was crowned in silver (an upside-down colander studded with three gaudy rhinestones) and robed in copper (a cape the young tailor had fashioned from a bolt of neat brown worsted).

"You're the first Catholic I've met here, Mr. Eastbrook," said Ina, teasing. "Isn't your costume rather a contrariety, though? Considering tonight's festivities."

"Someone has to assure the evil spirits don't overtake our merriment," Sam said, taking her cloak and hanging it on the hall tree. "Nice to see you again, Miss Shuford," he said, placing Doodle's overcoat next to Ina's. "My condolences on your father's passing."

"In here, everyone!" Guerine called from the drawing room.

"Let's not keep the *lady in waiting*," Sam said.

The costume Guerine had selected to transform herself this evening was a velvet, burgundy dress with a brocade bodice, the upper sleeves puffed to abandon, topped with a Juliet-style headpiece with veil.

"As long as you've been in town," she said to Ina, "and this is the first time you've stepped a foot inside my home. And to think you walk by here every day on your way to and from school. Shame on you. Magic Brew?" She offered Ina a cup of rosy-colored punch.

"Your home is very lovely," said Ina.

It was difficult for her to pin down the style of the Loftis abode. There were splats of Exotic and Colonial Revival, with an arresting combination of embellishments. Brass eagles, bronze horses, and gilded glass. The walls were webbed in a rich patterned paper with ferns. Large ferns. Ferns with the frightening wingspan of a game bird. And when Ina saw the heavy rug on the floor, laid down in a haphazard fashion as if for some shabby back-alley harem, she nearly gasped. In a room intended to be kept for brag, no less. Some folks' taste, she decided, resided solely in the mouth.

Arranged on the credenza was an impressive spread; deviled eggs and popcorn balls; meringues shaped like bony fingers; tea sandwiches cut into ghosts; and a molded beet salad that Bertie quipped she didn't have the *heart* to eat.

Guerine invited everyone into the parlor. Orange ocher flames pranced in the fireplace and sounded like someone snapping celery—if ever anyone had a reason to snap celery.

"And the rest of the party?" Bertie asked.

"Why, we're all here, every one of us," Guerine said in her usual harpy tone, and turned her attention toward Ina.

A corner of Bertie's mouth rose in scorn. She knew perfectly well Guerine's idea of a party: it was Guerine monologizing about lame Fraidy Hurdle's new extension shoe and a minute-by-minute recounting of Portia Irby's recent trip to New York City to consult a swami for muscular guidance, while she, Bertie, sat on her thumb and watched Sam, Guerine's gooseberry, gorge on potluck. She believed darn well that fella had a tapeworm. So the day her cousin had appealed to her for party advice, Bertie told her: "It's got to be a masquerade. And you can't be fickle about who you invite either. What's the purpose of having a gathering," Bertie admonished, "if you're not willing to be a little creative and, dadblamed, invite more than the usual two!" And Guerine had agreed, seasoned as she was to Bertie's tendency toward the cyclonic. But now, just look. Quite some crowd, huh? If it hadn't been for Bertie, Doodle would've been left out altogether and then Bertie would've been stuck with dull Ina for a date. That's okay. Guerine was in for a surprise.

"Do tell us, Ina," said Guerine, "what's it like without Miss Duncan's aid at the school? Just how, pray tell, are you able to manage those children all by yourself? I've always said teachers have the souls of saints. I imagine it's a lot like herding cattle. Wouldn't you expect so, too, Delores? I know I certainly would."

It would happen that the topic naturally turned to mammals. Ina was somehow moved to confess, "I made a promise to take my pupils on an outing next week if they did well on their lessons. But there are sure to be some disappointed children, since they're studying mammals and will be expecting—as children do—a trip to match their studies." She didn't drive, she noted, and a visit to a zoo was out of the question as one did not locally exist, and thus she had created a situation that was sure to be difficult to face come the following week.

"What about the monkeys at State Line Service Station?" Guerine said. "They had an advertisement in the *Courier* last Thursday, one of those gimmicks to get folks to buy Gulf gasoline. 'Come See the Monkey Family!' it said. Even had a picture of one of the little rascals."

"Well—" Ina tried.

"Sam could take you and the children," Guerine offered, "couldn't you, Sam? You could borrow your uncle's truck and take them on your lunch hour. Monkeys are mammals, aren't they? And State Line has a grill inside that makes toasted sandwiches. And Sam likes their toasted sandwiches. Don't you, Sam?"

Ina was caught short at the very suggestion. An unmarried, unescorted young woman (widowed or not) in an enclosed space with a gentleman—a gentleman who was soon to be promised in marriage to another woman. And to have that woman suggest it? It was highly improper. Think of the blemish it could leave on her reputation. She had known of lesser situations that had turned into scandals, and she couldn't take a chance on people in the community suspecting her integrity.

Sam, too, must've been caught unawares, for he leaned forward and clasped his hands and nervously wrung them together. "I'd be happy to. Though, Guerine, I'm not certain that—"

"Oh, poo about Mrs. Wheeler," said Guerine. "Let me handle her. Besides, this is part of the children's learning. And Mrs. Wheeler has known Sam since he was born. Hasn't she, Sam? For heaven's sake, Sam is just Sam."

How proud Guerine was of herself for suggesting that Sam take Ina and her pupils on a field trip. Only a confident woman could do something so unselfish. To recommend that her betrothed offer aid to another woman.

When she was satisfied that the matter was settled, she urged Bertie into discussing her recent train trip to Asheville—not that Guerine cared one iota about the Seventh Annual Convention of the Equal Suffrage Association of North Carolina, but the Battery Park Hotel was an interesting topic for a party. "Oh, do tell us, Bertie!" Guerine went on. And on. "Do they really put chocolate truffles on the pillows at night? What was the Turkish Room like? Did you get a chance to take the Moonflower Walk?"

Bertie could've cared less. She was only interested in relating the Association's ideas for advancing civilization. There was a notable guest address from the president of the National American Woman Suffrage Association, she said, and a resolution had been adopted during the weekend for good roads and the illiterate.

"Didn't you do anything *cultural* while you were there?" Guerine asked. "Take a visit to an art museum? Go to the opera?"

"Went to the Almo Theater one night."

"For a ballroom dance, I bet!" said Guerine, happy to have finally hit on something noteworthy.

"Good Lord, Guerine!" Bertie snorted. "Use your phrenology box. Do I look like I'd be going to a ballroom dance? I went to view a moving picture on suffrage called *Your Girl and Mine*. The whole premise, you see—"

Colon stood stock-still, his only arm off plumb, as his papa hitched a coil of rope around the waist of Colon's white drill jumpers. His mama slid a bow-back kitchen chair behind him and stepped onto the seat barefoot, ready to tighten a switch of false whiskers to his face. She looped the strings over Colon's ears and tied them into a bow at the back of his head. It had been a long time since the twenty-three-year-old had needed help dressing.

"Beats all I ever seen," she said. "A grown boy dressing up in children's figs. Where'd you get this ugly thing anyhow?"

"Bartered with a musk beaver," said Colon. He sniggled, and his mama found it necessary to swat his backside.

"Hold still, Son," his papa said, working at fastening an empty paint bucket to the coil of rope.

"I think you got the wrong end of that deal," his mama said, her face gone wry from the smell of boiled cabbage and mouse nest wafting from the ersatz beard. "I know one thing: I never thought I'd see the likes of one of my own younguns attending some jollification at the Loftises. You sure you invited? You know you as bad as your paw when it comes to cross-reading."

"Leave the boy alone, Maw."

By the time Colon was ready to leave for the party, he was outfitted in one hogskin glove, a leftover remnant of ceiling paper, and an eight-inch gray brush made from Russian bristles. The latter two items he tucked inside the empty can.

He grabbed his jacket and a light flannel baseball cap and started for the door, but then suddenly had a thought and went to his room instead. He put his chin to the edge of the dresser and splayed the tail of the beard on top, picked up the bottle of Lilac Vegetal, there among a slew of toilet preparations, and gave the scratchy pile a splash. Crisp and masculine, it would combat musk.

He was long accustomed to being without a left arm. He had no recollection of the accident when he was three, of playing on the bank at the corn mill, tossing rocks at the water wheel while his papa conducted business inside. He had to take his papa's word that he had ventured too close, that the cog had snatched his arm and ripped it and the shirt from his tiny body. And his mama's word, too, that he liked to've died. It had happened so long ago that he never gave the missing arm much thought—unless someone reminded him. That extension, he believed, was fated for something better; a comforting beacon for shy Chub Lake suckers. As far as he was concerned, the scar at the end of his shoulder was no more than a tolerable birthmark. At most, a negligible flower.

And rare was the occasion that his being rendered was off-putting. (His mama called him "diversified.") His personality immediately put people at ease. He was a good-looking, good-natured young man who took pride in his appearance, and drew the attention of pretty girls often. And even though he liked clean jokes and simple living, and looked up to his papa and loved his mama, he was far from simple-minded. He had a healthy degree of intelligence—was naturally witty, curiously perceptive, and had a gift for reasoning. He felt emotions on a deep, meaningful level. Would hurt him to see an animal suffer. Anger him to see someone taken advantage of. Make him jealous when the other boy got the girl. And feel guilty, sometimes, for speaking his mind.

A thrill ran through him (that or the banging of the paint can against his leg) as he walked toward the shed roof and spotted his Model O. He tossed the brush and roll of paper into the sidecar, hopped onto the seat, and kicked the motorcycle to life, snapped on a pair of goggles and drove toward town.

He had been looking forward to this occasion since the day before, when his friend Bertie told him he was among those invited to her cousin Guerine's party. That Miss Guerine Loftis considered him that close of a friend surprised him to no end. And if there was the slightest chance that Bertie's friend Doodle would be there, he didn't want to miss seeing her. The only requirement, Bertie had said, was that he come in disguise. The one-armed paperhanger was his own idea.

But not only did his bucket create drag, his whiskers proved problematic. The beard caught a tailwind and flapped in his face like a notorious sheet on a clothesline. It was dark out and hard for him to see. Unable to take his hand from the handlebar, he slowed down to let the whiskers unfurl, but once he resumed normal speed the switch of hair repeated its blinding dance. The best he could do was cock his head to the side and drive by one eye.

When he finally coasted to a stop in front of the Loftis home, he pulled his cap from his jacket pocket and set the bill low on his forehead. He adjusted the beard, patted himself to make sure the rest of him was there and discovered that, somewhere between home and here, his scrap of ceiling paper had flown the car.

When the doorbell rang, Sam excused himself.

"Give them whatever they want, Sam," Guerine said, and explained to the rest of the party how a trick-or-treater had rigged their porch the season before. "First one to step out the door the next morning and I ended up snared in a river seine. If it hadn't been for Papa, I'd still be out there swinging like the catch of the day."

Bertie made an indiscernible quip, something about the weight of a certain fish.

"What's that, Bertie?" Guerine craned her neck toward the entry. "I wonder who he's talking to."

Doodle bit into a meringue finger and bobbed and weaved near the archway to get a better look at the newly arrived masquerader. "Looks like Colon Clayton."

"That rough scuff of a mailman?" said Guerine. "I didn't invite him."

"I did," Bertie said.

"To *my* party? You didn't? You did! Well, he better not've brought Esperann

Tucker with him. I don't have near enough food. Have you seen that gal lately?"

"What would he be bringing her for?" Doodle asked, but no one heard the question.

"Look here, everyone!" Sam said, returning to the parlor with Colon. "We've corralled us another party-goer."

Guerine smirked. "And just what are you supposed to be, Mr. Clayton? The village rogue?"

Colon smiled and lifted his arm away from his side, waiting for someone to guess.

Bertie cackled and slapped her thigh.

"Oh, yes, I get it," Ina said. She had only met Colon once, a brief encounter at the Wheelers' picnic on the weekend she had arrived. She regarded him as a pleasant young man, one who seemed sweetly intent on getting Doodle's attention. And now, as she watched the two of them say hello, she was certain there was a heightening of color in Doodle's cheeks.

After a time of eating savories and engaging in railleries, Guerine called everyone over to a Sheraton-style card table where a Ouija board sat. It was a glossy, wood-veneer board lithographed with an arcing alphabet, a row of numbers beginning with *1* and ending with *0*, and a choice of *Yes*, *No*, and *Good-Bye*. A heart-shaped planchette with a circular window for viewing each pip rested on the board, and Guerine held it up and playfully waved it.

"Shall we divine the names of your future husbands, ladies?" she teased. "I, of course, will have to think of something else to divine." She patted Sam on the arm. "Who'll go first? Ina?"

"Oh no, let someone else, please. I'd prefer to be an observer."

Ina knew of talking boards, but had never once aspired to use one. Even if she did yearn for knowledge beyond her capability of understanding, she preferred her thoughts not be exposed. And perhaps, on a deeper level, she didn't want her feelings revealed so blatantly to herself—to have impressed on her the life she was forced to now live, that what she'd had with Harlan was forever gone, and to be reminded of the intensity of feelings she would surely never experience again.

Doodle backed away timidly.

"For cripes sake, I'll go," said Bertie, sidling up to the table and depositing herself into a chair.

"Well then, let me be your partner in this devilish divination," Sam volunteered. He took the seat opposite and instructed Bertie to lightly rest the fingers of her right hand on the pointer, just as he was doing.

"I'm not about calling up any future husbands, though," Bertie said to

Guerine, then drew a snipe on Sam, "so get that nonsense out of your mind right now, Captain."

"Then we'll call up the dead!" Guerine declared.

"Oh, bad! Bad luck, very bad luck," Doodle said, her hands buffeting the skirt of her dress.

"I think Miss Shuford here's got a good point," said Colon. "I believe you got to have some kind of training to use a device like that. You might not be able to get the spirits back from whence they came." He backed from the table in the same manner Doodle had, as if feeling a need to be at a safer distance.

"Applesauce!" said Guerine. "This is simply a game."

"Yeah, no, let's not do that, Guerine," Bertie said. "What if I ask it a question about the upcoming election instead?"

Guerine clapped. "Yes, that's good! Quiet everyone! We must be quiet in order for the spirit to hear the question. Go ahead, Bertie. Ask your question."

Doodle hurried over to the finger-food table and rifled in and around every dish, making a disagreeable clacket. Guerine told her to shush, but Doodle didn't stop until she had found what she was looking for, and began furiously shaking salt over her shoulder.

Ghastly! Ina thought. This whole scene! It was becoming clear to her that this was a poor choice of entertainment, especially considering Doodle's father had only recently died. She was disappointed that Bertie could be so insensitive in that regard, going ahead with the game without a care in the world, and she also felt a tinge of anger toward Guerine for suggesting that she call up the name of a future husband—knowing perfectly well Ina's status. All in all this was poor judgment on Guerine's part and it needed to stop.

"Bertie," Ina said, motioning toward Doodle by tilting her head. She wanted Bertie to see for herself just how visibly Doodle was disturbed.

"Sorry, country gal. Just having some fun."

"Maybe a game of whist?" suggested Sam.

"But there's six of us," Guerine whined. "How do you expect us to—"

From the corner of the room came a loud crash, and for a split second Ina was willing to believe that they had, indeed, summoned a ghost. But the perpetrator was soon determined. Colon's paint bucket had snagged the fringed paisley cover on a side table, pulling an entire collection of figurines to the floor. Each statuette was broken to tiny pieces, which put Guerine in a foul humor and brought an end to the evening.

"Oh boy! I've really done a hoopdedoodle this time." Colon bent to his knees and began picking up the larger of the painted shards.

Doodle rushed to help him while Sam went to the larder for a broom and dustpan.

"I'm sorry as I can be, Miss Loftis," Colon said. "Don't know as I've seen anything so nice. But if you'll tell me where I can find these, I'll surely replace every last one."

"Sears Roebuck doesn't sell Staffordshire, Mr. Clayton. They're one of a kind."

The party had reached a regretful end.

Sam retrieved coats and saw everyone to the door. He gave Colon a friendly slap on the back. "Don't worry yourself over it for a minute, Sport. Seriously. If you could only see the trifles she and her mother have tucked away in the attic— Well, good night all."

Stepping down from the porch, Colon rattled.

"I gotta say, that's one of the more terror-ific parties I've attended," Bertie said, unaware there was yet more grief to endure.

Her Model T sat lopsided at the curb, jacked on one side, the left front tire the victim of "side play." Removed and missing. A dupe in some harmless Hallow's Eve mischief. Bertie spewed out several choice swearwords. Only days before, she'd had the rear outer casings filled with tire cement and vulcanized for cuts and tears that had developed on the treads. The maintenance hadn't been cheap. She had a notion to kick the Ford.

"Colon, maybe you wouldn't mind seeing that Doodle gets home, would you? Me and Ina can walk from here."

Ina thought it was a ridiculous proposal. "She's wearing a dress. Wouldn't it be best if she came home with us? We can figure out a way to return her to home in the morning. When it's light out. When she can go by a more *appropriate* means of transportation." She hoped Bertie would understand her meaning.

"My work starts before the sun comes up," Doodle said. "If Mr. Clayton here is able to see me home, well then, I really ought to go."

Bertie reached into the Ford and pulled out a jacket and draped it over Doodle's shoulders.

"You're just going to let her go, then?" said Ina. "Like that?"

"Don't you fret, Miss Fitzhugh," said Colon. He removed his beard, reached for a spare pair of goggles from the sidecar and handed them to Doodle. "I'll be real careful. Why, I can practically drive this thing blind."

"And with one hand," Bertie added.

Doodle scooped the border of the dress and tucked the material between her legs. She hopped into the sidecar and slipped the goggles over her kerchief.

Ina stood by speechless.

"There they go," said Bertie. "Mary Pickford, our little golden-haired girl, and—"

"Douglas Fairbanks?" Ina said, shocked at the image of Doodle being sped away in a giant-sized Dutch clog.

"Actually," said Bertie, "I was thinking more Keystone Kop."

Colon grinned all the way out to the Shuford farm. The grin was a cross between the Cheshire cat and of someone who realizes he's just swallowed a bug. Every half mile or so, he would look over at Doodle and, in turn, she would look at him, and the two of them would nod at each other. The first nod could easily be explained—it was an indication the engine was too loud to carry on conversation. The second nod, Colon figured, was a shared opinion between them that the air was certainly chilly and just as loud. But after the third and fourth nods he didn't know what, exactly, they were nodding for.

He was glad he went to the party, in spite of wrecking a whole table of irreplaceables. How would he ever make it up to Guerine? Sam was sure a likable sort, always made him feel at ease, despite the differences in their upbringing. (Sam had the refinement of a quality saddlebred stallion, and Colon was more American draft, but lacking their impressive withers.) And Bertie never failed to treat him like family. He would've liked more time to visit with Doodle, though. He'd only seen her once since her papa died, the day he delivered a package up to the house because it was too large for their mailbox. He had found her out back doing laundry, stirring it in a black pot with a wooden paddle, and came up on her of a sudden and scared her. She was talking to nobody he could see, just herself and John's old hound.

"Does that dog talk back?" he had said.

And she had whirred around and seen him holding the package.

"Didn't mean to scare you," he said. "John must've ordered something from the Sears and Roebuck." He held the bundle out from his body. "Too broad to fit in the box, as you can see. Not heavy nor nothing, just too big for the mailbox."

"That's probably the new drinking fountain for my chicks," she said. "The other one's rusted."

"Rusty water's good blood medicine."

"Not for chickens, it's not. Foul water can give 'em gapeworms, and gapeworms will—"

"Block their windpipes and kill 'em." Colon nodded. "Yeah, I know."

They had stood there staring at each other awkwardly for a moment, before she finally let go of the paddle and took the package from him.

"You been getting on all right?" he had asked her.

It was her turn to nod.

"Not that it's none of my business," he said, "but it won't be long before it's time for harvesting, and I was just curious about—"

"How I'm gonna manage it myself?"

"Well, yeah."

"I'll manage."

"I just thought, if you were to need some help."

"I don't."

He scuffed a dusty shoe across a bare patch in the yard. "Reckon I'll be on my way then. Still got a few more deliveries yet. See ya, Blue." He patted Bugle on top of the head, then started toward the front yard.

"Bugle," Doodle said.

He turned. "What's that?"

"His name is Bugle."

And now look at her. Over there in that sidecar, nodding. Meant she couldn't wait for this ride to be over. Be shed of his company for good. And here he was thinking she had the prettiest beaucatcher curls he'd ever seen flying out from under her kerchief. Esperann Tucker had pretty curls, too, but he couldn't get past that fertile waste of a face. He knew it was ugly of him to feel that way, not the least bit Christianly, and if his mama caught wind of it she'd be swatting him with the first thing she got a hold of. But Lord knows, if a man can't even lift the merchandise, how's he gonna get it home? Onliest reason he'd gone to supper at Esperann's house in the first place was because her mama—a God-fearing post-mistress who was capable of making his work life infernal—wouldn't take no for an answer. And ever since then, Esperann had been hounding him. Girl would've made a good heeler though, because every time he came into town, plague-gone! if she wasn't running behind him choking on Model O dust.

He was kidding himself, thinking Delores Shuford could ever take an interest in him. A fool is what he was. Why'd he even go to that party at all? The only interest she showed toward him was in helping clean up that mess he made. His biggest flub ever and she had to witness it. Probably figured him for a rube. And acted as much, telling him it was best to drop her off at the bottom of the hill on some chance event he got his scooter stuck trying to maneuver the rough road. Before he could dismount and offer her his hand, she popped out of the sidecar quicker than toast, stammered out a "much obliged" in a childish treble and scurried up the hill.

He watched her as she went, her vapory shadow, the spirit of her yellow dress as it floated up the hill, and on a little further till she had reached the front porch, and then, with the prettiness of a pleated hand fan being slowly closed, she was gone.

Chapter 26

Bertie Deals with Snags and Lawyers

November 2, 1920–Election Day

*T*here was one heck of a rabid storm raging when Bertie woke up that Tuesday morning. Rain oscillated against the windows with every gust of wind, and put up such a brawl with the rest of the house that she figured water must be finding its way inside, puddling somewhere unseen. Let Miss Lul worry with it if that was the case. Even if they held out the rain, these walls could not contain Bertie's exuberance today. She was her own gust, a flurry to get to the polling place well before it opened.

She flung the bedcovers back and reached to the foot of the bed for her blanket-cloth robe and threw it around her shoulders. Plopping her feet onto the cold floor, she bent over. No sign of her *oomphs*, her favorite slippers that mired her toes in softened butter.

Her room in the attic wasn't as big as a rooster loft, though she was glad to be back to it after spending the heat of the summer downstairs in Alta Ruth's bedroom. Miss Lul liked to keep the extra bedrooms available on the chance a boarder would come to call, and sharing space with her younger sister had been hobbling. Alta Ruth complained that Bertie ground her teeth in her sleep worse than a Guernsey, and she didn't like Bertie piling her *Woman Citizen* subscriptions on top of the desk, or Bertie's pressed powder spilling onto the dresser. And what scrap of closet space Alta Ruth allowed Bertie for clothes, she insisted, was toward the back. So when Alta Ruth thought she could help herself to a box of French creams that the Equal Suffrage Association had sent to Bertie for helping to organize a parade, Bertie slapped her hand. Daye women weren't meant to go shares. "Get your own," she told her.

She walked to the dormer, barefoot, and looked outside. Across the street Guerine's house was an out-of-focus gray mass. Miss Lul's violets, she could see, were taking a spanking along the sidewalk out front, and the last of the leaves on the maple tree had been pummeled to the lawn.

The doors to the courthouse would be open early. She wanted to be there ahead of anyone else, to help any of the women who might need assistance, and offer encouragement to the ones who would have a tendency to hang back. Some, she figured, would be confounded by the whole process. The important thing, she'd be sure to remind them, is to get the cross mark inside the tiny square on the ballot card.

She scooped up a few toiletries from her vanity—a jar of Lady Esther face cream, a complexion mitten, a white bristle brush—and snatched the suit hanging on the back of the door. She saw the heels of her slippers peeking out from under the bed, sunk her feet into them and hurried off to the bathroom.

Her daily ritual, this bathtime routine, held a different meaning for Bertie this morning. She had always been particular in the way she cared for herself, never one to talcum and primp simply for the benefit of the dull-as-clay male. And not for the female persuasion either. She had no leanings toward one or the other, but was no less precious because of it. Romance was simply too viewy of a subject for her to fool with. If she was going to engage in anything at all, it was going to be front-page. When she stood in front of the mirror this historic morning, supremely unadorned, what she saw was eternally feminine. Not a bachelor maiden as some (or most) might think her destiny, but rather a new ideal. A woman all to her own. A woman whose spirits could not be trampled, who knew she had the right to a brilliant mind, and to remain independent, if she so desired.

"Hop in, girls," she offered, hustling her bosoms into a 38-inch embroidered camisole. She slipped into a pair of sateen bloomers and laced herself into a corset. A goodly number of women were starting to do away with theirs, but her abounding hips benefited from the light, pliable boning.

"Well, now, look at you," Miss Lul sang as Bertie stepped into the kitchen. "That your new suit you told me about?"

"You like it? It's all wool. Got the silk embroidery all around the back of the coat, too." Bertie reached into the cupboard for a coffee cup.

Miss Lul stood back with her own coffee in hand, scoping Bertie up and down at different angles. "Skirt's got a nice sweep. Very stylish *and* professional. Exactly the kind of suit my eldest daughter would wear on a day she's making history."

"We're all of us making history, Mama."

"I know, I know. But I'm just so proud of you, Beatrice. I hadn't told you before now and I should've."

Miss Lul was liable to start crying any minute, so Bertie told her she was in a hurry. "Where's that vacuum flask? I want to take some coffee with me."

"It's right here." Miss Lul opened a cabinet door. "Oh, but the cork's missing from it. I forgot I let Alta Ruth take some lemonade to a tea party one day, and she brought it home without the stopper."

Bertie shook her head. "I reckon I can manage somehow without spilling it."

"Here. I wrapped you up a peanut butter and jelly sandwich. That should hold you till later."

"You are coming, aren't ya?" asked Bertie. "You're coming to vote."

"Of course I am! No need for you to fret over that."

"And bring Alta Ruth with you, too," Bertie said, "even if it makes her late for school. I want her to be witness to all this."

The rain was still coming down hard as Bertie prepared to leave the house. She put on a pair of the four-buckle gaiters that were kept lined against the wall under the hat rack in the foyer, and took her raincoat from the hall tree.

Miss Lul held open the door. "Got your umbrella?"

"Hat's good enough."

Fastening the last button on Bertie's coat, Miss Lul handed her the container of coffee and watched as she made a dash for the Ford.

Bertie was relieved that she had put all the suffrage buttons and banners in the vehicle the night before. It was enough trouble juggling an open flask of hot coffee, trying to keep the rain from turning it into tinkle.

Giving the old gal a good hard crank, she scrambled onto the seat. But something wasn't quite right. The seat felt mushy, like her bottom was dragging from undue wear. She slid off the seat, stepped back out into the rain, and saw the problem immediately.

"Son of a—!" Not just one flat tire, but four! She should've known somebody would pull this kind of hokum to try and keep her away from the ballot box.

The car had to be jacked up and all the tire stems replaced, something she was able to do herself, but not without muddying her shoes, ruining her raincoat and wasting precious time. She cursed whoever was responsible, up hill and down dale, dadblamed him and deuced him till she was blue. When Miss Lul realized what was happening, she rushed outside and held an umbrella over Bertie while she worked.

Two hours later, Bertie arrived at the courthouse soppy and grease-streaked. The polls had been open for an hour.

"Somebody here owes me four tire stems and a coat!" she roared, blasting through the door, streaming a yellow banner behind her.

"I didn't have a thing to do with it, Bertie," Hoyt Yancey yelled in alarm.

"Quick to defend yourself, Hoyt. Means you must know something."

The usual disputables were standing around in amused contemplation when it struck her. Aside from her wet and wrinkled one, there wasn't one skirt to be found among the crowd, only a knot of aggravating men. Just as she was ready to comment on the peculiar nature of it, certain there was another scheme afoot, Colon burst in. He was out of breath.

"Bertie! I just saw Dorothea Merritt at the post office. She was here first thing this morning when the place opened"—inhaling, exhaling—"her and a bunch of other women. But they were told they had to have an affidavit in order to vote. And since you weren't here"—catching another breath—"they figured there was some truth to it, so they went on home. Is that right? Do they really need some kind of affidavit?"

All of a sudden Bertie had a clear vision of herself clinging to jail bars, because before the day was out she was surely going to kill somebody. She took a look at the men standing around laughing and grinning, thinking they had succeeded in staving Person County's women away from the ballot box.

"Is Dorothea still at the post office?"

"She was headed home," said Colon. "Said the weather was making her bursitis act up."

This predicament, Bertie decided, was not going to distract her from the job at hand. "Colon, listen to me. Sadie Reams is working my shift at the telephone office this morning. Run over and tell her I said to call up Dorothea, and to do it right away. Tell her I had some car trouble this morning, but I'm here now, and they don't need an affidavit or anything of the sort. That was just a misunderstanding that was spread." She looked around at the smirking faces. "They can vote on the same terms as the men. And tell her to call the other ladies, too, and tell them! We'll get this problem rectified right now, and still have plenty time for them to get back here."

"Will do!" Colon turned to leave, and Augustus Shaw shouted after him.

"Never figured a son of Broadie Clayton's would go soft!"

Colon stopped and looked at him. "I'd rather be without one swing than in your predicament, Augie—without a chunk of sense. There's some things that are just plain right."

"You wanna see right? I'll show you what's right!" Augustus Shaw hollered out. He elbowed his way to the front of the other men, but was held back by two.

"Colon," said Bertie. "You come back as soon as Sadie's made that call. Maybe you can see to it that nobody else gets that same mistaken impression as they're trying to enter the building."

"Gotcha," he said, and walked out the door.

Many of the women did return, those who were eager to vote, and by the end of the day Bertie noticed that the women took longer to vote than the men because they voted for each candidate rather than by party. Even Guerine made an appearance, if only to chew up scenery in front of Sam by overacting when she released her ballot into the box.

Overall, the vote was light. Of 557 voters, only 49 were women. It was by no means a loss, just a smaller victory than Bertie had hoped.

This campaign might be over, but Bertie Daye had a new fight to ready for.

Chapter 27

Colon Makes Good

*N*obody would've faulted him if he hadn't even done it. If anything, they would've thought him crazy for doing it at all. A brand-new Master Wingate phonograph. Free. (Well, minus the two dollars he had to spend for the key that ended up fitting the lock.) The only thing he'd ever won in his whole life. Not to mention it was made out of a high-quality, three-ply mahogany veneer, and the internal horn was every bit of the evenly formed spruce just like it'd been advertised—which is what you looked for in a fine machine such as that one, to provide an airtight sound chamber. It was a nice size phonograph, too, not much bigger than a suitcase. A small table model that was ideal for a man of reasonable means, like him.

It wasn't as if she needed a talking machine. But that wasn't the point. What was the point was what he needed—and that was to make up for breaking Guerine's expensive doodads. If she couldn't use the phonograph, that was fine, she could then sell it and use the money to replace all those precious gewgaws he'd broken.

He packed up the Wingate, glad that he'd saved the box, and included the shellac record that Mr. Cheeks had thrown in as part of the original deal. Wasn't likely he'd need that anymore. When he got to her house, he didn't knock, didn't want to come across as wanting praise for the deed, just left the box on the stoop with a note attached to it, and figured that was the last thing that would ever need to be mentioned about it.

This recording was not sold individually but came with the Wingate, which has but one tone arm, just like me! May this machine bring you much harmony.

Your friend in song, Colon Clayton

Chapter 28

Monkey Matters

The door to the schoolhouse scraped opened slowly, revealing Sam on the other side. It was just before noontime and the children were quietly working on their individual lessons. "Am I too early?" he asked, ducking inside.

"Oh hello, Mr. Eastbrook," Ina said, surprised to see him. "Too early for what?"

He closed the door behind him, and Ina felt a draft of cool air sweep over her ankles.

"This is the day Mrs. Wheeler agreed to," he said. "For your field trip. To take the children over to State Line for lunch and, well, monkeys. Didn't Guerine tell you?"

"Monkeys?" someone in the class whispered.

Guerine most certainly had not told her. Ina considered the matter forgotten after the party and never dreamed that Guerine would persist with her imprudent suggestion. And, too, Ina hoped her pupils had forgotten any mention of a field trip rewarding their good behavior. At most she had considered walking them over to Henry's father's hog farm to learn about the colors and characteristics of each breed, but that was potentially too upsetting to the tummy, not to mention the nose, so she had settled upon the interesting idea of taking them on an Imaginary Journey. By writing to the local railroad company for advertising pamphlets, and with the use of a few postcards, she would take them on a journey through the Rockies, or perhaps on a visit to Niagara Falls. They might even find a marsh to wade in and there they would discover miniature islands and bays. It would be like giving them firsthand information.

"Uh-oh," Sam said. "Guerine forgot to give you notice. My apologies."

"Is it true, Miss Fitzhugh? Are you really taking us to see the monkeys?"

one of the twins asked, his fervid excitement spreading to the other children.

"Yea! We're going to see the monkey family!" chirped Adele, turning to face Jeanette. "See? Didn't I tell you she'd find a way to take us?"

"Wait, now! Just a minute," Ina tried calming them. "I'm sorry, Mr. Eastbrook, but—" She realized her idea of an Imaginary Journey wouldn't garner the same enthusiasm as would a chance to come face to face with something that could use its tail to swing from a tree. She looked out into the schoolyard, saw the truck, certain that Sam must've gone to the trouble of borrowing it from his uncle. "—I just couldn't take a chance on them catching cold."

"It ain't too chilly for us," said Henry. "Is it, ever'body?"

"We walk home in weather a whole lot colder than this, Miss Fitzhugh," said the other twin.

If she was intending to talk them out of the trip, she made a mistake when she looked over at Etta. More and more Ina was becoming endeared to the child. She'd been working closely with her, slowly drawing her out of her bashfulness, encouraging her to talk each time there was an opportunity for expression, and extending other lessons of development to the playground by conferring the title of "slide captain" to her. Within two months Etta's silence had graduated to a whisper, the progress of which was pleasing to both teacher and pupil. And now the little girl's hazel-speckled eyes were fixed on to Ina, as if the child was certain that some sort of aberration would soon be revealed by her teacher.

"Hats, scarves, *and* gloves," Ina said, putting in motion a hectic stampede toward the cloakroom.

The children rode in the bed of the truck, but for Etta, who sat up front, snuggled against Ina. Sam helped the two of them onto the wooden seat, but not before swiping at empty Tootsie Roll wrappers until several littered the floor. Even the best-dressed men had shortcomings, and Ina wondered, by the fullness of his cheek and the way the corner of his mouth twitched, if he was secretly harboring a piece of the chewy candy.

The anxiety of being in Sam's company without another adult outweighed the sheer joy Ina felt in Etta's downy softness. Ina didn't speak for some time, and neither did he. She wondered if he, too, was uncomfortable with this arrangement; if he had felt pressured into the situation by an ever-eager-to-please Guerine. They had always felt free to talk on other occasions, but this was different. This time there were no other adults to diffuse any of the tensions that a man and a woman could possibly experience. He chuckled out loud, an indication to Ina that at least he was enjoying the talk and laughter coming from the children in the wagon.

Etta raised her head and whispered into Ina's ear.

"What's that, dear? I honestly don't know."

"Sounds like there's a point at issue here," said Sam.

"She wants to know if monkeys bite, but I'm afraid my knowledge of primates is limited."

"Let's see now," Sam said, taking an endearing paternal tone. "I don't know too many monkeys—"

Etta grinned.

"—but seeing they have the equipment, just like you, and if they got the inclination, well then, yes, they very well could bite."

"Mr. Eastbrook! You'll scare the child! Don't worry, Etta. I'm sure they're not harmful, otherwise we wouldn't be allowed to visit them. Isn't that right, Mr. Eastbrook?"

He leaned from the steering wheel and bent his head toward Etta. "Just to be safe, we should ask a banana." The little girl giggled.

When they arrived at State Line Service Station, the children jumped from the wagon in a frenzy, ready to run inside. It took some doing, but Ina managed to corral them before they got away.

"This is a learning opportunity," she reminded, "not a play day. And I insist you conduct yourselves like upright citizens. You're to stay together, walk not run, and you're not to touch anything unless you are asked. Do I make myself clear?"

Inside, Sam greeted the man behind the register. "Came to see what you have in primates, Mr. Dixon," he quipped, shaking the man's hand.

Mr. Dixon guffawed. "Right this way," and led them to the rear of the store, past a small luncheon counter.

The entire situation felt ridiculous to Ina. Here she was, trooping through a cramped, dirty country store with a bustle of children and a man who suddenly was making her nervous—and possibly she him—like they were there on official business.

"Only got two of the little fellas now," Mr. Dixon called over his shoulder.

"There were more?" Ina asked.

"Was four," he said, and stopped. "But I wouldn't want to say what happened to the other two"—he glanced down at Etta—"in the presence of children."

Ina squeezed Etta's hand and pulled her closer.

"Well then, here they are," Mr. Dixon said. "Play with the rascals long as you like. Need anything, I'll be up front." Sam thanked him.

"Aw, them monkeys ain't big as two squirts," Henry growled.

Between the pitiful sight and the awful outhouse odor, Ina's stomach began to turn.

They sat on the floor amidst a scatty mess of nuts and seeds and sawdust, collared and tethered to a wooden beam. One seemed especially listless, and the other little creature was scooping what he could from the floor, forcing the grainy scramble to his weary sibling's mouth. The sight was so upsetting, Ina felt ashamed for staring.

"Can we touch them, Miss Fitzhugh?" Lloyd asked.

She felt a touch of lightheadedness coming on.

"Perhaps we should eat first, Lloyd," she suggested. "Then afterward, if you wish, we can ask the proprietor some questions about them. Mr. Eastbrook, if you wouldn't mind, please, ordering sandwiches for the children?"

"Are you ill, Miss Fitzhugh?" he asked. "You look a little out of sorts."

"Only the gnawing effects of an insufficient breakfast. If you don't mind, Etta and I will have a seat. Shall we, Etta?" She led the little girl to a nearby bench, wiping it with a handkerchief before sitting down, turning her back to her pupils' field trip. Etta peered around her, curious to see what the two woollies were all about.

"They stink!" Adele said.

"Well, they're supposed to. They're monkeys," said Alta Ruth. "Monkeys don't bathe."

"They do too bathe!" exclaimed one of the twins. "Only it's more like cats."

The words alone, minus the picture to go with them, made Ina feel all the more queasy.

"Maybe this will be of some aid," Sam said, coming over with a bottle of Chero-Cola. "Grilled cheeses will be up shortly."

"You're very timely with the effervescence, Mr. Eastbrook. Thank you." She took a sip.

He shoved his hands into his pockets and surveyed the scene over Ina's shoulder. "They're not really so bad, you know. In fact, they sort of remind me of Miss Duncan."

"I assume you mean the monkeys, Mr. Eastbrook. In any case I'm going to pretend I didn't hear that."

He laughed, and Ina took another sip of Chero.

Lunch ready, she called for the children to come eat. One bite of hers and all she could taste was tepid grease, and returned the sandwich to its oil-spotted paper. The boys ate like horses, and it made her wonder what their diets were like at home. Henry was first to finish and promptly asked if he could be excused to sit with "the baby apes."

"I suppose that would be all right," she told him, pleased that he was making great strides with his table manners.

As the children focused their attention on learning every detail they could about primates—her knowledge of which happily remained limited—she and Sam carried forth in conversation.

He seemed more at ease now. But of course, why shouldn't he be? His own fiancé had made these arrangements. And in that respect, the very idea of anyone remotely thinking that Ina entertained any hope of sharing his affections was nothing short of laughable. Not that she did. Entertain any hope. Only she worried what other people might think if they saw them together. That someone could perceive such baseness was not so far-fetched, and her reputation meant more to her than her self-esteem. But despite her anxiety—she was eager for the children to hurry and eat that they could return to school and resume their studies—she was able to converse as if she were relaxed and enjoying the moment.

Mr. Eastbrook had been kind to her that first day at the picnic, sympathetic to what she was going through as the focus of everyone's attention, and of all the people there he had seemed more in keeping with the class of people with whom she was accustomed to socializing.

". . . and so you took over Eastbrook's Haberdashery when your father died," she said. "I think that's very admirable."

"What I really wanted to do was to paint the Sistine Chapel, but another lucky chap had already beat me to it."

They both laughed, and suddenly there came a stir of excitement from among the children.

"Uh-oh. Seems your boy Henry there just collared that monkey's bare posterior. And byjiminy, if that monkey didn't just slap him!"

Ina turned quickly in her seat and became witness to uncharted territory: a monkey gone wild, jumping on the boy's shoulders and boxing his ears. "Henry!"

Sam fled to the erratic scene and plucked the monkey from the boy's head.

"Henry!" Ina repeated, hurrying over to help. "Mr. Eastbrook, why are you laughing? Henry, what have I told you about not touching things unless you are asked? Did that monkey ask you to touch him?"

"No'm."

"Show some dignity, Mr. Eastbrook, won't you? Henry, are you hurt?"

"No'm."

"Then go at once to Mr. Eastbrook's vehicle." She pointed toward the door. "You're to wait there, in the wagon, until I can gather up the rest of the children—"

One suggestion in *The Rural School* is to "keep a subject before the mind for a month." She made a mental note right then that she would have the pupils concentrate the rest of the month on kindness; kindness to all things, including animals. Two months before the mind sounded even better.

She uttered her frustration aloud on the ride back to the school. "That child, if he doesn't set himself like flint sometimes. I wouldn't have blamed that poor monkey if it had cuffed him upside the head." Here she looked at Etta. "There are certain things you are never to repeat. This happens to be one of them."

"Boys will be boys," Sam said.

"Oh, please. You aren't going to quote that old rhyme about what boys are made of? You certainly didn't help the matter by laughing."

Sam gave a quick look through the rear glass. "Doesn't appear too flinty now. He's got a regular chorus going back there."

She had no interest in observing more of Henry's antics, but she could hear his voice. He was leading his schoolmates in a jangling rendition of "The Little Ford Rambled Right Along."

She glanced over at Sam. He was grinning and bobbing his head to the jaunty tune. Staying angry no longer seemed a viable option. He certainly was jolly, wasn't he? And a natural when it came to being with children. A boon companion, she'd say.

Back at the school he politely slipped something into her hand. "But that's from our school fund," she said, staring at the money she had given him for their lunch. "It was intended for such outings."

"Please, it's my treat. I would've paid double just to be witness to an occurrence like today. I don't know when I've laughed so hard! Oh, and in case you're wondering which twin picks his nose? Dolian."

Yes, she decided, Sam Eastbrook was truly a bon vivant.

Chapter 29

Bertie Gets Fired

Warren Gamaliel Harding Sweeps Up
Sixty Percent Of The Popular Vote!

𝓑ertie returned to work the morning after that tidal wave of an election, gripped by an encouragement that she'd never felt before. Times were changing for the better. People were finally coming to their senses. It put a bit more of the sass in her walk.

She slammed the door from the alley and stamped her way up the staircase to the office. As she bent to place the key in the door, she noticed the yellow flush from the lamp on Mr. Wheeler's curtain-top desk. She peered through the wavy glass pane, batting her lashes beyond the black capital letters of WHEELER TELEPHONE COMPANY, and saw Mr. Wheeler's thick figure hoofbeating shoe-leather over the hardwood floor. He had a smoldering cheroot in his right hand and was dragging on it like a furnace. Odd. For one thing, she'd always been the first to arrive each morning, and second, it was rare that B.C. showed his face to anybody outside his home before nine. Bertie—sorry that he'd ever made her privy to his daily habits—knew he had a fondness for his colored girl Rella's fried mush, but only after he had taken his morning coffee bitter black, read the *Courier* from front to back, and leisurely soaked in a hot bathtub while shaving with blades he had stropped himself.

As she pushed the door open and let it bounce against the rubber stop, she noticed the ashtray on his desk, filled with a confusion of cigars smoked down to suckled-on butts. He must've been there for a while, and the look on his face struck her as sour.

"Good Lord, B.C.," she said. "Least you could do is open up a window. And how come you didn't light the stove? It's cold as crystal in here. What's wrong with you anyhow? Corena finally come to her senses and throw you out?" She set her purse on her desk, then cranked open a window to rid the room of the stale tobacco.

"I'm sorry to have to do this, Bertie," he said, stopping in mid-sentence to get a firm footing on two boards.

"What say?" she said, paying no regard to his answer. She busied herself about the office instead, putting things in a general order as she did every cold morning before taking her place in front of the switchboard: striking a match in the little pug woodstove, opening blinds, sharpening pencils, sweeping around her work space, and doing a light dusting of the equipment.

"It's just that I've been getting a lot of pressure," he finally said. He took another puff on his cigar and started to pace. "Different ones complaining, you see. Folks calling at the house all hours of night, stopping by unannounced. It's become unbearable."

"Have you seen my y-end tube?" she asked. "I left it right here." She shuffled papers on her desk, lifting sheets to look underneath. "I bet it's that dern Sadie again. She's forever messing with my stuff. Leave her in charge for one day—"

"Truth is, you've always talked back to folks, Bertie. And courtesy is the kernel of this business. It's the focus, if you will. The navel. And you haven't made matters any better all these months with your suffrage antics. You've been driving everybody in this town crazy. I just can't have that anymore. A man's got to be able to show that he can handle any situation that comes along. Looks bad if I just let you do as you please. It's just not right. Bertie, are you listening to me?"

"Is there a point to all this, B.C.?"

"Yes, Bertie, there is. I'm gonna have to let you go."

"Let me go? What do you mean, you're firing me?"

"Maybe if things were different, then perhaps I could keep you on."

If things were different. She knew exactly what he was implying, and was on the fringe of stuffing that nasty stogie down his blubbery throat. "You mean if I'd been willing to clap spurs with you, that's what you mean!"

His look all but conceded.

"Fine," she said. "My sociability's about worn out anyway. I think I've rendered life pleasurable enough for folks in this town. Let 'em have Sadie. I guarantee she won't have near the same relationship with them that I've had." She went about the office collecting her belongings like a person stark-staring mad, smiting the objects on top of her workspace: her favorite gold-filled screw pencil, a nickel-plated nose protector she used when dusting, a desk calendar, a deck of Climax playing cards (for when business was slow), a copy of *Woman in Modern Society*, a pewter shaving mug that served as a coffee mug, and a Savoy-pattern spoon that Miss Lul had been searching for. "Just wait till somebody like Blanche Warren calls up and wants Sadie to time her Tilden cake. Won't she be in for a surprise! And you will, too, the first time you ask her to work overtime. Ha!"

When she realized there wasn't a box for carrying her things, she removed a drawer from the filing cabinet. Mr. Wheeler watched as she dumped its contents onto the floor and swiped her personal effects into it, purse included, and hoisted it onto her hip. She pushed past him and made for the door.

"Where you going?" he asked her.

"Wherever a person goes after they've been fired. That's where I'm going!"

"But the board's starting to light up. I figured you to finish out the day, at least until Sadie comes in."

"Well you figured on whippin' one slave too many, B.C. If you think we wear these dresses to let our brains fall out the bottom, then you better tighten your belt and buckle your boots! 'Cause we deserve respect, and you and your kith and kin are just gonna have to find a way to give it. Till then, answer your own damn board! And tell them ladies on the other end the truth about why I'm gone, too. When they stop in to pay their phone bills, tell them, 'Thank you, and by the way, you're too insignificant to vote.' You tell 'em that!"

Miss Lul was going from the oven to kitchen table with a hot dish of creamed eggs and frizzled dried beef when Bertie flew through the front door and dropped the drawer on the side table.

"That jackass!"

"What on earth!" said Miss Lul, the square skillet and hot handle pad nearly slipping from her hand. Ina and Alta Ruth were seated at the table.

"That beetle-headed bugger just fired me!" Bertie fumed, stomping into the kitchen. "Thinks he's a capital fellow, he does. A model man among men. Why, he's no more than a ratstinkingsnake is what he is!"

"Who?" said Miss Lul. "Mr. Wheeler?"

Bertie turned saucy. "Yes, Miss Lul. Mr. Wheeler. How many other low-life recreants you know?"

"For what reason? Why? Are you sure?"

"Put it however you want. Dismissed. Disemployed. Dejobbed. The short of it is, I no longer work for Wheeler Telephone Company."

"I don't know what you've done, Beatrice," said Miss Lul, "but roasting peanuts won't do. You're gonna have to make amends. Set the situation straight. He has no choice but to take you back."

"I've been fired, Miss Lul. Not crossed in love."

Miss Lul had several more utterances of disbelief, but Ina and Alta Ruth knew when to remain neutral. Ina stirred a spoon through her coffee without so much as a tinkle, and Alta Ruth plucked away at blueberries from a day-old flapjack and rearranged them into an upside-down smile.

Fortified with the anger of an upset hornet, Bertie hotfooted out of the kitchen. She carried the drawer up to her room and dropped it to a dull thud on the floor, then kicked her shoes into a corner and pulled the chair out from her vanity. She plunked herself down.

The best years of her femininity were spent in that dank dusty office giving service to this ungrateful community, giving them good memory and arms that were long enough to reach every line on the switchboard, working over when she would've rather been out with friends, hello-girling it when she didn't feel up to it. She was self-reliant, could handle any problem that came up. She had a clear voice and quick hands. She'd been the very heart of that place!

She let out an angry, nutcracking grunt.

The walls beneath her room's sloped ceiling consisted of a collage of calling cards and postcards, and letters still in their original envelopes. She snatched a handful of calling cards, pulled out her address book, and pored through every name of every person she'd ever met from attending canvassing suppers, mass meetings, conferences and conventions, and by participating in marches. Somebody would know of a position somewhere, don't think they wouldn't. When she finally settled on the name of a woman she'd met during a street speech, she took a sheet of stationery, her initials BAD welted and centered at the top, and began scribing a solicitous billet.

A reply came within a week. Word was that Alice Paul, head of the National Woman's Party, was in need of an assistant. This was better than anything Bertie could've imagined! The NWP was known for being warrior-like in its approach to the issues of suffrage, advocating the right for all women to vote. These were women who weren't afraid to fight. Quaker women. Women who'd been arrested. The perfect forum for somebody like her, an ideal opportunity to do something meaningful for the cause. There was still the issue of the colored vote needing attention and—Glory be! Now she was on a wise trail! She hadn't been able to make a difference on a local level in that stirring circumstance with Johnny Bob and Silvia. She didn't have the backing to see the situation through. A person has to start at the top if she wants to make things happen—in Washington, the D of C! She has to go where people change, exchange, and counterchange; she's got to be able to trade and switch, give as good as was sent, and all that mutual business. The only disadvantage she saw was she'd have to move there to do it. And what little money she made would have to go toward rent and other living expenses. Barely a smither would be left to send home for Miss Lul, and that was something she'd always prided herself on, that she was able to make a real contribution to the household, and see to it that Alta Ruth had all the advantages of other young girls her age despite having only one parent. But Washington, D.C.! To be surrounded by like-minded women, women working together for the same justification. That would be the ultimate swing around the circle! And executive secretary to the director of the NWP at that. Woo-whee! Wouldn't that be the cheese?

Making her usual cursory stop at the vanity, she sat down, took pen in hand and wrote a letter expressing her interest in the position.

Chapter 30

The Driving Lesson

*I*t was a Saturday morning over breakfast when Ina posed the question to Bertie.

"There's something I've been wanting to ask you. Now if the answer is no, that's fine. I just thought it might be a good time to ask, now that you're around more these days, and you have a little extra time on your hands, but I'll understand if you'd rather not, because I know that—"

"Out with it already! I'm no guessworker."

"I was wondering if you would teach me how to drive."

Bertie considered the proposition while drinking a cup of strong black coffee.

Ina further explained: "I was thinking that I might be in the market for an automobile, that is, if I can learn to drive one properly. It would make things handy if I ever needed to take the children on another outing."

"Sure," Bertie said. "I've got some time later this morning. We can do it then."

Ina had been sitting there conscience-smitten. She took a deep breath and broke into a smile the moment Bertie agreed.

At eleven A.M., bundled in hats and heavy coats, they met in front of the house where the Model T was parked along the curb. Bertie in a belted sport coat made of beaver fur that barely managed to cover her backside, and Ina in a full-length all-wool tricotine with large smoked-pearl buttons. The weather was spirit-stirring, brisk and piercing, and although the sun was out, Ina cradled her arms in an effort to keep from shaking.

"Now I know you're in the blush of enthusiasm," said Bertie. "I was, too, the first time. But there's more to motoring than just getting in and driving. Things like the radiator. It's got to have fresh water. And oil. You gotta make sure it's got plenty of oil. Don't do those things and you'll have a messload of problems down the road."

Ina nodded.

"Gasoline, too. Don't get fooled by some silly Ford song. You need to see that there's plenty in the tank. You won't get too far if there isn't. Also, you need to be especially concerned with the cooling system, otherwise known as the Thermo-Syphon System. Now, how it works is, the water has to heat up in order for it to circulate from the lower radiator pipe up through the water jackets, then into the upper tank, and back down again into the lower tank. And for that to happen, particularly in colder months such as this, you have to use a solution in the circulating system that won't freeze. That's what they call anti-freeze. Wood alcohol does the trick, too. It's simple, really." Seeing concern on Ina's face, she added, "Well, maybe we can go over these finer points later. Why don't you hop in and I'll give you a dry run, show you how to operate the controls. Then we'll crank her up and take her out for the real thing."

Ina stepped up into the vehicle, and bounced across to the driver side in childlike fashion. She wrapped her hands around the steering column. "One thing I've always been curious about is why there isn't a door on the driver side," she said.

"I reckon to keep the cost down," said Bertie. Not a matter worthy of serious consideration as far as she was concerned. "Now don't touch anything till I tell you to."

Ina dropped her hands to her lap.

"That's all right, I just meant don't touch the lever on the left. That's what sets the brake and the clutch." She then launched into the controls. She explained how the right foot pedal operates the brake, the left foot pedal operates the clutch; how the hand lever, when thrown forward, engages high speed, pulled back it operates the emergency brake, and set vertically between the two other settings is considered neutral. Once she figured that Ina had the basics down, she showed her how to crank the machine should the automatic starter ever fail.

They both stepped out and walked around to the front of the Ford.

"This is the part that'll take you some getting used to," Bertie said. "You gotta have enough strength in your arm, see, or you're liable to strain a muscle. Or in your case, break a bone. Especially if she kicks back and you don't get out of the way. A little practice, though, you'll get it down."

After Bertie gave the crank two firm pulls, the engine started. Then the two got back inside the vehicle, with Ina behind the wheel.

"What do I do now?" Ina asked.

"You'll want to go it easy, understand? First thing is to give her the gas by opening the throttle. Put your foot on the clutch pedal. No, no, the left one, that's your clutch. Good. Then throw the hand lever forward. Ea-sy, ea-sy. Okay, to start moving, just press the pedal into slow speed. Go ahead and do it, nobody's coming."

What she failed to mention to Ina was that taking her foot off the pedal would increase the speed, and as Ina began pulling the vehicle away from the curb, the excitement and confusion of being behind the actual wheel of a moving motorcar scared her. She withdrew her foot from the pedal giving the Model T a hefty swell of emotion. The vehicle spurted forward and barreled its passengers toward town.

"Go it easy!" cried Bertie.

Ina panicked. "What do I do? What do I do?"

"Put your foot on the pedal! Your foot on the pedal!"

Ina searched the floorboard. Her feet tried to find the pedals, but she couldn't remember what Bertie had told her, which pedal did what, and it wouldn't have mattered anyway because she was hemmed in at the ankles by a dark sea of fabric. And before she knew it, they were streaking by Mrs. Wheeler who was out walking Babette.

Dog and owner stopped and gave them a peculiar look.

"Oh!" Ina cried.

"Watch where you're going!" Bertie shouted.

Johnny Bob and his horse Thomas were coming from the opposite direction, the box wagon moving at a yawning pace. The Model T was headed straight for them.

"Gangway!" Bertie yelled.

Ina screamed and slapped her hands to her eyes. Bertie seized the wheel and jerked the car back into its legal lane. Too late. Before Johnny Bob knew what was happening, Thomas had pulled the reins hard to the right and veered the wagon toward the ditch. The back rear wheel sank into a rut, causing the wagon to shift and a load of potatoes to tumble out of the box.

Wriggling in her seat, Ina looked back. "Do you think he's okay?"

Bertie didn't wait for Ina to come to her senses. With one hand already gripping the wheel, she reached across and closed the throttle, finagled her legs over Ina's, placing one foot on the clutch, then the other on the brake.

The car came to a dead stop, and the two women were wrapped together like a loaf of braided bread. The bulk of Bertie was splayed on top of Ina, who, gasping for air, let out a little hiccup.

"This might be harder than I thought," said Bertie, wiping a squall of stray curls out of her eyes.

1921

Chapter 31

A Letter from the National Woman's Party

*I*t was the second week in January when Bertie received the letter she'd been waiting for. An official letter on official letterhead, an impressive cream wove, signed by a Lucy White, headquarters secretary of the National Woman's Party.

The letter stated that it was she, Miss White, who was in need of the assistant, not the director, but she hoped that Bertie would still be interested in traveling to the capital city for an interview. A basic formality, the letter stated, as Bertie's credentials were quite impressive. The organization still had important business to do in spite of the ratification. At present, they were in the process of planning a large ceremony in February to commemorate seventy-two years of woman's struggle and many caring hands and bright minds were needed. And they were formulating plans promulgated by Miss Paul for introducing another, even farther-reaching Constitutional amendment that will forever cement the concept of full equality for all citizens. Could she be there by Monday? They would secure her a room at a nearby hotel.

Hmm. Assistant to the headquarters secretary? Not exactly what she had been dreaming of, but not a bad place to start either. Especially in a city that didn't cultivate stupidity. Yes, ma'am, it was just like she'd thought all along—a person can't spend but so much time traveling a clouded road until finally the sun has just got to shine down on you!

Chapter 32

Ina Is Admonished for Her Snootiness

*T*he drawing room was softly lit. There was the floor lamp next to the Morris chair that Bertie was occupying, the supplement of two wall sconces, and the chandelier over the center table where Ina sat preparing her next day's lessons.

A light snow had begun to fall that evening, and but for the sound of a valve releasing steam coming from the marble fireplace, the house was quiet. Miss Lul was at a church meeting, and Alta Ruth had gone to bake cookies at a friend's house. It was a stilly hour in the Daye home.

Despite the counsel in her reference book, that a young teacher not expect to have as great an influence as a teacher with years of experience, Ina was encouraged by the improvements made in the classroom in the short time that she'd been there. Lately, when she called for order, the entire class became respectfully quiet, unlike in the beginning when one or two of the children (though more often it was three) constantly required reprimand. Even Henry had ceased with his usual prank of setting the clock forward. Boys especially, she had read, admire persons of a strong and robust statue. In any event, be it her stately form or her influential personality, she felt she had finally gained their confidence.

Normally she didn't bring home the children's seatwork (a teacher must apportion her time so she'll be bright and fresh for the next day), but this afternoon she had brought along the thread box that contained Etta's work material. Each of the children had a similar box for keeping their individual work separate, and at the end of each day Ina collected them. As she'd had an awakening interest in Etta, and as Etta was the only pupil who didn't outwardly long for the home-going hour, Ina was anxious to see how the little girl was coming along on her numbers. Today she had set Etta to bundling toothpicks in groups of ten with a rubber band to strengthen her skill in the use of figures. But time had run short and the school day ended before Ina could check on how well she was faring.

Seeing the contents of the thread box, Ina was disappointed. The work was less than first rank. The poor child had not grasped the number idea or its concrete representation. She'd had a growing concern that the little girl's home life was increasingly becoming a detriment to her lessons. Etta was always so rosy-cheeked, more than she should be, Ina felt, and her small youthful hands were already tempered by barn work. "Of what use is it for me to teach that child the likes of history when her mother has her milking cows and carrying wood," Ina mumbled. "And Lord knows what else."

She had only met Etta's mother on one occasion, on a day she had stopped at the Lester home after school to deliver Etta's forgotten lunch pail. From Ina's perspective, though Mrs. Lester was still considerably a young woman, her demeanor was that of a hardened scullery wench. She had been brusque, and Ina recalled how the woman had scrutinized her as they stood awkwardly on the porch after Mrs. Lester yelled over her shoulder and called through the screen door to Etta. "Quit burning daylight and get out here and get this pail!" Ina could see that the woman was up to and past the elbows in children: she had eight, including Etta, the others boys, and by Mrs. Lester's frozen grimace, and the way she held her arm over a protruding gingham waistband, another child was on the way.

A white cat, pure as milk, was standing off a corner of the porch, mewing. It jumped onto the porch, nearly missing its mark. "What a lovely cat," Ina had said.

"Like she would know it," Mrs. Lester had responded. "Dumb thing is blind. If it wasn't for Etta throwing such a fit over it, I'd have my husband take that worthless thing off somewhere."

"Diddy oughta take it out back and shoot it is what he oughta do," said one of the Lester sons, a tall skinny boy with mussed hair, coming around the corner.

"You hush up," Mrs. Lester had said to the boy. "If anybody needs taking out back it's you." She turned to Ina and shook her head. How grateful Ina had been when the door opened and out stepped Etta who timorously retrieved her lunch pail. Mrs. Lester must've noticed the look Etta gave to the cat, sitting in the yard as if considering its next move. "Don't even think about playing with that cat," the harried matron had said. "You got pigs to feed and a load of wash to hang out." It was a visit that had been distressing for Ina.

She set aside Etta's thread box now. "I simply don't understand it, that type of mentality. Absolutely deplorable! If that woman has no problem keeping her boys out of school to work a farm, why cannot her only daughter's chores be contained to the interior of the house? Work more suitable to a young girl, like setting the table or wiping the dishes? Or even sweeping the floor? She should be encouraging Etta to concentrate her mind on her studies, and for heaven's sake, urging her to routinely wash her teeth."

She felt herself burning with indignant displeasure, and half expected a reply from Bertie.

Bertie was listening, and not listening. She'd made an impression in Washington, as she was often wont to do when it came to making an impression. A natural-born NWPer, they could tell, and on the spot she was offered the job. In a matter of days she'd be heading back to the capital, just in time for the NWP's National Convention.

But for now she was catching up on lost reading, trying to concentrate on the latest issue of *The Woman's Cycle,* a monthly magazine that celebrated the domiciliated—all things homemade or homegrown, household tips, and recipes—that also housed a regular column called On the Subject of Women. It was this column, subtitled this month Women as Invaders, that Bertie was entrenched in. (Doesn't hurt for a suffragette to know what's brewing on the other side.) And right now Ina's mumblings were nothing but a source of irritation to her.

For the past week, Bertie had tried coaxing Ina into another driving lesson, insisting there weren't many opportunities left. But Ina either claimed fatigue or suggested they wait until the weather wasn't so cold. Her bon ton mentality was wearing thin on Bertie.

She would want to be conversational now, now that I'm up to my eye teeth in this noodlehead writer's claims, how women are bringing shame and disorder to the commercial world by taking jobs meant for men, and in the process causing salaries to be reduced.

"What a bunch of bull-hockey!"

"Pardon?" said Ina.

"Nothing. Article." She lifted the magazine in front of her face to indicate that she wasn't available for conversation—at least not the kind Ina would be interested in.

Yet Ina continued to talk (squawk). And the more she directed her words (gripes) to Bertie, the madder Bertie got.

". . . she's obviously ignorant of the term 'family limitation,' " said Ina.

Bertie tightened her jaw. You've got to be native-born to get away with talking down in the mouth about Person County folks that way, she thought, about our way of life here, like we're nothing but a bunch of ridge-running nitwits. She made a quick disposal of the magazine, plunging it to her lap, and began to rail.

"I swear, I think every one of you Blue Virginians think your scat ought to be bronzed!"

Ina was taken aback.

But Bertie wasn't finished:

"Just because you live in a Commonwealth and are choked with First Families and produce a dookie-load of apples! You know, Ina, ever since you came to town, you've done nothing but encourage yourself in snootiness. You have turned your nose up at everything and everybody around you. You act like we're a bunch of briar-hoppers."

"That's absurd!"

"The hell it is," said Bertie. "I don't have enough fingers or toes to count the times a flip remark has come out of that mouth of yours, about some-body or something another. And what makes it twice as bad is you don't even have the decency to say it to their faces. You wait till the door is shut and it's just me and you. For some reason you've decided I'm your second self. But let me just tell you: I ain't gonna be a sister-in-a-pinch for nobody, especially somebody who badmouths where I come from."

"I—I was simply stating a legitimate concern, Bertie. The children. You of all people should understand that. My duty, all along, has been to teach a good school. To help these children build their lives. Tell me, how can they learn anything of any value if their parents allow them—force them—to shovel dirt and plow fields?"

"Those fields are their lives, Ina!"

"But they don't have to be. No child, or woman for that matter, should be—"

Bertie's blood, on a normal day, had a tendency toward effervescence. But these days, since getting fired, every conversation had the potential of not only turning her into a soapbox orator, but of becoming a verbal contest of major proportion. She was irritable morning and night. Hence, difficult to live with. She knew where Ina was headed with the argument, and she im-mediately sat forward and prepared to spar.

"Should be what?" she said. "Getting their hands dirty? Making an honest living? Maybe you oughta tell that to Doodle."

"I think we're getting off the subject," Ina said. "I am speaking merely in terms of instilling interest in the parents, wanting them to take pride in the school and passing that enthusiasm on to their children. From what I've been able to discern, the school is in danger of retrograde—"

"Then quit quarreling with your bread and butter and do something about it," Bertie said. "Have you even considered coming up with a plan to improve any of the conditions? No. All I've heard you do since day one is rattle off one grievance after another. The school is for the pupils, not for the teacher. Not everything is about keeping up appearances. Most folks around here don't know, or care to know, that Richmond is home to the Virginia Historical Society, or that Virginia lays claim to Mount Vernon and Monticello. You think anybody gives a squat about all that pinkie-in-the-air junk? You better get wise to yourself—beyond your prevailing taste—if you plan on spreading your noble ideas to folks around here. Or, as you might otherwise refer to it, Teaching the Unteachable. You oughta think about others for a change, besides yourself."

As emotions will direct in these situations, Ina burst into tears. Bertie hadn't anticipated this. Even Guerine, the most sensitive person she knew, never resorted to crying. The second a tear appears, the sport is done for.

"Maybe you can't help the way you are," Bertie continued. "I imagine these are things that've probably been ingrained in you since childhood. We can't always help what we inherit. Some of us inherit strong wills while others of us inherit—different manners." Then, out of frustration, she picked up her magazine and retreated to her room, leaving Ina alone with her tears.

Chapter 33

The Baptism

$\mathcal{E}$motions ran the gamut in the Daye home during the week leading up to Bertie's departure.

Ina shrank into the background, still smarting from Bertie's bite.

Alta Ruth was all heart, impressing forcibly upon her older sister to leave behind a dollop of her almond face cream to tide her over till allowance, as she had recently discovered that it was known to clear the face of freckles.

Miss Lul was a hurry of temperaments, a series of unpredictable blusters. One minute she would blast Bertie with an angry tirade, the next she'd be using her sleeve to catch tears and telling her daughter how proud she was of her. She slept in intermittent fits. On the eve before Bertie's departure, however, she had come to the conclusion that what was wrought was wrought, that no amount of arguing would keep Bertie at home, and she would be doing herself a favor by helping her daughter pack. She was aided in this revelation by something she'd remembered finding amongst Brud's belongings years before. After retrieving the item from deep within her bureau, and a jar of her pickled Jerusalem artichokes from the kitchen cupboard, she carried each—one in her left hand, the other inside her right dress pocket—to Bertie's room. It may also be said that she carried with her an indulgent attitude.

The sun had gone down, and throughout the house could be heard the far-away sound of the Number Seven train as it headed toward Woodsdale. Miss Lul briskly climbed the stairs, her hair swept from her face into an unyielding bun, held in place by a half dozen straight hairpins and just as neat as when her day had begun.

She set the jar on Bertie's dresser. "Did you pack enough drawers? What about underskirts?"

"Plenty," said Bertie.

"You didn't forget your robe, did you?" she asked, and looked inside the gape-mouthed suitcase. "I wish I'd gone out and bought you a nice pajama set in spite of what you said."

"Nothing wrong with the ones I got," Bertie said, and went to the closet for more of her things.

Miss Lul began rearranging the contents of the case. "I don't know why I bothered to listen to you." She picked up the pair of folded pajamas and ran her hand across the material. "Just shy of ragged is what they are. Missing a button, even."

Bertie couldn't bother.

"Oh here, let's don't forget the pickles!"

"There ain't enough room for them, Miss Lul. Just leave them. Besides, they give me the hot vapors."

"A sunchoke doesn't care whether you've got room or not. This is a good spot for them right here." She considered slipping the other item from her pocket and hiding it among the clothes while Bertie's back was turned, but thought better of it. She sat down on the edge of the bed and sighed. If only she had prepared a speech.

"Beatrice."

"Miss Lul," Bertie called out, as if the two were playing a children's tag game.

"Come and sit with me for a minute."

But Bertie continued her search through the closet, flipping from one clothes hanger to another.

"Come—away—from—that—closet, Beatrice. Please!"

Bertie stopped and turned to look at Miss Lul. The deep lines across her forehead displayed a pattern of contrition, a look filled with pricks of conscience that was unfamiliar to Bertie, and she came over and sat down next to her mother.

"I knew it would be hard the day you left home," Miss Lul began. "I just didn't think you'd go so yonder."

"Mama—"

"Let me finish. You got to say your piece recently. It's only fitting that I get to say mine. And I want you to follow me carefully:

"A seed has two parents. Sometimes you plant that seed and it comes up different from what you might be expecting. With different characteristics and all. Sometimes it can run wild, be hard to control. Can have a different taste altogether." Miss Lul took a breath and dropped her shoulders. "I guess I'm not too good at this. The short of it is— What I'm trying to say is— You are Brud Daye's seed, but you're not. You're my seed. You are my seed, Beatrice, and you have proved it to me every day. Just look at you! You're on the path to righteousness." Miss Lul paused. She watched as Bertie picked imaginary lint from her skirt. Her silence said a lot. She had probably heard enough whispers over her shoulder, and Miss Lul felt that she didn't need to say any more about Brud than what she already had. It was a sad understanding between the two of them.

She reached into the pocket of her checked housedress and took from it a roll of money the size of a pint jar of preserves and placed it into Bertie's palm. "This was in with some of your father's things," she continued. "I've never touched it, as far as spending it goes. Would've returned it to the rightful owners a long time ago if I'd of known who they were. It's yours now. Because I know you'll do good things with it."

"That's a lot of money," said Bertie, staring at it blankly. "But I can't take this, Miss Lul. What about Alta Ruth? I'd rather this be used for her."

"I didn't say this was the all of it," Miss Lul said. She smiled and patted Bertie on the cheek, then stood. "Go on and finish with your packing. It's getting late and you've got a long day ahead of you."

At the bottom of the landing, Miss Lul stopped and urgently unwrapped a piece of Sweet Fern chewing gum.

"Lord give me strength 'cause I still have one more strong-willed daughter to rear!"

Chapter 34

Miss Lul at Odds

*W*ith Bertie having left the nest, what, besides raising Alta Ruth, was Lalura to do?

She'd been a widow since the fall of nineteen hundred and eight, after that fool of a husband of hers had managed to lose his head in that hunting accident. What kind of man would be crazy enough to wear a headdress that mimicked a turkey anyway? She believed he was rightly served (God doesn't take kindly to devils), although she never said as much to their children. To them he had been the pink of perfection, always up for giving piggyback rides at the end of a day, or bouncing them on his knees like a horsey, and she had allowed them their vision of what they believed their papa to be. In many ways it just seemed easier.

But in Lalura's eyes he was a conniving man with a gray heart. Not that he ever raised a hand to her. If he had she would've knocked him into next week, and could have too with any number of household items; the cast-iron bootjack he insisted on keeping in the entryway, or the tack hammer from his toolbox, or by simply whacking him upside the head with her sad iron trivet, which would've made a fine imprint of the "Dutch Girl" on his skull.

It was how Brud Daye treated the rest of the world that made Lalura come to despise him. He was a man who thought he was the above-and-beyond. To say he was a demagogue would be putting it mildly. He was a firebrand, a mischief-maker; a man who intimidated the weak and the feeble. He was a man who laughed at lightning.

She hadn't seen that side of him in the early days. His aggressiveness, she thought, was merely the sign of a man who wanted to make something of himself, and provide the best life he could for his family by seeing they had the biggest house, plentiful food, and the finest clothes. But not long into their marriage, Lalura realized that power was what Brud craved, and she began to suspect, though she had no proof, that his pushy nature went far beyond the simple act of collecting borrowed money.

There were nights he would leave home after dark, mumbling only that there was "some business to take care of." When he returned in the wee hours he would smell of smoke. And not the sort from a tavern, of cigars or cigarettes.

Curled on her side and pretending to be asleep, Lalura had visions of things decent people never dared utter. In her mind she could see a strangle-knot of rope worked onto the leafless limb of a tree, and if she listened real hard, she believed she could hear screams of agony. It made her nauseous to lie next to him.

One day, while in town at the milliner's, she overheard a disturbing conversation. She was in the back of the store with Miss Jessie, behind a curtain and seated at a mirror, being fitted for a new hat. Miss Jessie also worked from this room, and all around Lalura were wooden blocks and hat stretchers, seam press boards and pushpins, and every trim imaginable. A rainbow of veiling, horsehair, and ostrich plumes.

Miss Jessie had just returned from the northern markets where she'd bought her spring line. She had also used the occasion to "tie the nuptial knot," and she related the exciting events while making the final touches on Lalura's hat.

As Lalura playfully scolded her for not letting on earlier that she and Mr. King had been keeping company, the door opened and stunned the overhead bell, announcing to Miss Jessie she had customers.

Miss Jessie stuck her head out to say she'd be with them shortly.

"Don't worry with us, dear," said one of the ladies. "We're only treasuring today." Her friends let out a gay laugh.

With a thin curtain separating them, it was only natural that Lalura's and Miss Jessie's ears would perk upon hearing the words "I heard."

". . . said the two men were betting on who could throw the other down."

"What on earth for? Just to see who's the stronger man? How ridiculous."

"Well, from what I heard, that Brud Daye was the instigator. Pulled a gun on the Negro and had the gall to ask the sheriff to arrest him."

"I wasn't aware that Brud Daye had learned how to *ask* for anything."

Lalura was suddenly aware of Miss Jessie's fingers digging into her shoulders.

". . . and you didn't hear it from me, but you know good and well who's responsible for pulling that poor colored man out of jail. Calling him a lunatic and carrying him off to *the asylum*. How gullible do they think we are?"

Lalura imagined the women raising their eyebrows and passing knowing glances. Miss Jessie tried to keep her from leaving, but Lalura snatched the navy tulle from her head and threw it to the floor. The curtain billowed like a mainsail and Lalura flew past the women and out the door, tears blinding her all the way home.

That evening, she sent the girls over to her sister Maude's, which took a hefty amount of courage on her part, as her sister was often besieged by her obviously flammable mail-order tonic. She was coming down with something, she told Maude. Her head ached and her stomach felt galled. Whatever it was, looked to be shaping itself into a poignant sufferance.

Dinner was on the table when Brud arrived home. Lalura sat in the dining room and waited, listened as he worked his way out of his boots.

"Where are my little darlings?" he said, upon seeing only his wife at the table. She told him they were staying the night at her sister's.

He pulled his chair out and sat, and tucked his napkin over his collar. "Feeling under the weather, Miss Lul?"

"Disgusted."

"Yes? What's it today?" He began helping himself to soup. He dipped the broth from the tureen and ladled it into a bowl.

"You know, they say if you cut a baby's fingernails too soon he'll steal," she said.

Brud let out a guffaw. "Still believe in old wives' tales, do you?"

"Well, it makes one wonder, doesn't it, if something like that happened to you as a child. Maybe you were bitten by a snake. Maybe that's why you're a man of moral irresponsibilities."

"Woman, you're talking like a train hit you. Fix your plate now and let's eat."

"I'll tell you what I'm going to fix—"

"I don't like your tone, Miss Lul."

"I don't care!" She slapped the table, rattling the silverware, then stood and glowered at him. "I know what you do when you leave here at night, Brud Daye! And I want you to know it makes me sick! So many nights I have been on the verge of retching, the very image of you striking a match, hiding yourself behind a false face. I tell you this now: only because of the children will I stay, but don't you ever, ever touch me again. If you do, I will surely kill you." And she then whooshed from the room.

❊

Opening a boardinghouse was a natural transition for a widow with two children and no surviving family. For Lalura, it also allowed her to feel a closer connection to the community, being that Brud had never liked having company in the house.

After his death, she didn't waste time. She had the house wired for electric lights, opting for the more expensive G.E. Tungsten lamps—ninety-five cents for the frosted bulbs—instead of the cheaper sixteen-candle power Carbons which only cost twenty. (Didn't Brud always say "only the best"?) She smiled (no due given to whalebone pinching her ribs) the day she bent over and drove the sign into the yard: *Daye's Boardinghouse. An establishment owned and operated by Lalura Wise Daye.* And with glorious hibiscuses painted in the outer-most corners, too. What she had here, yes, ma'am, was a new *sublet* on life!

Chapter 35

Doodle Confronts a Brutal Winter

*T*he Shuford farm looked bleak during the long winter months. It had the appearance of want, a house in need of shoring up. Standing on the porch, or inside with your forehead pressed against the front window, you could look out and see a reach of sad-looking fields, as if a skeleton had arrived at the feast, and lift your head to an equally gloomy sky filled with dirty clouds that appeared to be smutched by cold coffee.

In spite of that, the homestead remained a place of tenderness; where her mama had cooked and cleaned, and mended the family's clothes with running stitches; where her papa had handed down a legacy of stories; and where life, in general, had been lived considerately and respectfully. For Doodle to be able to come inside now, in the shudder of January, and close the door behind her after another day of near backbreaking work, was like rubbing a soothing balm over her soul. If she closed her eyes and tried real hard she could warm her nose to her mama's fried apple pies, and hear her papa's catching laughter.

Gathering eggs earlier that morning, Doodle had noticed a crack in the hen house door. The wood had begun to check, and if left to split and separate would eventually expose her earnest hens to the bad weather and worse intruders with fur and tail. She spent the better part of the morning making the repair, and continued till the job was done even after a blinding snow began to fall.

Rural living had a forehand over town living in that regard, especially during a snowstorm. Country folk simply got on to the next chore. For townsfolk it was more of a trial, and Doodle didn't envy them in the least.

Snow had to be cleared from the streets to accommodate every kind of conveyance before regular business could commence, shoveled off the walks for every paw, pad, and pud, making the day that much longer. If the door to your fowl house needs patching, then you simply put on your shawl-collar sweater coat, pull a wool hat down over your ears, buckle on a pair of round-toed arctics, and trudge outside through snow calf-deep and set to work. Same as she had done.

But by mid-afternoon a rise in the temperature came and with it freezing rain, a reliable downpour that pocked the snow-covered ground and washed away patches until the surrounding fields resembled a worn and balding carpet, relegating the rest of her day's labor to the inside of the house.

She collected the starched laundry that had sat untouched in a basket for several days (other tasks had taken precedence), set the ironing board up in the kitchen where she could hug the stove, and adjusted the board to its lowest height. While the iron was heating, she opened the back door for Bugle who was scratching to be let inside. That dog had his own daily schedule. Every morning he would wake up happy, be quick to his feet and stretch, then look up at her and wag his tail as if to say, "Hot diggety! Another day! I hope I get the whole thing." He padded over to a good spot and relaxed into a soft puddle, and gave a self-congratulatory groan before nodding off to another sleep.

The shorter days filled the house with a palpable darkness and made it necessary to work by lamplight. When the iron was hot enough to gloss the starched fabric, Doodle pressed the right side of each article in a slow deliberate rhythm till every pucker had vanished and she could feel the silkiness of the starch between her fingers. Her neatly pressed efforts pleased her. A good time for contemplation.

Other than calling on Miss Cara Sue, she had done her best to avoid social contact of late. It was strange how she had been a hype of overactivity in the weeks soon after her papa died—the rare indulgence of a Saturday evening picture show, in spite of feelings of guilt whenever around Bertie, and later attending Guerine's Halloween party like a deprived child, for instance. It was a need to follow up work with waggery, as if fun were a mystery she had never been privy to. But that extreme mood had dwindled shortly after unburdening herself to Bertie, and she had since kept her focus strictly on the farm, a distance from town. And now Bertie had up and moved to Washington, D.C., practically on a minute's notice, and Doodle wasn't sure how to feel about that. She wished they'd had more time together before Bertie took off. It was unsettling in many ways, and a letdown for sure, barely getting adjusted to this new path their friendship was on and they'd hardly made a groove in it. She had gotten a postcard from Bertie, a greeting surely welcomed, but one how-de-do postcard does not a confident friend always make. In some ways, she supposed, her fate and Bertie's had been decided for them.

Her papa's tobacco field was another source of anxiety. She was considering ceasing its small production altogether. What vegetables the garden yielded would be more than enough to put food on the table and the surplus, along with her regular sale of eggs, would allow her a small income. It didn't make sense to create more work for oneself than necessary. And if someone at the Extension Service would get smart and organize a market closer by she wouldn't even have to go into town for provisions at all. The only reason it hadn't been done, she figured, was because the road in that stretch of county was yet to be hard surfaced. Still, she could mention it at the next field meeting, although the purpose of those meetings was to demonstrate new methods to local farmers looking to out-yield, and she was looking to scale back. Maybe the farm agent would be willing to suggest a better use of her acreage? Lespedeza made good cover for quail, and quail were cheery and ate bugs out of the garden, but she couldn't be sure just how polite Bugle was willing to be.

She finished the ironing and returned the board to its nook in the pantry, then took a pot of leftover navy beans from the icebox. After a paltry supper of beans and a dollop of apple butter on a warmed-over biscuit, she stood at the kitchen window and washed dishes. The moon illuminated the crystals that had formed along the edge of the barn roof, and every branch and twig was bent by the burthen of ice-beads.

At three A.M., she was awakened by a crash that rattled the windows and set Bugle into a fury of barking on the floor beside her.

She sat up and looked around the dark room, searching her mind for the cause of the deafening sound. An explosion? A muzzle-loader blast? A runaway millstone? Or were those silly figments from an unsettling dream?

"Bugle, hush! I'm trying to see what I can hear." He cocked his ears peculiar.

Did it come from the barn? she wondered. Drucie! Louise! She threw back the quilts, slipped off the mattress and into the boots at the foot of the bed. Not bothering to change out of her nightgown or buckle her shoes, she scuttled over to the door and snatched her coat from the peg. Bugle shot out ahead of her when she opened the bedroom door, ready to earn his keep.

But when she reached the central part of the house, the scene before her made her want to drop to her knees and cry: the top half of a pine tree lodged between roof and floor, and strewn throughout the room were pine needles and pine cones and the dead leaves that had been carried in with it, and enough snow and ice to fill a canoe.

"Come in here and make a mess of my house, you see if I don't burn every last chunk of you."

⁂

"That oil cloth was a good idea," Colon said, standing at the bottom of the ladder that was braced against the side of the house. "Least till you could get some help removing that tree. Boy, oh boy, I bet the sound alone was enough to rouse you up."

"Like a china cabinet crashing through the ceiling."

Colon craned his neck toward the roof.

The circumstance unequivocally called for a two-person cross-cut saw, but the last thing Doodle had wanted was to ask him for any help. What if he took her for some sort of temptress, or thought that he had taken her fancy and she was trying to use the opportunity to give him the draw-on? Good thing it was him who did the offering, seeing the damage as he had from the road. She knew better than to question the value of a gift, but there was a part of her that wondered about his motives, too. Seemed that he had made himself a curious fixture around here ever since her papa died. And then almost suddenly, as if the cold air had jarred loose a forgotten memory, it occurred to her that he might've surmised her papa's dying declaration: *If my daughter Delores should die without issue surviving her, then the land herein devised to her shall go to the only son of Broadie Clayton.* Well, she'd just see about that. Fine, if all Broadie Clayton's boy wanted was to be neighborly and help out in a time of distress, but she didn't have any plans to go dying, and if she did she'd go kicking and hollering before she handed this land over to anybody!

"Tinner snips and a peining hammer," said Colon, rummaging through a toolbox he now squatted over. "That's good, we'll definitely need them."

"I'd appreciate if you wouldn't get too comfortable with my toolbox," Doodle said, reaching over and sliding the box closer to herself. "I have everything organized, and if you go messing with my arrangement it will make it that much harder for me."

"Beg your pardon," said Colon. "Just wanted to be sure we have what we need."

"All's that's needed is to get that tree off the house, then remove that bad section of tin, splice in rafters with straight-on two-by-fours, and put a new sheet of tin on. And it's me, what I need, not we." She thought she detected a smirk on Colon's face as he stood, but he was quick to turn his back and retrieve the saw.

They sawed at sections of the tree for hours without taking a break. Colon was, it seemed to Doodle, a whirligig of energy. When he asked if she needed a rest, stubbornness caused her to refuse—she didn't want him thinking she was soft and slimsy. But she was cold and tired-armed, and after having set to work at three o'clock that morning, pushing pailfuls of water out the front door with the barn broom, and mopping up the remainder, then spending more than a full hour hauling away what she could of the pine tree from inside, she felt as weak as a wet bee.

Once the tree was removed, it was agreed that she would go to the lumberyard in town while Colon stayed behind and removed the fouled-up metal. The more they could get done to the roof before nightfall, the better.

She hitched Drucie to the buckboard and set out for town, but when she arrived at Roxboro Lumber she was confounded by an outstanding debt.

"Ninety dollars? I don't have ninety dollars."

"If it was up to me, Miss Shuford, wouldn't be no problem," said Mr. Barnett. "But, as you well know, Mr. Wheeler's the one in the saddle around here, and he's given me strict instruction: no more credit."

"There's a hole in my roof that looks like Goliath put his fist through it. I gotta have those supplies, Mr. Barnett."

"I'm sorry as I can be. I always admired your papa, ma'am, good man that he was. And in that regard"—Mr. Barnett began to falter—"I expect I owe you at least this much. You see, you ain't the only one. Other folks owe well over your amount. I'm telling you 'cause I suspect Mr. Wheeler's intentions are—"

"To foreclose on my property?" she said, believing she was finishing his sentence. "Can he do that?"

"Well now, I don't know nothing about that. All's I heard was him mumbling something about filing a claim at the courthouse. But I hope you won't go repeating 'cause really, Miss Shuford, I don't know no specifics."

Doodle felt as if she'd been hobbled. She rode back to the farm, dazed, without the necessary supplies, no eight-foot-long two-by-fours, no roll of tin roofing, or the barbed nails and roofing caps, just a useless stick of My-Te-Good Leak Mender that Mr. Barnett slipped her, presumably to assuage his guilt, but as far as she was concerned only added insult to the injury.

The whole situation was out of her reckoning. How could this be happening? Where was she going to get ninety dollars? Mr. Wheeler knew she didn't have that kind of money. And what right did he have to try and take her farm away from her?

As she neared the house she could see Colon on the roof. He appeared to be making head against a stubborn strip of tin. Just look at him, though, sitting up on that roof like he owned it! Made her blood want to boil. She gee'd Drucie and hurried toward the house.

"That was a quick trip," Colon hollered down to her. "Don't tell me Mr. Barnett's out of stock?"

She jumped from the buckboard and commenced to yelling and pointing. "I want you down from there! Right now!"

"But I haven't gotten that last piece of—"

"And you ain't going to either. In fact, you ain't getting this farm at all."

"Huh?"

"Didn't you hear me? I said, 'Get down!' I want you off this property. Now!"

Colon came off the roof and climbed down the ladder.

"Here, here's your coat," she said. "You can go put your charm on somebody else."

"My what? I don't know what's got into you, but you got to be the most mulish woman I ever met." He snatched his jacket and walked to his motorcycle shaking his head. "Pure-tee cast iron."

Doodle ran over to the buckboard, snatched up the tube of leak mender, and flung it at Colon as he sputtered off down the road.

Chapter 36

A Creative Vocation

_T_he opportunity had presented itself in the form of an advertisement in the back of a spent copy of _Motion Picture_ magazine. It was the bold lettering that caught Doodle's eye first:

WILL YOU TRY
THIS TEST FOR CREATIVE IMAGINATION
--BECAUSE IT'S INTERESTING,
PROFITABLE, AND
WITHOUT COST TO YOU?

Profitable and _without cost_ were the second thing.

She sat on a rag rug in front of the fire, her knees bent and feet tucked inside her flannel nightgown, the magazine pickaback on her lap.

Guerine had passed the used magazine on to her—like she did with all her secondhands—and Doodle, habitually embarrassed by Guerine's philanthropic display, but not wanting to appear ungrateful, always took them. If there was an article of clothing or an item she couldn't use, then Miss Cara Sue certainly could. Any movie magazines, though, she would keep for herself.

She had a quiet admiration for silent film actresses and found solace in Sunday matinees. Her bedroom walls were covered in hundreds of photogravures torn from Guerine's reach-me-down magazines. Mildred Harris, Catherine Calvert, and Lucy Cotton were among the untold number of angelic faces tacked from ceiling to floor. She secretly fancied herself most like Ann May, a tiny actress with large brown eyes, though Doodle considered her own features more along the lines of pale, not the least bit suited for silversheet dramas.

Her only witness to this rare moment of relaxation was Bugle. He was curled up and impartial on his bedding, an ivory spread with chenille tufting that she had taken from her papa's room and bundled on the floor for him. Laying on those hobnailed loops of yarn seemed a comfort to the hound, and every now and again, when Doodle would rustle a leaf of the magazine, or the wind would blow across the canvas that covered the hole on the roof, he would open his eyes with effort and blink sleepily at her.

She was still getting over a mild grippe that had seized her shortly after the incident with the tree, and tried not to feel as guilty reading nonsensical items as she normally would have.

No wonder why Guerine was so concerned with appearance. Nearly every other page had advertisements offering cosmetic treatments: a special *You Have a Beautiful Face—But Your Nose* soap for reducing conspicuous nose pores; a painless and harmless beauty preparation for hair removal that promised no electricity, whatsoever, simply ZIP superfluous hair right off—*It's Off Because It's Out*; and a beautifier for the face called a Vacuum Cup Device that resembled the rubber teat on a baby bottle, guaranteed to tighten flabby flesh and rid the face of frown furrows so long as one could commit to a few minutes of daily sucking.

The beauty advertisements were of little interest to her, amusing mostly, but she wouldn't have been opposed to trying a four-ounce bottle of Liquid Arvon if what it claimed was true, that it could, in as little as three applications, remove the scalp of dandruff. She scratched the back of her head and continued reading. Three dollars? Maybe a compound of sulfur and lard did make a smelly greasy mess, but it worked wonders for itchy skin and was as cheap as they come—a five-pound pail lasting from womb to tomb.

It was only when a log rolled off the grate in the fireplace and made a cachuck that Doodle quit with the scratching and prepared to toss the periodical aside. That was when the announcement caught her attention.

She read further, spelling over the advertisement carefully:

If you have the qualification of creative imagination, you should try your hand at learning to write photoplays. Find out if you are qualified. You will never regret that you took action to do so. There is a great field for new writers—a great demand for new plays. Producers pay from $250 to $2000 for "unknown writers'" first work, if good enough.

Writing for the moving picture industry by correspondence, she pondered. She could be another Peggy Fletcher, the woman pictured in the inset sketch, whose story "The Western Gate" had recently been sold for a feature production. All she had to do was fill out the coupon below and send it off to the Palmer Photoplay Corporation in Los Angeles, California, and in return she would receive the *Palmer Home Study Plan* that would teach her everything she needed to know to obtain the benefits of photoplay writing.

Well, why not? Why couldn't she do this? Why *shouldn't* she do this? Cecil B. DeMille himself was on the advisory council, and the advertisement said it was absolutely without charge to her, and that all correspondence was strictly confidential. She could try her hand at photoplay writing without anyone the wiser. If she found that she didn't have *Latent Creative Ability* or *Dramatic Insight*, so be it. No harm, no foul. (Her mind naturally took her to chickens.) But if she did? Two hundred dollars would sure feed a lot of geese. She could write in the evenings, after her chores were done.

She filled in her name and address, folded the coupon along the dotted lines, and rubbed her thumbnail back and forth across the crease, then tore off the coupon and slipped it into an envelope.

She thought the photoplay book would never come. One week, two weeks, and a sweep of days beyond that passed, till at last a bulky package arrived. It had been that and longer since she'd seen Colon, and it occurred to her, on the day she retrieved the package from the mailbox, the sender's address would've fallen under his notice, and maybe even engaged his thoughts long after he had delivered it.

She whanged the mailbox shut and walked up the hill with the package.

For several evenings she studied the material. Then late one night, an idea finally came to her. She sat at the table with a pen and paper and began to write, hurriedly but neat, afraid of forgetting details:

Carolina Hell Cat

Synopsis–

After the death of her father, Ruthie Humphries, a young country girl, is left all alone to tend to her family's tobacco farm. She is loved by Oscar Hawks, a neighboring one-armed sweet potato farmer. But believing that all men have but one agenda–to possess her and her property–she rebuffs him repeatedly.

While in town one day, at the grocer's, Ruthie learns that the proprietor–a money-grubber named

Dugan Steele who also owns the telephone company–plans to collect on her family's $300 debt by filing a claim at the courthouse. Knowing that she doesn't have the money, his plan will force her into foreclosure so that he can claim her farm.

When the bank comes to foreclose, Ruthie puts up a dramatic fight and proves that she is a veritable hell cat. The sheriff and his posse, however, come and carry her flailing and wailing off the property.

On the way to see his newly acquired tract of land, a grinning Dugan Steele is confronted by Oscar Hawks who runs out into the middle of the road and covers Steele with a shotgun. Steele brings his motorcar to a quick halt. But before Hawks can approach further, his sole intention to have a man-to-man talk with Steele, Ruthie springs up behind a rock and sails a butcher knife through the window of the vehicle. Steele clutches at his chest, gasps for air, then topples over and dies.

Doodle stopped writing. She laid the pen down and massaged her temple, then read fully what she had just written. On a second read, she scratched through the word *one-armed*. Too obvious a character flaw. It needed to be more subtle, something that wasn't quite so hokey. By now, it had occurred to her that her male characters were either dead, maimed, or intent on evil doing. She grinned, steadied her pen, and wrote in *one-armed* again. Under *sweet potato* she drew a line, wrote the word *pig* above it then immediately scratched through that and wrote *hog producer* with a ?. Not a problem, she would decide Oscar Hawks' occupation later. She drew a line through *money-grubber* and replaced it with *financial tyrant*. And reaching the part where the sheriff and his posse carry Ruthie *flailing and wailing*, Doodle determined that rhyming would be a sure sign of an amateur to a Hollywood producer. Kicking and screaming? Hooping and hollering? No. But that was fine, she would figure that out later, too. Point was, she was thinking.

Chapter 37

Colon's Conversation with Mr. Wheeler

Colon entered Mr. Wheeler's office.

"Afternoon, young man," said Mr. Wheeler. "To what do I owe the pleasure?"

"I was hoping if I might have a word with you concerning the Shuford property."

Mr. Wheeler, who was marking in an open ledger, stopped and looked up. "My time is very valuable. Am I supposed to know what this is about?"

"With all due disrespect, Mr. Wheeler, I believe you know very well what I'm talking about. That farm is the only thing in this world that gal's got. It's the only home she's ever known, and here you want to go and take it away from her. That just don't seem right to me. And beings you've known the Shufords for years and knowing how honorable they are, that by itself ought to induce you to stop with these proceedings."

Mr. Wheeler reared his back against the chair. "Friendship is one thing, son. Business is another. I can't help that that girl's family left her with a debt she can't pay. We all have to be accountable." He leaned forward and resumed his work.

"That's a shame. I was hoping we could come to an agreement," said Colon. "Reckon then you leave me with no other choice." And he went out the same door he came in.

Colon didn't know what it was exactly he was intending to do, but that "no other choice" business sounded like a good line at the time.

Chapter 38

Ina's Spring Awakening

At last, a morning when her feet didn't feel quite so cold. A glorious mallow-pink sun streamed in through the tall window, inched its way along the hardwood floor and up onto the canopied bed. While she slept it had snailed itself across her tenuous toes, over her well-turned ankles, up the full length of her serpentine legs, so delicate and graceful they were, like the turnings on a satinwood étagère, until her entire body was elongated in light. It was March. It was becoming pink chemise weather. Time for her to shed her heavy bedclothes and step from her long-sleeved flannelette cocoon.

She reached for the pocket watch on the nightstand and opened its cover. Even with the crystal broken it still kept precise time; the hands matched the same points as the porcelain clock on the bedroom's fireplace mantel. Six thirty-eight. Harlan once told her that it was a watch strong enough to be stepped on by the weight of an ordinary man and not break. She closed the lid and ran her fingers across the cold finish, then placed it back on the bedside table. She should be getting ready for school. Instead, she laid her head back against the pillow and mused on the feeble sounds coming from downstairs. Such a big house for only three women. And in the winter? *Le froid et calme.*

Despite her sister's urging that she should be with family at Christmas, Ina had chosen to remain in Roxboro the winter long. Her fear was that if she returned home to Virginia, even for a brief respite, she'd be filled with too many misgivings to resume her teaching post after the holidays.

And there was another reason that factored into her decision not to go home for Christmas. She was still imbued with anger at her parents for sending her off to Sunset Mountain the winter before to recover from her loss. It was the most crucial time in her life, a time when they should have been "weeping with her who weeps," and their insistence that she find solace singly she associated with parental abandonment. She was certain her mother would cry when learning of her resolve to remain in North Carolina, an image that caused her to feel a certain amount of ambivalence. But certainly her mother's tears could not compare to the torrent she had shed over the past fifteen months.

Whatever amount of salinity stained Mrs. Fitzhugh's cheeks, she saw to it that Ina wasn't without thoughtful offerings from home. She sent her a white pine crate so bulky that Johnny Bob and Thomas had to be sent to the post office to fetch it, an unwieldy parcel that took a solid steel pinch-point crow bar to pry it open.

Lying on top of the contents—an embarrassing abundance of her mother's excessive holiday shopping—was a gold-trimmed Christmas card with a winter scene, a majestic male cardinal nestled in a generous sprig of mistletoe, and inside the card a letter:

Thursday eve
Dec 16th 1920

My dear Ina,

I know you think I don't love you or I would have written long before now. Not so. I love you just the same as if I were to write you every day. Certainly miss you. Will be glad when you get your visit out and get home. Think it is so nice of Mrs. Daye to provide you with comforts and conveniences during your stay in their little village.

Everything is nearly the same as when you left. Lucia performed Charles Ives' Concord Sonata in church last Sunday. A little too eccentric for your father's taste, but nevertheless, you would have been so proud. Aunt Priscilla insisted that the evening dress Lucia wore was wool serge, when anyone could clearly see from that distance that it was a stunning quality of mohair Sicilian. Your father and I took her to have her eye glasses changed.

The rest of the letter described the contents of the crate. The cakes and candies, and, oh yes, the pastries! were to be shared and enjoyed at once, but the gifts to be placed under the tree. The Dayes did have a tree, did they not? And please assure her that it had not been flocked with spray-on varnish and cornstarch! Did she recall the Chas Montagues doing that very thing two years before and nearly burning down their house? Father was finally over his wariness of electric lights and would you believe has strung a faint scant strand. She ended the letter with a sentiment of having much love for Ina.

After Alta Ruth and Bertie had had a tiff over the hand-cut ribbon candy and the tin of peppermint cookies, the remaining non-edibles were placed under the tree in the parlor where, on Christmas Eve, the four of them sat and opened them.

For Mrs. Daye there was a set of pink- and blue-checked linen napkins.

For Alta Ruth, a handsomely bound set of Charlotte Yonge books with silk ribbon markers. *Nice* literature for a girl of nearly twelve.

And for Bertie, a bird in flight on a gold-filled brooch, a gift she took great delight in. "Yessiree, I like your mother," she had said, holding it up to the light before sticking the pin through the lace on her collar. "Not only is she generous, but she's also clever."

"You be sure and tell her that when you write her a thank you," Mrs. Daye said. "That goes for you, too, Alta Ruth. You girls are lucky to be getting more than a nickel and a pencil this year."

Ina wondered if Mrs. Daye was bothered by the extravagance of the gifts. Perhaps it bordered on insult to her, since she was unable to provide such things for her own children, but if so, Ina was unable to discern by her tone. Mrs. Daye didn't seem to be the type of woman to study and ruminate, the way she was always bustling about, full of energy, as nervous as a new broom.

It had been a simple holiday, primitive compared to what she was accustomed to, quaint, but one she would fondly remember; in the afternoon she and Bertie drove out to the farm to visit with Delores and take her a jar of Miss Lul's fig preserves; in the evening Alta Ruth taught her a hand-clapping game at the kitchen table as Bertie roasted peanuts; and on New Year's Day, when Guerine had come by with a generous sampling of her Glorified Excelsior Soup, eager for a taster but more for praise. Ina had taken a spoonful to appease her, but before realizing what she was saying had slapped a hand to her chest and spouted *Il goute pourrit comme le vinaigre!*, and Guerine, none the wiser, had accepted Ina's exclamation as the kindest, most gracious compliment anyone had ever given her. (And it would've been if her soup were in fact brine for dill pickles.)

But now it was March, and ever since the middle of January, when Bertie boarded and waved from a train bound for Washington, then wired home for the rest of her things, Ina had isolated herself, just as she had done after Harlan died. On more than one occasion, Guerine had invited her to dinner, but Guerine had a clubbable mentality and Ina desired to be far from any frenzy. In the evenings, she would withdraw to her room to read and plan lessons, but once there the grayness of winter deeply affected her and she would sulk. It was the mind, she knew, tricking her into a desperate feeling of homelessness.

She found that she missed Bertie. No one was more surprised of this than herself. She missed the energy that Bertie brought to a room, even her gruff demeanor, the manner in which she always had to be right. Their friendship had been swift, and now that Bertie was gone Ina had come to think of her in a different light. You could look at Bertie and tell she valued herself as an individual and not merely a member of the inferior sex. She was developing her mind. She was educating herself. And she wasn't willing to be held in a position of subjection by anyone.

And Ina was coming to admire this. She was beginning to feel more hopeful now. A sense that there was a purpose, a reason for her to be here. It was more than earning a salary, more than personal ambition.

After weeks of being "tried" by the pupils, she now felt more settled in her role at East Roxboro School. Granted, it had taken more than just a little enthusiasm and hard work. And another period of adjustment after the harvest was done and her classroom size doubled. She had been completely inexperienced at the start of the term and had thought only of herself. How will this help me? Will I become a better, stronger person for coming? Not, will I be a good influence on the children? Or, will I be able to inspire them to higher ambitions? But, subtly, that had changed. The children were learning from her, she could see that now, but just as importantly, she was certain, she was learning from them.

The thought made her spring from the bed, smiling.

After a quick breakfast of poached eggs and plum cake, she and Alta Ruth set out walking to the schoolhouse. Something akin to joy rose in Ina's breast. She took buoyant strides along Main Street as Alta Ruth tripped alongside her, trying to keep up. Tiny lavender and white crocuses had opened at the edge of one lawn, and crowded patches of buttercups in another.

As they turned the corner at Mill Creek, what had been a snow-slicked, muddy country road was now a dry and unyielding obstacle course with tracks made by equine hooves and automobile tires firmly fixed in the clay. Ina's gaze wandered to the stretch of woods on the crooked road. No flowers as of yet on the maples, and it would be a few more weeks she supposed before the dogwoods and redbuds blossomed. The contrast, when compared to Main Street, was stark.

"Strange how it still looks like winter along this stretch," Ina said, "yet it's as warm as a spring day."

"Good hide-and-seek weather," Alta Ruth said. "The boys'll want to play field ball at recess."

Ina unfastened the belt to her sweater coat and wrested her arms from the sleeves, while Alta Ruth offered assistance by holding her school bag, a hemp shoulder bag with a leather strap that doubled for vanity and utility. It contained the book Miss Duncan left behind, *The Rural School*, which Ina referred to daily, and a small blank notebook for jotting notes to herself, a dull lead Faber, a forgotten piece of hard candy wrapped in colored foil, a brown shell hair comb, and a silver compact with mirror and powder puff.

"This would be a perfect day for working out of doors."

"Doing lessons outside?" Alta Ruth asked.

"I was thinking more of beautifying the grounds," said Ina. "Some weeding and raking, that sort of thing. Those paulownia trees have littered the entire yard with their mammoth leaves. Just look at how unsightly. *C'est si epouvantable!*"

They were within sight of the laggard little schoolhouse now. No bigger than a box car, and with the addition of the pupils who had come after harvest, Ina felt as if she couldn't catch her breath some days, and she would get up from her desk and open a window. The pupils had to double up at desks. And the blackboard, for goodness sake, wasn't even real slate. Perhaps the only good she could say is the location was convenient, accessible to all the children. And the land it sat on, next to an acre stand of pine trees, near the crossroads of Main and Mill Creek, appeared to be well drained. But there wasn't much in the way of green, unless one considered the overgrown weeds; no lawn, no shrubs, no colorful flowers. The ground was desolate, with not a sidewalk to step on.

Not one thing has been done since I arrived, she thought. Someone has to take the initiative. That alone is a lesson in itself, and she smiled at her own notion. What an excellent opportunity for the children! Everything she had read (some pages were committed to memory) said that pupils need lessons in responsibility and cooperation. Giving them a chore to be in charge of teaches them to look at right and wrong and to change their own behavior accordingly. She was delighted with herself. She'd made a decision without consult.

The children were less than delighted. That housekeeping could be fun took ardent prodding to convince them. She expected resistance from the boys, but it was Victoria who came close to throwing a tantrum, so offended she was that Miss Fitzhugh would ask her to wrap her hand around a rake. Especially when she was dressed of such merit!

"Why, Victoria, I've seen you play jack rocks in similar frocks," said Ina. "And I can assure you that isn't the most sanitary of games, scooping up dirty round rocks from a filthy, germy floor." Which led Victoria to present another option: if Miss Fitzhugh would elect her to be in charge of sweeping the schoolroom instead, she would see to it that it was clean enough to eat from. Ina allowed herself to be swayed. The inside was even less inviting than the outside. It had continued to smell as musty as the first day she had opened the door, and the warmer days to come would only aggravate the situation.

After a morning session of music and songs—something lively to imbue them with the spirit—she and the children went to work. Their minds would be sharper at that early hour, she knew, and better able to handle the tasks at hand. The girls focused their energy on cleaning the inside of the schoolroom, and the boys focused theirs on the school grounds. Ina was skillful in her management of each pupil and divided her time between the inside and outside, like a player in a game of "anty-over;" she drew a bucket of fresh water and helped Etta and Adele get a start on wiping down all the desks; showed Victoria how to sweep without stirring up so much dust; helped Henry collect the trash to be burned; and assisted Alta Ruth in removing books from the shelves. Each task she undertook with an earnest determination.

By afternoon, a wave of fatigue washed over her and she felt faint. She was helping one of the twins—she thought it was Dolian but David corrected her—tidy the wood rack along the side of the house, after having just helped Lloyd and two of the new pupils rake up the last of the leaves. The last time she had done such strenuous work was on her wedding day when she wore seventy-two inches of scabious bridal veil with waxed buds and blossoms. For hours she had been involved in an action operation of trying to maneuver underneath its graceful train so as not to step on it and tear it. Why, even then she had nearly fainted!

She felt her way to a nearby tree stump and sat down, pressing a hand to her forehead. "Blessed candles of the night!"

"Are you all right, Miss Fitzhugh?" David asked. "Somebody, quick! Go get Teacher some water!"

Upon seeing her teacher's weakened state, Etta began to cry.

"Quit crying, you big baby," said Henry. "She's just conked out is all. Ain't you never seen a baptism?"

The rest of the children gathered round the tree stump, all armed with curiosity and some with cups of water, and waited for their schoolma'am to recover her nervous system. Happy is the teacher who comes to and sees that her pupils have been led to self-control.

After she had regained a generous supply of vigor and grace, Ina went about attending to Etta whose face she noticed was streaked with tears. She assured the child she was fine and, at four o'clock, at the end of a full day of fighting flies and dust, she sent her and the rest of the children home in good humor.

She stood in the schoolyard and looked around at their warm work. No longer did the little house look the picture of desuetude. The wild grasses that had grown along the sides of the house the previous summer and left to dry to thick bristly patches had been pulled, vines had been pruned, and the yard swept.

But still, she thought, there needed to be some type of ornamentation, something to gratify the eyes. Perhaps they could fashion window boxes out of wire hens' nests and plant them with geraniums. And dig a hole or two in the most unsightly areas and plant fruit trees, or native shrubs. It stood to reason that if she was going to insist the children pay homage to "The Brave Old Oak" during their morning musicale, then they should plant a brave young one of those, too. Not tomorrow, and probably not the next, but soon, very soon.

She went inside to collect her belongings. She draped her sweater over her arm, locked the door to the schoolhouse, and started for the Daye home. As she approached the Loftis property, Guerine came hurriedly out the front door.

"Ina! Yoo-hoo!" She stepped down from the porch like someone trying to dodge fallen hickory nuts, and made a short cut through the lawn to Ina. "I saw Alta Ruth earlier and she said you were still at the school."

"I stayed behind to do a few last-minute things. The children and I spent the day—"

"That's very nice, but I have some wonderful news that involves you!"

Whatever it was Ina couldn't imagine. But she was in a self-glorious mood herself and happy to be party to Guerine's elation. "By all means then, share."

"I am hostessing my very first dinner party," said Guerine, barely able to contain herself, "and you're invited. And it's not going to be anything like that silly Halloween party either. This is going to be the real thing, a sophisticated social affair. But I'm keeping it small, mind you, cozy, not like one of those cocktail smokers where people mingle with all kinds of shoulders. Those are too too icky. This is going to be very ah-teet-ah-teet. So you'll come, right? This Saturday? I know it's late notice, but Papa's got some business out of town and— Oh, I know exactly what you're thinking, but don't worry! Mama has agreed to chaperone. From upstairs. It's just that Papa doesn't like having people in the house too much, especially after that Clayton boy broke our curios at that last party. And Mama agrees, what Papa doesn't know won't hurt him, and I don't know when I'll have a better opportunity for such an occasion. Oh my gosh, that reminds me, I've got to get over to Bottomby's, their new spring dresses have just arrived! Cora Humphries claims she wears my size, and if I know her she'll buy the last one in Canton crepe just to spite me, even though she's got nowhere but her porch to wear it. I'll call on you later with the rest of the details!"

Ina laughed as she watched Guerine hurry back to the house. She couldn't help but like the young woman, flightiness and all, and for one night she could tolerate her and her corpus of gossip, along with her mediocre food. If Guerine was to be wed in the near future, she was going to need a lot of practice. And Ina was feeling especially charitable these days.

Chapter 39

Guerine's Formal Dinner Party

*H*aving taken a lunch tray up to her mama, Guerine sat down at the kitchen table with an easy action pen and a sheet of superfine notepaper. In her mind, for several weeks, she'd been planning a dinner party—the very thing needed, she determined, to knock the frost from Sam Eastbrook's engaging feet.

She had expected a ring from him at Christmas. Certainly no time like the present. Eastbrook Haberdashery was doing well. With Sam's uncle's recent retirement, Sam had settled comfortably into his position as owner and operator. But, when all he gave her was a pair of pongee turnover-cuff gloves, she was deplorably disappointed. To put a tent on that, they had to be returned for a larger size in a different color, without the delicately embroidered backs. So what had been at the least smart and stylish to begin with was now sturdy and useful with two Bolton thumbs.

She didn't for the life of her understand Sam Eastbrook. They'd been fated all these many years, had shared a desk at East Roxboro School and a back pew at Roxboro Methodist. She was his spark and he was her swain. They were inseparable. Just what did he think, that she was going to wait around until he was game? The time was ripe now. It couldn't be that he had any qualms about what kind of hostess she would be once she was Missus, could it? He'd seen how she conducted herself in social circles. For goodness sakes, she was a clubwoman! Perhaps if she gave a dinner party and invited all their friends he could, *would*, for once and for all, be put well at ease.

But the friend part presented a problem. One had to have them if one was to have a party. Few couples in town were her and Sam's age, at least none they socialized with. There was Kate Lewis and Pete Thacker, who, next to her and Sam, had the longest courtship in Person County history.

She jotted down their names. But, given a little more thought, Kate's personality bordered on vexing, and Pete had a reputation for believing every party to be a wet bargain and was always worse for it by the second course. Guerine grimaced, then sealed the couple's fate by glossing through their names with the black ink. Cheerio, Pete! Sayonara, Kate!

Ina was a given. But she would need an escort, a single gentleman to sit across from.

And then Guerine was struck by an idea. Why, of course! Mr. Gentry! How silly that she'd never considered him an acceptable companion for Ina till now. Guerine was awfully fond of the barber. Especially since he had shown himself to be bold as a lion, not hesitating in the least to chop off half her hair at her request when he knew, in all likelihood, he'd have to contend with her papa. (But what Guerine mistook for Mr. Gentry's fortitude was in reality the act of an over-timid man, who, when faced with the indefatigability of one Guerine Loftis, could not say no. Mr. Gentry couldn't even say "boo" to a goose.)

Guerine thought him an unequivocal and proper dinner partner for the young school teacher, in spite of being twice Ina's age. He, too, was widowed, and though he'd been a fixture in Roxboro for many years, he was not a native of the area, but originally from the eastern part of the state, a place where there are long stretches of shifty land and communal bathing in distasteful green water. How fortunate he was to have escaped it! And no one could deny that he had beamy good looks. So what if he was a gentleman of a certain age. He had a pleasant head of hair, and a nose that curved like a grosbeak's (Guerine liked grosbeaks). And he was a sprucy man, too. He kept his eyebrows restrained and his upper lip slick. Ina should be so lucky.

Four people. There. Cozy affairs were always best.

But what kind of food to serve? And how many courses? Four? Five? She pulled a cookbook from the shelf and flipped to the section titled Special Dinners. She skipped the two pages devoted to A Company Dinner (Chicken Salisbury was too Sunday-dinnerish), and the page labeled A Foreign Dinner (who in their right mind eats something called Salzburger Nockerl?). Oh, she was going to need help! Not only with the cooking, but with the serving of it, too. A hostess needs to be available to her guests at all times, her hands free of all things scullery. Nothing heavier than a silver goblet should grace them.

She bet her aunt Lul would lend Johnny Bob to her for one evening. He would need some decent clothes though. He simply could not wear those raggedy hitch'a'long britches he was fond of. After sitting all day in a wagon while Thomas dropped ploppies he would definitely have to do something about that smell. Sam might have a suit of tails at the shop he could borrow. And maybe Johnny Bob's wife could help, too. No, Silvia was likely to be at choir practice. If not her then, who?

Eunice. Yes, Eunice would be ideal. She liked being useful. She was good on her feet, seemingly took instruction well, and she didn't talk back.

On the morning of the dinner, Guerine was a collocation of jangled nerves.

She prepared to steep herself in the day's activities by wrapping a wide scarf around her head. Much needed doing and hair in the face would only hinder. Not only did the food need to be prepared, the whole downstairs needed a good going over. There was no need to worry with the upper level. No one, not even Sam, had ever ventured higher than the first stair tread. Her papa had seen to that. The silver had to be polished, the china washed, flowers picked and arranged, every little gewgaw dusted.

She covered the kitchen table with newsprint, and as she gathered the silverware a knock came at the back door.

It was Eunice, dressed for kitchen duty and holding a denim laundry bag in her hand. She was more than punctual, arriving five minutes earlier than the time Guerine had appointed.

"I knew I could count on you," Guerine said, rushing her over the threshold. "I've got most of the ingredients ready and laid out. Johnny Bob will be back from the grocer's soon. I had to send him back for one final item."

Eunice shoved the bag at her.

"What's this? Is this your serving outfit?" Guerine smiled. She took a peek inside the bag, pulled out a bibbed white dress and unfurled it with one shake. "This isn't what you're wearing, is it? My goodness, Eunice, this looks like a nurse's uniform." She draped the dress over a chair back and reached again inside the bag, drawing forth a three-cornered cap with a lawn scarf attached. "Why, it is a nurse's uniform! You're not a nurse! Where'd you get this? And where's the black dress I envisioned you in? The lacy collar and cuffs? The frilly white apron? I'm sorry, Eunice, but you cannot serve food in this. People might think it's a portent of illness! Why, it doesn't look French at all!"

Eunice shrugged her shoulders.

"I guess I'll have to call around to find you the proper attire. Let me get you started on something first, so we're not wasting all kinds of time. I should've known something like this would happen." She sat Eunice down at the kitchen table and went over the menu.

"Listen to me carefully, Eunice. I don't want to have to go repeating myself, there's just too much to be done today. Now, I bought a three-pound heel of round and had it sliced into eight pieces for making Steak Birds. You'll find them in the icebox"—she pointed—"but you don't need to pound the meat like you normally would, okay? Mr. Sargeant cut them thin, so all you have to do is mix up the dressing part, roll it up inside the meat, then tie each one tight with string. You've got your birds then, you see? And I want to make a Yorkshire pudding to go with it, too. That gets cut into wedges, and just before serving, we'll place them around the birds."

Eunice looked confounded.

"Think of it as a fancy spoon bread," Guerine explained, "except you cook it in hot drippings." She handed Eunice the piece of paper on which she had written down each dish, its corresponding cookbook, and the page number it could be found on, then pointed her to a stack of cookbooks that waited on the counter.

Next, came Johnny Bob.

"Mr. Sargeant says he doesn't carry caviar, Miss Guerine. Too expensive."

"What do you mean, he doesn't carry caviar? I've got a whole loaf of rye waiting for me to make canapés!"

"Yes, ma'am. Mr. Sargeant, he suggests these chicken livers here. His wife makes a dish called mock pate out of them and says nobody knows the difference. He wrote down the recipe for you."

She supposed it would have to do.

After several phone calls a suitable kitchenmaid's outfit was located. Mrs. Wheeler's hired girl Rella was a comparable size, and once her shift had ended for the day, she would be sent over to the Loftis's to change out of her uniform so that Eunice could change into it. Guerine hoped, by all accounts, it would be a light workday for Rella.

Despite Eunice's inability to speak, she had no problem communicating. When Guerine tried to show her a better way of doing a task, Eunice would give her a contemptuous glance then refuse by shaking her head. When Guerine saw her using a fruit knife to mince mushrooms and asked her to switch to the paring, Eunice, suddenly struck with Olympic ire, left an inflamed print of her hand on the back of Guerine's.

Guerine took leave of the kitchen—and of Eunice's feisty nature—and went off to conquer the rest of the house.

By the end of the afternoon the house was faultless. The dining room, the drawing room, the entire downstairs was ready to receive its guests, and the aroma of roasted beef could be met at every turn. The rugs had been beaten and the floors swept, the table was set, and a glorious arrangement of hothouse orchids demanded attention from the center of the table. The Loftis manor had never been so immaculate, so warm and inviting that even the silver was dazed.

Chapter 40

Even Ina Fitzhugh Can Have an Immodest Mind

$\mathcal{I}$na lay in bed, incapable of sleep. Her right arm was stretched toward the ceiling, elbow just shy of rigid, her slender fingers wrapped tightly around a beveled hand mirror. She was looking at herself. And at her hair, the way it was shawled about her shoulders. Silky locks like the petals of a lily resting against a pillow, still fragrant from a recent shampoo. Once a week she combed her hair over her face, freeing it of all its tangles, and lowering her head then over the basin she would wet her hair thoroughly. *The wetter the hair the more profuse the lather*, said the bottle's label.

She had come home from Guerine's party an hour earlier and gone directly up to her room, taken a seat in front of the vanity, and, slowly exposing tortoise shell prongs, coaxed a gold-plated filigree hair pin from her French knot. It was becoming fashionable these days for women to cut their hair, tending toward boyish bobs, a revolt against morals and certain manners that she had difficulty understanding. Guerine had done it, and she dared say the young woman had made a mistake. It wasn't the Bible she was thinking of. It was art, the image of a Botticelli, an unassuming Venus with a mane capable of covering the entire body. An untouched beauty.

And, for some inexplicable reason, it was of *him* she was thinking.

She pressed a cheek into her pillow and turned her head just far enough that she could, still holding the mirror high, see her profile. Lolling her head toward her other ear, she checked its opposition. She closed her eyes for a moment, let her arm relax, and placed the glass face down on the bedspread.

Bed. The only place she felt comfortable to allow herself the slightest immodesty of the mind. And even then it made her blush to consider what Harlan had seen of her flesh and what she had seen of his. And now here she was, in her sacred place, contemplating what she might care to see of—well, a very different side than what she had observed of him at dinner—and fantasizing what he in turn might care to see of her.

She rocked her head restlessly against the pillow as if in a vain attempt to shake away such flagrant thoughts and again raised the mirror, this time trying on several faces. It was helpful to practice faces since you never knew when you might need them. Just because she was a widow didn't mean she couldn't be hopeful.

The first was a smile that brought her eyelids to a dreamy hug around their dark pupils, yet caused a faint display of curved lines at the corner of each eye that resembled the growth lines on a Chesapeake Bay clam. Oh no, that would not do! Perhaps pensive would be more suitable. She could do pensive. She relaxed her smile and started over, this time pouting her lips by allowing her tongue to slide between her teeth until her bottom lip appeared twice the size of its consort and created a tiny gap barely large enough for a raisin's passage. Heavens! That wouldn't do either. Too indifferent. It also gave the impression of a lady who's been caught with the last sweet; it could even be taken for selfishness.

Maybe she would do better relating desire? But to do desire properly, one must have an image to work with.

It will start with an unguilty touch, she thinks. We will reach for the same thing at exactly the same time, our hands brushing ever so slightly, my pinkie aligned with his thumb. And what use would it be to belie my heart with my tongue, because the sudden warmth in my face will only give me away. We will be like Du Maurier's Billee and Trilby. Only, instead of a fascination with perfect feet, it will be an infatuation with hands.

Cursed hands! That they can be so sociable, so familiar, and yet so intimate, it seems virtually impossible to understand all that a hand knows. Enigmatic appendages are what they are, from the tips of their fingers to the very heart of their palms. And they never seem satiated. They want to touch what they care for, caress the things they desire, grasp what they don't want to lose, fend what frightens them. So many things they are capable of conveying. So much they are able to experience.

He had looked at her hands earlier this evening. Of this she was certain. She had nervously gripped the stem of her wineglass in one hand and allowed the fingers of her other to travel in a slow, scintillating sort of way toward the rim, and he had coughed. And this was not a productive cough.

Now, feeling her arm begin to tire, Ina lowered the mirror to the mattress and closed her eyes. She slipped into a dreamy state and placed her liberated hand onto—

—his lower back. He was openmouthed and up to his ears in the soft crook of her neck, just above her nightgown's drawstring neckline, the full weight of his body on her. She strained her head in the opposite direction that she could further accommodate his breath, and heard him whisper, *"Je veux vous."* (I want you.) Lifting the beveled glass and opening her eyes so that she could observe the heat of her expression, the look she saw instead agitated her. It was the painful elegance of someone who has just stubbed her big toenail, and she made quick to push him away.

This was it! She didn't even need the mirror to know that this was the look she'd been trying to attain. It was all there, she could feel it, the glazed eyes, the naïve way of nibbling one's lower lip. The look of a woman preparing for the throes of desire.

But what difference did all of it make? Young or no, the reality was, she, Ina Fitzhugh, was meant to be pitied. A widow to be pitied. For the rest of her life she would be denied healthy joys, be dismissed to cozy corners, find her comfort in cushions and flowers and cups of tea at twilight. She might as well have been a bachelor maid, the loneliest of all women—a direction in which Bertie herself seemed to be heading. She should simply accept her just due. There was no reason she couldn't make herself content with the life of a dilettante. There were multifarious activities and plenty of interests to keep her entertained besides romance and affection.

Oh, drat it all! She punched the mattress with both fists, refused to spare her pillow, then rolled onto her left side and tried sleep. But it was of little use. The evening at Guerine's had been fretful, one she did not care to repeat. The spectacle of seeing Johnny Bob in a suit of tails made for a smaller man, the sleeves lacking by an inch, and Eunice, her hair as wiry as a pot cleaner, shuffling from kitchen to dining room at the most inappropriate times—at one point, juggling a fourteen-inch silver waiter and a dinner castor with five crystal bottles like a clown on a tightrope. But it was that embarrassing predicament she had gotten herself into over dinner that bothered her most. How was she going to get out of it?

It had started innocently enough, when the topic of conversation turned from all things related to hairdressing—Mr. Gentry giving an exhaustive account of the demands placed on a barber nowadays, but not without offering his sincerest apologies to Miss Loftis, he was by no means referring to her—to the subject of education.

If only I hadn't complained so, Ina thought. But every word of what she had said about the school was true. The building was inadequate in every way imaginable. It was poorly equipped and overcrowded. If the parents of her pupils wanted their children to have a decent education, then another teacher was needed, perhaps even two. But the current structure couldn't handle one more body, she told her dinner companions, and despite Mrs. Wheeler's mention at their last meeting that money was scarce, it would certainly behoove the town to build a new school.

Everyone at the table seemed to be in accordance.

"The only solution I can see is to raise taxes," Mr. Gentry had suggested. "But that'd be a hard sale around here. Folks aren't usually too eager to have their tax rate increased. On the other hand—"

"Yes?" Ina said.

"I suppose a special tax district could be set up. Of course, you still have the problem of getting folks to consent."

"What do you mean, Mr. Gentry?" Guerine asked.

"Well, theoretically," he said, "and Sam, you correct me if I'm wrong, but if enough landowners agreed to have their properties included in a special tax district, which of course would have to be set up, and a tax was levied of, oh I don't know, twenty-five or thirty cents, then presumably you'd have the money to construct a new school and hire more teachers."

"Mr. Gentry! Aren't you the clever one!" said Guerine. "Sit down, Sam. Johnny Bob will do that."

"It's all hypothetical, of course," Mr. Gentry said, buttering a roll.

Ina stared intently at him. "But it is possible, you think?"

"Oh, definitely. But it wouldn't be easy. A person would have their work cut out for them. As a barber, I oughta know." His pun was rewarded with hearty laughter.

If only she had kept her remaining thoughts to herself regarding the school. If she hadn't so boldly revealed to everyone at the table her desire to be that person, the one Mr. Gentry had suggested, the very person who went door-to-door and secured the consent of every property owner in the county. If she simply could've restrained herself from saying, "It would be less daunting a task if I had a motorcar, though I suppose"—it must've been the wine—"being able to drive a motorcar would be useful."

"I'll help you, Miss Fitzhugh," chimed Mr. Gentry. "I'll be happy to drive you. We'll go from house to house. How's this Saturday?"

And here it was, the tight spot she had gotten herself into. *Et une belle situation difficile c'etait!* Nice man, the barber, kind enough. But she did not care a whit to be alone with him. Dressing for a formal dinner in the manner that he had? Short sleeves, the man's uncouth elbows exposed, and an open-end scarf that looked more like he'd tucked the tail of a napkin over his shirt collar than wearing a respectable necktie. And don't let her start in on his table manners—the man ate like a pelican. Sam, on the other hand, was a miracle of manners and toilet. Sam had worn a bow tie. He had taken smaller bites. Sam had, in every way, been a gracious host, tending to everyone at the table.

And that had to do with another crick in the evening she regretted now as she tried to sleep. She had accidentally put her foot squarely but publicly into her oral cavity after observing Guerine's lack of appreciation for Sam's considerateness. Could Guerine not see how attentive the dear man was? Pouring wine when he noticed a glass needing, dishing up a third helping, for heaven's sake, of Yorkshire pudding to that scoop-mouthed barber. Granted, her observations had been unsolicited, but when Guerine admonished Sam for an unknown time to "Please sit down, Sam! All your fussing, you're ruining the ambience," Ina, without thinking, snipped at her.

"I would think you'd be more appreciative of Mr. Eastbrook's attentiveness."

"How do you mean?"

"Just exactly what I said," Ina firmly explained. "That you would be grateful for his notice."

"Another piece of beef, Mr. Gentry?" Sam hiccoughed.

"Yesiree, don't mind if I do."

"Oh, don't let our nonsense bother you," Guerine poo-pooed. "Sam and I are used to giving each other a little side light in these situations. It's our way of being connected. You didn't find your steak bird too rare, did you?"

Ina stared at the bedroom ceiling and blinked. Perhaps she had been rather harsh on Guerine, if deservedly so. It wouldn't have hurt the young woman to be less of a raw wind. And as far as Ina could tell, her comment sailed right over Guerine's head.

And now that she considered it, she wondered if she had vocalized her concerns on the school matter specifically to incite Sam into offering his help? Because it was thoughts of Sam that shared her pillow.

Chapter 41

Life on Bertie's Own Account

$\mathcal{S}$ince moving to the nation's capital city, Bertie had spent little time in the cramped two-bedroom apartment she shared with three other National Woman's Party workers. And for that she was grateful. The apartment was potentially rife with danger. It was booby-trapped with furbelows. Daily, she had to dodge bust supporters, weave her way through a maze of drying stockings and silk knickers (as well as a cunning collection of hygienic and highly absorbent feminine requirements); walk through a permanent storm of face powder with caution, or risk tripping over patent leather pumps and lace oxfords left lying about, and God knows what else. Twice she had taken her chances. Once by walking barefoot, only to be surprised by a five-inch-long hair-curling pin that'd been lost to the sitting room rug. And on another occasion, at an ungodly early-morning hour, she accidentally skated toward the bathroom on a pack of reducing gum that belonged to the more fulsome roommate.

She was living among a mélange of estrogen, a 750-square-foot area overrun with the ardor of four big-boned women on a mission.

But the majority of her daylight hours—as well as a significant portion of her nighttime hours—was spent working at the NWP Headquarters. And for that she was grateful.

The NWP Headquarters was a place of frenetic activity. All the day long hectic feet went up and down the corridors, traveling between offices, running from desks to filing cabinets, jumping up and scuffling to answer incessantly ringing phones. Fast-paced talk, shorthand dictation, and weighty letters being typed and mailed to larger-than-life people. It sounded glamorous, and Bertie could've loved every minute of it—if she hadn't been assigned to Archives.

Her duties, in fact, weren't near as glamorous as she had envisioned them to be when she accepted the job. Her position as assistant to the HQ secretary had turned out to be merely one of several eager underlings who were assigned to menial tasks, and here she was tonight, already nine o'clock and working alone in a dark basement with the aid of a student lamp, poring through boxes of old papers and seeing that every document was filed into a recently donated cabinet, when what she really wanted to do was be a part of the hubbub that she could hear going on above her.

She kept reminding herself that the role she had was important. She was helping make history. She was responsible for handling letters that dated back as far as 1917, since the formation of the NWP, missives written to Alice Paul and by Alice Paul, as well as other significant members of the NWP, and these letters might some day be available for the whole world to see.

Oh, who the hell was she kidding! A numskull could do this job. The NWP—not to mention women everywhere—would be better served if she was campaigning out on the streets. Full equality for all women is what she should be working on. And she was about to steel herself to tell the higher-ups at NWP that she wasn't meant to be anybody's minion. Send her to Congress instead. She was a natural leader. Had she been born a horse she would've been leading a cavalry; if she'd been blessed with an ear for music she'd've been first fiddle; reared in one of those dark-skinned foreign countries she could've become something along the likes of a Grand Moobah, or a Chief Itch-and-Scratch on sacred land.

She heard someone on the staircase and looked up to see her friend Mel leaning over the banister. Mel—short for Marilyn or Madeleine or some other similar name that Bertie had trouble keeping straight—was the first person Bertie had met after stepping off the train. The NWP sure knew how to roll out the ol' hospitality rug, sending their very own press agent to collect Bertie from the station and bring her back to the headquarters at Lafayette Square for a tour. The two had hit it off right away.

"There's a group of us heading to the Ebbitt for a late dinner," Mel said. "Wanna come along?"

"Thanks, but I'll pass. I've got one more box, then I'm calling it a night."

"You sure? I'll wait. I know how much you like their anchovied potato curls. We could share a plate? Maybe even push some mustachioed old stogies off their stools."

Bertie chuckled. "Next time, for sure."

"Then I guess I'll see you in the morning."

"In the morning," said Bertie, returning to her task. She took a deep sigh.

It had been a day of missed opportunity. She supposed all this filing business was merely the "settling in" factor and she ought to just accept it. But damned if important things weren't taking place and none of them, she was sure, were down here. Getting ready for that ceremony, for one, which had been timed to coincide with the 101st anniversary of the birth of Susan B. Anthony. An event as big as that and she hadn't been trusted yet with the first detail. She had hardly even gotten a good look at Alice Paul since arriving, other than catching a glimpse of her this morning when she saw her shutting her office door. At least she thought it was Alice Paul. Or the arm of.

Well, she could grouse and grumble all she wanted tonight, but tomorrow would probably have a whole 'nother something in store.

Chapter 42

Bugle Witnesses
the Fowl Accident

*T*he dog could tell time. Which was unfortunate, since Colon had said he would be up to the house at eight o'clock that morning, big and pronto, to take Bugle fishing. Not that the dog knew the first thing about baiting a hook, but he was a fine companion for such an outing.

At a minute till eight, Bugle trotted to the edge of the yard and looked for his friend out over the horizon. At eight-o-five, he settled his hind end onto a soft patch of ground, but still maintained a sharp watch. At eight ten, hearing the sound of a vehicle, he stood up hopefully, but once he determined it was a motorcar passing by on the main road, he deposited his backside to the ground again. At eight fifteen, he scratched behind his left ear and dislodged a tick with his toenail. A couple minutes later, he chanced taking his eyes from the road and looked beyond his mottled shoulder to see how Doodle was coming along with her repair to the hen house. At eight twenty, provoked by a pesky mount of fleas, he nibbled at his ribcage, then respectfully straightened himself so when his fishing buddy arrived he'd be sitting there looking slippy. But five minutes later, and still no sign of the wavering burst of dirt that he had come to associate with Colon's motorcycle tires on the dusty road, he scampered back up to the yard and gave Doodle an earful of indignant arfs.

"Yeah? Well you be sure and tell him if he ever shows up," said Doodle.

She had so far declined Colon's offer to help out around the farm, but had agreed, if somewhat reluctantly, to allow him to take Bugle on regular outings. He had come across as genuine in wanting to pass time with the old mutt, and it was clear that Bugle had taken a liking to him, continuing, just as John had done, to meet Colon at the mailbox each day in time for delivery. The only difference: he wouldn't tote the mail back up to the house.

It was half past the hour now and Bugle was fit to be tied.

"Don't blame me," Doodle grumbled. "I didn't tell you to go and get all chummy with him."

She hammered a nail into the side of the hen house.

And then finally, what Bugle had been waiting for: the sound of Colon's Model O turning from the main road and climbing the dirt road, gaining speed as it neared the Shuford farm. His friend was coming! He trotted back to his original waiting place, playfully frisked at a family of geese (yard-chums to him), and incited the parents to hustle their goslings to the other side of the road where the pond awaited them.

Doodle continued to hammer, paying the whole scene no mind.

For that, she wouldn't notice the hackles on Bugle's neck, the way the hairs bristled at the motor's urgency. Nor would she see the accident itself, how it unfolded right before Bugle, the motorcycle rounding the bend at an ungodly speed, too late to avoid five of the eight goslings and their mother. And that godawful *yeek*.

Colon didn't even try to explain. To say that he'd been held up in town by Esperann—who had asked for his help with a menial task that he knew good and well she could've handled herself, but couldn't say no and hurt her feelings, and at the same time risk the wrath of her mother—what good would it of done?

"I believe I got 'em all taken care of," Colon said, returning the shovel to Doodle, knowing in his heart of hearts it would take time before he gained the trust of Bugle again. Doodle, he wasn't sure he ever would.

Chapter 43

Mr. Gentry Drives Ina Crazy

*B*efore she had a chance to comfortably settle inside the vehicle, the smell of Mr. Gentry's aftershave nearly robbed Ina of her breath. The assault sent a signal in short order to her sensitive stomach, which in turn relayed a mercurial message to her brain: it was to be the l-o-n-g-e-s-t day of her life. And comfortably settle? The seat was obstinate, a veritable boulder.

She hadn't noticed that particular off-putting aspect of Mr. Gentry at Guerine's dinner party, his liberal use of a toilet water that was reminiscent of stove polish. It was as if the man had rushed home from church to douse himself after sitting on a pew packed shoulder-to-shoulder; or, perhaps it was simply a matter of the interior of his machine having been marinated over time by pungent miscalculations. Whatever the case, it was a travesty that a barber should offend the nose. One could only think he had generously, erroneously, spiked himself for the sake of a sweetheart.

Sweetheart? Did he merely want to help her gain the trust of the community while gaining their signatures? Or did he have something else in mind? The very idea startled her, and she looked over at Mr. Gentry to see if she could discern his real intentions.

He flashed her an unctuous smile and she forced one in return.

"Lovely day," she coughed, after the motorcar pulled away from the curb. "A breeze, I would think, would be—most welcome." She had eaten very little the evening before. The anticipation of the reactions she would likely encounter from the community had kept her awake with worry most of the night.

Mr. Gentry apologized for not having lowered the top before picking her up. "I was afraid of you taking in too much wind," he shouted. "Sometimes these cowled windshields, they say they won't rattle or come loose, but that's not always the case. I'm happy to oblige by lowering the top, if you think it won't be too lively for you. Won't take but a second."

"That's not necessary, I can just as easily lift the window." She had seen Bertie perform this simple operation and was pleased to try it now. Despite Mr. Gentry's stuttering ejaculations that perhaps it would be better if he did it, she jiggled the window from its brackets, delighted in her fortitude. But before she could fully appreciate the task she'd just completed, she lost her grip and sent the isinglass crashing to the road and, from the sound of it, under the back tire.

Mr. Gentry set about reassuring her with his newly found eloquence: ". . . have always had a problem with that window . . ." He edged the vehicle to the side of the road, retrieved the tortured window, and proceeded to lower the canopy. When the top was at the middle of the retraction, he encountered a sticky situation. It wouldn't go forward and it wouldn't go backward.

"Perhaps if I were to help," she recommended.

Mr. Gentry wouldn't hear of it, resorting instead to a modicum of pushing and pulling as the underarms of his shirt began to show signs of stress.

"Mr. Gentry! Mr. Gentry, please! You might break it further if you don't stop."

Finally, he gave up, got back inside the vehicle and drove Ina to her first destination, the top hovering above them like a misplaced barn door.

They started at the far end of the county, and at each house, Mr. Gentry would wait behind the wheel while Ina went up to the door with her notepad and pencil. She gave the same speech to each person, and nearly every response was the same, curious stares followed by laughter. "Now who did you say you was again?" "What special tax?" "Nobody in they right mind wants to pay more tax. That's just crazy talk!"

When Mr. Gentry suggested they stop for lunch at the Dolly Madison, Ina acceded by nodding. Even a person who feels dejected must still eat.

She was discouraged that her efforts to procure a new school, such as they were, would be all in vain. And she was regretting that she had listened to Mr. Gentry's idea in the first place.

※

At lunch they ate, talked. Though most of the talk came from the outwardly nervous barber.

He scoffed at the parsley sprig that accompanied his veal cutlet, banishing it to the rim of his plate. "I'm not much on waste. Food's meant to be eat, not bibbed and tuckered. I just don't see the sense in all that curled celery and radish rose business, do you? That's what cakes are for. For instance, they've got a real nice Pollock here, but then they go and cover it from head to tail with lemon slices. I've told them before to leave that lemon fribble off, that all it's gonna do is go to waste with me, but then you know what they did next time I ordered the pollock? Delivered it to me, at this here very table, prinked with green pepper rings. And I have never been a man who likes his vegetables raw. See, a dish to me can be just as attractive without all that fancy trimming."

Trying to steer him toward another subject, Ina said, "That's an interesting ring you're wearing, Mr. Gentry."

"Oh, this here? This is a King Tut Good Luck ring. All the movie stars are wearing them. They call them Lucky rings for short." He took the ring off and handed it to her for a better look. "There's a lot of imitations out there," he told her, "but this one has the genuine silver finish. It's supposed to bring success, happiness, and love."

She couldn't hand the ring back to him fast enough.

"If you don't mind me saying, Miss Fitzhugh," Mr. Gentry said, forcing the ring back onto his finger, "a schoolmistress is, to me, the most admirable of women. I rank them among the likes of nurses. I think what you're doing is important, and the children will be better served because of it. Because of you."

Being in the man's presence certainly was a mortal challenge, and if she wasn't careful he could end up following her like a shadow. She took up her glass of water with a jittery hand and sipped. Perhaps she would do better navigating the conversation herself, keep it strictly geared toward the issues facing the school.

During the remainder of the meal, she became emboldened to try a different approach to acquire signatures. No one she had spoken with thus far had cared to hear about building a new school. What was wrong with the one they had? She would start fresh after lunch, at the next house, and focus, instead, on the elements that needed repair in the current building, without the mention of money for a new schoolhouse. She would incorporate a "tactic" she had been using on her older pupils when their inclination was to misbehave: speak to them about ideals and incentives. If she could appeal to their moral judgment, she would be instilling moral value, and thus accomplish her desired results more surely. In short, she would encourage the community to have the influence of heroes. And by becoming heroes to the children, they would be furnishing them with higher ambitions and stronger determinations to overcome the obstacles of life. And for that, they were to be commended.

Her new way of establishing a connection with the community worked.

By the time they had left the last house and headed back toward town, she had collected 112 signatures. That the motor was becoming uneven at a high speed didn't concern her, happy as she was, holding the names out before her and feeling pride in her accomplishment. And she wouldn't have heard the small explosions at all, a series of occasional "misses" of one or more of the cylinders, except for the awful odor that was strong enough to surmount Mr. Gentry's aftershave.

Ina placed her list of signatures on her lap. "Do you detect smoke, Mr. Gentry?"

To her surprise, they abruptly stopped. Mr. Gentry shouted "Fire!" and pushed her from the automobile. Only when she was at a safe distance, at the top of a gentle grass-covered slope, did she turn to see the hood ablaze.

Standing there, feeling the heat, she watched helplessly as Mr. Gentry swatted at the flames with his jacket. The fire grew, overtook the vehicle and, sadly, the man's coat.

"Oh, Mr. Gentry!"

Chapter 44

Bertie Meets Politics

*I*s Miss Paul expecting you?" asked Lucy White.

"Indeed she is," said the woman standing before her. "Miss Paul was noti-fied yesterday that members of our delegation would be calling upon her today at this very hour. We are representatives of the five million colored women in this country, and we've come to thank Miss Paul for her honor-able work in securing the passage of the Nineteenth Amendment, and also to bring to her attention specific violations during the recent election. Most of us have traveled great distances to get here. And at heavy expense. Our time is valuable as I know is Miss Paul's. Now, may we see her please?"

Miss White escorted the group of women into Alice Paul's office.

Oh, to be a fly! If it hadn't been for Miss White needing her to come up-stairs for another box of letters to file, Bertie wouldn't have even witnessed that much. Just the kind of sighting she had hoped she'd become accus-tomed to, the daily promenading of distinguished people right in this very office. She set the storage box down and plopped into the chair that Miss White had vacated, and prepared to take in the unfolding scene. But wouldn't you know, HQ Lucy had to go and shut the door.

"Miss Daye, would you please remove yourself from my desk," said Miss White, returning to claim her chair.

"Huh? Oh. Uh-hunh." Didn't Miss White know that this was one meet-ing she would die to be privy to?

But when Miss White invited Bertie to withdraw herself from Miss White's seat a second time, Bertie withdrew. Only, she didn't go far on the chance she wouldn't be able to hear what was happening on the other side of that door.

"Don't you have business that needs tending to, Miss Daye?"

"What's that? I'm trying to hear what they're saying."

"Other business, Miss Daye. Your filing?"

By the tone of the voices coming from Miss Paul's office, this was exactly the kind of great doings Bertie wanted to be in on. She should be in there right now helping them thrash it out.

"Miss Daye. Do I need to remind you that your business is elsewhere?"

Bertie turned to face Miss White.

"I would kindly appreciate it if you'd see to it at once," said Miss White.

HQ Lucy was pulling the wrong sow by the ear. But Bertie wasn't looking to fasten a quarrel on the woman, only trying to hear the one bubbling through the door. She hesitated, then snatched up the box and hiked it back to the basement. She would have to satisfy herself that NWP-plugger pal Mel would give her the details later.

Bertie lifted out the next set of papers, attached by a spring steel fastener, and was prepared to file them away to their respective places until the address on the top letter caught her attention. It was from a county in North Carolina not far from Roxboro:

October 1, 1920
The National Woman's Party
Washington, D.C.

Dear Secretary,

I am writing in hope you can help me before it is too late. I have been refused registration because I am colored, as have other colored folk in my county of Durham, and am looking for a way to send in my vote. The chair of this board requires all colored to tell him the correct number of licorice bits in a jar. I do not think he even knows himself. I am not a coal-blower. I am a member of Mount Sinai Baptist Church and mind no one's business but for my own. Please tell me how I can register and vote by mail before registration ends October 23.

Much obliged,
Mary Kendrick
Box 142
Bahama, N.C.

She finished reading the letter then folded it over the clip and read its reply.

October 10, 1920
Miss Mary Kendrick
Box 142
Bahama, N.C.

Dear Miss Kendrick,

Thank you for your letter concerning registration and how to send your vote by mail.

You must register in person in the state of North Carolina. Is it possible that you mistakenly tried to register outside of your own precinct? Our sources tell us that colored women in your state are being allowed to register. Therefore, we would suggest you try again, keeping in mind that registration will close on October 23.

In regards to voting by mail, you must apply to your county board for a ballot.

Please let us know if we can be of further assistance to you.

Sincerely,
Lucy White
Headquarters Secretary
National Woman's Party

Lucy's letter struck Bertie as highfalutin!—and little help to Mary Kendrick and the others who were being denied by the local officials.

Two more letters were attached. Bertie continued reading. Another earnest plea from Miss Kendrick dated October 15, followed by more fur-fur from Lucy White written on October 23, stating that she had brought Mary Kendrick's letter to Alice Paul's attention, but the only solution to the problem was one that wasn't available now. They needed to work at passing an Enabling Act through Congress—a law that would make the interference of registration and voting a federal offense—and they would be working for that passage at the next session.

A lot of good that would do Mary Kendrick now. This entire thing was disturbing. Unbalancing, in fact. Bertie read the letters again. She didn't like how Lucy White, Miss Headquarters Secretary, sounded. That busybody tenor she used around the office. She didn't much like Miss Lucy White, period.

Bertie revered Alice Paul. She had set the Shining One so high up on a pedestal it made her dizzy the few opportunities she'd had to lay eyes on her. To be in the presence of a woman who'd been arrested (willingly) on numerous occasions, attacked physically because of what she believed in, imprisoned, and, after starting a hunger strike, forced into swallowing feeding tubes—not to mention being responsible for securing the passage of the Nineteenth Amendment to the Constitution of the United States—was awe-inspiring. The very woman who, at the age of twenty-one—the same age Bertie was now—had moved to England and received the better part of her education with ladies who really knew how to rouse-rabble over woman's rights and suffrage. She had gotten roughed up by police over there and even wound up joining her first group of hunger strikers. Hunger changes a lot of things. Even if you bring it on yourself. Three years later she came back here with nothing in her belly but fire.

But now here were these letters that suggested, to Bertie, a contradictory side to Alice Paul. Bertie had heard staff grumblings about "throwing the baby out with the bath water"—losing support in the South if they fight to let black women vote, too. Was it possible that Alice Paul, with Quaker heritage, could have become so stretched that she had to care about white women's suffrage at the expense of Negro women? Was the NWP only publicly saying what colored people wanted to hear? Were they really Jim Crow's silent mistresses?

She thought back to the afternoon she had stormed from the registrar's office and had gone to tell Johnny Bob and Silvia that she had failed them. It made her wonder if maybe she had treated that situation like it was nothing more than a nuisance. She had given up too easily. And when this position at the NWP had presented itself, she had convinced herself she could make a difference on a much larger scale. But now, she wasn't so sure.

Chapter 45

Colon Brings Great Tidings

$\mathcal{D}$oodle decided to go down to the pond for a bathe. It was a day meant for exploring deep passions and curiosities, the morning was clear and bright, the sky a vivid cornflower. With a bar of soap in hand and a two honeycomb towels draped over her shoulder, she walked down the path that led to the pond. It was a special place for her, a five-foot-deep beaver dam pond where she had gone swimming ever since she was a little girl.

She walked through a patch of dewy fern and mint and spread out one of the towels and sat down, her back protected by a hedge of honeysuckle, and began removing her clothes. First, her shoes, and then her housedress and chemise, and a pair of ribbed summer drawers, ecru in color. She broke the surface of the water by miring both feet in mud, and slowly waded out till she was bosom deep.

For several minutes she floated, enveloped in a climate of sun-bathed balm. She considered the weeping willow along the water's edge and how she had swung from its branches when she was a little girl. Talmadge used to like to play on the bank, digging the wet clay and molding it into fun objects, then he'd allow her to decorate them with broken pieces of colored glass. But Ballard would often come along and stomp the treasures they'd made with his foot. The thought made her lonely.

She stirred her arms and paddled her feet.

Any day now she should be hearing from the photoplay people. What was taking them so long to respond?

She returned to the edge of the pond and retrieved the soap, and was sitting on a velvety slick log, lathering up, when the sound hit like a bucket of ice water.

"Doodle? You down here?"

It was Colon. She must've had her head under water, the reason she hadn't heard his motorcycle. And by the rustling on the other side of the hedge, he was fast approaching her bathing site. She crossed her arms over her bosoms, hugged them like they were two precious apples, and hollered, "Colon Clayton, don't you come any closer, you hear!"

"Don't want me to learn where your favorite berry-picking spot is, huh? Well, don't worry, I'm not about to steal off your blackberries. And you can blame Bugle for showing me where you were."

That dog, Doodle thought.

The rustling came closer to the hedge.

"I'm warning you, Colon! If you take another step, I'll scream! So help me, I will."

"Fine. Keep your secret," he said. "Just wanted to let you know you got a delivery up to the house."

"What kind of delivery?"

"Now that would spoil the surprise. How long do you expect to be?"

"I reckon that all depends on you."

"Come again?"

"It's not likely that I'll come out from behind this bush till you've made yourself scarce."

While Doodle was distracted with keeping Colon at bay, Bugle had seen fit to carry off her drawers and present them to Colon. He took the cotton from Bugle's soft mouth, and after holding them up to momentarily discreet inspection he grinned.

"Say," he said, twirling the drawers on his finger, "do you mind if I come by later this week and take Bugle hunting? I think me and him's back on track now."

Doodle was growing impatient. "Yeah, fine." Anything to get him to leave. Because if he defied her wishes and continued around the hedge to where she was, there would be nothing she could do to cover the area where her lower back met with a delicate, deeply creased, dimple.

Instead he thanked her, and she could tell that he had turned to go, but after a couple of steps toward the road everything went quiet. That's when she saw the little bunch of cotton fly over the honeysuckle hedge. The sight of the ribbed drawers left her gap-mouthed, and she held that look till the motorcycle dwindled to the distant sound of a bumblebee.

Once back up at the house, her delivery became evident. A wooden crate that sat on the porch, with no recognizable label. At first she was hesitant. She couldn't recall having recently ordered anything. Except maybe— roofing supplies! She dashed across the yard, figuring Mr. Barnett's conscience had gotten the better of him and he'd sent the supplies on credit in spite of Mr. Wheeler, but as she got closer she could hear some type of racket coming from inside the box. She stepped onto the porch and peered into the crate.

Ten purring turkey poults. And a 50-pound bag of starter feed keeping them company.

"Fool!" Doodle yelled at an absent Colon. "I can't raise turkeys!" You can't raise turkeys and chickens together, she continued to herself. Not without a lot of forethought. Good Lord, you have to be mindful not to track chicken manure into a turkey pen. Turkeys are prone to all kinds of diseases that chickens are resistant to. Blackhead, for one. But never mind that, I don't have a turkey pen to raise them in. The barn's full to the rafters and it'll take days for me to clear a reasonable size spot for them. "Fool!"

She stared down into the box. They seemed like content poults. Sounded like content poults. And they did have a profitable look to 'em. Lifting the box, she carried them inside and placed them in her papa's bedroom and shut the door till she could figure out what to do.

Chapter 46

Smoke and Mirrors

*A*t the Woolworth's lunch counter, over two slap-dashed BLTs, Bertie asked Mel if she'd ever gotten the sense that Alice Paul might have a slight case of yes-noism when it came to her commitment to equality for all women.

"I don't follow," said Mel, reaching over and helping herself to Bertie's egg cream soda.

Bertie told her about seeing the delegation of colored women who had come through the office, and about the letters she had discovered while filing. Two recent occurrences that were stirring up a lot of questions for her. "I'm thinking the NWP might be ignoring colored women altogether. If I didn't know better, I'd say Alice Paul believed that this depriving of colored women their right to vote is a race issue and not a women's issue."

"Really?" Mel said.

"You say that like you're not surprised."

Mel pushed her plate aside, then dug inside her purse for a pack of Sweet Caporals. She tapped out two, dared to light them both, then handed one to Bertie.

More and more, Bertie was liking this here redhead. She was a woman who clearly loved adventure.

Mel took a puff. "Miss Kendrick," she said, reflecting.

"You've seem 'em, then," said Bertie. "The letters."

"I saw *her*."

"Mary Kendrick, from Bahama, North Carolina? Here?"

"Bodily," said Mel. "Came to meet with Alice Paul and said she didn't want to talk to anyone but her. She had a young woman with her, a niece maybe. They sat outside Alice Paul's door for hours, waiting for a chance to talk to her."

"But she never got in, did she?" Bertie asked rhetorically.

Mel shook her head. "When I came back through the lobby later that evening they were both gone."

There was more that Mel had to tell, and Bertie—hard as it was to keep from interrupting—was intent on hearing.

There were other similar issues at hand, Mel explained. The Party was under fire for refusing to invite Mary Talbert, past president of the Federation of Colored Women, to speak at the upcoming ceremony. Since it was likely that Mrs. Talbert would be speaking on the anti-lynching law—a campaign that Alice Paul believed wasn't as much a feminist issue as it was a racial one and, therefore, Mrs. Talbert's appearance could upset the southern whites—Alice Paul had declined to invite her.

"I'd say you pretty much homed in on it," Mel said to Bertie. "What you witnessed yesterday was the mounting pressure to have Mrs. Talbert included in the program."

"Damn straight! White women can work hard as they want for colored women, but only a colored woman can represent colored women properly. Mary Talbert ought to be included. Given the same courtesies as anybody else. If she ain't, then something's wrong with that, Mel. Wrong—wrong—wrong!"

"You're not the only one in the Party who feels offended, Bertie. The whole thing is controversial. If you haven't heard rumblings yet, take comfort, you will. Mine included. Truthfully, I think there's more dissension within the Party regarding the race question than anybody is willing to admit. After yesterday's meeting, though, it looks like Alice Paul may be softening a bit. She's invited the National Association of Colored Women's Clubs to participate in the Capitol ceremony during the unveiling of the sculptures. One colored woman will carry a wreath on behalf of the organization and another will lay it."

"Be serious. A wreath? Pfft!"

"Well, you can't deny that she's in a slippery situation, trying to please everybody if she wants to keep their support."

"Listen—Alice Paul can't sidestep this issue," Bertie said. "Why do you think the NWP was formed in the first place? To put an end to discrimination against women. All women, not just the white ones." She shook her head in frustration. "Got a Congress that ain't doing a damn thing. Unless we get more of these slack-jawed windsocks from the North to recognize that Negroes are voters, too, then the NWP hasn't done its job as far as I'm concerned. Ain't no more than a tea and gossip group."

Just then their waitress strode over, and brought with her a sandy attitude. "Tobacco is not a food, ladies. If the manager sees you smoking, he'll have you both arrested. It's the same thing in here every day and I'm getting tired of it. Warning the likes of you scrappy gals from over at that military office."

Mel took one last drag on her torch of freedom before crushing it into her plate. "Only for you, sweetheart," she said, and released a contentious plume of smoke in the woman's face.

Bertie was too disgusted to care about anything but what her friend had just told her. Outraged might've better explained it, and she left her half-dragged cigarette to float in what remained of her egg cream soda. Miss Lul was right. Those things'll leave you with a bad taste.

They paid their ticket and left.

"I suppose to someone on the outside it could appear that Alice Paul makes herself busy when she doesn't want to deal with an issue," Mel said, once they were out on the crowded sidewalk. "But remember, Bertie, no matter what—she does pull the strings. And if I were you I wouldn't do anything crazy like trying to turn the house out of the window. Who knows? After the convention the National Woman's Party might even cease to exist."

Chapter 47

Enter a Stranger

*N*o one had ever presented Lalura Daye with a certificate of character before. What would it matter anyhow, so long as they minded their manners and paid their rent in a timely fashion? She figured she could look at a person and know all she needed. If they showed up on her steps looking like a second-shift cotton mill worker, she would simply point them to the Dowdy Inn. Let Eunice be the one to give them a talking to.

She was dusting the rose-patterned Fenton lamp in the parlor, and pondering a fish loaf for the night's dinner, when she heard the charming tone come from the foyer. Someone had twisted the finger turn on the brass doorbell.

When she opened the door, a fashionable gentleman was standing on the other side sporting a tailored suit and a felt fedora.

He introduced himself as Moses Joyner. He was in town on business, he told her, government work, and had heard while having lunch at the Wiggly Pig Diner ("funny name, that diner") that she might have a room for him to let. He couldn't say how long his work would keep him there, one never knows with the government, but he could provide her with excellent references. "I can gladly pay a month's rent in advance," he said, and pulled a silver money clip from his coat pocket. He spoke with a deep, authoritative voice, and Lalura, noticing his graying temples, figured him to be somewhere near his fiftieth year. Nothing about him suggested carouser.

"Come in, Mr. Joyner. Do come right in!"

After her newest boarder's first week of habitation in the Daye home, Lalura, armed with a feather duster and a fresh set of bed sheets and bath towels, went up to his room to change out his linens.

She did her best not to encroach on his personal belongings, even going so far as to considerately shut the door to the armoire when she saw the sleeve of what she believed to be his bathrobe hanging out, but not before noticing that he also owned a blue serge suit, a pair of khaki trousers, a tan driving duster, and wore a size seven-and-three-quarters fedora. She disliked people who meddled into others' business. As a girl she had told a classmate to "go roll your hoop" when the young friend had asked where she'd gotten her pretty pin set. And really, there was no need, no real purpose, for anyone to be looking through Mr. Joyner's clothing. It made no difference to her, except to say the man had good breeding.

But Lalura's curiosity continued to get the better of her. Mr. Joyner was still very much a stranger. He was up and gone every morning before she could offer him breakfast, and he had yet to sit down to one of her special dinners. This bothered her a great deal. Of all the men she had met in her life, this was one she actually wouldn't mind talking to. Where was he eating? Doesn't a man doing important government work need good nutrition? And what's so wrong with her being a little inquisitive anyhow? It wasn't as if she had malicious intent. Seemed to her that a little curiosity should be flattering to the person you're curious about. Means you consider them worthy of favor.

She placed the sheets and feather duster on the end of the bed, and walked over to the dresser and meekly opened the top drawer. Neatly folded shirts. She closed the drawer and slid open the one below. An array of silk neckwear and—

Undergarments!

She slammed the drawer shut.

The lift-front desk was certainly getting some use, and it pleased her to see the amount of paper strewn about. It meant that Mr. Joyner had started to make himself "to home." By all appearances, he didn't seem to be in a hurry to leave.

She wondered exactly what type of government work he did. Hard to imagine it could be anything of a secretive nature in these parts. A spy? Here? Unless—maybe he was sent to sneak up on working whiskey stills? Espionage in Roxboro! The notion made her chuckle.

Having dared to pick up one of the slips of paper, she began to read:

Condition of schools and lack of training of teachers—
1) Ellis Drumright School—one-room structure with plank door; shutters
    open when weather permits. Grades 1–6.
    Proposal to improve conditions:
    ⅓ of the money from state

⅓ from community
Remaining ⅓ to set up Person County Training School for Negro Teachers
**see Rev. Ragland

What's this? she wondered, and reached for another of Mr. Joyner's papers.

State of North Carolina
SECOND BIENNIAL REPORT
OF
STATE AGENT OF NEGRO RURAL SCHOOLS

MOSES N. JOYNER

State agent for the rural colored schools. That was an odd occupation for a white man, wasn't it? She took a seat at the desk and called up Mr. Joyner's image, the same small details that had made an impression on her the day he'd arrived. His pepper-and-salt hair with that beautiful ripple as if it had been marcelled, the glossiness of his dark eyes, the turn of his mouth. He was scholarly in appearance but with the freshness of a native face.

Lalura's jaw dropped. *No. He couldn't be. Could he? Mulatto?* "Well now, imagine that," she said aloud, a hint of a grin beginning to show on her face. "There's been no talk. Not in town, and certainly not in the house. And you know what? I wouldn't mind if there was. I don't mind it one bit." And then, struck with a clear image of Brud Daye banging on his coffin lid, clamoring to get out, she bent over in laughter. "Oh, the irony! I love it. I truly do love it."

At that moment a tap landed on her shoulder and she let out a keen gust.

"Alta Ruth! What are you doing sneaking up on me like that?"

"I thought I heard you talking to somebody up here. What are you doing?"

"I'm— Never mind what I'm doing! I'm straightening this place up, can't you see?" Lalura made as if to shuffle the papers into a neat pile. "I thought you were going over to Mary Dale's house."

"She wouldn't let me play with her Frozen Charlotte doll. That girl is stingier than a elephant with one peanut!"

"I seem to recall a certain somebody being that way when she got her TynieToy dollhouse," Lalura said, making herself busy.

"I showed her, though. I took her Frozen Charlie doll, the one she traded

Violet Daniels her Limber Jack for." Alta Ruth slipped an inch-long piece of glazed porcelain from her pocket and held it out to her mother.

Lalura took the porcelain doll in her hand and inspected it closely. It was a collectible, one of those ridiculous "gifts" that kept foolish women buying tea in ornamental tins. This one a curly-topped boy with clenched fists and blushed cheeks, and heavens to Betsy the boy was naked!

"And her mother doesn't know she has it either," said Alta Ruth.

"This isn't meant to be a toy," Lalura scolded. "You are to take this—" (no Christian woman she knew would collect these) "this tea cup doll back right this instant!"

Alta Ruth was none too happy. She snatched the doll from her mother and left.

"And don't think I won't be following up with a telephone call to Mary Dale's mother!" Lalura said. That child was forever working her into a dither, and she nearly forgot why she came into Mr. Joyner's room in the first place.

When she was finally back on track, she went to work stripping the mattress and replacing it with the fresh domestics. Somehow she needed to find a way to bring up Mr. Joyner's gallant cause to him in conversation. Without revealing, of course, that she had been snooping. What better way of getting to know someone? Particularly a gentleman nearly the same age—and very near the same polish—as herself.

Chapter 48
The Teacher-Her Perspective

*I*na stepped up to the outhouse door and braced herself. She didn't like it, especially today, with her stomach out of sorts. There were things in there—ughy and nauseating things. But there was, after all, no place for selfishness in the classroom. If she were going to teach her pupils lessons on the dignity of labor, she couldn't very well insist that they alone clean "the holy of holies." She must demonstrate a willingness to partake in some of the drudgery herself. So during their study period she had decided to don her hooded raincape and slog outside, with the intention of tossing a scoop of lime down this repulsive throat of human equalization.

She took a long inhalation and held it, closed her eyes briefly, then opened the door and stepped inside. The first furious assault of impure air was wrought by the gasp at evidence of someone's mischief—an immorally suggestive sketching thumbtacked to the flyspecked wall. She snatched the vile drawing and gave it a grave look. The eye is the second most serviceable of all the senses in committing an object to memory, bested only by the nose. But seeing is certainly believing. And every child who came into contact with this picture was sure to be poisoned. Children may learn by seeing, but believe you me, they are not satisfied with only seeing—they want to handle the object as well.

Who could've done such an obscene thing? It was a vision of moral bankruptcy. A rough and shagged conceptualization of an unclothed man and an unclothed woman. Deciphering one crotched figure from the other took no effort at all as the evidence was staring her right in the face—in the form of simon-plain genitalia, which made the exploits of the arrows that accompanied the drawing all the more unnecessary. The longer she looked at it the deeper she was stricken by the dagger of exasperation.

She was already of a bad temper this morning, knowing before she even got here that it would be a day to challenge even the most Christian of souls. She hadn't slept well the night before, burdened by a dream she'd had of Harlan. Though much of the vision was muddled, she perceived that she had done something in the dream to disappoint him simply by the expression of heartbreak on his face. From the moment she awoke she'd felt weighted down with an oppressive feeling of shame. It was incomprehensible.

Perhaps this was punishment for having a lapse of morality in secret contemplations. Her desserts for having less-than-chaste thoughts of another man. And Harlan, he was letting her know emphatically in that dream that she had less than an upright character, that it was to him she belonged. She'd felt it ever since that one indiscretion after Guerine's dinner party, and here it was again nagging at her.

In everything she did and said, guilt had become part of her daily presence. It was the source from which all her troubles leapt. She had been trying to piece together a life of self-support, and yet, despite this new lifestyle of connecting with people other than family, her feelings had remained wrapped up in Harlan. And Harlan was dead, having his own big adventure, and so what right would he have to be displeased with her? Wouldn't he want her to get on with her life? Wouldn't he want the best for her? At what point exactly can a widow just be a woman?

These feelings had left her with an aching exhaustion.

And then there was that long walk to the school in the pouring rain to contend with. Stormy weather and children do not mix. Too little pressure in the atmosphere leads to noise and confusion. All that motor energy stored up in the body must have an outlet, and there were more than a dozen of those little bodies back in the classroom that needed a good outlet-ing. Vigorous play on the playground.

She, herself, was in need of nerve rest.

As difficulties had cropped up in the classroom, she had taken them up with the individual as she saw fit. But this—this crude drawing that she now hastily rolled up—required that a lesson in morals be addressed to the entire room. It was one lesson she had hoped she wouldn't have to put into practice. Which reminded her, she needed to get back inside.

When she reentered the classroom, her pupils, already confined too long, had broken their bounds. They were behaving as if they'd been left hungry and abandoned and looking through a fence at a patch of ripe watermelons. It seemed that nearly all of them had caught the mob spirit. Henry was up to his usual degenerative tricks with a couple of the other boys, rifling through her desk drawer. Lloyd, interested in all things that move and anxious to see their outcome, was making a pest of himself by harassing Alta

Ruth with a caterpillar he had apparently picked up on his way to school. David was assisting Dolian in his attempt to swing from the stovepipe like it was a piece of playground apparatus. Victoria and Adele were arguing over nothing while the rest of the girls were laughing. And that wasn't the share of it. Others, too, were acting as if still in the "root and grub" stage. And someone had overturned the ink.

She'd barely been out of their sight for five minutes and nearly every one of them found it an occasion to act like *enfants terribles*! That'll teach her to place confidence in them.

She tore the dripping hood from her head and lit into a broad-voweled admonishment, shooing the children back to their original seats and behavior. "Get back to your desks! Every one of you, back to your studies! Assuming you can recall what you were doing before your thinking ceased."

When they were finally seated, she held up the curled paper.

"Can someone tell me who is responsible for placing this picture in the privy? Anyone?" She waited. "As much as you all love talking, now is your chance. No? No one wants to admit to knowing about this picture I'm holding here? I see. Well then—" *Well then, what? What is one to do now? Count to a hundred when angry, Ina. It says so in the book. Absolutely I will not! I will not stand here in front of them and count to a hundred. That's the most ridiculous thing I have ever read. Then offer them suggestions, Ina. Show them possibilities. If you want your pupils to act right, you've got to get them to think right. Do whatever it takes to elevate their thoughts. Try putting their roisterousness to good use. Dry formalism such as yours will only fail to accomplish the desired results.*

This inner argument served only to further frustrate her, and with breathless impatience she removed her raincape and hung it on the wall.

"Do not think that I will simply allow this occasion to go by," she said, and shoved the drawing into her dress pocket.

If she could find time enough to calm herself, perhaps show a shred of appreciation for what little labor they had expended thus far this morning, she might be able to come up with a better device for bringing out desirable activity in the classroom on rainy days, and even get them to refrain from misdemeanors altogether. (She could hear Bertie saying now: "In your hat!") For now, the best way, she resolved, was to go desk by desk and devote her attention to each pupil's study assignment.

"Nice effort so far, Lloyd. But you forgot to fill in this one—'The temperature at which water freezes.'"

"How is your letter writing coming, Alta Ruth? You need to go back and look at your superscription. We talked about how the form should be strict for a business letter. Remember? Easily fixable, though."

"This is a very interesting topic, Adele. Not a bad beginning. Although, I'm not sure how a horse can 'eat his head off.'"

Etta appeared to be vigorously at work. She had, in fact, remained in her seat during the classroom melee, just as Ina would've expected of her, absorbed in the task before her, oblivious to her surroundings.

"My goodness, aren't you the busy bee. Let's have a look. Etta? This isn't the work I approved for you. Your assignment is learning words, not making pretty pictures. Is this all you've done?"

Etta put down her colored crayon and slipped a sheet of paper from beneath her drawing. She handed it to Ina and Ina studied it.

"Compared to your penmanship last week I don't see much in the way of advancement. You certainly won't win any prizes this way. Where is your concentration? It's not as if I've asked you to write on lines or within spaces, and yet this is all you have to show? I'm terribly disappointed in you, Etta. And look at how you're sitting. Your arm is hanging off the desk. Your desk is for support, child. Now sit up straight and place both hands on it just as you've been taught."

Etta's pale face flushed in shame, but Ina was too distracted to give it much attention. She walked back to the front of the classroom.

"I can't understand for the life of me where some of your minds venture to. If pictures are such a desirable subject for some of you, then the question has arisen, when is it appropriate for us to draw? And what is appropriate for us to draw? I realize that we sometimes do things under the impulse of the moment, things that we wouldn't normally do, given time to think about it. But it has come to my attention that we must find a harmonious combination. Therefore, I think that this month's motto needs to be Self-Control. We'll make it the subject of our short morning talks. And the remainder of this week will be dedicated to self-control in the classroom, next week, self-control on the playground, and the week after that, self-control in our daily lives. By thinking, talking, and practicing self-control, perhaps it will leave on each of you a lasting impression."

Teachers must insist on civilized human intercourse. But she became suddenly breathless as she unconsciously placed her hand inside her pocket, feeling the offending picture. *Oh. Now that, is truly malapropos!*

Chapter 49

Mr. Joyner's Fillip

*H*e hailed from Charles City, Virginia, which was not a city at all as the name implied, more of a rural sanctum of farmland. But besides being rich in soil it was also rich in history; Thomas Jefferson and Martha Skelton were married there. But Mr. Joyner hadn't lived there since he was a boy, having been educated abroad and at Columbia, you see, and from then on had devoted his life to educational leadership.

Since 1916, he'd been employed by the North Carolina State Teachers' Association, which had organized a Rural Extension Department that same year to do special work among the rural schools for Negroes in North Carolina. And as state agent for said department—Mr. Joyner told that kind, God-fearing Mrs. Daye over breakfast one early Saturday morning—it had been his privilege to give aid wherever possible in creating a more wholesome school sentiment and to help, as far as possible, to create a cooperative relationship between the white school officials and the Negro schools.

In his travels, thus far, he had visited twenty-three counties: Alamance, Anson, Beaufort, Bertie ("such a coincidence," he said; "and oh what a good one," she said), Chowan, Columbus, Duplin, Durham, Edgecombe, Forsyth, Gaston, Gates, Greene, Guilford, Halifax, Hertford, Iredell, Johnson, Martin, Mecklenburg, New Hanover, Orange, and Pamlico. And now he was here in Person County, in Roxboro, to sound the alarm for better schools, better health, and a better community life for Negroes.

"The work does take its toll," he said, "but if permitted I could talk for hours on the subject." And for the next hour he did. While that good lady went about the kitchen in a sprightly manner and plied him with a breakfast that would rival a king's: cereal with soaked prunes, griddlecakes with huckleberries, eggs à la goldenrod, grapefruit cocktail, and don't forget the salt pork.

"Take the school I visited yesterday," he said, talking between bites. "A mere log hut where little or nothing is being done to improve the conditions. It consists of only one room, one teacher, and ten pupils of the primary grade. Whenever it rains, there's a downpour within, on both the teacher and her handful of shivering pupils."

"Sad," said Mrs. Daye, touching up Mr. Joyner's coffee.

"Thank you kindly. And the other sad thing is the old tow sacks that are pinned up around the room to ward off the cold winds. There is a stove but it has cracks and holes in one side, and I was told that during the coldest months live hot coals leap forth onto the floor and threaten to set the school on fire."

"How awful," Lalura said. "Here, Mr. Joyner. Do have more."

"Good gracious, I might never be able to rise again!" But he didn't mind if he did. "Especially given our churches," he continued. "We provide beautiful churches and comfortable pews for our own enjoyment for a two-hour service on Sundays, while our children are forced to dangle their feet from uncomfortable seats in cold and poorly ventilated rooms for five days a week."

It upset the lady to hear. And he took a break just long enough to have a sip of coffee.

"Sometimes," he said, "I fear that our leaders are too much absorbed in making money and tending to their own selfish interests to make themselves felt in the community."

"Not at all Christianly, is it," she considered.

He nodded, and wiped his mouth with the pretty red-bordered napkin she'd provided. "Yes well, however that may be, there are many throughout the State who stand ready and willing to hold up their hands and strengthen their knees. Much good has been accomplished already from their moral and material aid. But let me stop now lest I weary you." He laid the napkin on the table and prepared to get up from the table.

On his way out the door to his next appointment, Mrs. Daye handed him a basket she had packed with a carefully wrapped sandwich of her special peanut butter-and-bacon spread, a sheeny apple, and a prune-and-graham muffin she had tossed in for good measure.

"Blessings, Mrs. Daye, blessings! What a bright, attendant spirit you are!"

Chapter 50

A Privation

A change for the good was occurring in the tiny classroom of East Roxboro School. Over the course of a week, by adopting a more animated self, and adding variety to her pupils' lessons, Ina discovered that she had better success in holding their attention. Her solution for securing wandering minds? To think of the lessons as a banquet, and of herself as the caterer (per a wise suggestion in her handbook). If she were willing *to prepare and serve up so as to tempt every taste and appetite*, both she and her pupils would profit.

She started with a change to the afternoon recitation; an important event of the day—its purpose to test her pupils' knowledge on the day's lessons—which had lately turned into tedium. Altering the format from written to oral, and having them stand at their desks and recite answers aloud, enlivened the program. It benefited the rest of the class and seemed to have the effect of inspiring each child with the desire to know more. She was only sad that the banquet analogy hadn't been her idea, for she also made a priority of connecting the work of the schoolroom closely with that of their life at home, adding a lesson in manual training for the boys and domestic science for the girls. The interest in the new lessons was catching. She was even thinking of incorporating a tomato-growing club. The schoolroom now was a place of pleasure, not one of bane.

The only thing missing was Etta. She hadn't been in school all week. None of the children could recall seeing her since the Thursday before, when she had spent the better part of the day trying their patience with her annoying snuffles, and Ina had had to use her own handkerchief to wipe the neglected child's nose, which had produced enough mucilage to mend china. She had sent her home early. But after staring at Etta's vacant desk for six days, Ina began to grow anxious as to her welfare. She was willing to bet that the poor thing had been afflicted with enlarged tonsils. It would explain why the child was a mouth-breather.

She determined then to pay a visit to the Lester home after the day's closing exercises. After all, a teacher should become one with the neighborhood and strive always to enlighten. She would tell Mrs. Lester, in no uncertain terms, exactly how she felt. Mrs. Lester was doing her child a grievous wrong, was far too thrifty in her attitude toward caretaking when it came to her only daughter, and overly generous when it came to doling out heavy chores. She should be ashamed of herself for not recognizing the child's need for attention. How can a flower have the tenacity to thrive when its roots are bound in futile soil?

Whatever it took to get Etta back into school, she was resolved to doing, and walked toward the Lester property with the energy of someone trying to make up for lost time. Along the way she worked out another enthusiastic idea for the cause of education—a way to prevent unexcused, unnecessary absences. She could offer credit for home duties. Put a plan in motion to reward the children for work done at home, such as feeding the chickens, gathering eggs, wiping dishes, and washing their teeth. Perhaps then Mrs. Lester would take a more vital interest in her child if she could see how the school aided with Etta's homework.

There was no visible activity when she arrived, no barefooted children, no spouting of earthy curses. Not even a trace of the cat she had encountered during her last visit. Nothing was as before. The surrounding fields were empty and, despite the few articles of dry clothing strung on the line, the place looked deserted, robbed of its soul.

She stepped onto the porch and knocked, eager to see Etta's sparkling eyes.

Only it was one of the little girl's brothers who came to the door and peered out through the screen at Ina.

"I wish to see Etta, please," she said.

The boy didn't answer.

"She hasn't been to school for a week," she said. "I'm here to see that she returns. And I would think that you and your brothers should be in school as well."

He stared at Ina defiantly.

"My visit is purely one of well meaning, young man. Perhaps you'd rather I speak to your mother?"

"Etta's gone," he finally offered in an obstinate voice.

"Gone? Where gone?"

"Died. Day 'fore yesterday."

Ina stood silent, and after a moment uttered "I see" absentmindedly.

Custom dictated that she provide some semblance of comfort to Mrs. Lester, but suddenly she had no voice to ask to see the grieving mother. She backed from the door in confusion and bumped into one of the porch posts. She managed, holding fast to the railing, to ease her way down the uneven wooden steps until her feet found something that resembled solid ground. She turned and looked back at the house. The boy was no longer at the door.

Ina's numb legs began to move. Tears fell quickly, and she walked through them without knowing her destination, at one point stumbling to her knees.

But it was for the lost child that she continued walking. And for the lost child's mother. And she walked, doubting heaven. And she walked, doubting earth. Her mind shut to hope. And yet she walked.

❋

Sam was on his way home when he spotted her. She was coming toward him, in the opposite direction, the road between them narrow. It was too late in the afternoon for school to have just let out, and he wondered if she had stayed afterward to tend chores and was only now heading home. That he would know what time she left school, and cared to even ponder why only now she was walking toward home, caught him by surprise. What business was all this of his?

He took one last bite out of the Winesap he was eating and hastily tossed it over the hood of the vehicle. A distinct drop of rain splatted the back of his hand. He hoped the rain would hold off long enough for him to reach home, otherwise he'd have the nuisance of working the hard-to-turn steering wheel while dealing with the manual wiper.

As Ina's image grew larger and clearer, so did his smile. He slowed the vehicle to a funereal pace, hung his head out the window and called to her. "Hello there, Ina! Do you need a lift?" He couldn't get her attention. "Looks to be raining here shortly." But there was something wrong, he could see that now. She was crying. Her dress was soiled. She had obviously fallen, and he pulled over and got out, called her name once more, and when she still wouldn't respond he ran across the road until he caught up with her.

"Ina? Ina, what's happened?" He reached out and touched her sleeve. She became agitated, fending him off and shaking her head, unable to talk.

"Won't you tell me?" he pleaded. "Surely I can help."

Perhaps it was the rain that was starting to come down in a steady stream, but something in that moment caused her to stop and look appealingly into his face. He led her back to the vehicle, but once their sodden selves were under cover, he wasn't sure what to do, where to take her, or from whom to seek help.

And so he took her to his house. He had her sit at the kitchen table while he retrieved a damask towel from the linen closet. He wrapped the towel around her shoulders, and then wondered if by doing so he had taken a liberty, just as he had earlier when he touched her arm. He let the thought go and grabbed a Turkish tidy that was draped over a chair back to dry his own face. She was a friend, after all; clearly in distress, sitting there wet and shivering. Only someone with a soulless countenance could leave her to suffer.

He reached into the cupboard for the bottle of port and poured two goblets, placing one before her. "Here, this will warm you." He sat down across from her.

Shortly, she became aware of the towel and the water that was dripping from her hair. She pulled the towel tighter, its floral center snug around her neck. She took a deep breath and lifted the wine to her lips. He could see that she was starting to come round, and it wasn't long before she began to talk, in a manner so free it was as if the shower had ultimately washed away her reserve.

She told him about Etta, was convinced she had contributed to her death. She spoke of germs, germs on books and germs on doorknobs, germs being disseminated by common drinking cups; of her pupils putting pencils to their mouths and her failure to dip the pencils in aloe water, as the book had suggested to break them of the habit; of hookworms in water-closets; of Etta's blind cat and its being a metaphor for her own life—her personal misfortune and all the problems and limitations that had accompanied it thus far; and a host of other things that, as far as he could discern, had nothing to do with one another. But every word she spoke absorbed him, and no matter how frenetic, to him, her utterings were notabilia and he didn't want her to stop.

It was when she spoke of regrets that she began to cry again. And instinctively he slid his chair closer and took hold of her left hand. And she allowed it. He bowed his head to avoid looking at her. Into her eyes. Lustrous brown, lashes so thick and long they were fanned like an artist's sable brush that's been dipped, up to its ferrule, into oil. The warmth from her hand revived something in him and he felt the urge to place his mouth on the softness of her palm, envisioned it even, holding it there while she quietly sobbed. At that very moment, in that room, at that table, there was no past for him to recall, no future for him to consider, no commitments. No Guerine.

When he heard her say the name Harlan, he looked up and realized that her murmurings were now focused on her previous life. And it occurred to him then that she had never confronted the reality of her husband's death, and was only now beginning to grieve.

When she regained her composure and her philosophical tone, he drove her home.

As he pulled away from the corner he felt a gnawing disappointment that the truth of what lay in his heart, every thought he'd had of her since laying eyes on her the summer before, had not been reflected in her eyes.

Chapter 51

Guerine Bides Time

*G*uerine laid her book down when she saw a set of headlights go past the bay window. She got up from her chair and carried her curiosity over to the window.

The headlights belonged to a motorcar that came to a stop in front of the Dayes'. For an instant she thought it was Sam's. But one machine looked like the other and her Sam would certainly have no reason to go calling over there without her—the very notion ridiculous—so it couldn't have been him. Besides, if Sam stopped anywhere between his shop and home it would be for supper at her house, as he did most evenings, except for when he worked late, which was probably where he was tonight since he didn't show up for her delicious boiled fish at the usual time.

In fact, she hadn't heard from that rascal all day. It was just like him to put others before himself (though lately she hadn't felt like one of them). Busy building the business, always showing a determination to succeed. If it weren't for her insisting he take periodic breaks, why, the poor duck would starve! The sooner they got married, the better off he'd be.

She saw Ina step from the motorcar. Must be that dear Mr. Gentry behind the wheel. How kind he'd been to Ina, going above and beyond to help her in her efforts to raise money for a new school, driving her around the township for signatures, and losing his vehicle to a fire in the process. Wouldn't surprise her in the least if those two developed a twinkle. And all thanks to her.

Oh yes, that's why she thought it was Sam's motorcar! He had lent his to Mr. Gentry several evenings ago so Mr. Gentry could drive Ina out to RFD 3 to secure more signatures.

Not until she had seen the machine pull away and Ina close the door behind her, did Guerine retreat back to her seat and revisit her book.

Lengthy works of fiction didn't normally hold her attention for very long, but she was trying out something new. Mrs. Wheeler was forever promoting the idea at their Woman's Club meetings of being well read and expanding one's mind. And Guerine liked the idea of expanding her mind. Surely there was some value in it. Sam was an avid reader, and if she too became an avid reader they would have that much more to talk about after they got married. So when she heard of a book called *The Age of Innocence* that had been in *Pictorial Review* last year in four substantial installments, she ordered herself a copy.

But she found it difficult to sit through more than two pages. Her hands and feet forever wanted doing—a factor of her childhood bout with St. Vitus', she figured. And her mind. It carried on a constant dialogue, whether she wanted it to or not. That was the wonderful thing about perusing *Woman's Weekly* instead. She could drape the magazine across her legs like a little moquette rug and flip from one brief article to another. Flip, flip, flip. Just like that. Just like her mind.

It didn't help that she found this writer slightly offputting, a little too braggish for her taste, using words like *histrionic* and *maelstrom* and expecting an American to understand them. And this May Welland character was getting on her last nerve. What that woman needed was an old-fashioned pop upside the head. Couldn't she see that her husband was in love with her cousin Ellen? Why, anybody with half an eye could. Silly, silly, silly.

And then she remembered: the Ateco Cake Decorator! (A tenacious flapper was her mind.) Sam had a birthday coming next week and it occurred to her just now that she was intending to make something special for him, a memorable meal topped off with an out-of-your-ordinary birthday cake.

She shut the book and got up from her chair, and rollicked off to the kitchen on feet as swift as a foraging house finch.

Chapter 52

Ina's Malaise

*T*here are moments in every woman's life when she has a deep sense of standing at the center of infinity itself. She feels dimensionless. She has neither a beginning nor an end. It's a feeling that creates dizziness, and gives free play to the emotions as if they were no more than trifles. If she's of the dramatic type (and God love her if she is), it can make her want to tear her hair, to beat her breast, to give her sorrow palpable words. But how? And where, tell her, is she supposed to start?

※

It was during our honeymoon in New York City and I remember watching Harlan, absolutely adoring him from my Algonquin bridebed, as he performed his first order of grooming business in the morning: scraping a blade along the shadow of his jawline. A beautiful jawline. I wondered what thoughts filled his head as he looked at the same man in the glass at whom I was staring. I wanted to think of something clever to say, something I would save for a day far from then, perhaps when we had sons and daughters, or even later, after there were grandchildren and there'd be a quiet moment at home, just the two of us sitting on the porch watching a moon. "My dearest," I would say, "I hope you don't think this silly of me, but the first moment I laid eyes on you I was reminded of the Roman equites." And knowing Harlan's sense of humor his reply would've been, "Are they from Richmond?"

But only twice did that scene occur from that bed, for, one evening, after dining in the Oak Room, Harlan squeezed my hand and doubled over in pain. Appendicitis they told us at the hospital, then wheeled him off and performed a successful surgery. The two of us laughed and teased the day he was being discharged, a sheet of rain outside the window. He hugged me to him and kissed my forehead. Told me he was sorry I missed hearing that gent Wilson read his poetry. "We're making memories," I told him, "and that's all that matters. Stories to tell when we're old." Still, he promised he would make it up to me, an extra day in the city or better yet a long weekend in the near future, and he grabbed his coat and hat and just as I turned I heard the slump, the sound his body made as it hit the floor. An unforeseen blockage the doctor said. All the while I'm left standing there, confused, angry, wondering just how my knight could've slipped away so easily.

And now, Etta.

The one child most eager to be uplifted and inspired, who needed the touch of a loving hand, and the comfort of encouraging words, and I failed her. Because of my own selfish interests, I failed her.

Chapter 53

Guerine's Meditation on Love and Success

*G*uerine was bubbling over. She had just helped Sam celebrate his birthday with a glorious cake. It was the success she thought it would be—a Bride's Cake disguised as plain white with marshmallow frosting. What was the harm in not telling Sam the cake's original title? Soon enough she'd need to make a decision on one for their wedding, and there was no reason to worry him with those details. Leave that and the decorations to her.

After presenting him with his gift, a collection of copper cookware (she'd always wanted a set), the two had quietly settled in the parlor, Sam with the *Courier*, and her with her *Weekly*.

She tried to read the current edition's short story, really she did, but she found it too sentimental and turned the page to the latest design in slip-on blouses. She looked over at Sam. He appeared to be brooding. Whenever he was fully engaged in reading, he wore a serious brooding look, and he was wearing it now. This is what marriage was going to be like if she wasn't willing to broaden her mind. And if she had any say-so at all she was not about to become her parents.

She thumbed over to Digest of the News Women Want to Know. She had read this section the day before—after finally putting Miss Wharton in her place—and had come across a number of topics. Topics that sounded smart. Topics that were good conversation starters.

"It says here, Sam, that hotels in a number of cities are adding chapels." She said it as if discovering the newsworthy item for the very first time. "Doesn't say why, though."

Sam didn't reply.

"Oh here, Sam, listen: Did you know that rubber plants yield latex? That's certainly news to me. Seems like an awful waste, doesn't it? To turn such a beautiful plant into something as useless as an eraser."

Sam continued reading his paper.

She tried one more. "If this doesn't take the fig! According to this article, men object to the color yellow. Oh Sam, you must listen to this. Here's a young woman who says she asked all the men she knows, and some she doesn't, whether they like yellow—claims she reads all kinds of books on psychiatry—and according to her they all said no. Not one of them could tell her why either, except for one man who said he was a poet. Listen to what he said:

"*'We like to think of women as somehow mysterious. That may be why we like them to wear subtle colors. Dark blues, dark reds—all the colors not common in nature, we like. But bright, daytime colors destroy the mystery. We don't like the girl we are dancing with to look like a ray of sunlight when we are in a moonstruck mood. We want the colors in her garments, like her charm, to be something we can feel to be illusive.'*"

Sam was in a moonstruck mood, and Guerine's voice amounted to no more than a bee in his head. He couldn't read for thinking of Ina. Ever since he had offered her a ride home, she'd been the source of his distraction for days—several customer orders had even gone without tending. How quiet and somber her demeanor the evening he dropped her to her door. He hoped she was all right. He wondered if she was still troubled over poor little Etta's cat. If only he could find some way to see her, without causing any attention—

Guerine giggled. "Illusive," she repeated. "What do I care what a poet says when I know yellow to be an alluring color. Don't you, Sam? You like yellow. You own a yellow necktie."

"What's that?" Sam said, finally interrupted from his mind's heaven.

"I said: Don't you think yellow is an alluring color? Yellow is sunny and sunny equals success."

"Yes, Guerine. It's lovely. Perfectly lovely." And he buried his head once more into his paper.

His flat tone had a chilling effect on her. It suggested more than merely a preoccupation with his paper. For the first time ever, she felt that he wasn't being one-hundred-percent truthful, and then that awful phrase her mama liked to spout, "All men are fibbers," suddenly sprang to her mind. There were only two reasons for a person to lie—for protection against pain or to gain some advantage. But neither of those was Sam Eastbrook, and what on earth would he have to protect himself from anyway? And from her of all people.

It had to be her hair! Ever since she had bobbed her hair Sam's disposition had been a little off. That's exactly what it must be. For heaven's sake then, if that was the matter she would gladly grow her crown of glory back out. If truth be told, she had regretted clipping her tresses. Blame it on the fact she had liked playing with scissors as a child, would cut up anything she could get her hands on. She only bobbed her hair to be in style, more chichi, an interesting supper partner. But it had affected her own disposition and she was coming to realize that she didn't have the right frame of mind to wear short hair, always having to part it on the side. She missed the bun at the back of her head, and there was something sad about using a cut-glass candy dish to store unused hairpins.

She was glad that was settled. She would let her hair grow. Wouldn't Sam be relieved!

Chapter 54

Colon's Unfinished Business

*S*ome men are quicker to see defeat than others. Colon wasn't necessarily one of them. He had suffered a sizely whop to a tender spot the day Doodle ran him from her roof, down the ladder and off her property. Fortunately his give—whether the situation involved charms of the heart or more practical issues—had for the most part served him well. Another fella might've considered the matter closed.

For three days after the incident, after he had tended his mail route and returned home, all he did was sit and fidget. He had tried to keep it to himself, but his mood apparently hadn't gone unnoticed. He was seated at the kitchen table with his papa early the fourth morning, when his mama came at them with a broom. She had a dust rag tied around her head, and she seemed to be of a general sheet-flapping, mop-swishing disposition.

"Can't y'all scratch and fidget somewheres else?" she huffed, shooting a wide-eyed look at her husband.

Colon's papa sighed. "A man can't even light at his own breakfast table without being run off by a woman with a broom. Come on, Son. Bring your wishes. Maybe we'll have better luck out on this here porch." His papa pushed opened the screen door as Colon dutifully followed, and the two stepped outside. "Seems to be one of the few remaining places a man can get to where a woman can't bedevil him. Not that she can't really, just wouldn't want the neighbors seeing."

"I surmise so," said Colon absently. They both sat, and while his papa talked, Colon took in the sweet-smelling morning. It was warm and slightly breezy, the sky a watered-down blue. A perfect day for a young man to consider his future. The trees were heavy, and the branches on the hydrangea were rubbing up against the house.

"Womenfolk like to have the upper hand, son. Take your ma in there. Makes her feel good to think our coming out to the porch was her idea."

"I thought it was," said Colon.

"Don't be too sure. The one thing a man has to learn early on when it comes to women is timing. We got out from underfoot just in the nick of time. Any longer she would've set us to task."

His papa's voice continued to flow, but Colon's thoughts continued to meander. Maybe all this talk about women was his papa's way of telling him it was time to think about moving on, and moving on meant moving out, establishing a life for himself under a different roof, one with all the excitement and all the barbs that come with being a man.

There had been many times in the past few months when he'd been aware of some strange attraction to Doodle. Mostly he'd had doubts—she was temperamental, had more phases than the moon, and could sure be unreasonable. Yet because of her he was losing sleep. But how come? What was it about her that he found fetching? There were plenty other gals prettier than her, in the traditional sense, with chirkier personalities and winning ways. He could have nearly any pick of that lot. Esperann crossed his mind, but he didn't necessarily believe her to be the best example. Sure, she'd had success on a horse, racing a bowlegged Mr. Don't Stop Moving at the county fair (he seemed to recall her flashing a green ribbon in his face), and that kind of thing, he recognized, could certainly catch some fella's eye. But a woman with tack made little if no impression on him.

Come to think of it, maybe Esperann was a good example. At least he knew what kind of woman he didn't want. And Doodle had caused him to look even closer. At himself, and at Doodle. There was something time-honored about her, the way she carried herself. She was unassuming-like, without the least bit of consciousness of herself, though her stance was as firm and rooted to the ground as that majestic bur oak he'd grown up with. It was something he had never noticed in a woman before.

Her voice had a soft drawl, too, and he could easily see how a sound that pleasant would allow a man to draw a long breath after a hard day. Not to mention her eyes, pure and tender, yet at the same time a little in the way of aching. Made him want to reach out to her point-blank and be sentimental, in a manner like the leading heroes do on the great screen. He just knew behind those big brown eyes of hers were a million tantalizing emotions. And the way she wore her hair without a lot of fussing, all natural with soft ripples and curls. Even the times he'd seen her perspire, it stayed fluffy and sanitary. It had the fragrance of a thousand flowers and it glowed like the sunset. Why, it was downright electrical. And her hands—he'd noticed them when she had wrenched the toolbox from him and accidentally brushed his hand—were surprisingly smooth to be so hardworking. Which made him think about the rest of her skin. That, he imagined to be as soft as the pond water he'd caught her bathing in.

If a man put all those things together, it was understandable why he was restless. Wherever he was he thought about her. In town, at home, on his Model O, or over a fishing hole with his papa catching a brag of brim. So he knew darn well he wanted something more with her because she was making him plumb miserable. To him, she was the divine expression of beauty.

"Yessir, a woman like that can easily get away from a man, quicker than a bobcat," he heard his papa saying. "Why, Son, that kind of woman's a blessing if you ask me. She's what you might call conspicuous. Special. Like a wood duck during breeding season. And every conspicuous woman needs a considerate man behind her."

Colon stood up and made his way over to the steps.

"Where you rushing off to, Son? Thought we might take a couple poles and go sit down by the crick."

"Sorry, Pa. Not today. Gotta see about a roof on a birdhouse!"

She was tending to the turkeys when Colon came puffing up toward the house. He had a look about him, one she had never seen before. His whole bearing was obstinate, the expression on his face fixed, as firm as a rock.

He handed her a slip of paper. It was a receipt from the lumberyard, and it was stamped PAID.

"Mr. Barnett will be delivering the lumber and the rest what's needed to repair that roof," he said. "I'll be back on Saturday to finish job." He turned to go, but remembered one more thing. "Oh, and you can get uppity if you want. Makes no never mind to me. I'm gonna fix that roof, whether you like it or not." He didn't give her a chance to reply, simply made rudders out of his legs, straddled the seat of his cycle and sped off.

He waited till he was beyond the mailbox and down the hill before breaking into a jaunty little diddy that, if she could've heard him sing, would've sounded a lot like a Lester O'Keefe dancing song. "Doodle-dee-doo! Doodle-dee-do!"

Chapter 55

Miss Lul Receives Good News

*L*alura cradled the envelope in her hands and gloated over it as if it were a planked whitefish she'd just taken from the oven. It was addressed to her by Bertie's familiar round fist. That child of hers hadn't written her a legitimate letter since she'd been in Washington, D.C., (even though she had written Bertie with regularity), only mailed home occasional postcards of street scenes and churches, and of a few federal buildings, with abbreviated sentences on the back that didn't convey in one way or another whether she was happy or homesick, well-fed or overworked. And she only telephoned every three or four weeks, and because Alta Ruth would be so wrought up to talk to her, and Bertie was always in a hurry to be somewhere important, Lalura hardly got a word in. The last communication had come on a Field of the Dead postcard from Arlington National Cemetery with the sentiment: "Still in the land of the living. Love, Bertie." Her and her offbeat humor. She had nearly given Lalura a fit, and now here was a letter from her as thick as a panned squab. That girl was always doing the unexpected. Just what fly-by-the-seat-of-her-pants news was she about to share now?

She tore open the envelope, unfolded its contents, and commenced reading.

Bertie began with a long apology for her lack of communicating. She hadn't taken a day off to relax since she'd gotten there, except for the day that she was writing this letter ". . . and before you go and accuse me of gallivanting all over this city, every one of those postcards was purchased off a lopsided rack at a hole in the wall lunch counter that doesn't know the first thing about making a decent grilled cheese."

She gave a page-by-page account of her work at the NWP, and her excitement over participating in a ceremony to celebrate the passage of woman's suffrage back in February. The event had coincided with the 101st anniversary of the birth of Susan B. Anthony. In March she attended the Southern Women and Race Cooperation Conference, where she had learned about the Inter-Racial Commission, which was created by a large denomination of Christian (yes, it didn't hurt her to spell it) women who felt a deep sense of responsibility to do something about the friction between the Negro and White races. The original purpose of the commission—she quoted from their literature—was *to study the whole question of race relationships, the needs of Negro women and children, and the methods of cooperation by which better conditions might be brought about.* It had given her an idea, something she'd been thinking about for a while, and she wanted Miss Lul to hear her out before poo-pooing the idea. She believed that the NWP was doing great things for women. But their priorities and her priorities had now come to a fork. There wasn't one person at the National Woman's Party, as far as she could see, that was pressing hard enough for voting rights for Negro women. And someone needed to take a firm stand in that regard.

"There's a great opportunity here, Miss Lul," Bertie's letter stated. "By the two of us working together, you and me, we can help bring about a better understanding between the races in our own community. The women members of these state committees still haven't all been named, and I'm not saying we have to get on board with this particular commission. We can start our own agency if we want, so long as we can agree not to use the words *Christian* or *missionary* in the title."

Bertie went on to describe her proposed plan in detail, and soon Lalura's mouth was gaping with wonder, for she, too, had been thinking about a similar thing. Ever since Mr. Joyner had come to live under her roof, she had been trying to find a way to approach him about how she, too, could make a difference to the Negro community.

She read Bertie's postscript and soon was crying. Her oldest girl child was coming home! And apparently she was bringing a friend named Mel with her. "My goodness, that girl is full of surprises. With all her overwrought sensibilities and insatiable ambition, I always figured her to remain a hard-boiled virgin." She'd have to ponder that one later. There was plenty of space for the young man, and Lalura would see to it he got a nice room—so long as he didn't turn out to be one of those slybooting so-and-sos or she'd be quick to toss him out on his ear. The important thing was Beatrice Abigail Daye was coming home!

Chapter 56

The Growing Pains
of Evolution

$\mathcal{A}$nother high-tide day at the NWP and Bertie was glad to see Friday evening on the horizon. She'd spent the week, along with the other members, moving the National Headquarters out of the Lafayette Square building to a new (temporary) location on Bond Street. She couldn't exactly say that she was sad to be out of that dust hole she'd been working in. Wouldn't surprise her if she ended up with lungs full of chokedamp from being down in that stale-smelling place every day. Already it had stripped every bit of luster from her hair.

The building on Bond wasn't the only thing temporary for the National Woman's Party, Bertie figured. Lately she'd been feeling an urge to get on back home, to Alta Ruth and Miss Lul, to Doodle and Guerine, and everything else familiar. Over the weekend she would sit down and write to Miss Lul, run some ideas by her, worthy causes they both might want to consider devoting themselves to.

But right now she could hardly wait to head back to the apartment and get out of her dingy clothes. Treat herself to a quick rub-a-dub is what she was gonna do the minute she got there, too, swipe a little mixture of castor oil and cologne water through her scalp, pull out something fresh to wear, and she'd be ready for a night out. Dinner with Mel and a few friends, then a late-night game of Set Back afterward, something she had looked forward to all day. Mel never could seem to remember to keep six cards at a time, or that the joker was the one you always wanted, the highest of them all. But not everybody was cut out for playing cards, and Mel's clumsy foozles (dealing cards up instead of down) sure did make for good laughs. And Bertie felt in need of a lot of that lately.

As she made her way toward the cloakroom, she heard two voices coming from the office that had been designated the mail room. She wouldn't have thought much of it—there was always someone working late, and more unpacking yet to do—except that one of the voices was Mel's, and Mel was to have left an hour earlier for a meeting she told Bertie she didn't have time to explain but would see her at the restaurant.

The secretive nature of the conversation coming from the mail room made Bertie stop.

"Sure, honey. Didn't I say I know him? Know the man personally and I'll go see him first thing in the morning like I said I would, set up a meeting between him and Miss Paul. Woman won't know what hit her. Right now, though, me and you got some seeing of our own to do."

"Not so fast, Senator."

"Don't be shy, Red. We got us an understanding. You want the Coloreds to be on equal ground, don't ya? That's what you said you wanted. And I said I'd take care of it, too, didn't I?"

"You did, Senator. And the missus will be glad to get the colored vote, too, because I know she supports it."

"Aw, come on now, Red. Don't you trust me?"

"Soon as I make a note of that birthmark. Peculiar place to have one of those, isn't it?"

"You can trust ol' Earl here. Now go on now. Make 'em jump for me. You don't get Earl red as a poker and then don't come through for him. Earl's gonna be so good to you, honey. He sure is. Goddamn is he gonna be good to you!"

There came a guttural groan. Then a slow, rhythmic thumping, a table leg against the wooden floor.

The weight of the circumstance taking place, only paces away, nearly carried Bertie off her feet. Her back collapsed against the wall of the outer office, and every inch of strength she felt she'd ever had up until then flooded right out her body. Her hands did their best to hold her steady as she tried to repress the violent sobs eager to work their way out. Her body shaking, expecting too that any minute her lunch would rise over the distress of the blatant sounds coming from the other side of the wall, the humiliation of the rutting and grunting that her friend Mel was willing to suffer. Every last base throb of it.

Bertie's mind flashed to Alta Ruth. This was a far cry from Person County peanuts and kissing foolery. What women were willing to endure, every indignity, physical pain and suffering, all to express their beliefs. Jailing. Painful, humiliating force-feedings. Foul insults from filthy men. Rotten fruit and vegetables lobbed by unsympathetic women. They were regaled as "wild women," treated like second-class citizens. And, in spite of it all, there was obviously no cost too great for one of the most committed.

Chapter 57

The Plan

$\mathcal{M}$r. Joyner had found a sympathetic ear, a friend of Negro education. And at this moment she was perched at the front window like an Eastern Screech awaiting its prey, hiding behind the convenience of the drapes. All the day long her mind and body had been a remarkable get-there of activity, and the eagerness she felt for her male boarder to return only added more fuel. She had very pointed business she wanted to discuss with him.

Today had been one of the most beautiful days Lalura could ever recall, and the reason had not a thing to do with the weather. She'd had an epiphany, plain and simple. Bertie had given her much to think about. And so too had Mr. Joyner. When he revealed the condition of the so-called graded Negro school to Lalura that morning back in the kitchen, she had been appalled. His words had ignited a secret wish. For years she had wanted to make some type of amends to the colored community for the pain Brud had inflicted, but it was a problem much bigger than herself and she had never been able to see her way around it. Ignoring a bullock in the parlor might be easier. Hadn't she always believed domestic service should be recognized as an occupation, though? Wasn't she on good ground with Johnny Bob and Silvia? She'd always treated that relationship with respect. But she'd been quiet about her views on the race question, had chose to keep them to herself. Folks could either know how she felt or not, and if they didn't then that was their loss. Maybe that was part of the problem. If a person, in her heart, stood with colored people in their search for every right they were entitled to, wouldn't her silence then be grave and dishonest? Her own daughter was a perfect example of someone trying her best to bring folks together. The girl was fearless. And Lalura was already seeing that same type of fire in Alta Ruth.

Presently, she saw Mr. Joyner round the corner, and hurrying away from the window she began busying herself in the living room under the pretext of dusting. She could distinctly hear him whistling a cheery tune as he ascended the front porch steps, but she waited for him to step inside the foyer before affecting surprise.

"Oh hello, Mr. Joyner! Is it that time already? My, how one's work can get away from them. I'll have dinner on the table shortly." As a good hostess she offered him a nougat to tide him over, and he happily accepted. But in the wake of his dignified exit up to his room, Lalura had the slightest inclination that Mr. Joyner's mind was occupied with something other than her cooking. Sad but true. Such great efforts that kind gentleman was going to. Imagine the burden he was carrying on his shoulders! It's a wonder he wasn't footsore and tired. Made her glad for arranging the evening as she had—sending Alta Ruth to go find fun and popularity over at her friend Mary Dale's house. And Ina, bless her heart, hadn't taken a meal outside her room since that poor little girl had died, which would make it only Lalura and Mr. Joyner at the table for supper. It pained her to take advantage of a terrible situation such as that, but the timing was just. This was her gilt-edged opportunity. She was ready and more than willing to offer her moral and material aid to Mr. Joyner. She still had the major portion of Brud's nest egg, and she wanted to turn it toward this fine cause. It's the only thing she had thought about the entire day.

She didn't even allow the good gentleman the pleasure of one slurp of her velvety potato potage before she outright declared:

"They'll come here to study their lessons, Mr. Joyner!"

"I beg your pardon," he said, the hot broth still on the safe side of his pucker.

"Those children at the graded school," she said. "I'll open my home to them during the week. Monday through Friday. They will come here and have their lessons. They simply cannot continue to attend a rumble-tumble school building. And I won't take no for an answer. If the white children in this community can enjoy the benefits of a good school supported by a special local tax like the one Miss Fitzhugh is pushing for, one that my own daughter will reap benefits from, then why can I not push the same for your children? Who's to say we can't do our own gerrymandering? I don't know how long you intend to stay on, Mr. Joyner, but between the two of us I know we can get the word out. We'll get every influential thinking North Carolinian on board, everyone who is in favor of giving the Negro children of our state a fair chance for education and happiness and a life of usefulness to themselves and society. Yessir, Mr. Joyner. That's exactly what we shall do." Having expended her breath, she noticed that Mr. Joyner's soup spoon now lay noncommittal on the stamped linen table cover.

"Dear Mrs. Daye. I'm not sure I know how to respond." A look of amused interest came over him. "Except to say—What a capital idea!"

It was the divine spark that Lalura needed to fetch her breath.

"Fact is," said Mr. Joyner, laughing, "it's not the only one presented to me this week. You see, a matter was brought to my attention some days ago regarding an acre of land here in Person County. Reverend Ragland is looking to put a school into operation there for students preparing for the ministry, as well as for boys and girls who are seeking a high school education. And, as things will happen, I bought that acre of land for the reverend's school today."

"So then, you'll be staying?" Lalura prompted, for Mr. Joyner was giving her something else altogether to think about, and she studied him with an intentness that she never had studied a man before.

"I believe many great things will be taking place for the Negroes in this county over the next few years, especially where education is concerned," he said. "Your plan, for one. And I can't tell you, dear lady, how it pleases me to hear it. But much is still needed. I'm finding a number of irregularities here while out in the field—not only problems with buildings, but with the educating of the teachers. Not all is in harmony with fairness and justice, and I think my work here is only beginning. So yes, to answer your question, I suppose I will be staying on in the Courteous City a while longer. For as long as a man of my age can be of use to someone."

For the first time in a long time, Lalura could feel the color of modesty. All the way up to her eyes.

Chapter 58

A June Night

"A JUNE NIGHT"

BIGGEST MUSICAL REVUE
EVER STAGED IN ROXBORO

SNAPPY GIRLS! SNAPPY COSTUMES! SNAPPY REPARTEE!
With a cast of 40 people

Benefit of the Roxboro Woman's Club
Reception to follow

When the show ended and the curtain fell, and after the applause died down, everyone poured out of the theater and into the lobby for the reception. The Palace had never been so crowded. Tonight's benefit for East Roxboro School was a huge success, the enthusiasm honor bright.

Even Ina's emotions nearly resembled giddy. Construction had begun on the new school and the building was to be a reality by the start of the fall season. It was a definite cause for celebration.

"Bertie'll be sad she missed this," said Guerine.

Sam adjusted his tie. "Don't be too sure. More likely she would've preferred a challenging game of cards over tonight's affair. When did you say she was coming home, Miss Fitzhugh?"

"Another couple of weeks, I believe."

"What's taking her so long?" said Doodle. "I thought she was on her way back days ago."

"She's apparently educating herself along the way, according to Miss Lul," Guerine said. "One of those crazy missions of Bertie's, sounds to me. Probably trying to hit every women's rights convention between here and there. Personally, I like to think she's gone on romantic holiday with that gentleman friend she's proposing to bring home with her."

"A gentleman friend, huh?" said Sam. "Fancy that."

Doodle, too, found the notion peculiar, made evident by the wrinkle above her brow.

"Be a dear will you, Sam, and hold my throw?" Guerine said. "I must excuse myself to the ladies' room. Don't look now, Doodle, but there's your favorite messenger. Looks a little windblown if you ask me, like he arrived by pigeon."

"Guerine," said Sam.

"Don't everyone wait for me," Guerine said. "Go help yourselves to the array. I won't be a minute."

He was hanging back from the rest of the party, hovering near the punch bowl when Guerine pointed him out to her. Sing small if you have to, but get on over there and sing something, Doodle thought at that very instant. Everybody's got to be willing to tuck their tail at least one time in their life. Now's your time.

She worked her way through the confusion till she stood face to face with him, the tallest object between them a prism-cut punch bowl resting in a fancy stand.

"Snappy show," she said, and briefly touched the handsome glass bowl.

Colon nodded. She thought he even might've shuffled his feet.

"Look, I didn't really come over here just to be sociable," she said. "What I was wanting to do, see, is to make matters up for the way I been acting, and to thank you for all you've done for me. My papa, I know he would've been appreciative to you himself, what for all you done. So. That's all I got to say, I reckon."

He hadn't said the first thing yet, which made it hard for her to know what he was thinking.

"You gonna keep standing there like that and looking at me like I'm crazy or what?" she said. "Ain't you gonna say something?"

He set his cup of punch down and commenced to dipping up another.

"You just gonna ignore me? Fine. That's just fine," she went on, her voice getting louder. "Even the likes of me can beg pardon for being an ass, you know. Least you could say you accept my apology."

He offered her the sparkling cup and in spite of her jumbled irritation she accepted.

"They say the humble pie is awful good here, Miss Shuford." Colon took a quick sip. "Myself, I believe it's the best I ever come across."

"What?" she said. She saw that he was grinning now, and it didn't take long before it spread to her.

☀

Throughout the performance, they had stolen glances at each other. A harmless child's game was all, a silly *passetemps*. So Ina wasn't surprised when, after Guerine had excused herself to the ladies' room and Doodle had gone over to say hello to Colon, Sam joined her in contemplating a soiree of desserts.

But it was with an air of aloofness that he joined her over by the tables. Conversation did not come easily for either. The brief periods of silence between them were palpable.

Something about their friendship had changed. She could feel it. And she could feel that he could feel it, too. It was—uncomfortably comfortable.

"What do you suppose it is?" he said.

"Difficult to say," she said.

"Black Forest," he decided.

She laughed and leaned closer to examine the uncut cake. "It most certainly is not! I'm sorry to tell you, Mr. Eastbrook, but Black Forest has cherries, and this one has no cherries." He reminded her of a garçon, a bullfighter even, with Guerine's shawl draped over his arm. Few are the women who cannot be won by a handsome tailor and his trim.

Something was happening to her. Of this she was acutely aware. It was the first blush of a suggestion, a physical insensibility that seemed to be rising from the pit of her stomach, and one she would gladly have acted on if given the chance. She watched him closely, her curiosity aroused, as he ran a finger along the base of the cake and brought away a tantalizing dollop of icing.

"Really, you shouldn't!" she said. But she was being insincere, for she liked the manner in which things had now turned, this acting out of character, this disregard for what or whomever polite was around them, and the way the icing momentarily disappeared into his mouth. The excruciating smile it produced on his face, and the conduct of his eyes, how they danced when he offered, without the slightest hesitation, the remaining icing to her lips.

It was all so delicious.

Standing in front of the bathroom mirror, Guerine took a small compact of solid perfume from her handbag, and was about to give her earlobes and wrists a good dosing of Sweet Pea when Eunice came in and scurried up next to her.

"You'll have to wait your turn, Eunice. I refuse to move from this glass until I have checked every angle. Have you seen Cora Humphries' olive-drab trapping? Far be it for me to say, but that woman's got the belly of an ostrich."

Eunice tugged at Guerine's sleeve.

"Just a second!"

Animated, Eunice made a wild gyration with her hands.

"Like I have time for your riddles? Sam is out there, waiting on me."

Provoked by Guerine's dismissive attitude, Eunice stomped her foot, shook her head and motioned toward the door.

"Well, don't have a pet," said Guerine, finally permitting the wrought-up woman a fritter of her attention. She watched as Eunice then brought her hands to Eunice's own throat and made a sign that looked to Guerine like a bow tie. "Sam?" said Guerine. "What about Sam? Sam is what? Sam is choking? Oh my word, Sam is choking!"

Clearly, Eunice was having trouble getting her point across. She hooked Guerine by the arm, shook her head at the young woman to assure her it was something else altogether, then urged her over to the bathroom door where they stuck their heads out like two box turtles after a summer rain.

Guerine followed Eunice's finger across the lobby floor until it stopped at the dessert table and wagged accusingly. "Oh for heaven's sake, Eunice! Is that all? I gave Sam permission to start eating without me. Don't you scare me like that again, you hear?" But Eunice refused to let her move from their post until Guerine had followed her pointer slightly to the right of Sam's shoulder where Ina stood. Sam must've been acting his usual charming self. Ina appeared to be enjoying herself. She was laughing. But who didn't when in Sam's company?

She looked down at Eunice who was peering up at her and making a spoony face.

"Don't be silly," said Guerine. "That's nonsense! I declare, Eunice. You don't know what you're talking about. Remind me to never listen to you again."

But before she withdrew to the porcelain basin to soap her hands, something besides Sam and Ina's fascination with the dessert table caught her attention and held her there. It was more than their mutual like for pretty sweets. It was the dovetailed nature in which Sam's icing-cloaked finger came to settle on Ina's lips.

When she looked down, Eunice was gone, and it was with an inordinate amount of trepidation—she had the skinful, cloying feeling of having been fed a diet of cake—that she pulled back the door to the washroom and returned to the reception.

Music played throughout the lobby, the type of soft music that caters to ardent lovers. Nothing, however, can comfort a man more, on an exciting evening such as this one was turning out to be, than a good sampling of highly seasoned beef whorls, tantalizing olives in blankets, and a most delectable cream cheese dunk. But helping himself to a salami stick—on a tray-full of tasty-looking salami sticks—Sam accidentally knocked over a glass of orange shrub. It had been set there by Kate Lewis, a sprightly young woman with a head full of ringlets the color of Walnettos, who had turned her back for a moment to reach for a spoon. Turning around, she saw her overturned glass, the orange sherbet no longer floating in harmony atop the fruit punch, and a scrambling Sam Eastbrook trying to clean up the mess before it ran down the edge of the table.

"I say, Kate! Was this your shrub? I'm terribly sorry."

"My fault for even setting it there, Sam. Here, let me," she said, and came to his aid with a stack of napkins. "How've you been? I was just asking Pete the other day if he'd seen you lately. Oh, do watch there, Sam! You'll have it all over your shoes if you're not careful."

"Golly, such a waste of a good shrub. But business, yes, business is good," he said, wiping the stickiness from his hands, then tossing the napkins into a receptacle at the end of the table. "How I do love shrubs myself. The perfect refreshment on a warm summer night. Here, Kate, let me get you another." He felt someone bump into his shoulder and saw Pete standing by his side. "Why, hello there, Pete! Enjoying the party?"

"Did I just hear you make a reference to my girl's bubs?" Pete slurred.

"I beg your pardon?"

"Honestly, Pete!" said Kate.

"You got an eye for her, don't you?" Pete said, scowling at Sam. "Tell the truth. You been looking at her for years."

"I most certainly have not," said Sam. "No offense, Kate."

"None taken, Sam," she said, and then focused her anger at her male companion. "Pete Thacker, are you so bent that you'd make a fool of yourself in public this way, and embarrass me in the process?"

But Pete persisted.

"I invite you to kindly step outside, Sam. Just me and you an' me. The two of us putting up our dukes like gen'lemen." Pete swayed, and bungled two lightweight fists into a breath's width of Sam's face.

"Don't be ridiculous," said Sam. He gave a weak laugh. "You've misinterpreted the situation all round. Come on now, Pete, maybe you should sit down. Besides, Sport, you couldn't pull off a sockdollager right now if your life depended on it."

"Don't you 'Sport' me, you—" Pete attempted to hook Sam's jaw with a right jab. Sam ducked, avoiding the sloppy thrust.

A clumsy scrimmage ensued and the crowd began to mill around them. A little shoo-fly flask fell from Pete's jacket and clattered onto the floor. Colon saw what was happening and jumped in, caught a draggletailed Pete by the waist, but Pete continued swinging and trying to lunge at Sam.

"Stop it, Pete!" Guerine yelled, rushing to the scene. "Stop it! He isn't in love with Kate, you sap! He's in love with Ina."

The outburst stilled everyone at the reception—with the exception of Doodle and Colon, who together echoed, "What?"

"Who?" said Pete, who by now had fallen to his keester at Colon's feet.

Sam looked to Ina, then to Guerine. "Guerine," he tried.

"Really, Sam, it's all right. It's really all right. I've suspected for some time. Just took me a while to get used to the idea is all.

"Well"—she paused—"if y'all will excuse me, I believe I've had enough of celebrating for one night."

She held off crying until after she reached home.

There, she closed the door behind her and quietly turned the key. She stood there reflecting, one hand on the knob, the fingers of the other pressed to the keyhole, willing Sam to follow her home. At any second he would knock. At any second she would be opening the door to him standing there sheepish, and he would promise her that the whole thing had been a big mistake. A doozy of a misunderstanding, but a misunderstanding nonetheless.

But after a spell of standing wait and looking at the Waterbury on the mantel, her palm all the while turning wilty, Sam didn't knock, and she went over to the divan and sat down. Robbed of her honey! A man so firmly knitted into her daily existence, their bond she had believed to be as strong and durable as those Hercules braids he used for trim. The color drained from her face and she laid her head against the cushions and wept.

Oh, how love can wrench you and turn you into a complete dummy! How did a thing like this happen? Why didn't I see it coming? Sam could've beaten me blue with his hickory walking stick and it wouldn't have hurt near as bad as what he's done to my pride and soul. To think of all the time I've spent. All these years. The surprise lunches, the special dinners, not to mention the pleasure of my company, and he wasn't even worth it. Love, dove, schmove! Who can understand it? I won't deny that Ina is pretty, but so am I. I'm as pretty as a flower, and I've got snap. I'm a girl with great spirit. Poets rave about girls like me in springtime. What does she have to offer opposite that?

When she was done berating Ina and Sam into the cushions, she sat up and wiped her eyes. She was exhausted and her head ached, the reality of the night's events still swirling around her in a heavy fog. She carried herself upstairs and went straight to the bathroom and looked at herself in the bevel mirror. What a pitiful spectacle.

She washed her face, hoping it would make her feel better, then crossed the hallway to her room in search of sleep, knowing that when she woke she'd be facing "the drab dawn of a dead tomorrow."

Chapter 59

Le Epanchement-or, Ina and Sam Exchange Commerce

*T*here had been no verbal agreement to meet, only a look shared between them—all destined lovers share a *coup d'oeil*—that suggested this moment was inevitable.

As Ina approached the door, she could hear music coming from within the house, a piano playing "Dreaming Dreams of You." This was senseless. She'd never been secretive in this fashion before, had until now lived her life straightforwardly. But forbidden fruit had never had so much appeal. She didn't want to hurt anyone, and her hand seemed to be restraining, but before she had a chance to knock, Sam opened the door. He'd been waiting, and without delay, reached out to her.

Inside, neither lover spoke.

For months they had been a warm shadow in each other's heart, but they had analyzed their feelings for so long—Are they honorable or dishonorable feelings? Are the two of them even in possession of their faculties anymore? Or are they merely fools?—until they had reached a point where they'd lost the ability to speak of love at all.

Yet here, now, they found the sweetness of togetherness. There was the initial embrace, and there were soft kisses, and there were urgent kisses, and kisses of whimsy, and there were imploring eyes, and hungry hands caught up in hair, and rapid chest-swelling heartbeats beneath an oh-so-very-long line of ocean shell pearl buttons.

The rest was a situation of great mystery.

Chapter 60

What a Man Thinketh

*J*na departed on a promise before the small hours of morning. Sam watched her from the door, and when he could no longer see her, he went into the study and lifted the lid of the Victrola. He placed a record onto the turntable—Graveure singing "The Want of You"—then slumped into the elbow chair thoughtfully. Guerine once laughed at the concert singer's voice when Sam had tried sharing with her his appreciation for the baritone (he believed *beastly* was the word she used), and had further spoiled the moment chiding him to choose something they could laugh to, like a minstrel song, or Ted Lewis's Jazz Band, something with snap and swing.

He reached up, switched on the lamp, and examined his surroundings like a man preparing for his last sleep. This house and all its belongings he had inherited upon the death of his parents three years earlier. The firescreen that his mother placed in front of the bare hearth every summer, the singular, colorful parasol she had painted onto it herself; the lambrequin draped over the mantel that she'd made from a remainder of moss-green velvet from his father's shop; the writing table where his father ministered to the family's accounts, the butler's trolley along the wall that housed a tray of light-colored aperitifs and dark-tinted digestifs; shelf after shelf of books enveloped him, and the nose of his father's pipe tobacco still lingered there in the silk damask shades.

But of all the flourishes it was the Victrola that he most cherished. Just as food was capable of calming his nerves, music consoled him during times of crisis. It was his safeguard. But no matter how many boxes of raisins, or sleeves of crackers, or apples or arias it took, he'd best plan on nerving himself. After what had occurred tonight, there'd be no turning back.

It wasn't as if he had set out to destroy Guerine's honor. He'd been raised to believe in decency. His parents were the epitome of human goodness, and they had given him every advantage. But the influenza couldn't see fit to spare either one of them air, taking first his mother and, within days, his father. And that was one of the things about Guerine that he hadn't been able to understand, the one characteristic of hers that perhaps disturbed him the most—never once had she approached the subject of their deaths. She carried on as if it had never happened, even though everywhere you turned people were wearing those stark-white gauze masks. He accepted it as a product of the way they both had been brought up. A man's role was to be that of protector, to deal with the burdens of life in order that a woman's thoughts could remain unclouded. And what could she have said to him anyway? Still, he couldn't help but wonder whether she'd even considered how such a rapid and cruel loss had affected him.

He had tried to live an ideal life, had tried to honor his parents by showing strength and noble character to the outside. If it hadn't been for their passing in such a vicious manner, he and Guerine probably would've been married by now. Maybe in that regard it was a hidden blessing. It had allowed for postponement. And Guerine had accepted his reasoning of needing time to settle into his father's business (though, he was already a darb at tailoring and knew the business inside and out).

On so many levels he felt that Guerine was like a child, in her general way of thinking and in her affectations. All the years he'd known her she'd remained in a state of puppyism. Her naïvete used to be endearing, but now he found it irritating. He had hoped by now that she would be a different person, more interested in ideas and other cultures, and less in her looks. When two people keep company, there's a point at which there's no reversal—unless you're willing to play the deuce with it. So you make the decision to go further and fare worse. The only thing you gain is a contented acceptance for things as they are. Mostly what he felt for Guerine was . . . protective, like a brother. That was it! In that way only did he love her. He had reached a point in the relationship that he'd never before considered—he had grown weary of her. She had become, for him, a habit. Deceiving her now was just as bad as if she were already his wife. But then, she had never been an object of passion for him. Her kisses had never burned. Certainly not what he'd expected after his experience with Mrs. Charing, the woman who could have been his piano teacher until she and her husband left town in the middle of the night.

The memory of Mrs. Charing became heavy. He fondly recalled the afternoon that she came into his father's shop to check on the status of a special order she had placed for her husband's birthday. His father apologized for the delay—Mr. Charing was a large man and a 48-inch measure took the conscientious tailor a bit more time—but he offered to have his son Sammy deliver the article the moment it was ready. His father was easily smitten with Mrs. Charing—she'd been a stage actress in her youth and spoke with a fine Italian accent. (No one could deny that the Eastbrook men had a weakness when it came to beautiful women and romance languages.) Sam was at the helm of the sewing machine in the back, putting short stitches in tunnel belt loops on a pair of beaver brown pants, but he could hear their conversation, as well as the stress Mrs. Charing put on next-to-last syllables.

Lessons in exchange for Mr. Charing's double-breasted mohair driving duster? Lessons a sixteen-year-old Sammy cared nothing for but would eventually agree to so as not to disappoint his father. "Why yes, of course," he could remember his father saying. "My wife and I would be very grateful." That's when the young Sam saw Mrs. Charing looking at him through the part in the curtain. Her intense stare, the way she was biting the fleshiness of her bottom lip, caught him quite off guard. His foot slipped from the treadle, throwing the machine out of time, which caused him to prick his finger with a No. 7 needle. *"Grazie!"* she said to his father, then turned on her heels and walked out the door.

The day he mounted the doorstep for his first instruction he could hear her playing the piano. He remembered being reluctant to knock, but he had with him Mr. Charing's duster to deliver so thought he'd better get on with it. The music stopped and he could see her figure on the other side of the leaded glass. She was smoothing her hair. When she opened the door she was smiling. "Good afternoon, Signor Eastbrook," she said, and then led him inside, toward the rear of the house, into the master bedroom. She showed him the exact spot to hang Mr. Charing's birthday present, and then led him over to a lowpost Cannonball bed where she wasted no time in seducing him with charms that surpassed all musical tutelage.

As his neck tensed and his teeth locked, she taught him coloratura, performing deliciously lingual trills, runs, and scales befitting Luisa Tetrazzini, a melody of what was, to him, an earth-shakingly unfamiliar operatic lay. When it reached a crescendo to its *finé*, she breathlessly proclaimed his performance *magnifico*.

Ah, Mrs. Charing. Signora. Was I the cause of your suspect departure?

He appreciated the levity of the reflection, but by the same token the episode with the older woman had left him stunned. The act itself had been awkward, devoid of harmonious meaning. It was impatient and impure, and produced in him a confusion of feelings and thoughts that ranged from utter elation to absolute remorse. Within minutes he had gone from feeling very much the two-fisted man to believing the foul action was an indication of his entire character. It was a circumstance, a weakness, that he fought in his heart from that day forward. And with Guerine, his attention to living a life of decency—his redoubled commitment to their shared celibacy—felt justly earned. She had been the remedy to what he'd believed were the defects in his soul.

But there remained the persistence of the issue at hand: the pain he had caused Guerine.

He stood from the chair and paced the room. What was he to do? How could he lessen the pain he had caused her? It was far beyond any box of chocolates. He tried to console himself with the thought that she would re-bound. Guerine always sprung back from every misadventure (witness the prosaic nature of her departure this evening). He would have to go see her, at the least try to explain. Surely she would understand that time displays character.

As does the meeting of the right person.

Ina was his affinity. In her he had found his inspiration. He'd hardly been able to take his eyes from her earlier this evening. But it was not only to-night. So many times he'd been by Guerine's side, finding himself indulging in the sweetness of Ina. And tonight, Ina had come to him as though he were something for which she hungered.

The feeling he had upon opening the door and seeing her standing there, in all her radiance, was the sensation one gets in a quickly falling elevator. The reflection in her eyes was the finest view he had ever seen in the world.

What they had shared tonight, the prolonged caresses, and the slow, ten-der breaths they had courted with sweet golden phrases, was purifying, and had resulted in a better understanding of his carnal experience with Mrs. Charing at age sixteen. It was the necessary cultivation of his slowly evolv-ing self. And now, for the first time in his life, he knew he had fallen truly in love.

He walked over to the window and leaned against the frame. The sky was taking on a reassuring cast, and he began to feel a rush of excitement over what was to come. There was a supreme understanding between them. It was clear that he and Ina were about to embark on something splendid. He had every intention of asking her to marry him.

Chapter 61

Birds of a Feather

*M*el never spoke of the incident, and Bertie never mentioned it. To dwell on it made her feel god-awful, but to have lived it, it seemed to Bertie, was enough to traumatize any woman for life. Returning home was a natural decision, but when Mel jumped at the chance to join her, Bertie immediately began to feel a sense of recovery. The Person County chapter of the Woman's Inter-Racial Commission (or whatever they'd decide to call their organization) would definitely need a publicist, and Mel was the best around. She could charm the stink off a skunk.

They took the train from Washington to Alabama, then made several stops—a roundabout journey through Georgia and South Carolina—to sessions and meetings and conferences, all dedicated to finding a solution to race prejudice, each as stirring as the last. By the time they arrived in Roxboro, they figured, they'd have a clearer idea on a course of procedure and be ready to work.

When they boarded the last train home, impassioned by all they had witnessed, they plunged into an exhaustive talkathon.

"I'll want to check out the local paper, too," Mel said. "See if they need an editor." From that point she spoke freely of her upbringing; she had inherited her finesse as a wordslinger from her mother, a teacher of Latin; her father had a strong work ethic, was a Wall Street type but encouraged liberal thought in his daughter in spite of it. She had graduated from Bryn Mawr where she'd been a girl of sober-minded simplicity and forced to room with a girl who cared only for superfluous drink and dressing pretty.

"I've never seen someone as fascinated with the taste of stingo as that gal," Mel said. "We called her Ginny."

"Because she drank gin," Bertie said.

"No, that was her name. Virginia."

Bertie had never laughed so hard. And when it came her turn, she surprised herself. A less exciting tale hers was, but she didn't stop talking until she had revealed everything about herself that she could think of, turning every bit of her conscience inside out for Mel to see, including the one thing that was eating her up the most: her acceptance of who Brud Daye had really been.

"You have nothing to be ashamed of, Bertie."

"I don't think that's the way it works."

"You just stick with me," Mel said, giving a playful tug to Bertie's dress sleeve. "A little time and I'll shake some sense into you. By the way, you weren't planning for us to stay with your mother, were you? I mean, on a permanent basis and all."

"Well, I—"

"Good. 'Cause I was figuring I'll buy me a house. Good investment, my daddy says. And I'll give you cheap rent. We'll live like a couple of Boston sisters, you and me. Give people in that town of yours something to talk about." Mel settled back against her seat and closed her eyes.

For the remainder of the trip home, Bertie began to see a faint picture of the pair of them, her and Mel, years forward, living under the same roof, helping each other muddle through life. And with that picture came an emotion—a sense of calm—she had never experienced, much less considered. And not at all a hard one to take.

Chapter 62

Guerine in the Gloom

*I*n the days that followed, Guerine moved through the house as if walking on the bottom of an ocean. The smallest activity felt beyond her capability, and she refused to go anywhere and be seen. If it hadn't been for tending to her mother, she wouldn't have so much as gotten out of bed. It seemed to her that for the first time in her life she was finding everything to criticize, whether it needed to be or not. Before this horrible nightmare, she had never allowed herself to be depressed in such a manner—sagging cheeks, drooping mouth, frown furrows. There had been too much in life to be happy about. Sam, most importantly; the ring at Ingram's Jewelers she'd had her eye on that nobody else was buying; and her new friend, Ina. But it was those very things that now brought blood raging to her face. Life as she knew it had ceased, and she was plunged in grief.

Who to be angrier with—him or that woman? She couldn't fathom how Ina could do something like this. And to her of all people! Had they not had the perfect friendship? Had she not rolled out the red wagon on her arrival? Gone to the trouble of making bacon tidbits for her? Shared her famous Excelsior Soup with her? Did all those nice things for her and then some, and this was the thanks she got—taking the only man she'd ever loved and shaming her in her very own town. On no occasion, not for the world, would she ever forgive her. She'd rather feed on shattered glass!

She'd barely been able to eat. Every day she was surrounded by poison as she relived that June night. Pressing on her body like a ton to a cornflake cookie, it was a wonder she didn't collapse.

And then there was the morning, a week after the dreadful event, that she carried breakfast up to her mother's airless room and shed the awful news. That in itself was regretful. She was intending to wait it out a while longer, but was prompted into telling after her mother's comment that Guerine was growing crow's-feet.

"Oh," her mother said inertly after hearing of the breakup. "Well, all men practice deception. What you need is shockless electricity, Ga-reen. It's perfectly painless. Just a pleasant, invigorating jolt that'll drive all your aches and pains out. You plug it into a light socket, simple as that. Now hand me that bottle of Nervine."

Guerine heaved a heavy sigh. Her mother. Always quick with a magic cure—and always in need of one.

It was only when Bertie returned home from Washington did the fire fade from Guerine's cheeks and she began to feel better.

She was in the kitchen, mashing up her mother's afternoon roughage, when she heard rapping at the front door. She had every intention of ignoring it. Just the mailman after all, delivering another fix-your-liver-change-your-life device for her mother. Whatever it was could wait. She had yet to see a product that could shake that woman from her foolishness. But the irritating rap-tap-tap continued and out of frustration she slammed the potato pulper to the counter, stomped through the house, and flung open the door. But no one was there, only a wooden case propped against the doorframe, and she bent over to pick it up. "What on earth—"

"Ta-da!" Bertie sang out, jumping into view.

"Bertie! You scared the dickens out of me! The zither?"

"They say music mends a broken heart," Bertie said.

Guerine began to cry. For the next hour, while Bertie supplied her in handkerchiefs, Guerine poured her heart out to her cousin, telling the whole tragic ordeal.

"I loved him, Bertie! I would've done anything for him."

"I know. But sometimes it's not the person we love as much as their reflection. We Daye-Loftis women have a tendency to not look further than our noses. Sadly."

"We had plans."

"You'll have others."

"Only not with him."

"You wouldn't have been happy with him."

"I'm sure I would have."

"The man never stops eating. He would've eaten down the walls."

"But I like to cook."

"Yeah. But have you considered that might not be your long suit?"

Guerine looked at Bertie, groaned, then grinned. Having this moment with her cousin was heartening, and she hadn't realized until now just how much she had missed her. The one person in the world she could always count on, who had helped her since they were children get past the worst of any pain.

Guerine blew her nose and chuckled. "You're darn good, Bertie. And you're right. I didn't look an inch beyond my nose, did I?"

"Maybe a quarter," Bertie said, handing her a fresh cloth.

After Guerine was alone, she went over to the window and looked out. She felt that she had come through the darkest part of it. Before, she hadn't believed that she could ever take another risk for the rest of her life. Now she didn't feel quite so weak in that regard. She was feeling stronger now. Maybe someday she could take another risk. Maybe someday she'd lavish, once again, the cornucopia of her wholesome gaiety on some lucky one— someone, obviously, who could appreciate it.

Chapter 63

Ina's Cherished Ideal

*I*na propped the broom against the bookcase and laid the empty dustpan close by on a shelf. A strand of hair had fallen into her face and she reached up to tuck it behind her ear. She looked around at the recent changes in the old schoolhouse. Light was coming through the window, catching gleams of floating dust.

The one-story frame building had been transformed, practically overnight, into an ideal residence for this newly appointed principal of the newly built East Roxboro School. The community had generously donated furnishings that turned the now-retired schoolhouse into a comfortable home: an oilcloth floor covering and a set of cream curtains, an iron bed and oak chiffonier, breakfast table and chairs, a single-door ice chest and decorated dinnerware, and an overstuffed parlor suit among them. The effect was softening, but the pride she had expected to feel was overshadowed by a sentiment of sadness.

She thought about the first time she had seen this place. She had walked the half mile to get here, had stopped at the end of the path that led up to the schoolhouse to relieve the pressure of her left shoe on her heel, and when she looked up had seen the tiny white building, snug against a wide canvas of lush green paulownia leaves. Leaves large enough to swaddle a baby. It was a tranquil scene, but she had been too irritated to appreciate it then. All she had cared to think about was how her life had been altered and with whom or where to place the blame.

What marvel time. For her to go from the self-involved person that she was in fear of permanently becoming, to someone who is learning to expand her way of seeing things—because she realized now that a person spends a lifetime learning—and to understand others with tolerance staggered even her belief. She was beginning to look more outside herself. And she liked herself better for it.

She reached for the broom and carried it out to the small porch, nearly stepping on a maple kazoo that one of the children had apparently left behind. Possibly it had dropped from a box the day the textbooks and desks were packed up and removed. She was surprised she hadn't noticed it before, but reached down now and placed it inside her dress pocket for safekeeping. She resumed with sweeping, and looked up when she heard a motorcar turn into the yard. Bertie. She tightened her grip on the broom handle, certain she was about to receive a harangue for the mess she had made between Sam and Guerine. Never mind the one between Guerine and herself.

"Came to see if there was any truth to the rumor," Bertie said, shielding her eyes from the sun as she walked toward the porch. At the bottom step, she stopped and looked at Ina. "I understand East Roxboro School just hired themselves one helluva principal." Her face broke into a grin. "Congratulations."

"Thank you, Bertie. Welcome home." She invited her to come onto the porch and sit.

"Sorry I haven't been out before now, but things have been crazy since I got back," Bertie said.

"It just so happens I understand crazy," said Ina.

For a short while, they sat in the rockers drinking sugar-sweetened lemon juice with ginger ale. Bertie made a sport of the ice chips, and Ina found comfort in the warmth of the sun.

"Oh, I've been meaning to thank you," Ina said.

"Yeah, what for?"

"For leaving behind some of your literature for me to read. Winnifred Harper Cooley."

"Ah," said Bertie, "*The New Womanhood*. That's a classic. Glad you found it." She fixed her eyes out toward the yard, the cast on her face of someone who had faith all along that this day would come—that Ina would eventually come around in her way of thinking.

Ina let Bertie have her moment of glory before changing the subject. Then finally, "So," she inquired, "do you think she'll ever speak to me again?"

Bertie lowered her glass to the arm of the rocker and shut her eyes as though she were contemplating. "Guerine always bounces back," she said. "I reckon what you're really asking me, though, is if I think she'll forgive you. She will. When she's ready." And then it was time for Bertie to go.

As she drove away, Ina continued to sit and look out at the lushness that surrounded her. The sun was dissolving into a beautiful summer evening, gold turning to crimson, and crimson melding into purple, blanketing her and the little house. It had been a regal day.

She was happy here. She had made strong friendships and was grateful for every blessing that had been bestowed upon her. This place—this community—was where she wanted to put her energies. She wanted to inspire her pupils to higher ideals; to make the school an inspiration for better country life; to awaken the neighborhood, every home in the district, and uplift them to better things in which interest never before had manifested itself. There were so many opportunities here that she couldn't imagine ever giving up this veritable Garden of Eden.

Lately, she was feeling a legitimate desire for her own growth as well, a chance to explore a whole array of mental and spiritual instincts, all the ones that have for ages been starved in women. Sam's proposal only complicated that.

His proposal when proffered had caught her off guard. After their night together, and confronting the impulses of her heart, she determined that it had been merely a weakness in character, nothing more, and that Sam would likely agree. His seriousness on the matter afterward, though, betrayed any notion of that. She still had not given him an answer. And he was adamant about getting one. The opportunities set before her now seemed so much wider than those of a married woman. Did she really want to be dependent on a man for her bread? And who's to say that they wouldn't grow weary of one another? Why why why, she wondered, do we yearn for things, and would give all and everything we have to attain them, but then once we've gotten them they don't seem all that important anymore? Perhaps the old maxim was true, that anticipation is more valuable as titillation than the actual having. She was coming to believe that she might prefer the constancy and comfort of being economically independent to that of a union with someone who would have a right to her being. She had no visions of becoming a path-breaker in the sense that Bertie was, only aspired to become a wholly developed individual. And if married, she would have to give it all up. Everything. Her pupils, her work.

And really—could anyone, truly, take the place of Harlan?

It was decided then. Her decision would mean another change was foreseen, another time of renewal. They couldn't simply go back to the way it was before. She didn't know how Sam would take the news at their next meeting, but she hoped that he would understand and, in time, forgive her. He was a romantic, but he was strong.

Tomorrow, she would try again to meet with Guerine. And the day after that if she still needed to. And the day after that, and the day after that, until Guerine, if nothing else, would at least hear her apology.

Her mind then turned to something less remote. The gentle swipes of a white cat at her feet gained her attention, and she reached over and lifted her onto her lap. "Well now, you're just in time for dinner. Anything special you have *your* heart set on?"

Chapter 64

A Daughter
of the Soil

*I*t was the morning of a new moon. The favorable time for planting late peas. Doodle sat outside on the steps drinking coffee and making notes for her new photoplay, as Bugle satisfied himself by playfully nipping at one of the hens in the yard. She looked down at them and smiled. Mr. Palmer had rejected her "Carolina Hell Cat" photoplay, said it too closely resembled a Willard Mack story, but praised her efforts and said he'd be interested in seeing future work. Recently she had started a new one, an ironical comedy drama, a light and farcical story with a vein of melodrama running beneath. She was thinking of calling it "The Man Who Understood." This time, give Oscar Hawks an arm up. He'd be the perfect character.

The day was looking to be rich with sun, too beautiful for a person to be ill-natured. The sunflowers were already turning their fat, bulging faces toward the yellow lamp, and throughout the furnace of the day, she would watch them bend on their stalks as they faithfully followed its curve. Rain had come through the night before and given the rows a good soaking, and everything that was green was flourishing. Even her geese and chickens and turkeys were accepting.

This was the throb of life, she thought. Months it had taken her to exhaust her pride, especially when that pride involved Colon. And it was Miss Cara Sue who had set her right-now straight one afternoon, no different than if she'd been Doodle's own mama. "That boy ain't about seeking to rise above anybody's shoulders," Miss Cara Sue told her. "He used his own savings to pay that debt off. Alls he wants is to be anchored to that farm and the self-owned woman he loves. I don't know how you can expect for a single woman to run that farm in the same manner that a whole family could barely make a go of. That's foolish pride is all that is. And it's not giving up to grab on to reality, especially for a chance at happiness." She sent Doodle home with a full dollop of wisdom and half a spit-roasted rabbit to think on it. The old woman's tough talk had taken some of the starch out of Doodle, and if not for that, she doubted that Colon would be the comforting fixture he had become around here.

It stood fair to say that a strong, devoted affection was germinating within both of them. Working this farm together, the way they did now, they were getting close as two whirligig beetles, and she believed it wouldn't be long before Colon's presence here every day was graven—at least by New Year's Day, when superstition demanded that a man be the first person to put his feet in a house to assure good luck for the coming year. Already he'd surprised her by planting a sweetgum. If they could keep the deer and other critters from eating the young plant, he told her, then one day he'd cut a notch out, and soon as the sap rose they'd have themselves a fine-tasting chewing gum. Not only was he a man about town and country, she thought, but he was solid comfort and kind words, too. And he was inspiring in her the need to be completely known.

Today he was coming to help her plant peas.

Yesterday, Bertie had come. Doodle was so thrilled to lay eyes on her she came close to imposing a hug, but neither of them had ever been much for open arms and quick kisses, so they settled on sweet tea and cracker pie at the kitchen table. When it came time for Bertie to leave, Doodle felt out of sorts as though something was missing. That gal, always in such a flurry! Like the world would change before she could get there to fix it.

"I still think you oughta see about having a telephone installed," Bertie had called over her shoulder while walking toward her machine. "It'd give me a good chance to tweak the nose of B.C. Wheeler." And Doodle, at that very moment, had an overwhelming feeling to give her that hug after all. She ran down the steps, almost missing the last one, and out into the yard after her. "Bertie!"

Bertie turned around.

"Are we all right?" Doodle asked, her heart racing. "Me and you?" It was a question that had been bothering her deeply.

"Always," Bertie said without reluctance. A single word full with tenderness and easy to accept, it gave Doodle a feeling of contentment. This wasn't going to be a friendship deterred by hurdles, and she let Bertie simply be on her way.

Now, Doodle looked out across the broad green landscape with silent wonder. It was a crazy world, but even with its trials and all its labor she was glad to be in it. Just to be. To witness daylight break and watch each day unfold; to live among every star and cloud and leaf, and every single blossom. Here a ladybird beetle lighted onto her hand and, at first, her impulse was to flick it away, but she resisted. She watched as the spotted insect calmly and slowly negotiated the valley between her thumb and forefinger. She held her breath when it spread its wings, waiting to see the direction it would fly. Then up, up, up it twirled, teasing her to follow, until at last her eyes came to rest on a familiar burst of dust on the offing. Bugle knew what was happening well before she did.

She stood from the porch and watched as the hound scamped off to greet Colon. It didn't matter to Bugle if a man had prospects, so long as he had an open soul. Dogs know things.

Chapter 65

Guerine's Glow of Hope

*G*uerine splashed in her morning bath, reveling in the dainty luxury of Bathasweet. She was singing the refrain to "Bubbling Over," and took every word of it to heart. "Bubbling over, bubbling over, hope with me is bubbling over all the time." She couldn't recall if she'd ever thanked Colon for the phonograph, but she would have to be sure and do that the next time she saw him—and thank him for including that sweet little number with it, too. She believed that song had been written just for her, and as long as she had a say, hope would forever be bubbling over in her, because, in the human heart, there must be a hope that glows! How else did a person recover? One has only to stop dwelling on the past and look to the future for happiness.

There was risk in happiness, true, but why deny oneself the least little bit? Bliss can be. Yes, that would be her motto! And what better way to start than by visiting an old friend. As a girl of spirit, one must pave the way for others. Things could be worse. She could've been born with a short limb or a harelip.

She yanked the rubber stopper from the tub, watched the water burble to oblivion, dried off, and finished dressing. Anyone looking at her dressing table could see she was a woman of loveliness, a possessor of bottles and jars that healed and velvetized and helped retain beauty. She finished with a light tamp of pink complexion powder, then looked herself in the glass. She had the charm of Mary Pickford in *Pollyanna*, and it tickled her very much that she had managed to create a little mystery about herself.

Her mama called from across the hall. It was time to harness her into her latest obsession, a body brace she was giving a thirty-day examination that guaranteed to develop lungs, relieve curvatures, and replace misplaced organs.

"Hand me my tonic, won't you, Ga-reen. I'm hardly able to drag," Mrs. Loftis said feebly after being hitched up like a bull.

"You didn't have all this trouble, Mama, till you started guzzling that ridiculous tonic," said Guerine while fluffing and rearranging the bed pillows.

"Not so. I have disorders of the nerves and it's the only relief I get. If you'll remember, I wasn't hardly able to get a good night's sleep before. Now go and fetch it for me, please."

Guerine searched the top of the bureau for the brown bottle of Rub-My-Tism. She unscrewed the crown and handed the bottle to her mama, who put it to her mouth and swigged. Guerine shook her head. She, too, could've relied on some type of restorative at any time—goodness knows, there were all sorts of bottles of the stuff lying about in the house—but she was determined to put her faith in something else.

"I'd say by now you've got a de-ranged nervous system, no thanks to the two bottles you've worked your way through this week," Guerine said.

"That's no way to talk to your mother. Now be smart and pull that blanket 'cross my feet."

Guerine did as she was told, then let her mother know that she was off to town and would check on her later. When she went across the hall to retrieve her purse, the bell rang, and with the energy of a confident young woman, she grabbed the purse and hurried down the stairs.

"Oh. Hello, Sam."

"Hello, Guerine. I was hoping we could talk." He stood on the other side of the threshold just as she had imagined him on the night she had returned home. Looking sheepish, as if he'd just had some peculiar experience.

"Now's not a good time, Sam. I'm just on my way out." She tucked her purse under her arm and stepped out onto the porch, pulling the door to.

"But I'd like to apologize."

"Maybe another time, huh, Sam? I'm in a bit of a rush right now. Something important to see to." She breezed past him and hurried down the steps.

"Please, Guerine. Won't you let me try to explain?"

She turned back toward the house. "Oh, Sam! Don't you worry yourself about it. Really. It's nothing a little Blueberry Buckle won't fix. Gotta run now, Sam!" And she swept down the sidewalk, under a sunny sky, the light streaming all the way down Main Street, and with it the noises of a village wide awake. Soon she spotted what she was looking for and stopped for a moment to regard him, as well as take a quick peek at her wristwatch. He was locking up his shop, the same faithful time as always, on his way to the Wiggly Pig for lunch.

"Mr. Gentry!" she called out. "Whoo-who, Mr. Gentry! Why, you're just the one I'm looking for!" and walked friskily until she managed to catch him.

Chapter 66

Another Daye's Call

*T*he first couple of days back in the Daye house, Bertie and Miss Lul regarded each other's new friend with the suspicion of a mother bird looking out for her blind and naked chick, and took turns interrogating each other in private. "Who are her people?" Miss Lul insisted on knowing. "What else do you know about him?" Bertie demanded of Miss Lul. Back and forth, till eventually they were in tune.

Once satisfied that they all were working toward similar goals—it had already been established that they would be opening Miss Lul's house as an interim school for Negro children as one constructive measure—neither Bertie nor Miss Lul wasted any more time getting the local chapter of the Women's Inter-Racial Cooperation up and rolling. There were the large details that needing tending to, as well as the small, and after supper one evening, as soon as the dishes had been cleared from the table and soaped and put away, the two sat back down with a box of soft lead Faber's, two pencil tablets, and a large pot of coffee, ready to brainstorm:

"Mr. Joyner will return directly. I've asked him to join us this evening," Miss Lul said. "We need his expertise."

"Mel's, too," said Bertie, returning the like. "She only went up to polish her teeth. She's a very conscientious person."

"I thought we were done with this foolishness."

"We're square."

"Good, then."

"Fine."

After a minute, the two subjects of parry returned, and ideas and suggestions were promptly tossed about for setting forth committee plans.

"If we're going to work at settling racial differences, there has to be mutual change," suggested Mel, already scribbling notes. She tapped the rubber eraser thoughtfully against her cheek. "We should think of it as taking in one another's washing."

"I firmly agree," Miss Lul said, impressed with the young woman's analogy. "It has to be far-reaching. The current racial conditions are a challenge to the Christian faith."

"To be sure," said Mr. Joyner.

Bertie gave him a cool look, as if he had just let out a hot, blowy hiccup.

Mr. Joyner cleared his throat. "Necco, anyone?" he said, offering a roll of the wafers to his table companions.

"Don't mind if I do," said Mel, helping herself to a clove.

"Nope. No thanks." Bertie glanced down to examine what she'd written. "We'll start by including representatives from every civic and social organization in the community."

"And a select group of Christian-minded women, too," Miss Lul said. "What would an interracial group be without them?" She looked over at Mr. Joyner and nodded.

Bertie spoke as she wrote: "Women of spiritual existence."

"There has to be frankness of speech," said Mel.

"And let's not forget confidence," Miss Lul said.

"We have to call attention to every possible cause of friction," said Bertie. "Justice in the courts, for one."

"And education, too. Jot that one down, Bertie," said Miss Lul. "Sacredness of personality is the basis for all people, whether they're white or colored. Don't you agree, Mr. Joyner?"

"Ab-so-lutely," said Mr. Joyner, who had up until that moment shown a great deal of reserve. "Members should be urged to create mutual respect in the hearts of the children of both races. Which reminds me—you'll have the bus at your disposal when the children aren't using it."

"What bus?" Bertie said. She looked at Miss Lul.

"Things have been so crazy around here since you girls arrived that I haven't had a chance to tell you. But Mr. Joyner here and I have gone in together and bought a school bus. That way we'll be able to transport the children here, then back home again. And at no cost to the county."

"Huh. Planning to stick around Roxboro, are you, Mr. Joyner?"

"Now, Beatrice," said Miss Lul.

"Indeed, young lady," he said. "I believe in her future growth."

Bertie looked him directly in the eye. She had been concerned, at first, that he might be some big-time lady chaser, but was beginning to be convinced otherwise. It was looking to her like Mr. Joyner's desire and ability to carry out work on behalf of the Negro people knew no bounds. Favorably impressed with Miss Lul's special friend, she, too, gave the man a nod.

"Well, ladies, looks to me like you have everything under control here," he said, the chair legs lightly scraping the floor as he stood. "If you all will excuse me. Mrs. Daye, I'll look forward to our engagement tomorrow evening."

"Chamber music at Trinity College! I wouldn't miss it for the world, Mr. Joyner."

Bertie arched an inquisitive eyebrow at Miss Lul.

"What? Even folks our age need a little recovery if we hope to be efficient at our daily tasks."

By the wee hours of the morning, over a table stained with coffee rings and dusted in Goody's Headache Powder, eyes dry and stinging from too little sleep, the women had established a full list of guidelines and a date for their first meeting.

The Roxboro Women's Inter-Racial Cooperation inaugural meeting attendees weren't sure what to make of it. In spite of being puttied by refreshments, they either nervously tapped the balls of their feet or tugged at necklaces—those who were wearing them. The room was as fidgety as a bucket of bait turned onto a hot rock. Cora Humphries bounced her melon-style opossum muff on her lap while forcing a smile at her girl, Geneva, who stood at her side twisting a lock of her hair. Myrtle Suitt all but hid behind her chin-chin fur collar, afraid to look at anybody. When Mrs. Wheeler spilled her hot cider on the floor, her girl Rella instinctively hurried off to the kitchen in search of a mop.

"Come back, Rella," Miss Lul called after her. "Leave it be. I'll clean it up later myself."

"Let the girl clean it up, Lalura. It won't take her just a minute."

"No. I won't have it." Silence caught the room.

Bertie stood at the sideboard and looked around at every woman, taking in splinters of conversation as it emerged from the tension.

"Geneva, I want you to be sure and get Lalura's recipe for these little lemon spritzes. And quit twirling that pilly hair of yours! It's like cutting your fingernails in company."

"Remind me when we get back to the house, Rella, we need to clean the silver. See the tarnish on this dish?"

Bertie took a deep, futile breath. She imagined how the colored women, particularly those still in their aprons, could easily, even eagerly, start to busy themselves throughout the house by flipping mattresses, dusting knick-knacks, and removing spots from the furniture with camphor-moistened cloths to avoid any possible confrontation. Or retreating as a group to the confines of the kitchen, just as Rella had tried, to polish silver and stew blue plums for pie filling. The meeting was in danger of branching off in an undesired direction. If she didn't do something quick to set it on the right path, the only promises to be exchanged among the women that day would be of recipes and offers of employment. Maybe this whole thing was crazy. Probably the only reason any of them had shown up was curiosity—to see what Brud Daye's leftovers were going to do for an encore. If she could at least get them to look at the "Negro problem" from a different point of view than in the past, she would feel that she had accomplished something today.

Mel came over and gave her elbow an encouraging squeeze. "Bertie."

"I know, I know. Time to start the Daye Family Side Show." She finished off one of Miss Lul's fussy baked bean sandwiches, washed it down with a swig of lukewarm cider, then picked up a document from the sideboard and held it out in front of her.

It was Miss Lul's idea that she start off the meeting by reading from a script, believing if Bertie had tried to wing it she would surely scare the bejesus out of everybody with the spontaneous nature of her tongue. "But it'll sound stilted," Bertie had argued. And Miss Lul had countered, "Like it or not, Beatrice, it comes down to poise. You have a purpose now. And you are gonna have to prove to people that you can take whatever they throw at you. Courage isn't always in overwrought colorful language. Now get Mel to help you. I'm sure between the two of you that you'll write something that will appeal to the sound faith and grace of every woman who'll be there."

The best she could hope for now, was that some small piece of what she was about to say would grab at least one woman by the button.

"Miss Lul and I," she read, starting off loud to get their attention, "find ourselves with a deep sense of responsibility to the Negro race. The women, as well as the children. And yes, the men. Not only do we recognize the clashing between the two races, we detest it. And we believe that many of the problems can be erased—" She paused to look up. They seemed to be listening. Myrtle Suitt had come out of hiding. Even Geneva had given her hair a rest.

Bertie looked back at the document she and Mel had prepared on ruled octavo, and continued, "—but not without exercising consideration, justice, and sympathetic collaboration. And that's where the Inter-Racial Cooperation comes in. Think of it as the elbow grease that's needed for washing away the injustice that Jim Crow has wrought."

From there, she read a list of every imaginable cause of friction, ignoring the broken tones and muffled chatter that was filtering through the room. When she was done she opened the floor for questions.

"So it's your conviction, then, that our town has a problem?" said Mrs. Wheeler.

"That's certainly a revelation to me," Cora Humphries said.

"I've never noticed any friction. Have you? I'm sure our girls here would've brought it to our attention a long time ago if there were."

"I think what Miss Daye is saying is that this is often subtle but far-reaching," Myrtle Suitt said. "I, for one, can appreciate her vision."

"I don't mean any disrespect, dear, but you have to admit it seems awful peculiar that she, of all people, would be claiming to understand the Negro mind," said Cora Humphries.

Bertie thought her head was going to explode. Here it was again—another train wreck that she ought to have seen coming. Just listen to them! Everything she put her hand into always turned into nothing but pure cussedness. And now she had gone and dragged Miss Lul into it, too. She didn't know whether to cry or scream, or go over and open the door and escort every one of them out.

But then an elderly voice spoke up. The room fell silent in stares of disbelief at the speaker's gumption.

"You mentioned lynching," the woman said to Bertie. It was Anna Belle Lunsford. She went on to further say she was the great-aunt of Dock Jones, the young colored man who'd been taken off to somewheres by the authorities and it'd been near'bout fifteen years since his loved ones had laid eyes on him.

Bertie felt every eye in the room trying to gauge her reaction. The shame of her papa's legacy, what he had done to the people of this community, was right there before her, looking her earnestly in the face. She couldn't ignore facts.

"Yes, ma'am." Bertie nodded.

"How, if I may ask," the woman continued, "will we correct that?"

Bertie looked down at the supplied words, raking her teeth over her painted bottom lip until she could taste burnt carmine. She could read, verbatim, the language that was there before her—*As women we require those who are charged with the administration of the law to prevent lynchings at any cost.* But her instinct called for her to do otherwise. She squeezed the papers in her hand, gazed into the faces before her, one by one, and straightened amid the startled silence.

"You know, I'm pretty fortunate," she said to the room. "I know what my faults are—though most of them are attributes." Her candor brought laughter. And then she looked at Dock Jones's great-aunt. The woman's face—its spirit, its obstinacy—made Bertie feel all the more encouraged.

"I will scrape, and I will scrub," she said at last, "and I will scratch, and I will gnaw, until every crime against every Negro has been reduced to powder. But none of us can do it alone. The only way we're going to survive is by pushing ahead together." She glanced over at Miss Lul who had tears streaming down her cheeks. Maybe it was Miss Lul who'd been her inspiration all along.

Bertie thought of the apple and the tree, and she could feel that a great constructive movement had begun. And for the first time in too long, she smiled.

Acknowledgments

$\mathcal{M}$y deepest gratitude to my literary agent, Erin Malone; my editor, Erin Brown; and her assistant, Lorrie McCann, who possess the courage to shepherd new work and new workers and the skill to make good things happen; to Cyn Kitchen, the Cyster I never had and always needed; and to Pam Duncan, whose friendship is as honest and real as her lovely novels. To my husband, Jim Shamp: Without your support this book would not have been possible.

Other conspicuous women—and steadfast men—have shaped my life, and therefore, my book. Thanks to Judy Hogan for encouraging my early efforts while teaching me craft and classics; to Lynn Pruett, who led me to the Spalding University MFA program; to my friends and mentors at Spalding, in particular Ellie Bryant, Luke Wallin, Robin Lippincott, and Neela Vaswani; to Lynn York, for sharing her wisdom and enthusiasm for this writing life; and to Jill McCorkle and Lee Smith, for their generous support and encouragement.

For braving the manuscript in one form or another, thanks to Verna Austen, Denise Heinze, Paul Hiers, Silas House, Matt Jaeger, Cate McGowan, Margaret Phillips, Heather Shaw, and Brad Watson.

Thanks also to the Durham Arts Council for sending me to the Sewanee Writers' Conference, and to the denizens of the Vermont Studio Center for the fellowship and the time and space to finish this novel.

In my effort to bring the past to life, I relied on a number of publications including: *For Rent—One Pedestal* by Marjorie Shuler; *The New Womanhood* by Winnifred Harper Cooley; *The Southern Lady: From Pedestal to Politics, 1830–1930* by Anne Firor Scott; Floyd Clymer's *Model T Memories* including "The Ubiquitous Model T" by Les Henry; *Photoplay Plot Encyclopedia* by the Palmer Photoplay Corporation; *The Rural School: Its Methods and Manage-*

ment by Horace Cutler and Julia Stone; *By Her Own Bootstraps: A Saga of Women in North Carolina* by Albert Coates; and Dover Publications' *Everyday Fashions of the Twenties, As Pictured in Sears and Other Catalogs*, edited by Stella Blum. Also of great help were the Model T docents at the Henry Ford Museum, the *Roxboro Courier-Times* (N.C.), and other period newspapers and magazines.

Special thanks to Duke University, University of North Carolina, and Person County libraries, the Alice Paul Institute, the Library of Congress, the NAACP, the League of Women Voters of North Carolina, and the Person County Historical Society for their assistance.

And finally, thank you to my father, Holmes Adair, for always freshening the wellspring of stories about Grimma Lizzie, a free spirit, hello girl, and peanut vendor.